W9-CCE-111

The Longest Way Round

by Burt Cole

Subi: The Volcano
The Longest Way Round

The Longest Way Round

Burt Cole

New York
The Macmillan Company
1958

First Printing

Library of Congress catalog card number: 58–12074

The Macmillan Company, New York
Brett-Macmillan Ltd., Galt, Ontario

Printed in the United States of America

A mi querida esposa, Tina Varela

Cand'as pedras desen gritos
i-o sol parase d'andar
i-a mar non tivese agua
eime de ti d'olvidar.

Contents

The Jaguar

One

A WHILE AGO I bought an MG midget roadster. It's a little English car, two seats and an open top. Well, it was more a whim than anything else, not that I am allowed to have two-thousand-dollar whims (my mother thought it was a racing car and was going to call the man to come take it back, until I explained it was a graduation gift from her and my father) and then I got married about that time, to a girl I had gone steady with in college, and I forgot about the car, except for the essentials of transportation.

What I remember of it was that the catalogue or driver's manual called the carburetor "carburretter," or something like that, and the fenders were called "wings." The dashboard wasn't the dashboard, it was the "fascia," and the windshield was the "wind-screen." The car had four forward gears instead of three, very quick steering, hard little springs that bounced you all over the road—and a lot of other things about it, things I could describe now that I know more about the type of car, but that I barely noticed then. It was a TF 1500 and I drove it as though it was a '53 Chevrolet, which was the car I had before it.

Never mind: I had it for only two or three years and then everything went to pieces, so I cashed in some stocks left to me by a dead uncle, and I came to travel Europe. I sold the MG and my mother suggested I buy a car in Europe on the tourist plan, as some of her friends had done. These friends all bought large Mercedes Benz touring cars, but she was more in favor of the Volkswagen, a famous little beetle that will only go seventy downhill and then doesn't like it. But it runs forever and you don't have to put much gas in it. My father arranged to have one waiting for me when I got off the boat in Cherbourg in August, driven there by a German lad who had brought it and my International Papers all the way from Wolfsburg. I understand this is not the usual arrangement, but my father probably has stock in Volkswagen; he has in everything else.

Before we go any further: my name is Captain Cord and I am twenty-five years old, having graduated late from college—by preference; I liked it. My first name is Andrew, but I was in college so long they finally had to make me president of the fraternity, and the president was called Captain on all but formal occasions, when he was called Most Honorable Senior Leader of our Souls (when he wore a cloak with moths and a steel helmet with wings). The Captain part stuck, maybe because it alliterated with my last name. My last name has always irritated me, and the Captain began to irritate me too when all my friends took it up outside the fraternity. Now I am even called Captain in my home-town (small, rich, outside Hartford) and I have even got into the habit myself.

While I was in college I majored in English literature, and that was considered a snap course, so I was considered a playboy, though I had only four suits and seldom went out with girls, except for Jennie. My first year I drank a lot, until one day I drank too much and went into the infirmary. A friend of mine, a colored boy who worked in the frat-house kitchen, brought me a bottle of red wine in the infirmary, on the theory that if all the gin I'd been drinking hadn't killed me, the wine wouldn't either. But now I have an old man's kidneys and don't drink much any more.

I didn't drink much through the rest of college, for that matter. I became an intellectual. This sounds very Scott Fitzgerald, but I guarantee I was no more stuck on myself than the next person. I did get introspective, though. My mother said it was my terrible experience in the war, but I hadn't seen any war; I was a file clerk in a quartermaster depot in San Francisco. I didn't drink there, I was not intellectual, I was not introspective. Too young. Later, when I got to college, I was very intense about what courses to take to prepare myself for Life, in case my father made me go to work. He would have, too, if it hadn't been for my Uncle Fred; and he will, when I get home. If I get home.

When I landed I shot straight south in the Volkswagen with

American Express Traveler's Cheques, and crossed over to Perpignan by way of Chartres, Orléans, Limoges, Toulouse and Narbonne. The first sight of the Mediterranean comes between Narbonne and Perpignan. I stopped the car and thought about Odysseus, if he had reached this far. If I am to tell you everything, I have to report that I began to cry. It was the first moment I had had to sit and think about myself, where I was, why I was where I was, and what I would do all by myself three thousand miles from the nearest human who knew me by name. I was all ready to get rid of Jennie: I had worked toward it and nerved myself and asked for the divorce and got it. And I am sure if I hadn't set about getting rid of her, she would have taken steps to get rid of me. But we had been married three years, since I was twenty-two and she was twenty-one, and in that time I had formed habits. And now I was lonely.

Between Narbonne and Perpignan there are only flat stretches of wasteland and desolate vegetation, and there is also a wind called the mistral that will rock the heaviest car back and forth on its springs. Sometimes there is the forlorn figure of a man with a sickle chopping weeds back from the road's edge, and now and then there is a ruin of a town where people walk back and forth on the streets very slowly and their shoes make no sound at all. They do not speak. No one blows horns. To ears that have heard nothing but a Volkswagen engine whining behind the rear seat for two days, there is no sound at all; and the sun boils down out of a light blue sky the clouds mix into edgelessly.

Perpignan is different, but you can't stop there during the tourist season if you are on a budget, so I went on following Le Perthus signs until it was quite late, until I came to a town where there were a few people still walking around and a café still open. I think the town was Le Boulou, but it didn't matter and I couldn't ask anybody. I don't speak any French at all, though I studied it for four years in high school and can still say the first ten words of the Lord's Prayer.

I stopped in the café that was open and sat by the window looking out at the lonely lights in the street. Men were playing cards at one table, and the waiter was working with a broken machine on the wall—for a franc it dispensed a small quantity of gasoline for cigarette-lighters. He kept his nose in it and shook and banged it, and I would not have got my cup of coffee if I hadn't gone over and interrupted him. I ordered it and sat down again looking out at the watery lights, and he brought a cup of slop over and banged it down so that it slopped on the table. I had come all the way across France without stopping and was dead tired and had not even heard the French language spoken, much less gotten down to the grass roots of French life. I had not yet formed an opinion of our allies in the present world crisis; but here was a Frog I would have liked to crack across the point of the nose. Maybe he thought I was a German, because of my German car, my short haircut, suede jacket, and heavy shoes. "Come-beans?" I said. "Three hundred francs," he said. I did not leave a tip; I wasn't dispirited enough to leave a tip.

When I got outside I found that the trunk of my car had been pried open and the spare was gone. "Oh bat shit," I said. "I'm going home." Luckily I had locked the car, and most of my belongings were in the rear seat, not in the trunk, which is up front in the Volkswagen. They thought the valuables would be in the trunk and had ripped it open with a crowbar and taken the spare, the bundle of tools, and some shoes.

It was half-past two then. The lights of the café were beginning to go out behind the thick dusty windows as I stood looking at the empty trunk and remembering that I was a whole ocean away not only from people who knew me by name, but from anybody who would even speak to me voluntarily unless he had the American dollar sign in mind. All the electric signs were out and I couldn't locate a hotel or a garage. After driving steadily for more than twenty hours, all I wanted was to lie down and sleep and try for a fresh morning wind. But there was no place.

I crawled through the town at two or three miles an hour with my head out the window looking for lights. I knew there was nothing beyond the town but another twenty or thirty miles of empty night-time countryside between there and the Spanish border.

A man waved the car down and half crawled in the window to smile at me, a big rotten smile as trustworthy as a cat's, and he asked me what I was hunting for. "A place to sleep," I said. He spoke English after a fashion. There was an excellent garage and a private bedroom down the next street, he said. At least he didn't try to get in the car. He was dirty and dressed in a smock and beret and he touched me enough even through the window. I let him run ahead of the car down two or three turns of dark alley until he stopped and pulled open a creaking double door in a mud wall. My lights shone into a kind of shed full of old crates and broken bicycles and primitive digging tools. He was going to take me up above and put me to sleep good. And who knows what would happen to me and my car and my clothes—I thought that anyway at half-past two—between the dark walls with the dark shuttered windows?

"Drive in," the man said, leaning in the window and trying to open the door from the inside, panting and smiling his rotten smile.

"This won't do," I said. "I want a place where I can take a bath. A legitimate hotel." He said there was a bath; he himself would heat the water for me. "This is Board House," he said. "Pension. There are no better. Accommodation of astonishment."

"The car won't fit in your garage," I said, "and you haven't got room to accommodate my astonishment. I'm going on."

"Oui, oui," he said. "The best hotel you will find. What you want? What else you look for more too late?"

"I'm looking for love," I said. I had to put the car in gear and start driving away with his arm in the window still touching me, or he would not have let go that night. He had misunderstood me; he was in a position to offer me love too, I gathered. Whatever I wanted.

Things are a lot better than they were. When I arrived in Europe I did not have a friend in the world, and stopping the car to sob on the bleak coast in high summer is not the worst I did. Months passed before I quit brooding, and sometimes I still think I am not reconciled, but that is just my pride smarting. That summer the divorce had not yet taken place, and several times I was on the point of wiring Jennie to stop all the processes and prepare a table before me, I was coming home, and we would give it another try. But it was a very complicated situation, and I changed my mind every three days about what I was going to do and how I felt.

At first it was a dim place lighted by weak European light bulbs that I looked into whenever I tried to figure out the shape of my future and how I was going to spend my time alone. There seemed to be no particular reason to be in any particular place, so I hardly stopped moving. I drove all day from dawn to dark, barely willing to stop even to eat. Everywhere I went I looked for a bar that didn't exist, to drink a beer in, or a hotel that wasn't built yet, where I could spend the night comfortably. There was nothing to do but keep moving. Because no man can leave any woman, no matter how amicable the goodbyes, no matter with what mutual good wishes, without its being a bad thing. Unless he goes to a different woman. I didn't even want a new woman. I didn't feel like stopping the car long enough to hunt one up, think of the things to say, and probe around for an in. So I passed down the Spanish Mediterranean coast, shifting gears around the Spanish highways that wind like cramped snakes from bump to pothole, and as I drove I thought about Jennie and contemplated the bright face of death. Then I contracted Wanderer's Woe and spent three days in a beat-up auberge running a high fever and drizzling diarrhea into a porcelain bedpot. Nobody came to see me either.

The Woe is probably caused by drinking water. I've had it a couple times since then, though not so severe as the first time. I drink the local water wherever I go, figuring either to die or get used to it, rather than carry around bottles of Vichy water or drink nothing but wine. I drank the local water even while I was sick and I was on my feet again in three days, driving south with a huge headache and a taste of oil in my mouth and a sharp hollow pain bolting across my midriff every few minutes. I drove even faster than before.

Barcelona saw the car go by; Tarragona and Castellón offered nothing much. I stayed in Valencia one night, got sick between there and Alicante and stopped in a place called Villajoyosa to dump and fill. Next Murcia and Lorca and Almería. Someplace along there I saw a blue English Jaguar, a coupe with a lot of headlamps across the front bumper, two exhaust-pipes, and an escutcheon that said: *Brooklands 120 miles per hour*. That's a fine thing, I said to myself. It was baby-blue with dark blue upholstery. It was lower to the ground than the Volkswagen and twice as long. It looked more warlike than automotive.

Like most of my generation, I am intermittently car-crazy. Not that I am a hotrodder or anything like that, but I recognize that a car is a necessary part of adolescence and early youth. I have known some young men who did not own cars, and they were sad cases indeed. I had a wreck of a Willys once, then a Ford, two Plymouths, the '53 Chevvy, the MG, and then the Volkswagen. That's all. But I used to amuse myself by customizing a little and tinkering with the spark and doing some of the routine servicing myself; I even put dual pots and a straight-through exhaust on the

Chevvy just before I got rid of it. So I like cars, and this blue racer fascinated me. I went on a distance and then turned around in the road and went to Germany.

I did not want to stop moving. The trip from Cherbourg to below Almería had taken me some fifteen days in all, counting the three days I was sick and the day I went swimming on the beach at Alicante. From below Almería where I turned around and went the other way it was another five days to Frankfurt am Main. I was just as much alone as ever, but felt a lot better all the same, because I had some purpose now. At least I was going somewhere definite to do something definite. If I hadn't seen the Jaguar I would have gone on down and passed through Gibraltar and come up the other side through Portugal and out the top of Spain to France again, and then where would I have been? On the point of leaving for Norway or Holland or Italy, I guess. Or it might have been something else; maybe the Volkswagen would have broken down and forced me to hole up somewhere; or I might have fallen in with other tourists or somebody else who had some idea of what to do. I might have gone home. I might have gone to Paris to raise a beard. But the way it worked out, I saw the baby-blue Jaguar coupe and remembered the MG, which was a sports car whatever you say, and I turned around and went north to Frankfurt.

When I reached there I stopped in the biggest hotel I could find and got a room and a hot bath and put on one of my two suits. Then I asked the desk clerk if there was a Jaguar shop in the city. He said he didn't know but he looked in the telephone book and said yes there was; he wrote the address on a slip of paper for me to give to the taxi driver and I went out.

I had no more trouble with the Jaguar dealer than I did with the clerk or the taxi driver. The only thing that's easier to spend than four thousand American dollars is a larger sum of American dollars. Not only that but the dealer turned out to be an American named Rudge, who dealt mainly with tourists and American Army personnel. He had a system worked out for volume sales whereby he scooted me around in my own Jaguar to talk to the Used Volkswagen people, the Tax people, the Auto-Club people and the Police people all in one afternoon; and the following morning an enormous Frankfurt cop, of the original rubber-hose team, delivered the plates, and Rudge and I drove over to the ADAC to pick up the Carnet de Passage, and Rudge handed me the keys and the driver's manual and said: "Well, sir, it's all yours. Where are you off to now?"

That stumped me. The car was brand-new, black, shiny, with twin fog lamps, twin wing mirrors, windshield washers, dual exhausts, a high-compression head, high-speed crankshaft damper, wire wheels, bucket seats, lead bronze bearings, a hot clutch and racing tires. It set Uncle Fred back almost four thousand dollars and left his nephew with only five thousand to live on till something came up; it was drawn along the road by two hundred and ten horsepower and was supposed to be able to top a hundred and thirty miles per hour with a good tailwind. But I didn't know where to go with it.

Well, I didn't want to appear an idiot, so I said, "I'm going back to Spain." And then because it occurred to me in the same moment: "The amount these toys cost, it's the only place in the world I can afford to live from now on."

He remarked I would have got a better trade-in on the Volkswagen (I got only six hundred dollars for it, with ten off for the missing spare) if I had not been banging it around Spain. Not that I had been able to do much damage in the three weeks I had had it, but the next buyer would want to know where it had been driven, and Spain has the reputation of being hard on cars. As for the Jaguar, Rudge said I would soon break it in half, I would scrape the under side off on the crowns and bumps, and I would spend thousands of dollars yearly on new springs, but that was my business. A mechanic who was bolting on my license plates also asked me where I was going, and when I said Spain, he grinned and said something in German to another mechanic and they both laughed.

"You have our address," Rudge said when I left. "We will try to get parts to you by mail, but it's not a very good bet."

I had my first tryout in the new car on the Autobahn between Frankfurt and Karlsruhe. I had no trouble finding the highway, but once on it I immediately ran out of gas. There's so much to do when you're buying a new car—seeing that the windows roll up and down and the heater blows and the lights all work—that I hadn't remembered to put in any gas. With the Volkswagen you wait till the motor starts to misfire, then you plug in the reserve and go hunt for a station; there is no indicator. On the Jaguar there is a big legible indicator and, more than that, a red light. This light had been glaring at me ever since I left Frankfurt, but there was such a jumble of buttons and levers and gauges that I hadn't noticed. Besides, it is no easy trick to sit down in a car with two hundred and ten horses and buzz calmly away with one elbow on the windowsill and a cigarette in the other hand. There were a lot of new things to learn. For one, to make the Volkswagen go at all you have to tromp on the accelerator good. Not so with a Jaguar. On leaving the dealer's I remembered to press lightly and not feed too much to the twin carburetors, but once in gear and moving I forgot a couple times and bore down so hard that all the valves clicked and my head snapped back. Once I almost rammed into an Opel Kapitan.

For another thing, the gearshift was stiff as army socks and now and then second wouldn't engage. And then there was the revolution counter. You're led to believe that if you exceed 2,500 r.p.m in the first thousand miles, or 3,000 in the second thousand, you have a dead horse on your hands. If you shift too soon the motor lugs, and if you wait too long it winds too high. Not that you can do any serious damage, because the car is delivered with an angle iron bolted under the accelerator and secured by a lead seal. This meant that a lot of Volkswagens and tincan Auto Unions and even U. S. of A. Pontiacs went sailing by me, whistling derisively at my poor low crawl. I was roused. My mother said that even when I had the Chevvy and put pipes on it I was speed-mad. But it is not exactly that; it is seeing other cars go breezing past that gets under my skin. Or maybe it is the suicide complex a friend of mine in college said I had. He was on oddball. He fell in love with a crazy girl who lived on the hill above the college town, and she tried to cut her wrists, and he went off all one summer vacation without a nickel in his pocket, and when he came back he never went to see her. But he was a very intelligent person and he said I was accident prone and self-destructive and hated my own face. It was from him that I learned to be an intellectual. We used to sit all night in the frat-house kitchen eating stew and kidney beans and discussing politics, the end of the world, and love. Neither here nor there.

When I ran out of gas on the Autobahn it was at a good time. The water temperature was up above eighty and it made me worry. Heat is the worst enemy of a new engine. I managed to coast into one of the escape roads where people stop to have picnics, and locked up the car and hitched a ride to the next gas station with an American Army major and his wife, two kids, and a Scotty dog. They were going to Switzerland for furlough. I got off at the next gas station and the attendant there made me leave ten marks deposit for the five-liter can he lent me to carry the gas in. I decided I was better off in Spain where people aren't so suspicious. From the station back to the car I got a ride in a big double lorry. Every truck in Germany seems to drag at least two large trailers behind it. The driver of this monster was younger than I and covered with scars as though he had been knocked apart by an avalanche and then sewed together by a shoemaker. I started to give him some marks to pay for the lift and he looked at me so mean that I was sincerely nervous.

The Jaguar wouldn't go even after the gas was in. I was about to hitch back to the gas station again to look for a mechanic when one of the ADAC Auto Club patrols came along on a motorcycle with a sidecar full of tools. He found the fuel line and blew the bubbles out of it somehow without burning himself, and thereafter the engine fired. He wouldn't accept a tip either, but smoked a Chesterfield with me and we had a long conservation about the Jaguar, him in German and me in English. He approved of the car, I could tell that. Then I went on.

I forget a lot of the trip and of course I was concentrating so much on driving that I didn't see the scenery; it was all I could do to catch the road signs going by. I remember there were some problems about the five-hundred-mile free check-up. I had a voucher for the service, given me by Rudge, good in any licensed Jaguar establishment, but I decided to do what I could on the road without stopping for a whole day until I reached Barcelona, where there was an accredited Jaguar garage. There was one in Strasbourg, but I arrived there too late the first evening. I stopped at about four hundred and fifty miles on the odometer and changed the oil and put in a new filter I had bought from Rudge; then, very late at night, I don't remember where, I stopped and broke the angle iron off the accelerator. From then on I fairly scat. Not exceeding 2,500 r.p.m. though, or hardly. There are a lot of long straight roads between Strasbourg and La Junquera, where everybody turns into a Spaniard, and it was about then that I got the hang of the car and started getting the gearbox worked in. I drained and refilled the rear axle in one place, got lubricated in another, and stopped to shorten the play in the clutch in a third, all without much trouble. It rained once and the wipers worked fine—two speeds—and then I was in the vicinity of Narbonne and knew my way from there. I went through Le Boulou in daytime and it didn't look too bad. I didn't see the man with the rotten cat smile and didn't stop in the bar where they hate Germans. I went on and stopped in one place to stare at the hazy Mediterranean inlets and let the engine cool off some just for luck. I was feeling a lot better.

I would always be friends with her, after the divorce was final and she was married again and had two kids or more, and every once in awhile a package would come and the kids would holler: It's from Uncle Andy! In the package would be a carved coconut, a stuffed marmoset or a live one, an elephant's tusk, a guitar, a shrunken head—something arriving in a box covered with exotic stamps, while the second husband did a slow burn. I wonder where he is now? Jennie muses. I didn't think he would go away forever. He always liked to travel. My, what a pea-green enviable life. Oh well, I must go and darn my second husband's smelly socks.

There are villas all along the Mediterranean coast, mostly in Italy and France, the Côte d'Azur, but it seems the big money has not yet discovered Spain. Yet the Costa Brava in the province of Gerona combines stupendous mountains with changing handsome seas under a sun that always shines. It is one of the most beautiful places I have ever seen. I often think that someday I will go back there to live forever, in one of the smaller villas under the olive trees, with lizards in the walls and black goats under the windows and the fishing boats coming and going on the tremulous Homeric blue sea off the end of the terrace. I was there one day on my way back from Germany in the new car, and for all I knew at noon I might have stayed there until I became a local monument; but in the evening the olive trees turned ghostly and the sea began to mourn and I went on. Last summer I went again with company and liked it better, but that evening I couldn't put up with it and I jumped in the car and went down to Barcelona. It was nothing like arriving home after a journey.

I could not get rid of Jennie. In a world where nobody knew me by name except Rudge, she was the only one who did not call me Captain or even Andy, but some fool nickname that meant me and nobody else. And in a country where everybody I saw was more or less dark, she was the blue-eye blonde just short of a barber's calendar, so that I was always fat with how she looked when we walked into a place and people stared at her. She had short blonde hair that curled around her ears, and long legs; and her breasts were high with a dark declivity between them. We would lie on the couch in the living room, when we had a living room, and I would put my nose in the hollow and run my hand up her calf. Then she would close her knees on my hand and ask if I felt secure. Sure I feel secure, I would say; and she would say: You can't escape unless I exhale.

We had our own bedroom down the hall. That was when we lived in a small apartment over a candy store to be away from both our sets of parents. I worked in a soap business; had been at it for two and a half years. When I took the job, I believed I would stay at it forever, just to earn the money (a wart's worth at a time, as a matter of fact) that would give me the privilege of coming home at night to find her cooking over our stove. She had a knack with recipes she got out of a special cookbook for people with experimental palates: sometimes we would have bananas with sour cream on our pork chops and it was better than you would expect. Or subgum fried rice with chestnuts and roasted eggs. I was full of the idea of turning into another Charley Kenilworth. He was a sixty-year-old guy in my office who had worked for the company since he was twenty-two and never asked for more than an increase in his wart's worth every so often to keep up with the cost of living. He was a hardnose old Presbyterian who wouldn't borrow a cigarette if he was out of them, and he had had the same wife ever since he was twenty-seven and he bought a new car every five years, and he had two sons, both married and gone. He lived a nothing life and I was prepared to follow his example and lead one, too, for the sake of coming home at night to eat shrimp soup and beef roasted with sherry, to watch television or go to the movies or to some friend's house for bridge or television and come home to bed afterward with my wife.

We had a nice apartment and a circle of acquaintances and the sporty little MG, and we scarcely ever visited our parents: mine were too rich and hers too poor and we didn't get along with any of them. We lived our own life and would have lived it so for sixty years, only things didn't work out that way. That night in Barcelona I remembered the roll of flesh above her breasts and the hand-knit socks and the glasses she put on to read, and the bed with the bookshelf and radio behind our heads, and the knees and the hips and the stomach with the slightly off center bellybutton that she had, and denied she had. All of it was very good and getting better, but somehow it got worse instead. That night when I arrived in Barcelona I wondered again where she had gone off, where I had gone off, and I reviewed everything and saw a couple of ways the trouble might have been avoided. It was late so I put the Jaguar in a garage and went to a hotel.

Everybody was very polite in the hotel when I said I had come to Spain to learn Spanish. I was dead tired. I went up and took a shower and got in bed before I remembered I hadn't eaten anything. It was twelve-thirty but I wasn't hungry. I lay in bed thinking about Jennie. Finally I got up and went out. First, I thought I would go to the garage and sit in the Jaguar, because while I was sitting in it, fondling the wheel and touching the buttons, I did not feel anything except pleasure in the machinery. Then I thought I would go get something to eat; and then I thought I would go to a whorehouse if I could find one. First I went to a bar.

It was not a bar on the Ramblas, the broad paseo full of tourists; it was down a maze of twisting cobbled streets between cramped shops, moulding rusty gateways, and high thin scabbed walls stained by centuries of garbage and urine, rainless damp, heat, and cracking chill. The cafés and bars opened like tunnels into the leaning walls; they were dusky and full of shabbily-dressed men, shoeshine boys, express coffee machines wringing out slow drops of murky coffee, flags and bullfight posters, and big aproned women now and then masked with darkening pancake. I sat on a stool in one of these places and the women asked if I was American Navy. But they were all too heavy and obvious and the best of them looked a little grimy around the nostrils. They were all named María, or its variants. I bought a bullfight poster for two dollars; it was full of gorgeous colors and I thought someday when I had a house again I would hang it on the wall in the gameroom; but later I left it somewhere. The girls lost interest in me when I would not buy them a drink, and I sat listening gloomily to the music.

Three men were on a platform over the bar ringing guitars, and a boy with white teeth and side whiskers—probably the business boyfriend of all the girls in the bar—was singing gracefully, with many high notes and throbbing vibratos, but nobody listened to him. At one of the back tables sat an old man, with seven or eight other men gathered around him, leaning on their elbows and listening to him. He sang, too. In a tight voice he ground out from the cords in his throat exclamations of pain and bereavement, scarcely audible beyond the table under the light bulb. His listeners were solemn and critical, as though the old man were singing to educate, not amuse, them. They were deeply thoughtful and stayed motionless through long tormented modulations, only at the very end nodding approval or murmuring a single Ole.

I didn't stay long. But before I left a man came in and asked me in perfect English if there was anything he could do for me. I said no and he tapped the bullfight poster rolled up in my coat pocket. "I could obtain tickets for the bullfights tomorrow if you wish," he said. "There is a very good corrida."

I told him I wouldn't be in town the following day. I would, but I didn't want any guides; they're too hard to get rid of once you do business with them. He was a stumpy little old fellow with black teeth and hard round eyes, and he reminded me of my father when the telephone bill comes in. I asked him where he had learned English and he shrugged and said he had always known it. He didn't look like a Spaniard; maybe he was somebody left over from the last war. I bought him a drink. He said: "You will not reconsider my offer to get tickets for tomorrow's bullfight?" I said no.

"I recommend it to you," he said. "The bulls are from Jaen; they are to be executed for having been heard to recount an improper joke concerning a Falangist meeting in a gypsy cave. One matador is to be gored medium severely in the left thigh for having referred to El Caudillo as El Cosquilleo. Haplessly, he cannot prove that it was a slip of the tongue."

I could have asked this hard little malcontent, but instead I went out to the Ramblas and got a taxi. The driver leaned back to look at me and I made some international gestures. It took some doing, but finally when I showed him some money he nodded and drove on, and then all I had to do was sit back and relax and try to see where I was going. The name of my hotel was the Brigánt and it was on the broad promenade street named the Ramblas; my name was written in my passport and also on my driver's license; but beyond that I was lost. The place he took me to was a building in a nice residential district. He let me out at an iron door, took my money and was gone before I even rang the bell.

A woman answered. She was heavy and ugly and I did not want to go in; I felt headachy and tired and the drinking-water pain had shot across the top of my stomach once or twice already that evening. It was not worth the trouble. I am not a broad-jumper; I have to work up to it, and I haven't much experience of whorehouses even in my own country, only enough to know that they are as mechanized as the ones in Spain. Here they had seven girls who filed out and stared at me and then went back in without even smiling. I had a hell of a time explaining to Madame that I wanted the light little round-armed one with yellow hair and blue eyes, that looked Frenchy and walked on three-inch heels. She came back in and we did not even get along well together. I think what I wanted was sympathy and they did not sell that. I went away feeling worse than before, lonely enough almost to ask the taxi who took me back to the hotel to drive me to another place, for another try. I think I had the idea that I would spend the night in some cathouse drinking beer, that I would rent a room in the same building and live there in bugs and dirt, and the girls would come up to chat with me in their off hours; I would learn Spanish and be friends with them and never touch them.

I only wanted somebody to talk to.

Two

CONSIDERING I wanted a divorce, and asked for it, and got it, the way I felt and acted those first weeks in Europe was a disgrace, but it is not worth arguing. The reason why everything suddenly fell apart runs into a theory of the psychology of the American female and the American male and ends up proving that there are no set patterns, that everybody is different; too much has been said in the public prints on that score anyway. Enough that she wanted me to be something that I wasn't, and wanted it bad enough that my refusal to be it spurred her to fight me, and that I fought back. If I hadn't won I would be Charley Kenilworth now. For the last six months we were toe-to-toe, hitting as hard as we could in our separate ways, and I hit harder. I hit her last. Then I went tooling along the shore of the Mediterranean moaning for her.

I think I have it fixed. The part about wanting to talk to somebody has gone away, and I am not so desperately lonely any more. I have people to talk to; I have a life again. I live with a Spanish girl and we get along. We live near a small town and everybody thinks we are married, so we are on speaking terms with everyone except the proprietor of one grocery store who cheated us when we first arrived and so lost our business and our friendship. We have friends in the city, and I know several young men with automobile and motorcycle interests. The little village bar we frequent is pleasant and full of people with whom to pass the time of day, and our neighbors on the farm alongside us come over sometimes. The only thing is, these people all speak Spanish, and while I can now talk a blue Spanish streak and make myself understood in spite of infinitives and errors in gender, I still sometimes get a powerful urge to talk English with somebody. But that's not a major problem.

I am more or less stationary now. Mari and I go for trips in the car, sometimes with a friend if he or she is willing to curl up in the jump seat with no leg room and very little headroom. But I don't run from dawn to dark as I did. My feeling for the Jaguar has changed too. When I was in love with it I used to touch it all over and feel under its skirts and fondle its fenders when I was not actually driving it. I washed it two or three times a week and waxed it at least twice the first month I had it, and I put stickers on the windows and Spanish-flag insignia on the bumpers and glass waxed the faces of the gauges. It stood for a lot. Maybe it is getting back at me now, as a matter of fact. I have just passed the worst four or five days of my life, automotively speaking.

Mari and I and a friend named Manuel Ortega, who is in the business of selling earrings and brooches to specialty shops (he is about my age and has a big English motorcycle that I can borrow sometimes), went up to Andorra this past week end. Andorra is a little republic or principality or something in the Pyrenees between France and Spain—two-by-four big and you never read anything about it in the newspapers, but it has two or three towns and a government all its own and the best density of automobiles per family in Europe, outside Germany. The scenery is picturesque and the standard of living high and there is a thriving contraband business, so I'm told.

We set out one morning over a back road that was supposed to lead us to the main highway that goes to Andorra via Seo de Urgel, but before we had gone ten miles something started going *clonk* in the rear suspension. I stopped right away and made everybody get out and wait in the road with the luggage piled around them. I drove on a short distance, hitting all the bumps I could find, and the rear end continued to go *clonk,* so it wasn't the weight or the luggage. Manuel and I screwed the spare down as tight as possible, hoping it was only that; but nothing doing, still the noise, so I decided to turn around and go home rather than risk a two-hundred-mile jaunt into the mountains where there wasn't even a service station, much less an accredited Jaguar agency.

On the way back, passing through one of the little towns above Más Nou, what should jump out in front of the car but a fat woman. This is simply not understandable to people who have never driven through Spain, through the winding streets of towns full grown long before the invention of the internal combustion engine and still not convinced of it. The streets had been laid out for donkey carts and two good-sized automobiles can't pass each other in some places; one has to back up. And the people, like this woman, don't really believe in motor cars. She was walking along and quite casually decided to cross the street just in front of me, without looking in either direction, not even the one in which she was going. I had already seen her but it never occured to me she would wander out in front of me. I jumped on the brakes and stopped short. The car has good brakes; they are carefully adjusted every five hundred miles. I stopped almost dead. I hit her, but only with the last five inches of forward motion, and anyway she had a bottom like a bolster. She plunked down on the cobblestones and turned white. I turned white, too, Mari said later. A million people appeared from nowhere.

The woman was only frightened. So was I. Dozens of people rushed to pick her up and she dragged them all with her on her instinctive struggle home. She was blubbering in Catalán, the local language. Manuel jumped out of the car with me and alertly took down the names of two or three men who had seen everything and were willing to swear the woman had stepped off the curb without looking. Manuel explained later that he got the names because innocent foreigners in big high-powered cars are sometimes held for considerable ransom. Then I went to the old woman's house and her son let me in. Everybody was grinning and the old woman was simultaneously crying and laughing at not being dead. The son gave me a glass of cognac to steady my nerves, as he gave one to the old woman to steady hers. This, by the way, is a good example of the Spaniard's readiness to help out a stranger—a readiness so automatic it made these people forget it was one of their own family that had been injured. Spaniards are some of the best people on earth.

So all was well, except it was by no means over. The rear suspension went on going *clonk* between there and home, and I spent the rest of the afternoon under the car but didn't find anything. We finally tried sitting Manuel in the other corner of the rear seat and the noise stopped immediately. So the problem was not exactly solved, only postponed. The next morning we left again for Andorra. It is a long trip, most of it in second gear. There is no use trying to explain the roads. A bad road, full of holes, anybody can understand, but it overtaxes the imagination to visualize mile after mile of consecutive hairpins. Not sharp curves: hairpins. Closed U-turns writhing along the sides of the mountains through a changing landscape. The sandhills and stony hummocks along the coast changed to Norway forests of heavy pines. We left spring behind in Cataluña, its coocoos and cactus and lemon trees and almond flowers. Up in the Pyrenees it was still winter and the snow was a foot deep on the shady sides of the mountains. Down below the roads were long steep valleys with occasional lost villages flung into the bottoms. The slopes were white with snow and empty except for occasional solitary clay houses halfway to the sky. We stopped and took pictures of each other under the pine trees, but none of them came out when we had the roll developed because of the glare on the snow or something. On the way to the top, where the road passes between big rocks called the Puerto Tosas, we slipped and skidded two or three times, with the edge of the drop to the valley never more than a few feet to our left. Once past the Puerto the snow thinned out and vanished. We went faster. The car bends very neatly around even the sharpest curves in a reasonably fast gear.

Along came an enormous diesel truck loaded with telephone poles, towering thirty feet in the air and leaning over.

I had a choice of: one, ramming full into this monster; two, holding to my right and trusting him to avoid me and so fall off the mountain; or three, take to the ditch. We were lucky to be on the mountain side of the road or we would have gone over. The road was not wide enough for two cars, much less a car and one diesel truck. I took to the ditch. There was almost enough room on the shoulder. I knew just about what I had. The worst I could do was scrape along the shoulder and bend the exhausts or punch a hole in the radiator. As it happened I did neither, only filled up the jacking sockets with gravel. Both offside wheels went into the ditch and we slid to a stop while the truck trundled on around the corner and vanished. It could at least have stopped to tow us out.

Manuel and I crawled under to look for dripping oil, leaking water, or dangling springs, but found nothing. Mari sat in the car fluttering and breathing hard. Poor little Chiquitín—she was more frightened than anybody. She is afraid of cars and when I drive fast she hunches up in the corner and stares at the onrushing road like a bird at a snake. Her husband and sister were both killed in the same auto wreck some years ago. She knows I like to run a little when there's a good stretch of road, so she won't say anything, but I know she's counting her beads. This car goes very fast. Sometimes I even scare myself. I have made a couple of mistakes already, though none of them serious. Mostly it is a matter of brakes. You come to a flat stretch and wind up to about ninety, and then suddenly the stretch comes to an end, usually in a curve and hill combined. The choice is to jam on the brakes and burn up the linings and maybe skid, or else let up on the gas and wait for wind and road resistance to slow you down to where down-shifting and braking is at least an engineering possibility. Once or twice I have shot into these corners and felt my inside wheels lift a little off the ground. Once or twice I have found myself in four-wheel slides on roads too narrow for such shenanigans. So far I have not yet met any big diesels in the middle of one of these corners, but sometimes I sit in the garage in the morning warming up the motor and thinking: maybe there will be a truck on the other side of today's blind corner.

We put rocks under the front and rear wheels to make a sort of ramp to climb out of the ditch on. Probably I could have driven straight out without them, but I was worried about my springs. Between the fat old woman and the diesel I was nervous to the point that I drove the rest of the way to Andorra at a modest thirty-five. Just as well, because it started to rain at the frontier and did not stop raining all the time we were there. The roads were buttery. Every time I applied brakes the rear end seemed to swivel a little. Thinking back, I tend to shake my head over the whole trip, from first to last.

As far as the excursion goes it was hardly worth it. It rained all three days. Manuel went out some mornings to sell earrings to the local shops, but most of the time we just sat around in the fonda where we were staying and played parcheesi.

Most of Andorra is just a long steep valley with the twin towns of Les Escaldes and Andorra la Vella crammed into the last half mile, like something shoved into the prow of a canoe. Our posada stood with its back to the mountain and the first morning I looked out I saw rain falling on the town, but snow falling on the pine trees above on the slope. A river ran straight through this town, about thirty feet wide and foaming its way amid boulders and fallen trees, so that the noise of its flowing was a constant roar in the streets, in the houses, in the bars, and the bedrooms, like a noise in the head. Only once did it stop raining, and then only for a few minutes. From a balcony we watched the next storm come wallowing up the valley like a low dirigible, massive and gray and solid enough to hit like a stick.

It was cold. However, with water cascading from every rock higher than eye level, electricity was dirt cheap, so we put three coil heaters together around the card-table and sat playing parcheesi in relative comfort. Manuel and I were so bored we wouldn't even think of any way to alleviate the boredom. Mari wanted to go to the movies, but I had come to visit a funny little principality in the mountains and would not hear of wasting my time on movies, which I could do anywhere. Most of the three days we argued. Mari is a kind of Christian Communist, and every once in a while would make some remark like: If the gold of Spain were distributed as God wills it, there would be enough for every man to have a house and a mule and to keep his family decently. When Manuel and I tried to drill a little economic theory in her head she would turn stubborn and cite the case of some acquaintance of hers as though it proved everything. Women always do that. If you explain something as true and proved as Gresham's Law to them they always have a friend who spent his gold and hoarded his 1917 rubles. I am at a disadvantage when I argue with her because naturally I can't talk Spanish as fast as she can, and then she thinks she has put one in my eye. This makes me sullen. Two of the nights in Andorra we went to bed and said "Rest thyself" very curtly and settled down back-to-back to sleep. The third night she tickled me in the popliteal and said: "Cariño, art enraged?"

I will explain about Mari soon, but I haven't finished with the series of mishaps on the Andorra journey, and the weather counts as one. The first two nights I put the Jaguar in the garage and it only rained; but the third night I left it in the street, since we were planning to leave early in the morning, and it snowed. Somebody skidded during the night and when I came out in the morning there was a red mark and a dent on the left rear fender. The Andorranos abroad at that hour must have thought I was out of my mind: I stormed up and down the whole length of the street with the copper-and-hide mallet from the tool kit in my hand, looking for a red vehicle with a corresponding bump. I never found it or there would have been a murder. Luckily the dent was not deep and with the red paint scrubbed off it hardly showed. But it is still there and every time I look at it I am reminded of Andorra and the hairpins and the diesel and the fat old woman. I don't think I will ever go up that direction again.

I was shaken. Dents, bumps, near misses, gravel in the underworks, miserable weather and grit from Manuel's feet in my back seat, litter in the seams of the upholstery . . . and then we went home by a different route and had to pass over thirty kilometers of rock garden where a new road was being put in. We went through an absolute wilderness and passed through a deep canyon that is a real natural wonder, but I scarcely noticed. The road was a tank trap, with steep slopes to groan up in second gear, running a temperature in the radiator, and too many stretches where water sluiced out of the rocks and into the road as though to wash us over the precipice. It kept on raining. Near Tiurana the Guardia Civil stopped us and made us drag every goddamned thing in the car out for them to inspect. There are secret customs checks all along the Spanish highways, but they usually don't bother foreign cars. This was a lonesome outpost, though, and maybe they just thought it would break the monotony to stop somebody in a fancy car. They were officious and extremely thorough and on top of that one of them called Mari *Tu* instead of *Usted,* which was disrespectful. They all carried sub-machineguns with their fountain pens stuck in the muzzles.

We spent the rest of the trip from there to Barcelona cursing the Guardias and reflecting on the sad plight of the Spaniards who are about fifty per cent cops of one kind or another. Or so it seems as you walk down the Ramblas. There are more uniformed and formidably armed cops than lampposts. And still more in civilian clothes who go around listening to conversations in bars to catch people breaking the law against talking politics. But a tourist has to be here for some time before he notices anything.

We let Manuel off near his house and then drove on toward home, some twenty miles outside the city. The trip was not yet over. There's no arrangment for draining the roads when it rains, and lakes collect. In the dark I could not see them coming. I went to pass a Renault that was popping along at about fifteen miles an hour between Badalona and Más Nou, and I went *floop* into one of them about a foot deep. The car slewed and I could see nothing through the windshield for a moment—I was cursing the mud flung all over my clean engine—and I changed down a gear. With the clutch out the engine died. And there we were. Maybe the distributor got wet somehow. The rain was teeming down. I sat without moving for a moment, debating whether to punch Mari in the nose or just run away screaming into the hills. Then I pushed the starter and the engine caught. I suppose the engine heat evaporated the water off whatever was wet; anyway, it started. We drove on. I stopped in the next service station and opened the hood, but everything looked all right to me. We went on very slowly. Between there and home a tire blew.

We were in the middle of nothing, on a road that cambered down to the sea on one side, with no room for a passing car on the other. Changing that tire was a nightmare. The jack lifts both wheels on one side at once, and I was afraid the other two wheels wouldn't hold the car up, that it would slip off the jack into the sea. Then I found the spinner hub on the flat wheel hammered down so hard I couldn't get it off. Then, too, you can't jack up a Jaguar without having the door open, and the rain was running in on my red upholstery. Moreover Mari kept asking stupid questions. To be fair, any question sounds stupid when you are changing a tire in the pouring rain. The spare turned out to have only about fifteen pounds of air in it, so we skidded wildly every time I braked between there and home. When we finally got home I put the car in the garage and locked it and did not take it out again for three days. It was dirty inside and out and underneath, dented and scarred, underinflated and overheated and dry in the bearings. Only a mother could understand my feelings.

A day or two after my return I noticed an itch in my armpit. Wash your armpits, Cord, I said to myself. I did, but the itching persisted. Then my groin began to itch. I spent an ecstatic night or two. Then an informed source—a friend living on a slum street in Barcelona—put me straight. He said I had crabs. Life is full of wonders.

When we are not traveling we live about three quarters of a mile from a small market village on the road between Barcelona and France. The beach is flat and runs for miles beyond a barrier of huge gray stones the Highway Commission, or what passes for it, has put up to stop the waves. The terrain rises slightly, and four or five miles behind our house the mountains begin again. Our house is high enough that we have a clear view of the Mediterranean over the roofs of the houses along the highway. We face in the direction of Italy, more or less. It is an empty sea; there is not much traffic except a few fishing boats and an occasional American battleship far out.

We don't live in a villa. There are some fancy houses in the vicinity, but they rent very high and are normally in use only during the summer or during Holy Week in late March when people come out from the city. These villas don't have much in the way of foul-weather conveniences. Not that our place has either; there is only one small fireplace in the living room. We live in a farmhouse actually. The family who used to live in it has moved down to the pueblo and operates a sweet shop, a bar, a barber shop, and a pharmacy. The sons didn't want to be farmers. The farmland itself is rented out to the neighbors in the white house some two hundred yards from us; they raise potatoes and cabbages and other vegetables I don't recognize and they are generally swarming all around our house with ploughs and shovels from first light on. They draw water for their crops from a round pool four or five yards deep and the same across (we swim in it when the weather is good and the water is clean) that is on our property; right in front of our house as a matter of fact. We are awakened every morning by the neighbors saying Hoo to their horses. They also have a cow and its calf, hundreds of rabbits in pens, a flock of geese, some ducks and two lambs, one black and one white, that run free and have lately taken to visiting us when we pull our hammock-chairs out in the yard and sit eating our meals in the sun. Directly in front of our house is a fig tree and a little to the side is a lemon tree, loaded at the moment with fruit. We try to eat some, but what can you do with a whole tree full?

The inside of the house is what you might call unspoiled provincial. That is, the Catalán family that lived here had their own ideas of how to decorate and we have not touched anything, neither the mouldy stuffed squirrel on top of the radio, nor the cross-eyed China lions on the window sills, nor the paintings of the Last Supper nor the busts of Mary Mother. Paint is peeling off the walls in the rooms that are painted; the rest of the rooms are nude white plaster with crucifixes here and there. We have any number of straight chairs and two woven basket-chairs and then the hammocks, or beach chairs. In the kitchen there is a big wood range with a firebox just the size of the lengths of olive wood we buy to put in it; and along the side, built into the counter, there is a square pit for making small charcoal fires and a sink with three faucets, all running cold. The floors are tile and freeze your feet through your shoes on a cold day. The light switches are hung loosely on the walls in the most unlikely places and sometimes the whole system goes on the fritz. All the wiring was loosely festooned around the walls some fifty years after the house was built, in the apparent conviction that electric lighting was just a fad that wouldn't last.

To leave the house you pass out through the adjoining garage, because the front door hasn't been opened for twenty years and probably won't open any more. It's about a foot thick, made of solid oak, secured with bolts and chains and padlocks, and it has swelled up to fit its aperture as tight as a block in a stone wall. Once outside and in the car you drive over a thousand yards on a cart track before reaching the asphalt. In wet weather this track is a bog. Even when dry it is not easy to negotiate, on account of the holes and ruts, and the mattocks and ploughshares our neighbors leave lying around.

You'd gather the place is in a mess, but we both like it. Once you realize you can do without a lot of things you once considered indispensable, you are really more comfortable than before. We have plenty of room; the kitchen is warm and dry in bad weather; the garage accommodates the Jaguar and all my apparatus for maintaining it. We can hear the sheep and goats go by, ringing their bells early and late, and the beach is close. There is an almond orchard to one side of the house and a mixed forest of pine and grand cactus behind it. There are few bugs, hardly any lizards, and we always have friends around—if not somebody from down in the city or the village, then the folks from next door, or else the two lambs and the Siamese cats.

The girl I live with is named María de los Ángeles Florentina Quintero García, as near as I can make it out. To explain her I have to go back to the evening I arrived in Barcelona on the way back from Germany with the Jaguar brand-new and in need of its free checkup. I had almost nine hundred miles on it and that was four hundred miles past time to make a lot of general tests: tighten the body bolts, clean the carburetor filters, and check the brake unions, axle bolts, clutch and so forth. The morning after my arrival I drove the car up to the Jaguar garage high in the new city and left it there. I came out on the sidewalk with nothing to do until the following afternoon at four, when it would be ready.

In my state of mind I wasn't fit to sit down and commune with myself in the Brigánt Hotel. But there was no point going to movies since I wouldn't understand them, and I didn't have any idea where to go for long walks, or where to eat, or what to do, and above all I didn't have anybody to talk to.

To begin killing the long day I decided to walk back to the hotel instead of taking a taxi. It must have been all of three miles, but as I say, I didn't have anything else to do. I passed down through the new city, which is just that: built mostly in the last twenty years or so. It features a lot of sloppy modern architecture and the intersections are equipped with very modern rond-points. There are garages and shops and hospitals and apartment buildings and broad desolate streets, and if it weren't for the cafés and an occasional braying burro you might think you were in some airy and semiabandoned suburb in Queens. This is all in direct contrast to the old city, which extends from the Plaza Cataluña down to the harbor and dates back to long before Columbus. The streets down there don't look wide enough for a single normal-size automobile, but they are packed with trucks, horses and carts, two-stroke motorcycle-engined vehicles of tin-can construction, taxis, tourist buses, and a great many riotous scooters and motorcycles all traveling at considerable velocity and puffing clouds of blue smoke.

Pedestrians of all descriptions surge along excitably on sidewalks a foot and a half wide, knocking each other off into the paths of lumbering trucks a hundred years old, and black and yellow taxis either just as old or brand spanking new. On the Ramblas, where I ended up, lines of cars inch between curbside stalls full of gorgeous flowers on the one hand and swarming trolleycars on the other.

By the time I got to the Ramblas I was steaming. There was a bookstore on the corner that advertised foreign books, so I went in and bought a pocket English-Spanish dictionary and then sat at a small table in an outdoor café and tried to reconcile the grammar sections with what I remembered of the two years of Spanish they made me take in college. Not thinking, I ordered coffee and a waiter sweated an exprés out of one of those Rube Goldberg machines and brought it to me, and I sipped it without looking and almost gagged. "Meelk?" the waiter said.

"All right," I said. "Café au lait. Café leche." That was my first conversation in Spanish. The city continued to heat up. After a time I went and found a taxi and had my second. "Vamos, comprendez? You voy rapidad, understand? Hacer viento. No? You speak any English? No? Listen: Señor, you marche le taxi, entiende? Woosh, cool! Un promenade." I had had it all figured out, but when he didn't understand me the first time it threw me off. What I wanted was to ride around and see the city with the windows open to make a breeze. The heat of the sun was wilting my aplomb, giving me a form of bud blast. We struggled with each other, and the doorman from a nearby hotel came over, and two blind men selling lottery tickets ambled up to see if they could help. The taxista climbed down from his seat and gabbled and after awhile we had a fair crowd. Everybody tried to help. The doorman spoke French and I said "No française" until I was tired of it. The rest all talked to me in their equivalents of Español Fácil and then they presented their conclusions to the taxi driver. He and two or three other men talked earnestly and rapidly in the Catalán dialect, trying to figure out what I wanted by the way I was dressed. They all got excited and gestured with rigid hands. Under other circumstances I would have let it ride at the first failure rather than spend half an hour at it, but these were the first people who had noticed me in a week, and I caught something cordial and tough and friendly in their attitudes that did me good.

Finally I looked in my dictionary again and found Paseo. "Paseo," I said to the driver.

"Paseo," he said. "Sí."

"Solamente un paseo," I said.

"No más?"

"No más," I said. "Yo pagar." It was all arranged. We jumped in and said goodbye and the crowd waved. We went downhill through the traffic to the waterfront and the driver started the tour off by pointing out the statue of Columbus, and I think he tried to get me to believe he was a native of Barcelona. There was also a little boat that I couldn't see very well through the iron gates, and he said it was the *Santa Maria* en verdad. Then we went up a long broad street to the Plaza España and into the park on top of the hill. From the very top there was a view of the sea and the harbor and the city smoking to a cinder under the brass ball of the sun. Then we went down out of the park by another route to Columbus again, up the Ramblas past my hotel and turned onto another wide avenue, and pulled up at a tall gargoyle of an unfinished church with which the driver seemed modestly pleased, as though he had built it himself. It was the church of the Sagrada Familia and I have not yet run across anybody Spanish who doesn't think it's beautiful. To me it looked as though it might suddenly run into a puddle of caramel and melted butter in the sun, it was that confectionary.

After that we took a longish trip I hadn't planned on. The driver leaned back and said: "Tibidabo?" I said: "Sure, very nice," but it turned out Tibidabo was a place name, and the place was a good way away. Our taxi was a battered, rattling old Citroën with many pink patches of repaired metal on its fenders and sides. We went up from the new city along another of these winding-around incredible roads and on the eventual summit there was a small church and a bar and some amusements. The taxista pointed intently at the church until I got out and walked up to it. In front was a huge cast-iron Christ without any halo. Signs all around said in English, French, German, and Portuguese that Christ counted on the generosity of visitors of all faiths and nationalities for the final benediction of His neon halo to shine over the city below. The church, more signs explained, had been built around a little decorative prayer stall on the highest point of the mountain. In these days the only thing higher was the high end of the Atalaya, a carnival-wheel affair of two cabins on either end of a steel beam, that revolved shrieking girls, just like anywhere else in the world.

"Montserrat?" asked the driver; but I wasn't going to be caught again. "Dónde es?" I said, and he pointed inland to another mountain visible from where we stood but some twenty miles distant—or maybe fifty or a hundred by car, depending on how many hairpins there were. "Muy bonito," the driver said, referring to Montserrat, which looked hard and craggy as a yellowed old tooth in the burnished landscape. I have been there since that day, and it is really a weird sort of mountain of perpendicular granite shafts, with an air of having come from somewhere else. There isn't a hint of its peculiar geology anywhere else around. On top there's a monastery of some kind, and a thousand spectacular vantage points, and a legend of a Madonna found in a cave which refused to be carried downhill, making itself too heavy to lift.

I got the driver to take me back to the Ramblas, as I was getting hungry. There was some trouble in the end, and we had to get an interpreter from a nearby travel agency. The idea was that he claimed he forgot to put down the flag when we started off, and without the machine ticking he would just have to estimate the fare. This is an old gag, and when he estimated, it came out enough to cover not only gas and oil, but also depreciation on his car and the cost of repairing two cigarette holes burned in the upholstery. I paid the equivalent of six dollars and forty-two cents when everything was explained; I would have paid it anyway. He was cheating me in a casual and friendly way, and when he had driven off I missed him.

I still didn't have anything to do. I decided to go to the bullfights after all, but first I wanted to eat. At last I was hungry. There was another friendly waiter in an expensive restaurant near the top of the Ramblas; he spoke a little English and warned me I could probably not eat the English mixed grill and a paella both. He brought me both, though, and then stayed to watch when I ordered a second portion of the paella, paella being a mound of yellowed rice full of fish chunks, chicken, beef, oysters, pimientos, and enormous shrimp called gambas, complete with heads and feet and feelers. Paella is more or less the national dish, and varies in form wherever you get it. In good restaurants it is approximately as I have described it, but a national dish is no good unless you can adapt it to individual tastes and means. In very poor houses it is only rice and three thin crayfish.

This was the first time I had tried it and I liked it very much. Spaniards eat a lot, heavy meals, but my waiter was not accustomed to foreigners with such big appetites (I have a heavy appetite normally and in this case hadn't eaten much since Cherbourg) and he hung around waiting for me to get sick. When I didn't he said something to another waiter, which, now I think back on it, was: "I evacuate ten times in the milk; this one has the stomach of a goat."

That afternoon I went to the bullfights, and discovered that neither Hemingway nor Tom Lea nor Tyrone Power nor my imagination had prepared me for it. First I decided I could stand whatever sun still shone in the last few hours of the afternoon (the show didn't start till four), so I bought a seat in the Sol instead of the Sombra. My place was down front in the second row, but on a narrow concrete ledge burned white and shimmering, hard as an anvil. My second mistake was not to rent one of the canvas pillows men were hawking at the entrances. Everybody else had one. The third mistake, after I had been sitting for half an hour and was soaked with sweat and dizzy, was to buy and drink what looked like a bottle of orange pop. It was warm and thick and completely unfamiliar, and it gave me a few vigorous moments keeping it down. I didn't have any sunglasses and could hardly see.

After a long time a group of people came out a hidden door in the arena and paraded around in costume to the music of a band I couldn't locate. I finally saw it way up top in the shade where there were hundreds of Spanish soldiers in wooly uniforms, eating peanuts and drinking out of wine skins. At the end of the parade came a team of horses dragging hooks in the sand. A little while later the first bull ran out the door, stopped dead, and looked all around. Little men with red capes ran at him from all sides and he chased one after another until he was tired. Then a man came up and stuck two sticks full of colored ribbons in him and ran away, leaving the bull twitching its shoulders nervously. There was a man next to me who jumped up and shouted Ole when this happened, and everybody looked at him. My head ached. I felt I wasn't entering the spirit of the thing, but I didn't feel like it. More people came and stuck banners on the bull. Prepared for a barbarous spectacle, for bloodlust and cruelty, I kept waiting for something to happen. The bull did not seem particularly upset, but it obviously did not like the horses, padded up in big quilts. It butted them so hard it knocked them up in the air, and some fell and had to be hauled to their feet like old ladies out of plush armchairs. But the horses didn't seem to mind either; they took it in good part, suffering hideous internal injuries, probably, but I've often heard that their vocal cords are cut, for Christ's sake, so they can't scream.

When I shaded my eyes with my hand I could see a little, but I was still apprehensive about my stomach. The bull kept running after the red cape wherever he saw it. The torero led him in circles. Blood was running down the bull's sides in a red sheet; it was tiring. Anticipating to a nicety the exact moment the bull would learn better and stop chasing the flag, the matador leaned over and stabbed his sword down through the top shoulder on the near side. The bull collapsed onto its front knees and lay down, sort of doglike. Another man jabbed the bull twice between the horns with what looked like an icepick, and then the team of horses came out. Men hooked the carcass to the horses and dragged it away while the matador walked around the ring with his arms in the air, his hat in one hand; the women in the audience threw their shoes at him. Not in disapproval; they probably just didn't have any roses.

One bull, I think it was the fourth, ripped the matador's pants up to the crotch; he had to go behind the barrier and tie a handkerchief around the rip. But every step he took it spread out and looked sillier; it was practically indecent exposure, so he went irritably under the arena to change his pants. The new pants did not match his chrome-plated jacket, and he was nervous. The bull caught him in the crotch again and flung him end over end in the air. Apparently he wasn't hurt, but the new pants were ripped in the same place. They were so tight I didn't see how he could walk in them anyway. Now he was more nervous than ever. When the moment came for the kill he missed completely and the sword sliced down the bull's side and let out a further waterfall of blood. People were beginning to whistle, which is the equivalent of boos, and the soldiers in the top tiers were shouting. The second thrust went into the bull but did not kill it. The matador walked around the panting bull in a jerky circle, and then stabbed again, missing the heart again. Everybody was whistling now. When the two passed close I could see blood all over the bull, and the sweat on the man's face and the silky sheen of his drawers showing through the rip. Long strings of saliva were hanging from the bull's jaws and his sides worked like bellows and his back legs trembled. The fourth thrust went part way into the huge red shoulders and clanked against bone; the sword sprang from the matador's hand and leaped in the air. He would not bend down to pick it up; he retreated and waited for a flunky to hand him a new sword. I felt like protesting. It seemed to me that by all rights the bull had won the fight long ago and he ought to be let off, to go live out his days in a green field and tell his grandchildren about the time he flung a famous matador ten feet in the air and damn near exposed his exterior plumbing to a capacity crowd. But he was not to be let off. The matador came back with the new sword and stabbed again. This time the bull fell down on its forelegs and looked all around the arena, as though hoping somebody would come down out of the crowd and lend a hand. Eeverybody was screaming and whistling and things were flying through the air; the arena sounded like one vast birdcage. The matador finally kicked the bull and stalked away in a fury. That was apparently the signal for the phlegmatic one with the icepick to come out and finish up.

The band played. Men in ragged clothes began cleaning up the blood and footprints in the sand. The bull was hooked up and towed away, but the matador wouldn't leave the ring; he was protesting the booing and the crowd was booing his protests. I got up and climbed through the people toward the exit. It was only intermission, I know now, but I thought it was all over. Four bulls dead seemed like enough for me. There were vendors and technicians in the shade under the stands discussing the riot up above. They stared at me but I was thinking in terms of getting out ahead of the crowds so as to find a taxi. "Old bull," I said affectionately. "Threw him right up in the air and de-pantsed him."

I guess I turned down the wrong tunnel and made a half circuit under the stands before I saw an archway with sun shining in it and made my way out from under the uproar that was still going on, louder than any Big League game I ever attended. I was in an unroofed passage between wooden walls, and by a gate the horses were standing and the ragged men were smoking in the cool shade. The street was just ahead. I saw the last bull dead in the passage and men tearing the hooks out of its legs. Then there was a commotion behind me and I saw twenty or thirty people being hustled up the passage by an almost equal number of Policía Armada. Most of the people were infuriated Spaniards but six or seven were taller people with sandy hair and cameras with their attachments strung all over them. The women were lean and fidgety, the men sunstruck and fitted out with baggy pants. To me they looked like traveling English. There wasn't much room for them to pass by but I pressed the wooden wall; and they crowded past and the rear-guard policeman prodded me into a dead run with the end of his truncheon.

There wasn't anything like a police wagon in the street; instead we were loaded into an ancient cattle truck, and away we went. I wormed over to one of the men who looked English and asked if he'd mind telling me what we'd done. "Throw cushions at that filthy matador," he said, all exhilarated. "Demn fine bit of business. Couldn't hit him though. Too far away."

I remarked that the police had just picked me up in the corridor, that I had left the arena before there were any cushions thrown, that I hadn't thrown any, and he said: "I don't suppose it matters. Phyllis didn't throw any either, did you, Phyl?"

One of the lean women said: "I didn't throw anything at all. Why was everyone throwing things?"

"You see," the first Englishmen said, "when the torero doesn't stand quite close enough to the bull to execute his rabadilla, the crowd whistles. Then they throw cushions. All these fine fellows were throwing cushions, so we threw some, too. Now I suppose we shall have to pay a fine. Are you an American?"

I said yes and he said: "Oh well then, I suppose you can afford it. Are you staying in Spain long?"

Phyllis said: "If you are staying for any length of time perhaps you'd like to buy our dog. We have a dog bought from a bootblack in San Sebastián, you see, and now we find we can't take it home unless we place it in quarantine for six months. It would be ever so much kinder if we found a home for the poor brute."

All the English had been drinking sherry in the sun. But it didn't hurt our case any. The Policía whisked us into a different room in the comisaria from the one where they put the natives, and the judge imposed a fine on us. "I eempose a fine," he said pleasantly. "One honderd pesetas each person." The English asked each other what that amounted to. The men were named MacLean, Fitch, and Braisted; the women were named Phyllis, Angela, and Ruth. I told them it was just two dollars and fifty cents in American, and Angela said: "Oh that's simply eighteen shillings. I'm quite familiar with American money; Carleton had simply wads."

"Come and have a drink," MacLean said to me when we had paid our fines and the Spanish customers had been taken below to start serving their sentences. The English and I went out together. It was evening by then; the evening paseo had begun. The entire population of Barcelona in its best clothes walked slowly and with a roaring carnival noise from the upper city to the harbor and back again. "You people go along to the Café Luna," Braisted said. "I'll go to fetch the old Singer and Tossup."

MacLean caught me by the arm and said: "Listen here, old man, I'll pay."

"Oh top-hole," I said. "Who are Singer and Tossup?"

"That's our dog," Phyllis said. "No, the car is. We have a Singer Nine and one can only fit five in it, but we came all the way from Bordeaux with six, and now we have the dog. We call him Tossup because it was a tossup whether he would be a German shepherd or a dachshund."

"Or for what he did with whatever we fed him for the first week," Angela said.

"He isn't either," Fitch said. "He's a police dog. A lobo, as they say here, exactly what the bootblack said, although we thought it meant wolf."

"Wolf means lobo in English," MacLean explained to me.

We all strolled up the Ramblas together. The Café Luna was in the pretty plaza at the top. People were ambling in all directions with and against the dozens of traffic lights and across the symmetrical centerpiece of the park. In the café we pulled two small tables together and sat on the sidewalk under an awning, and waiters came with cloths over their arms. Fitch ordered a bottle of champagne. "Look here, old boy," he said, "you drink a toast to us to show how sorry we are you were dragged into our little beano this afternoon. Quite sorry about your fine."

"Doesn't matter a bit," I said. Braisted never left to go after their car, which was still parked outside the Plaza de Toros with the dog locked in it. Following the bottle of champagne we descended to the lower city in single file through the crowds. I was glad to be talking English and was willing to follow them anywhere they went, at least till they began to snub me. They were all new in the city, too, and the problem was where to go. MacLean, the expert on Spain, said that a night club was out because decent women couldn't go into Spanish night clubs; all necessary women of the non-decent kind were there already, supplied for a stag clientele by the manager. Phyllis and Angela wanted to go to a movie. Women always want to go to movies in strange towns. I see the point. If there is one place in the modern world which is the safe hub of human life, it is the movies. Except for different languages and ventilation systems, one movie is exactly like another if it is in Pawtucket, Rhode Island, or the Belgian Congo, and the quiet people sitting around hypnotized might be Parsees or Pennsylvanians or Picadillians. Phyllis and Angela probably wanted to go to the movies because they were weary of being far from home in an exotic city full of foreigners. But we didn't go anyway. While we were debating in the middle of the sidewalk a little man in pegged pants came up to us and said: "Good night, misters and madames. You need interpreter? Guide? You wish to see spectacle?"

"Do you suppose it's like a Paris Exhibition?" Angela asked.

"Ignore the fellow," Fitch said. "I don't like the sound of it."

"Barcelona is a little Paris," Phyllis said. "It says so in the Southern Voyagers' Guide."

The small man's name was Ramón; he was a legitimate guide and also a pander. He had arranged to collect a commission from whatever dive he brought tourists to. Practically everybody who is not either a cop or owner of a bar is a guide in Barcelona in the summer time. Or else black-markets Lucky Strike cigarettes. "Gitano caves?" Don Ramón said. "Geepsy caves?" Later on he told me he was Andalucían. His fawn-colored suit was covered with a thin film of grease, his teeth were terrible, and he wore his hair in a big pompadour from which little ends fell out and coiled around his ears.

He took us to a place where there was an orchestra and a heavy woman in a red-spangled bathing suit who did bumps and grinds so wrenchingly that even the other Flowers of the Night sitting around looked disgusted. This place was called the Cairo and it is in the guidebooks as one of the two or three best clubs in the city, but it was only two-by-four, and besides it was one of the places MacLean meant when he referred to Bachelor Night Clubs. Not that it was a brothel or anything like that, or that diddling went on upstairs; only that decent Spanish women would never go to such a place, and a night club without women would be silly, so the management arranged to have women. The women were not exactly prostitutes; they only sat around drinking, and if they could get somebody to buy the drink they got a cardboard token from the waiter, and at the end of the evening they redeemed the tokens for pesetas. Of course if they met somebody in the club, and he bought them drinks and danced with them and started to make improper advances, what they did about that after the club closed was no concern of the management's.

This place was expensive, and the women were, generally speaking, rather pretty, but beyond that it had the same reek of black tobacco and European water closets, and the same rapacious waiters as any other dive. Moreover, it was almost empty when we arrived. Nothing begins in Barcelona until at least midnight. The orchestra was small and spasmodic. MacLean danced once with Ruth, but everybody else pulled to the side and gave them long hot Spanish stares, till they began to trip over each other, so they came and sat down again. MacLean said: "By heaven, one'd think they'd never seen a white man before."

Ramón sat down by me. "You like leetle girlfran?"

"No," I said.

"Hombre, everyone have girlfran," he said. "You like one leetle girlfran talk and sing?"

"No," I said.

"Oh go on and get a girlfran," Fitch said. "Don't want to be odd man out, do you?"

A little later a thin girl came out and began to do a typical Spanish dance. First she danced alone, then with a dark weirdly graceful boy about four feet high and slippery. I was looking at her and Ramón said: "You like that one for girlfran? She is good fran mine, clean girl, no puta. Bailadora, she is arteesta." The girl had endless long black hair and enormous eyes. When she danced she did a turn that threw her hair forward over her face and gave her a look I will swear made her look more Spanish than even Ramón's haircut. The Englishmen watched her too, and MacLean said wolfishly: "You might as well have her brought over to the table, old boy. She'd certainly add a bit of something!" Ramón beckoned to a waiter and whispered and the waiter went to the bar and spoke to the boss. Ramón said to me: "She come quick. Good luck for her. Spanish man think she is too skeeny. We speak: only dog like bones."

I didn't think she was skinny. It is not strictly true that all Latin men like big fat earth-mother women with cannonball breasts and a behind like a mat, although among the carters and diggers and taxistas maybe a case could be made. Men of the upper class like their women a little subtle, like good horses. Anyway, this girl wasn't at all skinny by American standards. She came out in a cocktail dress and I could see the conformation of her body under the fabric, but nothing more; not like the woman in the red bathing suit who slid around the floor with one leg forward, wriggling her pelvis at each table in turn. When my girl came closer I noted that her nose had no indentation at the top but was straight from the brow down, like ancient Greek noses. She had huge dark eyes.

Ramón jumped up and placed her a chair next to me. "You like one drink?" he said. I told him to order a bottle of champagne. This isn't as silly as it sounds. Good champagne costs about seventy cents a bottle. The girl smiled at me and laid her hand on my wrist and said something long and rapid. "I don't speak Spanish," I said. Ramón jumped in and said: "Oh he speak Spanish very wal, habla muy bien." I had been trying out my few words on him during the floor show.

"No, no," I said. "Poco, poquito. Casi nada." Long and involved, she spoke to me. Ramón translated for awhile, but then he went back to working for the English, who were drinking more than I. The champagne in the Café Luna, and the two small cups of cognac, and then this last bottle of champagne, were all working on me, and besides, I felt a touch of the Water Woe once or twice. I danced with the girl, whose name was Carmen, and everybody pulled to the side to watch us, but then they filled back in and enclosed us after they had looked me over. Carmen swung her legs around a lot when she danced; once she kicked me in the shin. "Lo siento," she said. She kept on talking Spanish. She said something was something in summer, verdad? I said verdad. She spoke again and at the end said, No es así? I said Sí. "Usted habla muy bien el español," she said.

At the table she wrapped her arm around my biceps and smiled in my ear. Ramón said: "I tell you she is nice clean girl. She go with man one time, maybe two times one year. She is arteesta. Five hundred pesetas."

The night before I had been with the little Frenchified girl in the house above the Plaza Cataluña; as far as du-bien-au-corps goes I was fixed for some time. But I was still looking for something. At least I could dance with her and try to get to know her a little first. I said to Ramón that I would think about it.

"And you give me little teep, no?" he said.

"Drink some more champagne," said Fitch, who had ordered two more bottles.

"Don't get him so drunk he forgets to buy the dog," Phyllis said.

Braisted said: "Oh my God! The dog! He has probably wet all over the seats!"

"I'm dizzy enough already," I said. It was one of those occasions when what you have drunk lies quiet for awhile, and then fumes up and takes you by surprise. All day I had been feeling moody and thoughtful and couldn't imagine getting even a little bit stoned. I was starting to feel good, though. One thing I noticed was a lot of blood in my head.

Carmen and I danced again, and this time I kicked her. She was about a foot shorter than I, which put a cheek on my chest and a bosom in my solar plexus. You can believe it or not, but I was thinking about Jennie.

When Braisted went for the car, Ruth went with him. She had not seemed to be enjoying herself, had neither danced nor spoken, nor drunk much of the champagne, but on the way out of the club she hiccupped and I saw her stumble and almost fall. The doorman caught her and she hung on him for a moment like a wet flag on a pole.

Carmen left me sitting at the table and went to change into her costume for her next appearance. By then I was distinctly blurry. Ramón switched chairs and leaned on me. "She say," he interpreted, "that she go with you for cariño, for love, but she have a seek mother. Four hundred pesetas and she pay hotel. She say to me she can not go out Club Cairo until four o'clock, but for you she go three o'clock."

"Tell her to make it three hundred pesetas and two o'clock," MacLean said, rising. "Maybe she'll come down to yesterday and gratis. I say, where's the old w.c.?"

"I'll show you," Fitch said. "It's down a noisesome flight of steps and through a corridor where thousands of Spaniards jostle one and say, Passez! Passez! Not a patch on the one in Marseilles, though."

So I was left alone with Ramón and the two women. Phyllis said: "Tell us, are you really going with that girl? Angela, Mr. Cord is going off with a prostitute."

"Jolly dee!" Angela said. "Tomorrow you must tell us all about it."

A couple of long scrawny birds, bobbing in their champagne glasses. I missed the voice of the announcer and the fanfare of the band and Carmen's entrance into the spotlight. "That's the girl now," Phyllis said. "Oh this is good fun!"

She didn't dance that well either; but the four-foot-high boy with her was a miracle. He was sullen and scowling and arrogant and he stamped and danced till the veins stood out on his forehead. But she was slower on her feet, amateurish by contrast. "She is a very nice girl," Ramón said. "Skeeny."

When MacLean and Fitch came back from the old w.c. they said Pardon us a tick, and took the two women with them out to the street door where Braisted and Ruth waited in the Singer Nine, and I didn't think anything of it. Phyllis came in with the dog on a chain. It looked to be a German shepherd puppy about five weeks old; it was wriggling and wetting and whimpering. The ears and feet were huge. You could tell at a glance it would grow up to be a monster. Then Carmen appeared with a jeweled comb in her hair and a dress made of so many layers of polka-dotted material she could hardly sit down. She talked to Ramón and Ramón said to me: "You must speak now. She want to go out Club Cairo, she say what you want to pay?" She had gone to change back to the cocktail dress and the arrangement seemed to be that I was to wait in the bar across the street till she came. "Where is everybody?" I asked. The waiter laid a bill for one thousand five hundred and sixty-three pesetas on the table and turned his back modestly. Ramón went over to talk to the boss and I was alone except for the dog. "I don't suppose you and I could struggle for the check," I said to the dog. Then Ramón came back and he said: "You no forget, you geev me little teep, no?"

The next thing I remember was the stares again, in the Bar Vaquero across the street. When you enter a place where you are not well known, the stares you get are a form of salute. Even if you are not a foreigner but only somebody from another part of town, the men all give you this prolonged intense scrutiny from your shoes to your cowlick. It takes some getting used to. There's no hostility, appraisal, challenge, not even curiosity; just stare. Total and unconscious as the sun looking at you on a clear day.

In this particular bar there were few women, a lot of men in working clothes, a limpiabotas with an ornate shine kit, and a blind man playing an accordion. The limpiabotas came over to me and immediately started to oil up my good Italian slippers with some gunk out of a beer bottle. I gave him a handful of pesetas and made him quit. At that he wanted to rip my heels off and put new ones on. I was sitting at a table and therefore when the waiter came up Ramón said I ought to buy something, so I ordered another cognac. Meanwhile the blind accordionist had come to me unerring as a beagle to stick his tin cup in my sternum. It was getting pretty expensive; I was glad I had left the rest of my money in the hotel. Ramón had already called up a taxi; it stood chugging at the door, the driver smoking a cigar. "I don't suppose we could take a trolley," I said. "Tramvia," I explained.

"Hombre, you want to take pretty girl to bed in tramvia?" Ramón said, profoundly shocked.

Things were going around and around. I have the impression I gave the shoeshine giant more pesetas for not nailing tin taps on my heels and toes. Then Carmen finally came along, dressed in a light blue thin dress and white cotton gloves, and we got in the taxi. Ramón had to come with us because the taxi was about eight feet high and I couldn't get in or out without assistance. On the ride she must have asked him how much money I had left, because he handed her my wallet, which I didn't know he had, and she counted out some money and gave it back to me. Then we pulled into a garage underneath a building and got into an elevator full of signs that said: Phohibido Descender.

"I go," Ramón said. "Señor, you have good night, eh? Tomorrow I take coffee in Bra Gato. You come drink one coffee with me, no?"

Then the room, perfectly appointed, with a big bed and a big bathroom with a hot shower, tub, and fluorescent lighting. There were even flowers in vases on the night tables, and the rug was thick as a fall of snow. It was a better room than I had in the Brigánt, which was "A" category. Afterwards I learned that there are no better rooms anywhere than in the unpretentious little joints on the back streets, with their simple signs: Habitaciones. That is, if you don't mind the water running in the pipes all night long and an occasional racketing bedstead in the next room.

We talked Spanish some more. "Me voy a lavar," Carmen said. "Bueno," I said. She left the door open and I saw her sitting straddled on a low fixture that had hot and cold running water, like a sink. I had one in my room in the Brigánt too. Some sophisticate I am; I thought it was for washing feet.

Whether it was the champagne, or the nature of the room (the light switch had three positions: one for normal room light, another for a dim red glow, a third for an eery blue light—and the ceiling was glass, painted with life-size reclining nude girls, all fat and abandonada), I did well enough, in spite of my prejudice in favor of long warm companionships first. I was pleased. Carmen was pleased. "Dios mío," she said. "Hemos hecho un niño!" I was proud. Primitive women think a simultaneous climax is what does the conceiving. She jumped up to wash again and said something and indicated with her finger that her brains were whirling. Mine, too. I was stuporously asleep and did not know it when she came back to bed.

All pretty disgraceful from most points of view. When you've lost a thing, and don't know what it is, and go looking for it, not knowing where to look, how to recognize it, or even if there is any, you can get into some weird fixes. Everybody is looking for love. If somebody loves you, it means you are worth at least something to somebody (and the smarter, the richer, the prettier, the more discriminating that somebody is, the worthier it makes you). Even if you don't love anybody, you go looking for somebody to love you. A lot of people only love people who love them out of sheer gratitude for being loved. A lot of times neither loves the other but both think they are loved. To love somebody is nice but it's not indispensable, and certainly there's no point in loving anybody if that somebody doesn't love you.

I am getting mixed up. Nobody knows what love is. There are as many kinds of love as there are people. I happen to be a spoiled, lazy, moneyed no-goodnik type who does not often want the responsibility of loving somebody or of being loved, so you know what you can expect from me. Or rather, nobody knows what to expect from me, including myself. The intellectual oddball I used to talk to in college did not believe in love at all; we used to sit up all night talking about it. He said love was a lie, like God. There were several different feelings: lust, loneliness, timidity, maternal instincts and nest-building instincts, each one existing separately, that societies of a more advanced type arbitrarily lumped together and called by the single name: Love. Maybe he was right. He would have taken what I said about making yourself feel important through being loved and expanded it into an all-inclusive motive for human activity. He would have said that everything a man does is to make himself seem more important and thus more worthy of being immortal, since the one thing everybody is most afraid of, first, last and always, is death.

I am only intellectual to the point where I recognize I don't know anything. I don't know what love is, whether it is what makes the world go around or just a fiction, but I always want it and look for it, maybe because I am still young. I also know I am afraid to die. I know I'd live longer if I ate yogurt and stopped smoking and went to bed early. But I don't eat or stop or go. I also know you can die of bending around the corners of Spanish roads at sixty miles an hour. You can die between one moment and the next, with all your business unfinished, if things turn out that way. But what is there to do about it? Everything happens to you sooner or later. I stepped on an ant this morning, but that doesn't mean I came all the way across the Atlantic to snuff out this ant's life. Why should I expect the next diesel truck or typhoon or love affair to *not* step on me? Everything is haphazard, and if one thing doesn't happen to you, something else will.

Anyway, I got back to the hotel about eleven in the morning. I took my time getting back because I still couldn't collect my car and move on until four that afternoon. I woke up in bed with Carmen and felt lousy. It had not been worth it. It hadn't been what I was looking for. I was not afraid of venereal disease or of being arrested or shot by an outraged husband or brother, or any of the usual consequences. Maybe I was thinking about the damage to my personality, my conscience; but that sounds moral, and I am not very moral. I didn't grow up that way. When I was little I was a scamp, and in my teens I was a hoodlum, and in college I was a playboy, so what else could I be upon attaining my majority but a bounder? All the same, I felt some shame at getting stupid on cognac and champagne and doing something dull just to blot out my thoughts. Those same thoughts were back with me in the morning anyway. It was purely a frame of mind that gave me a brown low-down headache, a sweaty feeling in my shirt and socks, and a fog around the corners of my eyes.

Walking along the wide streets of the upper city, I was in a mood to commit Yoga suicide; that is, just stop, just quit, let everything drop, just quit breathing and talking and moving from place to place, what's the use?

By the time I reached the Ramblas again the sky had heated up, the walls were melting. The flower stalls were open and the trees were full of birds, and there were tourists all over the paseo with complicated cameras. I went to the hotel, figuring to go upstairs and take an aspirin and some kaopectate, get my passport and go to the bank, because all I had left in my wallet was a five-peseta note that had been ripped in half and stuck together with postage stamps, and I had to cash some travelers' checks.

Ramón bounced out of a chair in the lobby; he had the Englishmen's dog on a stout chain. "Señor, last night you forget your dog!"

He explained that the English had left for Málaga, and in token of their appreciation for an evening pleasantly spent, they had given their dog to the quiet American, absolutely free.

" Bat shit," I said. "I don't want it."

"Oh yes, señor," he said. "It is a gift. You owe me nothing. Unless you like give a leettle teep."

I asked him how he had found me. I forgot he had had my wallet last night with Brigánt cards in it. He said: "Señor, the beast smell its path to master. You like this dog. See, is muy inteligente. He do many trick. Watch. Hola, bicho, speak English! Sit! Speak!" The dog clanked its great chain and turned in a circle, squatted down and peed.

We had an argument that lasted half an hour. He tied the dog to the leg of a chair and tried to get away, but I held him by his coat. He said the dog was mine and I said I had never seen it before. The manager of the hotel came over and Ramón presented his case in Catalán. The manager looked doubtful and said I might keep my dog in the hotel one night, but certainly no longer.

I said: "I don't want to keep the goddamn dog anywhere. The last thing I want is a dog. Help me tie it to this guy's belt and chase them out the door and we'll be rid of them both."

Ramón broke for the exit but I held him firmly by the tail of his coat. His feet slipped and slithered on the mosaic floor. I started to laugh. A lot of clerks and chambermaids clustered round.

Finally Ramón said: "How much you pay this hotel? Tha's too much. You like to live in good pensión? You live in my house. Very cheap."

That's how I met Mari. I didn't expect to stay in his house; I only thought once I got him there it would be me escaping and him stuck with the dog. Besides, it might turn out to be the worst kind of firetrap, full of pimps and prostitutes and the decent poor, twelve in a room with cats and cockroaches. I was leaving the city anyway as soon after four o'clock as I could. So I went along, dog on the chain.

The building turned out to be one of the big new apartments in the new city, respectable and clean, with even an elevator, up only. For these apartments you have to pay ten or twelve thousand pesetas trespaso just for the privilege of moving in, but once you are in they can hardly get you out, and they can't raise the rent. The woman who rented the apartment Ramón lived in had been in there for fifteen years and still paying 1943 rent. I will give her a false name—Carmencita—not because I want to fool anybody, but because I will get all mixed up if I give all the women their true names, which are practically always María. Carmencita moved into the house when it was first built, paying trespaso with the money her husband left her when he went off to the Spanish civil war and got killed. She has a twenty-five-year-old son, Manuel, who owns the B.S.A. motorcycle that I borrow sometimes, who has a job selling costume jewelry. Ramón lives in the apartment and pays rent, and she has two other boarders who come and go. Carmencita does laundry, sews dresses, and sells her son's jewelry to her women friends. Then Ramón sometimes brings tourists to stay at the house, pensión-plan. So Carmencita is not badly off, as Spanish widows go. Later on I stayed in her place a couple weeks, was blandly overcharged, and slept on an appalling bed, the mattress obviously stuffed with cannon balls. Moreover, everybody in that house sleeps till noon, so if you get up before that time you have to sneak around like a mouse and there isn't any breakfast coffee. Not only that, but the cooking won't sustain human life, in my opinion.

Carmencita is a nature-cure fiend. She owns this enormous medical book written by a German in the year 1871, which is full of plates showing nude men with mustaches sitting huddled over smoke pots, with blankets over their heads. She cooks only vegetables and eggs and will not serve meat in her house. Given a chance she will explain her whole theory of health and strength from beginning to end, and document it with a wrenching story about the time her son Manuel fell off his motorcycle and gave himself a concussion and she cured him with cold showers, boiled artichokes, and vapor baths. He was going around a corner and his rear wheel slid out from under him at about eighty kilometers per hour. The doctors said there wasn't much to do about the back of his head except wait and see, but this may only be an index of the calibre of Spanish doctors. Manuel could not move anything below his waist for a week and he was delirious. She drenched him and smoked him and fed him artichokes and he lived, and is now perfectly normal except that if he looks up at anything high he falls over. Not dizzy or faint, just falls flat on his back. And then gets up looking irritated. The cure was wasted effort anyway. Manuel raced bicycles before he bought the B.S.A. and he fell off the bicycles all the time too. He has had four broken bones, not counting his head, and some of his teeth are gone and he is a mass of smaller scars. He has fallen downstairs and off trolleys, and has tripped over just about everything you can think of; and dogs always bite him. Sooner or later he is going to kill himself. He's one of my best friends in Spain and I will be sorry to see him go.

He and his mother both have dark sparkling eyes, clear and sharp as glass beads, which they say is the result of the nature diet. On the other hand, Ramón lives with them, has eaten and slept with them for five or six years, and he has a bad stomach and milky eyes and an unhealthy night-life appearance. The two boarders are fat and greasy and eat out at noon, steak and pork, ravenously. The only other person in the house at that time was Mari. She was working as a servant. Ramón got her a job cleaning up and washing dishes for Carmencita when she came to the city from Galicia, a baby in her arms and no money in her pockets. She was married but her husband ran off with her elder sister and the two were killed in an automobile accident. She was left pregnant and without a nickel. Mari is one of those women who can't resist a louse, which is apparently why she married this husband in the first place, and probably why she is sticking with me.

When I came to the apartment the first time Mari was scrubbing tile floors on her knees. She did not speak to me nor I to her. I didn't know she belonged to the house till we sat down for lunch and she served the table and then sat down to eat with us. Then I thought she was a daughter, although nobody said so. In Spain, live-in servants are treated pretty much like family.

Manuel and I talked, through Ramón, about motorcycles. We ate green salad, a stew of peas, potatoes, and artichokes, omelettes with fried onions, and pomegranates for desert. Then we had coffee and resumed the argument about the dog. Ramón insisted it was mine, and I denied it. I asked Carmencita if she wanted it, and she threw up her hands. A city apartment is no place for a dog, in Spain or elsewhere. I explained to them that I had a kind of temporary disease and couldn't stop traveling, certainly not to house-down with a dog. I said I could stop hardly long enough to let the motor cool, because when I was not moving I thought, and I did not want to think. Probably they decided I was posing, but I honestly did not want anything on my mind but the road and the gears that were still stiff, and the tachometer and the countryside shooting past too fast to be anything but a blur of sandhills and rocks and pine trees. "Where are you going?" they asked. I didn't know, I said through Ramón; I had no plan. I was just walking downhill with the wind, I said, and had to explain what I meant. "I'm not going to face any opposition," I said. "I'm not going to argue with anybody or do anything difficult; I'm just going to do the easiest thing, even if it turns out to be running the car off the cliff."

Ramón and I got very annoyed at each other about the dog. I figured the English had given it to him. Nobody is allowed to give me dogs without asking me if I want them. He said they had left it for me, it was my dog, he had only been kind enough to deliver it, and why should he be responsible for it? He had reason on his side, of course, but so did I. It was Ramón's problem; he should give it to some other tourist, not try to load it on me. "All right," I said finally, "throw the cur out in the street. It's not my business." This was what it was coming to, and the only question remaining was who was going to take on his conscience the job of abandoning the dog. The same as the problem of ownership. Ramón wouldn't do it, he said it was my affair. This proves Ramón has a soul, in spite of his greasy Andaluz haircut and rotten teeth. You can tell a man by how he goes about abandoning puppies. But I was getting sore. I finally said I would take it with me as far as the city limits and put it out of the car near a farm or something, where it would at least have a chance to survive traffic and maybe get adopted by a farmer. "Good," Ramón said and folded his arms and told the rest that I was going to fling the poor dog out of a speeding car. Carmencita looked at me reproachfully.

"Be reasonable," I said to Ramón. "What can I do with a dog?"

"No es my dog, señor," he said.

"Well, it's not mine either."

There was some conversation in a mumble from the other side of the table, and then Ramón said: "Mari say she take dog, if you want."

Everybody except Carmencita was relieved, and she and the girl worked out the details. The dog and all its messes had to be kept in Mari's room, she had to take it out for regular airings and feed it the table scraps, and in general keep it out from under people's feet. I had to laugh; I don't think they had any idea how big that dog would be when it was full grown, with jaws like a wolf, or how much more than table scraps it would need to keep it alive.

Mari says now that I came into the place eight feet tall and yellow-haired and dressed like a prince (in a pair of surplus khakis, as a matter of fact, and a polo shirt and an old camel's-hair jacket) and she was too shy to speak, but thought that if she offered to take care of my dog I would look at her. This might only be the way European women have of puffing up your ego a little at no steep cost to themselves. At any rate, I did look at her, and she ran off into the other room. She came back sidewise through the door and grabbed up the dog, scolding it when it nipped her. She sat and held it and rubbed its neck, and it lapped her on the chin. She was about five feet six, dark as most of them, with long hair ragged around her ears from scrubbing. She wore a bata, a housecoat, and a pair of Manuel's old sneakers with no laces. Who would look more than once? She hardly said a word. And I'm sure she was sorry she had ever opened her mouth about the dog before I was even out of the house.

At four I said goodbye to everybody, and Ramón came up to

me and mumbled: "La señora, she cook good for you?" I paid less than I would have at any good restaurant, but then the food was worse, too.

Then I went back and checked out of the Hotel Brigánt and went by taxi to the Jaguar garage. The mechanic conveyed the intelligence that the car was in perfect condition, but they couldn't do anything about the rasp in the steering post. This sound persists; it's a noise of dry metal scraping against metal, like something wearing out. I didn't think it worth the trouble either to look up all the words in the dictionary or run around after an interpreter to explain it to him, so I let it go. The steering may break some day when I am lumbering along about a hundred and ten miles an hour, but it hasn't happened yet, and I am ever the optimist. Besides, I am selling the car soon now.

Three

I CLAIM the title of Europe's speediest tourist that awful summer, unless there was some other poor idiot all alone and roaring around in a high-powered car with no place to go, trying to outdistance his own brains, and afraid to stop anywhere for fear of being shut up in a dim-lit hellish hotel room with nobody even aware of his existence except a few servile non-English-speaking waiters to whom American spells t-i-p. Say what you will about the charm of the Old World, if you go past it fast enough it might just as well be Route 40 across Ohio. Except that whenever you stop to eat, sleep, buy gasoline or cigarettes, there comes a look that passes between natives that says as clear as bold face type: *Here is a foreigner. Joy! Let us impoverish the son of a bitch!*

Or maybe it is all in my mind. It did cost me plenty to stay alive and keep moving, but then I made no attempt to meet anybody halfway or even behave the way I should. I am not much of a tourist. I know there is a whole lot I missed in the countries I passed through. I read in a travel book about much of it, things I passed by at a distance of only a few miles: the Augustin Museum and the Church of St. Sernin in Toulouse, and Brantôme Abbey, and the caves near Souillac, and the whole city of Tours, and the resort of Biarritz—not to mention Paris, which I was in, but barely saw.

When I left Spain I had the idea I would travel around leisurely and see Europe at the height of the tourist season; I would go to all the places there were foreigners and look at what they were looking at, so as to have a reasonable report to make to my relatives, some of whom do the cathedral-and-tomb circuit every couple of years. But I shot straight through from the border to Narbonne, though there was good excuse for that: I had already seen that part of the country and hadn't noticed anything worth stopping for except good old Le Boulou, where they ripped open the trunk. When I got to Carcassonne, however, I stopped.

From the main highway I saw the walls and battlements and crenels up on the left, and I followed a stream of American heaps with tourist tags on them. The city inside the walls is pretty interesting; there are winding streets and tea shoppes and souvenir stands and the big castle in the middle, with a dry moat and a drawbridge, and everywhere you go somebody says: Daddy, take a picture of me standing by the lion! Men pop out of the narrow streets and flip half a mile of postcards on a string at you. The sun was shining but it wasn't too hot; there were women in the streets with market baskets. There was a drugstore and a little hotel buried in its own moss, and a lot of placards telling about sieges and history. I thought: Boy, this is interesting. And then I thought: Oh the hell with it.

I got in the car and drove on toward Toulouse. Toulouse is a great art center, and there is probably a house where Toulouse-Lautrec lived, or an atelier, or a collection of his paintings. The truth is I don't remember which town was Toulouse. I think it was where traffic was routed around a square and at the far side there were two signs pointing in opposite directions, both of which said Limoges.

Superficially, it was because of the two signs that I went on, to see which one led to the next city; but I would have gone on anyway. And that might not have been Toulouse but Montauban or Cahors for all I know. On that trip practically all the towns were the same: walls. Walls with small doors and windows in them and a stream of cars passing between them and a few apathetic people standing around. I remember thinking maybe I would unbolt the back of the passenger seat and lay it on the floor; this would provide a space almost six feet long, from the firewall to the rear of the back seat, and I could sleep in the car. As I drove I kept looking for a nice side road with a few trees and maybe a running stream, where I could park the car and bed down.

I never found the right place, so I drove all night. At about midnight I found a restaurant still open and decided to eat something. There was a crummy-looking hotel next door where I might have slept, except as I got out of the car I saw two handsome types standing furtively in a doorway, wearing sunglasses in the middle of the night, pointing to my car and obviously saying to each other how much they could get for it once they had forced the door and crossed the ignition wires and driven it over the border to Switzerland. So I ate pheasant in the little restaurant at a table by the window and went on. At noon the next day I was in Paris.

I remember the long straight roads. Looking at the map I judge that from about Brive all the way to Paris I was on the straight good-surfaced roads that I roared over in the middle of the night at about eighty miles an hour without slowing down except for a darkened town or two. On the odometer there was a little over two thousand miles when I started the run. I entered on the straight stretches and went easy for a long time until I noticed there weren't any curves; then I wound up as high as I dared—about 3,500 or 4,000 r.p.m.—and really made tracks.

After awhile it got light and there was a wind that rattled the windows in their frames. Morning traffic materialized, but not much of it, and I was ready then; my reflexes were tuned to a hundred miles an hour. I scared some people but didn't hit anybody, and had only one close call—on a narrow stretch with a parked truck on one side and no way for me to get by without running into a French Ford that was coming peaceably along on the other. I don't remember who saved the day, but I shot through. I saw the other driver's face; I could swear his eyes were shut. In the view mirror, I saw he had pulled over to the shoulder and stopped. I hoped he had a little snort of Napoleon in the car with him; I wished I had.

The only thing that happened beyond there was that one of my twin horns went out of business. I stopped in a garage and the mechanic deduced what the trouble was after I pantomimed him under the car and made him listen while I tooted. He fiddled in the fuse box and fixed the horn for a nominal fee—three dollars. Then I went on.

Close to Paris there was a lot more traffic, and after swerving and averting and bearing down heavily on the brakes for awhile I gave it up and slowed to thirty, crawling in through the Porte d'Orléans about noon, as I said.

I didn't see the Place de l'Opéra, the Vendôme, the Champs Elysées or the Arc de Triomph, the Etoile, the American Express, the Louvre, Notre Dame, Bal Tabarin, or any tombs, and I only saw the Sacre Coeur from a distance. Getting into the city was enough for one afternoon.

I was hungry and circled around some cathedral about nine times looking for a place to park, then finally turned down a long straight avenue jammed with Vedettes and Citroëns and Renaults, unable to make a left, until the street petered out in a cul-de-sac and I drew up. A young man in a beret, a long coat with wooden buttons, a big pipe, and sandals, and a bushy beard was lounging in a doorway nearby. I was certain he was an American. I put my head out the window and said: "Where am I, buddy?"

"In Montparnasse," he said. He came over and leaned his elbows on the window and gave the interior a once-over. "Of course, I'm only a poor student," he said. I told him not to worry, with the car paid for in cash I was probably poorer than he was. He asked me what my top speed was and then didn't believe it. His preference was for the new Citroën DS-19. Personally, I prefer having my rear wheels push me than my front wheels pull me. "Air-oil suspension," he said. "Automatic clutch." He didn't seem to have anything to do but smoke his pipe, so I said if he knew of a likely place I would buy him a drink. "I'd rather," I said, "go someplace where I can park the car right in front and keep an eye on it." He said it was all right, that Parisians were basically very honest. Sure.

He took me to a place called a Brasserie, but it was not, it was a bar. His name was Gilman, he said, and he was a sculptor going to welding school on the G.I. Bill. This isn't as far-fetched as it sounds, because he was doing modern sculpture and was already having occasion to burn copper and cast-iron tubes together to make forms. He showed me some formal portraits of his work from snapshots in his wallet: all the sculptures looked like big iron TV antennas with Kitty Hawk wings, except one that looked like a New Orleans wrought-iron fence. This last was a balcony adornment, he said. "Of course, I dislike having to work up commercial projects while my serious work is still in the balance," he said, "but things are not as cheap as they were. One must live. For instance, you'll pay at least fifteen dollars for a decent hotel-room in Paris. Remind me, before you shove off, and I'll give you the address of my place. If you can't find a hotel I'll put you up. It's only an attic, but what's Paris if you don't visit an artist's attic?"

I said it was accommodating of him, but I wasn't sure I was going to stay. We went on talking about his work, then French roads and automobiles again, and he asked where I was from. New England, I said. "No, I mean where in Europe?" He thought I was Armed Forces. "No?" he said. "With those German tags I thought you were from Mainz or somewhere. It's the G.I.'s who usually come around in sports cars. But then they have special tags, don't they? You mean to tell me you're just touring alone? Very exciting. I was thinking of doing the same thing this coming summer. Unfortunately, I don't have enough money to buy a car and travel both. Look here, if you ever feel the need of a traveling companion, drop me a line. I could split expenses with you. I have a lot of camping equipment. We could see most of western Europe in one summer. What do you say?"

But he was going too fast for me; I caught a false note. There was something about him that bothered me. I should have known by the beard, the pipe, and the sandals, but then with real artists it's sometimes hard to tell. He prodded me about why I was going from place to place, alone, spending a lot on gas and oil and not even seeing Europe.

"I'm looking for love," I said. It's what I tell everybody; it's closest to what I think I'm doing. I should have guessed when he offered me a bed in his garret. About some things I am very naïve.

Gilman suggested we take my car to an alley he knew of and park it in front of the studio of some friends of his. They would keep an eye on it for me. And since they would invite us in for coffee and schnapps, I would get a chance to see a real Paris studio. They were two successful abstract painters who had had shows in New York as well as in Paris galleries, and their joint workroom was decorated with any number of interesting objects, from Salem Samplers to Lapp phallic symbols. After we had a drink with his friends he, Gilman, would take me to the Deux Magots and the Steer on the Roof and other celebrated joints. We would dine in

Montmartre, where the Bohemians lived. "Is it a date?" he asked. He used the word in the same sense I always used it to mean dinner and dancing in exchange for a goodnight kiss. I am not the sort of person who gets infuriated or nauseated by queers—I think that is protesting too much—but I was sore at him. I was disappointed. The first chance I'd had to talk to somebody on an equal footing in my own language, and I had to turn it down. I felt moody and depressed again and almost left the city that afternoon.

I paid the tab and walked away. He did everything but crawl after me on his knees. It wasn't pleasant. "You do need a friend," he said. "Don't be lonesome." I got in the car and he wheedled in the window. I said: "Oh get away, goddamn it." He got nasty; he straightened up and said: "You think you're a tough guy? I warn you, don't threaten me. I haven't been bending iron for six months for nothing. I have formidable biceps."

That made me laugh. In fact I laughed so hard it lifted me halfway out of the dumps and contributed to keeping me in Paris another day. I went haw-hawing down rue Vauclaire or Vauclain or something like that, too fast for traffic, and suddenly the Simca ahead of me braked. I swung to the left to avoid ramming him, and the car I met there swerved toward the curb to avoid hitting me; it ran full into a parked Panhard. The Simca ahead of me had braked sharply to let a taxi get past, and then it scooted on, but a Versailles behind the car that hit the Panhard swerved over in my lane, and I gave it up and squealed around a right-hand bend. Ahead of me I saw a river-bridge and the Eiffel Tower.

If it hadn't been for the taxi that jumped out I probably would have left Paris that same afternoon with no impression of it except what Gilman had given me, since I was headed in the direction of the Porte d'Orléans and felt the old familiar urge to move. But when I saw the tower I felt vaguely interested and thought I'd stay the rest of the day at least. I thought: Maybe something good will happen to me because of the taxi and the unpremeditated right turn. Something terribly good might happen this afternoon and I'll stay in Paris a couple of years.

Because I figured I might as well be in Paris as anywhere else. My experience of European travel is that one place is just about like another when you are alone. The way it worked out, I left the city the next morning, but all that afternoon I had the superstitious notion that some fate was working on me because of that unpremeditated right turn. Let's face it: I was expecting to meet a girl.

I parked in the street in front of the Eiffel Tower and went underneath it to look up. Then I decided I would eat lunch on the second stage, where a sign said there was a restaurant, so I went back to the car and got a tie and the camel'shair coat. I bought a ticket for the elevator. This elevator rides up at an angle at first and gives a rather giddy sensation; it is fastened at the side instead of the top, a seemingly precarious arrangement. The car was full of light-meter types in summer-weight suits and two-tone shoes, and their women in cotton print dresses. Everybody said: Isn't this something! but we creaked up between crummy girders and the car was so hot I was dying. Besides, I might as well admit it, to my stunted esthetic perceptions the Eiffel Tower is an architectural monstrosity; it looks like a madman's oil well.

When the car stopped we got out on the second stage and a singeing wind blew up the women's print skirts and sailed the men's Palm Beach hats out over the Mother of Cities. I leaned on the railing for a while looking up. The clouds soaring over the top gave me the impression that the whole structure was falling over. You can get this impression looking up at any high building when the clouds are blowing, but up there it was so acute that I actually lost my balance when I let go the rail.

From the second stage it is a far drop to the ground. A better tourist than I could probably tell how high the whole works is, how much it nods in a gale, and so forth; but I don't have the knack of picking up such details. This is not a snide remark; I think it is valuable to have the kind of intelligence that catches facts and holds them gummed until the time comes to prove something or interest somebody. I have the other talent: I can pass through any structure, town, or crisis without remembering a single significant detail. Especially when I am preoccupied, as I was those days, running back and forth in strange countries, looking for somebody to take my sniveling self to its bosom and caress the top of my head and murmur. I leaned on the rail awhile looking out at Paris, France (big clouds on the westward horizon, pink and purple and boiling, and mingling to the north over the Sacre Coeur with a layer of industrial fog that gave a nice silvery color; and below me was a green woods and a long boulevard with people walking, and squares and plazas and churches in all directions), and I thought: I want to come here with *Jennie!*

But it was too late for that. Too late. Think in those terms and it will ruin any sight-seeing. I leaned on the rail thinking: Too late, and then I went into the restaurant. It was full of couples. There was a couple with a Midwestern accent that were the most honeymoon couple I have ever seen; they made the waiter set both places on the same side of the table so they could pat each other while they ate. They murmured and knocked heads and every so often one would tweak the other on the thigh and then look coyly around the room as though they had done something awfully risqué. Then there was the businessman from Australia telling a Frenchwoman all about his travels while she leaned on her wrists and glittered her eyes at him; he ate pressed duck with both hands and leered. He was willing to stay in Paris a long time and let his ranch fall to ruin in the hands of aborigines if only Paris would be nice to him. Here he winked. Then there was a strange-looking French girl with a strange-looking light chocolate Negro with a face smooth as putty; they were both dressed in plaid pants, ruffled white shirts, string ties, and black jackets, and both wore wedding rings made of twisted snakes.

They all made me feel more lonely than ever. I ate a dish of mushrooms in a fancy sauce, some tiny meatballs with a licorice flavor, mashed potatoes, and a complicated salad. There was a girl next to me sitting alone. Not bad looking, but her hair was done up in a bun and she was dressed in a schoolmarm suit of a gorse or horse color. So I had a chance meeting all right. I asked the waiter where Notre Dame was. He didn't understand me. The girl said apologetically: "I don't believe you can see it from here. It would be over on the other side.

We progressed through pleasantries. She had seen all the major churches in Paris. "Will you be here long?" she asked. I said I hadn't decided yet whether I would stay or go.

"I'm leaving tomorrow," she said. "I'd like to stay longer, but a week from Sunday I have to make my report on the churches of Paris to the International Presbyterian Youth Fellowship Progress Committee Congress in Racine."

So there you are. Not that I have a word to say against cheese country virgins who get sent to Paris by church committees, but my experience is that they have different ideas about love than the average youth from fifteen to ninety. I ate my meatballs and complicated salad and marched on without any coffee. I was worried about leaving the car parked in the street too long. There were signs in the elevator that said "Beware of Pickpockets"; and where picks operate there are likely to be other specialists. If it had been the Volkswagen I wouldn't have worried, because the boulevard below was full of AAA Cadillacs and Chryslers that looked like much richer pickings, but a Jaguar is almost up in that class. They wouldn't get anything but a lot of old clothes, but all the same they might have broken a window or forced the trunk, like last time.

On the descent I didn't see anybody the proper age, the proper pulchritude, and unaccompanied. The indirect approach wasn't doing me any good. Probably a more enterprising tourist would have struck out for the Latin Quarter or entered the nearest American bar at nightfall. But that wasn't what I was looking for. Plain garden variety sex I had tried in Barcelona and it had left me flat. For this reason the average international beauty wouldn't have been any use; and I didn't have the patience for anything else. How do you start the afternoon in a strange city and finish the evening in bed, after what the books call a mutually satisfactory sex-experience, talking this-and-that with somebody who is *fond* of you?

I don't know exactly what they meant when they used to talk about "free love." Love without getting married, I suppose. From the term itself, and my own notions of love, I work it out that there is a kind of love you encounter in novels, movies, and plays, where two people are thrown together and they come up In Love, wholesome and pure. But it's the kind you never see; it's not real. Real love isn't free, it costs. It is a business matter. On a very simplified basis, you buy it at night and it costs a fixed amount and lasts till morning—or forever, of course, if a price is agreed upon. It used to be a shocker to say that marriage was legalized prostitution; but it would be more exact to say that prostitution is a form of substitute marriage. Even that is not exactly it, because even when you buy a woman you are hoping for love thrown in. Somebody to hold your arm. Somebody to sit and talk with. Somebody to share the Eiffel Tower and the dinner dishes with. Or it isn't any good. You can buy a naked hole in the naked earth wherever you are. But what a human needs is another human to sit around with, to live with. And you have to buy this, too. Jennie never understood that.

One of the things that fouled us up was my romantic ideas. I have a very highly developed sense of romance and I won't take Hollywood or musical comedy for an answer. The average person's idea of romance seems to be two people of the opposite sex meeting in a clearing in the woods or in the middle of a city and slowly walking toward each other, looking deep into each other's eyes. You know sex tension is mounting because the music gets louder and the chords are longer. Then in one last chord they fling their arms around each other and smooch. Close-up. But this is not love or romance, and it is certainly not marriage. It is just sex tension. Against which I have nothing to say—sex tension puts people together. But it is only the vestibule to the rest of it: love, romance, marriage, home, mutuality, companionship, et cetera. Most people mistake the vestibule for the home. Inside the home is the intimacy and togetherness that everybody wants. How stupid it is when old married people, who are already living a close companionable marriage, who already have shared jokes, who have seen each other in rumpled underwear, and who eat every meal together—how stupid it is for them to believe they ought to stare in each other's eyes and moo. Whether they know it or not they are already living love and home and romance and marriage all the while they are picking their teeth, cracking old jokes, and casually considering each other basic fatheads.

What I am getting at is that I was not even looking for love, as I thought I was. I was hoping to meet somebody, sleep with her, start in right away eating meals, joking, thinking fathead, and living real romance—that is, marriage. But I wasn't willing to stop long enough to pay up: to spend time, money and attention on a woman. What I wanted was free love—love for free. But subconsciously I knew all the time that it didn't exist. I don't believe I would have accepted it if I had found it. Because whatever else I am, I am preeminently monogamous. I didn't know this either at the time.

I jumped into the car and toured the Left Bank until I found a café with tables outside and tourists sitting around. I sat in the café and ordered a Ricart. I had to talk to somebody.

I heard a man saying to his wife: "I don't know. They've got a speedometer that says a hundred and forty."

They were looking at the Jaguar. I smiled and said: "Don't you believe it, sir. The last three dots are never touched."

"That your car?" he said. He was about forty, his wife the same.

They were sunburned and fatigued and dressed in casual clothes. He carried a big leather bag of camera attachments and she a wicker basket of travel books. "We're going to Sweden," he said. "Have you ever been to Sweden?"

"No, sir," I said. "I'd like to go. Maybe I will some time this fall before the weather gets cold."

The wife wouldn't speak to me; she distrusted me. The man and I talked about European roads and I said I bet he hadn't seen anything like the roads in Spain. Then the wife pulled on him and whispered something in his ear. "I hope you have a good trip," I said moldily as they left.

I sat in the café about an hour more. I had eaten at three so I wasn't hungry. Along about seven I went to look for a hotel. The Jaguar I laid up overnight in a public garage, with pantomime pleas to the attendants not to sit in it, push its buttons, open its hood, or displace its wing mirrors. They did anyway.

I walked along narrow streets full of young couples until I found a place that said HÔTEL in dim flickering letters on a glass door. Old Madame made me fill out forms in French and I wrote everything in the wrong place, but she couldn't tell the difference between my name and my home-address, so that was all right. I got a room in the triangle of the building and looked out through two windows onto the street. There was a red rug and an armoire and a big soft bed. A breeze was blowing in the windows and I stood for awhile looking out at the Paris twilight and the people walking. Lights came on, the traffic slowed up, and cooking smells floated among the chimneys. An accordion was playing in a café across the street. I started to bawl. This was the last time. I report it because it hasn't happened since. Besides, it was not really bawling, just a lump in the throat and a hard round thing in the stomach. Besides, Paris is supposed to be a sentimental place anyway.

In the morning I got the car, warmed it up, and buzzed out of Paris by the Porte de St. Cloud, bent over the wheel and one big foot in the carburetor. It was not even traveling; it was driving the car for performance, for speed—shifting from first to second at fifty and second to third at seventy-five, and into fourth wherever there was any kind of stretch for really letting it flat out. It drummed and shook and scattered around corners like a handful of pebbles, and I got up to swimming valves a couple of times by forgetting to shift up while passing tottering trucks. Chartres was one problem and Tours was another (I didn't see the cathedral in the one or the cathedral in the other) and I stopped for gas in Châtellerault and bought a bar of chocolate for breakfast

Beyond there it rained and I backed off to seventy on the stretches and a little more than thirty around the corners, as the roads were slippery. Then it dried off in the vicinity of Poitiers and continued fine and I stood on the loud pedal once more, listening to the loose window stutter and the timing chain whine and hearing a new rattle in the tachometer cable and hoping I could get to Bordeaux before something burst and before I had time to wonder where I was going.

In fourth gear along one piste with the needle ticking one-o-six, two cars came at me from the other direction, one passing the other. The guy passing had underestimated my speed of approach and by all rights and reasons he ought to have had plenty of time to pass, but I bore down on him so fast he didn't have time to complete the pass or drop back, so he swung off the road at the last instant and I sang between the two of them. He shot left off the road and into an Esso driveway, racked around the pumps, and slid out on the highway again. I went on, nervously saying Ho ho ho to myself into the rear view. I was sweating though.

Then in another place a truck was apparently stopped ahead of me and I didn't pause to wonder why, I just tooted and went past and cut the nose of a car that was turning left in front of the truck. I was going about ninety-five or six and didn't see any point in stopping to see what this truck was up to, so I blew the horn and went around. At that speed I couldn't tell whether the car in front was a Volkswagen or a Porsche, but probably the former, since the latter would have cornered faster and would have his front wheels out in the road further and I would have bashed him a hundred yards into the field and killed us all.

I was a little shaky and so pulled into the next gas station and checked the air, the oil, the water, tightened the spinner hubs and bought a Coke and a can of paste wax I wasn't sure I would ever have a chance to use, and in general stalled around to give the brakes and oil pump a chance to cool down.

Then I went on.

Sometimes just before I drop off to sleep at night I still think about that ride down from Paris—the speeds the Jaguar will reach, the condition of the roads, the fallibility of tires, steering knuckles, and human judgment—and my heart starts to pound all over again. I visualize the car speeding as though I was outside it; it roars along with the word ZOOM written out behind it, like in funny papers. Another car enters my imaginary scene and gets in the way. Then the impact. It never gets any further than that. I close my mind. But by this time all my muscles are tightened up to withstand the shock of the collision, and I have to get up and sneak downstairs (Mari won't let me get out of bed at night; she's afraid of the dark) and get a sandwich to draw the blood out of my head.

The thing is, the best of Europe's highways are full of hazards. There are potholes that can wrench the wheel right out of your hands; there are winds that swoop down out of nowhere, especially in the south of France, and actually blow your car across the road; and everywhere you go there are solid walls of trees planted along the edge of the road. Maybe they were just pleasing adornments of the landscape in the day of the horse, but to a car going anywhere over fifty miles per hour they are an impenetrable wall of thick trunks between you and the open fields where you might be able to flip over two or three times and still come to a battering but non-fatal halt. Then too, single-lane traffic is all that fits between these carefully planted walls, so that if there is a truck ahead of you, you have to be very sure there's nothing coming the other way before you dare go around it. But the biggest hazard is probably the different kinds of traffic. In the States and to a great extent in Germany on the Autobahns, everybody is moving at approximately the same speed and you can make pretty accurate judgments. In other places in Europe it's different: on the same piece of road with you there might be a Mercedes 300 SL going a hundred and forty miles an hour, a Citroën going eighty, four or five Quatre Cheval Renaults doing about sixty, and an assortment of 1910 Daimlers, Fiats, Austins, Fords, and Dodges in the thirty-to-sixty bracket; and some trucks, diesels or gas, going at anywhere from ten to eighty-five; plus a few motorcycles either pottering at twenty or splitting their sides at seventy-five; some Mobylettes, Mo-Peds, racing bicycles, plain bicycles, horses with carts, plain horses, and finally pedestrians. And each one has his own individual velocity. You never know who is just up ahead doing what.

Once between Angoulême and Chevanceaux I got badly fooled by a motorcycle; I moved to pass it and it turned out to be an N.S.U. scooting along at better than eighty-five, which left me out in midstream with egg on my face, a curve coming up, and nothing to do but squeeze back in behind to avoid a group of wandering minstrels walking down the road leading a blind mule. Simultaneously I almost got rammed from behind by a pink convertible I had previously seen in the mirror but had not figured was due to catch up yet. But it was going faster than anybody else at that point. It was a Lancia Spyder, the first one I'd seen. At the moment he had the edge of r.p.m. and while I was sorting things out he shot between me and the minstrels and scat. It took ten miles to catch up with him and another five to pass him. I had ample time to read his Royal Automobile Club insigne on the rear bumper.

A little further on I noticed a rattle in the clutch pedal that bothered me. I slacked off and reached Bordeaux about six that evening. It was still light. Luckily the Jaguar garage there was still open so I left the car and went to the nearest hotel. I slept like a stone from eight o'clock on, and next morning by eleven the car was ready, greased and oiled, and I left for Biarritz. I reached there too early in the day to stop and have nothing to do with myself for the rest of my life, so I ate lunch in a fancy casino and then went down to the beach. There was nothing down there except some Cannes bathing suits, so I came back and went to an accessory shop and bought a pistol-grip spotlight that I didn't really need.

Then I went on.

And so on. There's no point detailing the whole trip. I always had the idea I would stop in the next place and hole up for a month or two and remake my life. All the way from Paris I had been promising myself that the time had come to stop racing around, to sit down and think things over and come to terms with myself. I would rent a room in a pensión and garage the car semipermanently and do some swimming and café-sitting and fishing. But when I looked around Biarritz or Angoulême or Chartres or any other place, all I saw was dry towns full of tourists and hostile natives, with the heat well over ninety in the shade; and I couldn't bear the idea of not moving, so I always went on. After Biarritz I said to myself that I would go down to the summer resorts around San Sebastián and Satander, since living was cheaper in Spain. But when I got to the former it was again too early in the day to stop, so I went on to Santander by the corniche road that runs along from Deva to Bilbao. The scenery along there should not be missed. By anyone who has somebody to see it with. For me it was too stupendous and dreary to bear.

I went on to Santander and arrived late, slept and woke up determined to stick around a few months learning the language and making friends. But by noon I was traveling again.

I went through Burgos and a series of smaller cities to Madrid and could not stop anywhere, but went on through Guadalajara and Zaragoza and Lérida to Barcelona province again, where I am now. It's hard to explain. Whenever I try to think of a logical explanation for how I felt, I always think of the Escudo Pass between Santander and Burgos. Anybody who has been up that way can understand how I felt. It is vast and desolate and bare, three thousand and some odd feet in the baked sierra. Not soggy any more—anything but damp; there is no moisture—but lost, brittle, and miserable as a dry stick in dead soil, in a hot wind in the late afternoon.

What I am gettin at is that I was back in Spain for no better reason than that I was still running away from the moment I would have to sit down and recognize myself for what I was, and acknowledge what had happened to the large plans for my life—the moment when I would have to build new plans.

I once read in the papers about a woman who spent all her summers for ten years scouring the Rocky Mountains for the body of her husband, who crashed there somewhere in a private plane. And I have an aunt whose husband died of sea food poisoning while on a trip to the West Coast, and she couldn't rest until she had gone out and brought his body home. There are lots of people like that, who when their husbands, wives, children, or parents die are inconsolable and will not even try to remake their lives unless they can see and touch and finally bury their dead themselves. What I had to do was perform an autopsy on the corpse of my marriage and palpate the stiff organs and open the gizzard and then come to a decision, whether to cremate or bury, and go through with one or the other, and say goodbye.

In the Absence of Jennie

One

Mari and I lived through the warm months, till the end of November, that is, on the Costa Brava, which I know a lot more about, touristically speaking, than I do about any other place in Europe, with the exception of low parts of Barcelona. Brave doesn't convey exactly the meaning of the word Brava as applied to the coast any more than it conveys in English what they mean when they say a bull is brave. In the dictionary it gives not only courageous but harsh, ferocious, and savage. There is also the sense that something *bravo* is a thing in its own right, and not to be trifled with. Pride fits in there somewhere, too. Both in connection with bulls and coasts the word has something to do with the Spanish idea of forceful individuality. Just as every man is *himself*, by God, so is every bull entitled to consideration on its own merits; and this particular coast is to be respected for its own geological unity, whether you like it or not, ni más, ni menos!

The coast belongs to the province of the city of Gerona, which is the last large city on the Mediterranean coast before you get to France. It begins when you swing off the highway at Malgrat and make the short trip over to the beach to Blanes, and runs from there all the way up to Port Bou at the border. Between Blanes and Port Bou there are no more than a dozen considerable towns, but there are another dozen smaller ones right on the sand, and many more villages or hamlets a short distance inland. None of the towns was ever a big tourist attraction like Nice or Sitges or Málaga, but almost all of them had had tourists at one time or another. I hear that before the war there used to be a regular bus service for intellectuals coming down from Stuttgart to Tosso de Mar. Right now Playa d'Aro is the big tourist center, with Tossa second and I suppose Lloret third; but there are tourists everywhere during the summer like fleas on a rabbit, and they are too mobile a crowd to make any kind of census possible. However, the coast is full of indentations, some of which cannot even be reached by land, so there is room for everybody; and you can always go five miles inland and be free not only of tourists but of the twentieth century as well if you choose. Old stones and olive trees and not a soul in sight. There are also northern towns where hardly anybody goes, except maybe Salvador Dali, who has a house in Port Lligát. Taken all together from Blanes to the frontier, the coast is brave enough, in the sense I explained, to be creeping with tourists and still remain enormous and melancholy and stupefyingly scenic and empty as another planet.

I saw a long stretch of the coast one time from a fishing boat, on a night I went out with some locals to drag nets and incidentally pick up a few cartons of Lucky Strikes from a shrouded launch. We came back at dawn and turned right up the coast off Lloret and chugged north till noon, and I will never forget it. The cliffs rose out of water so clear I could see thirty feet down to a bottom patched with white sand and forests of black weeds where tiger-striped fish swam. Beyond Tossa we steered toward the rocks and in one place passed underneath a forehead that loomed a thousand feet high; it beetled out over the boat and a few pines clung in cracks and there were stains where seabirds had nested for centuries. Between us and the open sea were several needle-thin monuments with breakers beating around their bases and cutting them to inverted plumb-bob shapes. All along that stretch were huge walls of reddish and grayish stone, yellow chalk, granite, and agglomerate rock, pocked with grottos, caves, slides, and explosions. Sea and wind had worried the once plaster smooth barriers into impossible shapes, pinnacles and plateaus and stalagmites, canyons and shelves. From where we were I could see a succession of promontories fading to pale blue toward Cabo Creus. In one vast notch of shaved rock I saw a patch of drab olive grove and a whited village like a scattering of sugar cubes.

This stretch is the geological crescendo of the coast, and there is nothing like it for living sinewy rock and wild water and windy trees. But if you go far enough up toward the other end, near Cadaqués and Rosas and L'Escala, there is a part that is all ghosts: a weird metal landscape of low bleak brown hills, totally deforested hundreds of years ago by the monks of San Pedro, and remote rocks at the end of the land, with only a few sepulchral towns; the rest is silver olives and tortured cork trees. There is even a gloomy ruin: Ampurias, founded by the Phoenicians, lived in by the Greeks, then the Romans in the third century B.C., next invaded by the Visigoths, and finally knocked apart by Norman pirates in the ninth century, and covered with sand by the winds thereafter. The government is digging it out now, probably unearthing archaeological treasures, but in the evenings, when the workmen wander home and the sea laps at the rocks and the sea wind comes in and turns up the phantasmal gray-silver undersides of the olive leaves, it is no place for anybody alive.

On the other hand, the middle stretch, from L'Estartit down to approximately San Feliu de Guixols, is a gentler and more cordial landscape than either the Cadaqués end or the Blanes end, with a big handsome blue sea and several comfortable towns, and long bright beaches equipped with striped cantinas and quick-change casetas. To these towns the Michelin road map and Kodak types come flocking. There are A-category hotels, banks, telegraphs, cheap pensions, souvenir shops, and bars for everybody. Especially bars. There's a bar for almost every tourist and if they were all closed you could still get a drink in any food store, restaurant, or curio shop. Excursion buses run to and from the nearest cities and make connections with the coastwise railroad. The weather is almost perfect and the sea is warm as tepid bathwater from mid-April to late November. I've heard it's almost as warm through the winter months too, but have never tried it. The hills slope steeply down to the sea and are covered with luxurious vegetation, including a hundred different species of prickly pear, examples of which are collected in a frightening kind of botanical zoo on the estate of Dr. Carlos Faust in Blanes.

From spring to fall these towns boom. Probably the most typical scene along here is a rubber inflated dinghy full of loud Englishmen off a white beach strewn with Barcelonese, Gerundense and Frenchmen eating butifarra and drinking red wine under parti-colored parasols. The cars parked under the pines are Spanish-assembled Seats or English Austins, with a few German tourers thrown in. In the typical midcoast town there are as many foreigners as Spaniards in high summer, and more artists than either. By artists I mean not only the people who make a living in the cinematic, graphic, or literary arts, but those who would like to as well. The total population of foreigners has to be divided into two groups at any given moment: the transients who are staying for a day or two, and the residents who plan to stay there the whole summer or even forever.

The town we lived in was probably typical as any, though smaller and we had no beach to speak of. Smaller, and somewhat isolated, but it had been Discovered, so we had a respectable population. The place was called Es Cruylles, which is not important to remember, as all foreigners called it Port Doughnuts when they referred to it in other way than Town.

Some of the towns seemed as clearly restricted to Frenchmen as though they were marked; others were for sturdy German types who brought in cases of beer and sang in groups; still others were full of oil painters almost to the exclusion of anybody else. One town seemed to have had nobody in it but dipsomaniacs from all over the world. Our own town was full of literary types, and we had some difficulty being accepted at first because neither Mari nor I are up on Motivational Trends or the Influence of William Wycherly. Our cafés along the waterfront were always full of writers and aspiring writers talking shop. This was partly because Jocelyn Strangewolf lived in a villa on the hill above town. Even I had heard of him. I thought he lived in England though. I believe he is a lord or a knight.

About three days after our arrival I was talking to a playwright named Cobra Haddad and he volunteered some information about Strangewolf. I said: "That's a hell of a good name. What's his real one?"

It amused me to ask this of Cobra Haddad, which is about the falsest name I have ever run across on a more or less standard Caucasian chassis.

"That is his real name," Haddad said. "And he has put it to some of the world's worst popular literature, and yet to one of the marvels of this century's fiction: a book which no one can read but which takes its place on the shelf alongside Gargantua and Pantagruel, *Finnegan's Wake, Remembrance of Things Past,* and *War and Peace*. Only ten thousand copies were printed, nor will it be necessary for the publisher to reprint while Strangewolf still lives. He himself owns more than two thousand copies. There is a joke that stacks of *Sursum Corda* are used in place of chairs in the villa upon the hill."

I asked what he was like. "He is rich enough now to be boorish," Haddad said. "He will speak to no one to whom he has no desire to speak, nor will he exchange even casual pleasantries except with the natives, who revere him. He has discarded courtesy, as he has discarded reading and social intercourse, as impediments to his work. Nor will he discuss or display his current work. Nevertheless, everyone who is no one makes the pilgrimage to his shrine, which you see there upon the hill. He retreated here after the war; he leaves Spain only to attend to well-spaced business matters in London. I occasionally go up to visit him, presuming upon an ancient correspondence. Usually I am received. You may accompany me one day if you are anxious to meet him. Otherwise you will only see him racing by in his automobile, unless you are received into his coterie by virtue of work of yours which has been declined by all publishers on the grounds that it is incomprehensible."

"I don't write anything," I said. "What kind of automobile has he got?"

"I knew him in London in 1930," Haddad said, "when his first poems were published. I was seventeen years old and working for the publishers. He touched my head as he passed and said that I had the hollow gaze of one who could see far. Actually I was suffering from pleurisy and had not eaten. I followed his career closely the next ten years and wrote him interminable letters afire with the heat of my ambition, which letters he was kind enough to answer in terms of contempt for the theatre as a dead form. When I achieved sufficient critical sense to evaluate his work, I discarded him as a fraud, which the rest of the world belatedly did upon publication of his one great work. Now he has reached the pinnacle of success: his name is a stink in the nostrils of criticism; publishers avoid his serious work like the plague but vend his earlier cheaper wares in every corner drugstore. The cafés here wriggle with intelligent young men and women who have paused in their intense circuits of the globe to speak to him, to solicit his encouragement, to induce him to read their experiments, and to sit over a Pernod below his hill and deprecate him."

Later on I bought a Penguin edition of one of Strangewolf's early books and read it, but I don't remember much of it except that it was about a girl trying to marry some idiotic duke with a monocle who was traveling in Albania with three nuns. On the back of the book it said he started with *Lonesome Hunting,* a thin sheaf of poems in 1924, then *Anchoring,* another thin sheaf in 1925, then twelve light novels between 1925 and 1934, interspersed with film scenarios, radio scripts, critical articles, two critical books both entitled *Brands in Flames,* and hundreds of short stories and poems for American slicks. Then between 1934 and 1944 another dozen light novels in uniform, all of them going into reprints. Next, eight years of seclusion with rumors of a big work-in-progress, and finally *Sursum Corda.*

Gregory Kline, a poet who was living in Port Crullers that summer, said he had read *Sursum Corda* but didn't dig it. I asked him what the author was like. "A sleeping mountain," he said. "A man who writes giggling pornographic novelettes of English diplomats going gracefully to the dogs in the tropics, and of silly young girls trying to marry Oscar Wilde. Also, a man who chants twelve hundred pages worth of unreadable rhythms, in the midst of which a single coherent sentence is as rare as a June-Moon lyric in Béla Bartók's *Concerto for Orchestra.*"

Anyway, because of Jocelyn Strangewolf our town was discovered, and we had a large population of picturesque types. I met them all during that summer, the ones who came and went and the ones who were staying as long as they could. Most of them I met in the Bar Gaucho every morning at ten. This was where the mail was dispensed. There was one bus every day that came up from San Feliu and dropped off the mail, and Señora Viñals, the wife of the town taxi driver, was postmistress and she distributed it. The first day I went up I sat in a wicker chair next to a big gloomy Swedish girl about nine feet high and she pointed people out to me as they came in. There was a Finnish painter who lived there the year round and spoke eight languages and painted pink mountains and went swimming every day. And two Dutch queers who were writing a movie script with no words or music in it. And a retired Dublin policeman who had served in the Indian Army and was writing his memoirs. And Carol Bond, an Englishwoman who wrote detective stories. And Pete Merriam, an American girl who had written a successful sexy novel at seventeen and was vainly trying to write another. And old Mrs. Brewster, who lived on a yacht moored offshore with three sick Malagueños who wore knives in their belts—she was composing a new Bible that reconciled all the scientific advances of the last thousand years with the Hebrew J'H'V'H. And a lot of others.

The Gaucho bar was in the middle of the town and didn't have a view of the sea. It was up the hill among the twisty dirt streets and stone houses, and it belonged more or less to the locals. Generally speaking, the foreigners hung around the cafés on the water's edge. The Gaucho was popular with the local old men who went there to play chess and futbolin and get away from the noise of tourists. But in the morning, when the jangling old bus from San Feliu arrived, everybody tracked up the hill and crowded into the bar. New visitors generally came by bus, too, as well as dry goods and guitars and food stuffs people had ordered from Gerona or Barcelona. So there was always a mob. Señora Viñals grabbed the leather bag of mail away from the bus driver and carried it inside, and everybody followed her. The foreigners all called her Madame de Mars, because two of the beauty marks of her youth, one on either side of her forehead, had darkened and attentuated with age, until they were dark brown little pods on the ends of cords of skin, resembling the antenna of an insect. Her spectacles had blue lenses like a welder's goggles, and side lights to keep the dust out, and they too contributed to her interplanetary appearance. She had no teeth at all and rouged her lips in a perfect circle.

She pulled the leather bag onto a table and took the envelopes and rolled newspapers out and spread them in front of her. Everybody had to wait his turn. She went through the whole stack for each customer, bending down and peering cautiously at the addresses through the blue goggles. "Villa Harmonía," said the two Dutch queers. "Vee-eel-ya Ar-mo-*nee*-ya," she said, turning over every last letter in the stack and peering at it. "Nada," she said at the end. "Nothing for you."

"Villa Alegre," I said. That was the name of the house we lived in. She never bothered to learn the heathen foreign names, just remembered us by the houses we lived in. "Vee-eel-ya A-*leg*-gre," she said, beginning again from the top and turning the letters over one by one. I never got much mail, aside from an occasional letter from my mother asking was I eating properly, but I rarely missed a mail call. The old men of the town, suspending their games, would sit back in their chairs and meditatively roll black tobacco cigarettes and stare. We always had half a dozen young but rather strict and buck-toothed girls in town hoping for a chance to meet Strangewolf. The old men always looked these girls up and down with total unblinking concentration. They stared at all the women—at elderly ladies, at Carol Bond and Pete Merriam, and even at Mrs. Brewster, as though they had never seen any of them before. They also stared long and carefully every day at the three beards that came into the Gaucho: the curled reddish full beard of Gregory Kline, the poet who worked and lived in a tiny windowless farmer's hut up the road; the stiff sparse French beard of Jack Pangs, the American electrician who painted abstracts of electrical diagrams; and the crisp square chinbrush of Marcel Climant, the Parisian surrealist who wrote bleak novels about anarchists in jail.

The foreigners milled around the unhurried Madame de Mars shouting for their mail and saying good morning to each other (for most of them El Gaucho was the first call of the day) while the oldsters sat and took it all in and never said a word. They sat over their chess boards and green felt card tables, gnarled and attentive; they scarcely moved. Once I noted old González (who was a public charge; everybody took turns feeding him) with his king held in the air over the board. To my certain knowledge he held it there, halfway out of check, fron the time the leather bag arrived to the time the last piece of mail was distributed.

To add to the confusion, everybody came to the Gaucho accompanied by his dog. Kabut, the Ethiopian, owned a terrible black dog the size of a pony, and kept it on a thin leather leash. Fuhta Brag, the Finn, had a tiny little old man of a dog which he claimed understood six languages and Catalán. Old Mrs. Brewster, who lived alone on her yacht with the three knife-carrying Spaniards from Málaga, kept four dogs of her own, all white but all formed differently, and she took in any other dogs that came along and fed them all on the octopus tripes she fished from the sea with a wooden pole. Sometimes I brought along Siguiente, our dog, but it was not accustomed to other dogs or people either and would not stay still; if put on his chain he howled and peed and in general made a nuisance of himself. In addition, the village was full of more or less communally owned dogs of all sizes and shapes and mixtures who attached themselves to anybody who gave them a friendly look and would follow after them until hit with a rock.

After mail call most of the foreigners went down to the Bar Royal on the waterfront. It was actually no more than a long porch propped up by cane poles, with nothing between it and the low jumbled rocks of the beach except a strip of asphalt where the local bravos occasionally disported themselves on their motorcycles. During the summer season round wooden tables and basket chairs were spread all over this porch, and in the evenings men with guitars and other instruments would sing habaneras. Sooner or later all the artists made either a sketch or a full-dress oil portrait of Pepe, the master of the Royal, because, as Jack Pangs said: "It is a tremendous face! It is all there: tragedy, humor, triumph, bitterness, ignorance, work, sex, joy, bereavement—"

Pepe's face was lined and awful; when he smiled he showed brilliant white teeth.

"—grief, pride, folly, intelligence, sensitivity," Pangs droned, "envy, irony, curiosity, despair . . ."

"Oh pipe *down,* Jack," Pete Merriam said. "It's just those teeth and you *know* they're false."

That same morning there was an intense youth from some intellectual center in Minnesota who said he had been thinking all night about the riddle of Jocelyn Strangewolf. "Look," he said. "All the greatness of us dissipates in our early years. Most of us have lost the three things necessary for true genius: shameless enthusiasm, terrible shyness, and the habit of masturbation."

"—hope, gregariousness, fear, sadness," Pangs said, "enthusiasm, shyness, and masturbation; I forgot them. Health, neurosis, diarrhea . . ."

Meanwhile Charles Kolp was working up a bargain with Pepe and some of the regular waiters; they were to start bringing him a different drink every time he came. Kolp was a tall fleshy American Negro who rarely wore anything but a bathing suit. He was probably working on something, but nobody knew what; he spent most of his time skin diving. "One is limited by the names of the drinks one knows in a foreign country," he said. "All summer so far I've been drinking Cinzano in the daytime and cognac at night. I intend to try everything on the shelf and remember its name, so I'll know what to ask for to fit my mood."

On the shelves behind the bar and under the bar, on hooks and ledges above and in wooden racks on the walls were bottles of all shapes and colors, some of them covered with dust and cobwebs. There were fig aperitivos and lemon ferments, cane-sugar extracts and green gins, sap-and-molasses mixtures, speckle-horse whiskies, liqueurs made of every possible fruit, and a broad range of yellowish drinks that all tasted like licorice, one of which was absinta. To start Kolp off on his project we all ordered something different. Pangs got a kind of tequila. I got kirsch, which I didn't like. Pete Merriam got something called caña. "Oh God!" she said. The waiter brought her some water. Carol Bond recommended an egg broken raw in a glass of milk, with vodka. Pete spat on the ground and staggered around the table clasping her stomach and breathing hoarsely. "Oh God!" she said again. The glass was passed around the table for everybody to try. I noted that when I brought it close the bouquet closed off my esophagus and respiratory tract by reflex action. I could only get my tongue in. "One coult ged used," the Dutchmen said. "It hass a goot flavor." Pete, who had drunk first, was all right again, although she said her throat would never be the same.

A couple of tables away Gregory Kline sat with the son and heir of a Chicago meat-packing family who had come to Spain to hunt up natural materials for his art; he was a sculptor. On the table in front of him he had an enormous gnarled cactus root full of eyes and whiskers and elbows. He was working out of one of those beginner's oil painting kits with bottles of turpentine and linseed oil and little tubes of garish colors. He was carefully painting the tentacles of the root blue and red, and the knurls green; and in the thick wet paint he was imbedding sequins. Around the table were some seven or eight local children and their dogs, absorbedly watching every move. The sculptor, Tom Fast, was one of the semipermanents in Port Doughnuts, except that he had no place to live, neither room nor villa, nor did he stay in María Molina's pension on the hill. Usually he slept in the pine trees by the sea, out in the open in fine weather or under his cart when it rained. He had ticks all the time. He got his meals in the Bar Royal or the Bodega: gambas and sandwiches of the hard red local sausage. Since he owned no door to lock he carried all his possessions around with him in a farmer's two-wheel cart he had bought for that purpose. In the cart was a green army surplus duffel bag full of overalls and polo shirts and shoes, also a wooden box full of international papers and miscellaneous articles. The rest of the cart was full of natural materials, some worked, some not. He had odd-shaped stones, lengths of worm-rotted driftwood, big three-pronged fishbones, lobster baskets, broken anchors, crusted amphoras, crooks of olive and cork wood, pieces of glass, carved fence posts, conch shells, and primitive farming implements of interesting shapes. The Materials of his Art.

Kline, who sat with him, scratched in his huge beard and indicated parts of the cactus root he thought needed a touch of color. Later everybody looked up to see what the uproar was about and saw Fast trying to smash Kline's head with a chair and Kline holding Fast around the hips and trying wildly to knee him in the groin. Some locals were standing nearby concernedly discussing the unsporting tactics of both, and the dogs were barking; the children had run away to stand in a row in the sun by the sea.

About this same time Lola Wingfelt Curtis was talking to Jaume Pujol, the poorest man in town. He had seven children, the oldest just seven, and his wife was pregnant again. Jaume went out every day in a leaky old rowboat, with a rusty harpoon gun and a face mask, to fish. He always went alone and exhausted himself underwater and when he surfaced usually had to chase a quarter of a mile after the drifting boat, sometimes with a big live mero struggling on the end of his dart. Everybody said that one day he wouldn't come back in the evening, and the empty boat would drift up the coast and smash, and then the woman and the eight children would starve to death. Lola Wingfelt Curtis had been writing pulp stories under different psuedonyms for twenty years; she sold her rights outright and made enough to live abroad. She figured there was a story in Jaume's plight. "Tell me the story of thy life, Jaume," she said.

Jaume shrugged. "There is no story, señora." He was dressed in worn corduroy pants without pockets and of late without buttons either, the fly strung shut with fishline. His shirt was the gift of a tourist who had gone fishing with him some years earlier. He had no shoes for week days in summer. Lola Curtis sensed a tragic flaw, I guess—a dark star in Jaume's life, which, with proper rearrangement, might be the kernel for a story of a young girl's Disastrous Marriage, small town Midwest scene.

"But no man becomes as thou without great trouble, without great reason," she pursued. "Tell me why thou has fallen so low."

Jaume pursed his lips. Her Spanish was very good; he could

not mistake her meaning. Though impoverished he was not shamed, not deshonrado, not without pride. He rose from the table and leaned his garlic breath on her. "Señora," he said, "I defecate in the milk of your mother. If ever you capture a man, bring him to me, and I will break his head for the insolence of his woman."

At that moment Tom Fast and Gregory Kline started to fight, and Jaume stalked away from Lola Wingfelt Curtis's table. He entered the fight and with his sinewy swimmer's arm dealt Fast such a palizo that he sprawled over the table, flipped completely, and landed on his stomach on the ground; then he dealt Kline such another that he upended into the cart with his feet in the air and his head and shoulders buried in stones and driftwood and lobster traps. The rest of us watched silently as Jaume dusted his hands and then padded arrogantly all the way down the waterfront past the various cafés, jutting his jaw and shaking his fists and shouting: "Son-a-beetch los extranjeros!" When he was out of earshot we gave him a sincere round of applause.

If this gives the impression that there was always something furious going on in Port Crullers, it is misleading. The general impression I retain of the place is one of bottomless tranquillity, the dust lying flat on the road, the sun shining, a cart going by, a motorcycle in the distance, and a dog or two snuffing around; maybe a few people swimming up near the lighthouse and an occasional hawk gliding out over the sea and then returning to the rocks without so much as swooping. A good part of the day there wouldn't be anybody in any of the bars, or at the Bodega—they'd all be working on their opuses or trying to catch fish or taking siestas. Every foreigner seems to think he has to take a siesta.

Even when people did congregate, it usually only amounted to a drowsy buzz of conversation punctuated by the creak of an occasional cart and the hourly timbreless clanking of the church clock. Once or twice a month somebody would give a party in his villa, and on Saturday and Sunday nights there was the Grand Paseo, when everybody in town walked back and forth on the asphalt in front of the Bar Royal. But generally the foreigners only got together between ten and noon in the morning and between six and nine at night; and then it was just conversation. One thing I have noticed about literary and artistic people is that they haven't got any roofs to their mouths. No sooner is an idea generated in the upper part of their skulls than it falls flop on their tongues and has to be articulated, as though it couldn't live without immediate light and air. Not that some of their ideas weren't interesting, but sometimes I had to smile.

A little American by the name of Sammy Carpenter had rented a big villa all for himself that summer in the mistaken idea that in solitude and concentration he could write a book as confusing as Strangewolf's; but he had already got himself into several different kinds of trouble by the time Mari and I arrived. In the first place he was spending all his time in the Bar Royal defending his literary ideas and scheming how he would astonish everybody as soon as he got to work. In the second place he had somehow got himself mixed up with Pete Merriam, under the very nose of Luis Pallarés, a Catalán financier who was also contraband commander in chief in our area. Pallarés was Pete's protector, if that is the word. In the third place, he got into an argument with a motorcycle racer who was passing through Spain on his way to England to compete in some race or other. It seems at a party in the Bodega the motorcycle racer had given everybody leave to call him by his nickname, which was Crash. His real name was Ace Gibson, he said. Sammy said: "Ace 'Crash' Gibson. They're both nicknames. What do you want two nicknames for?"

Gibson said: "The same reason you got four eyes, Four-eyes." They were both a little drunk. Mari and I were at the party—it was the first we were invited to—and witnessed the argument. The two arranged to meet the following day on the asphalt and slug it out mountain style, no holds barred. Nothing ever came of that, but Sammy had to listen to himself being psychoanalyzed for days afterward. He got a lot of advice on how to integrate, how to sublimate his aggression and how to lick Gibson.

Cobra Haddad told him: "There is no such technique as fisticuffs in this part of the world. The idea is purely Anglo-American. It is a moronic business. A pugilistic display for sport is one thing, but to set out to strike a hard human head with your bare hand—a tremendously complex apparatus consisting of over fifty small bones and fragile members—is clearly idiotic. The nearest pole, stone, chair, club, or cooking utensil serves much better. If nothing is at hand, use elbows and feet. Remember, a blow to the groin incapacitates one's adversary more surely than the most adept uppercut. There is also the solar plexus; and the shins are handily vulnerable to a well directed attack. But the fistic attack is an outmoded form, like chivalry. Mr. Gibson may employ it; he would seem to be a romantic rather than a realistic type. Therefore, if he offers to approach you in the orthodox boxing stance, ignore it and kick him squarely in the genitals. As he bends forward, bring the blade of the hand down sharply on the Atlas vertebra. Once he has been felled, kick with the heel of the shoe rather than the toe, directing your blows at the temples and throat, with a further kick or two to the groin. Do not allow yourself to be swayed by the urge for a K.O. It is not necessary to render your opponent unconscious, only to cripple him beyond retaliation."

Lola Curtis said: "I think it's all a silly business if you ask me. Two grown men flailing away at each other like school boys."

"Don't I know it?" Sammy said. "But I can't back down from him if he really wants to fight."

"Cor-rect, by Jeezuz," Kolp said. "Never take no crap off no man."

All this time Ingrid, the gloomy nine-foot Swede, was staring at Sammy; then she said: "I remember a case similar to this in Nurdsvaag before the war. A youth named Pvrtr was grown to be tall and dark and strong, in this very small town. He adopted a swagger when he was twenty, and wore a trench coat with a high collar. It was his custom to depart from the village for long periods of time, to return with much money. It was said of him that he rode the railway trains and robbed the rich in the first-class compartments. He became known among the townsfolk as the Highwayman. Then one day there returned to the village a young man named Urhlf who had been absent for many years with the Merchant Service. He had visited many exotic lands. He too swaggered and he wore a sailor's jacket with a high collar, and a peaked cap. He wished to be called the Sea Rover. These two young men hated one another from the first. When they met they snarled like dogs. Once they fought together fiercely in the main store, and demolished a barrel of mackerel. Always they challenged one another to duel to the death. Their mothers begged them to use reason, but neither would lose face to the other. At last the Sea Rover was found in a barn with his skull cleft by an axe, and the Highwayman was arrested and hanged."

"All in order," Gregory Kline said. "Better to be hanged or die of a cleft skull than live a poltroon."

"I never knuckled under to no man alive," Kolp said. "Never will, neither."

"Ridiculous," Lola said. "Men are all alike. You wouldn't work so hard getting into trouble if you had to clean up the mess afterwards."

"Beg pardon," Kline said. "Everyone concedes the impossibility of explaining the idea of Honor to a woman. It is like exhibiting delicate water colors to a stomach. Woman, who is concerned with the well being of her tripes and the issue thereof, has no inkling of the rankling deposit left in the seat of male emotions, the breast, upon defeat, retreat, ignominy."

Marcel Climant suddenly applauded. "Que musique! Eenkling! Reenkling! Defeat, retreat! Formidable!" Everybody was disconcerted, and he seized the opportunity to quote something long and euphonious in French, to which everybody listened, continentally, without understanding.

Kolp said: "Anyway, no man ever made me back down. I don't take any lip."

"It's all balls," Tom Fast said. "I agree with Lola. I haven't got any pride. If he's bigger than me, the hell with it. I'm not going to get my nose broken just to prove I'm brave."

But Cobra Haddad rapped the table. "You don't see the point of Ingrid's story. It is not a question of bravery or cowardice. It is Fate. The Sea Rover was doomed to die at the hands of the Highwayman, or vice versa. Certain men are destined to struggle against each other as the cat goes in fear of the dog, or vice versa. What a man fears he attacks. Sammy fears Mr. Ace 'Crash' Gibson; he must therefore fight him to the death. Mr. Gibson fears Sammy, and so must attack. There is no question of one or the other being a coward. When two men fear each other one must attack the other as the other attacks him, and the two go locked in struggle downward to their doom."

"Fiddledeedee," Lola said.

Kolp said: "What's Gibson afraid of? Sammy's just a little shrimpy guy."

"He fears what we all fear," Kline said. "To be ridiculed. We do not have any understanding of it because we only vaguely remember having honor. We are adults. Most of the human virtues are adolescent. At the end of adolescence the human becomes cowardly, indifferent, selfish, dumb, and greedy. He spends his life in the hunt for tiny satisfactions. Those few who, for one reason or another, don't mature, become artists or are hanged or have their skulls cleft. By artists I mean inventors, hermits, fanatics, adventurers, and criminals as well as creators of art forms. One of these atavists might put himself in jeopardy for the sake of honor—no mature human would—the idea is to smirk and scorn. Honor is for children, who treasure odd little items in their sticky pockets; and for the eternal adolescents, who perhaps believe less strongly in the human virtues than the rest of us, but who personify them."

"What's that got to do with Sammy and Gibson?" Lola asked.

"Of course," Ingrid said. "They are the unmatured. Great men."

As a matter of fact, Ace Gibson was an ape type with a big English EMC motorcycle who didn't have a spark of greatness in him as far as I could see, though in a dumb sort of way he was a nice enough guy. And Sammy Carpenter was a mousy little man with a big larynx and little ears who may have personified some of the human virtues, but he didn't personify the ones that make headwaiters notice you. From all I could see, he fell in with Pete Merriam practically by accident, when she was half drunk and neither of them meant anything by it; and he was only in trouble with Luis Pallarés, the Catalán smuggler. Certainly Pete wasn't making him any trouble. By accident I heard them talking one morning, about a week after the night they went out in the rowboat together—a parasol screened me from them. She said: "You're very sweet, Sammy. Excuse me if I bawl. I think you might even marry me if I took you up on it. But I won't. I don't want to marry you. I'm not in love with you. And you would never forget Luis. How could you? On top of that, I'm not sure any more that I'll get a divorce from Raymond. He's been doing much better. He may come down to see me this winter. His mother says he has made a lot in export. In the flannel business, you know. Not only that, but if you married me, you'd begin to regret it in a year or two. I know you, Sammy, and I know myself. I want a home and children. You want to live wild and free. It would never work. In years to come I'll think of you dashing about the free spaces of the earth, wild and free! That's how you'll always be, Sammy. Free! Alive!"

Poor little Carpenter. All this while she was living in Pallarés' villa, and he came out from Barcelona to stay with her whenever he had time to spare from his own occult concerns. One heard that he had villas in all parts of the world, with a mistress in each one, but nobody believed that except Spaniards, who think Spanish men and foreign women are capable of anything. Admittedly he had bags of money in banks all over the world, mostly dollars and Swiss francs, good hard money. And he went from place to place in his private planes; he was supposed to have three. It was said that he financed practically all the smuggling between Africa and the Spanish peninsula, and even that he had something to do with shipments of Indian hemp to California. But what was most memorable was the substantially documented fact that he had financed both sides of the Spanish revolution in order to stay in business no matter which side won. And since that time he had not only collected his money from Italy, he had even got back eighty centimos on the peseta from Soviet Russia.

I met him later on; he didn't look like anything particular to me, certainly nothing like a ruthless international financier. He didn't look subtle or magnetic or mysterious at all; he looked sincere and tough, like a farmer, his face chipped out of some hard, dignified material like the bare rock mountains of Spain. I liked him on sight.

But my best friend among the foreigners, or at least the one with whom I had the closest association, turned out to be Strangewolf, of all people. I didn't know anything about his life or his work, and certainly we didn't have anything in common except cars. I saw his car before I saw him; it was a gigantic 1937 4.3 liter Alvis, light green with dishpan spinner wheels, eight headlights and an engine hood a mile long. Very hairy if you like the classic rather than the sleek cars. First I only saw it going by in a cloud of dust. Once I passed it going down to Barcelona while I was coming up. But I didn't see it close at hand until the day Cobra Haddad came by repeating his offer to take me up to the white villa with him. I went along because I didn't have anything else to do that morning, and Mari was working in the house—cleaning out the old stove, with carbon all over her and sweat on her forehead—and it always made me feel like going far away whenever she set to work. She was always very conscientious about housework in Es Cruylles, because she considered herself under surveillance both by the Spanish women and by the foreign women. She was afraid the former would think her a useless or even a loose woman if she didn't work like the ideal Spanish wife, and she liked to believe that the latter (women who sat around all day in the cafés doing nothing and declaring that the ideal Spanish housewife was a slave and lived in feudal bondage) would envy her and her fine house and the fun she had running it. She wouldn't let me help her with anything. She was very proud of how clean the place always was and how prompt the meals. Anyway, that day I left her busy and happy enough, rasping away at the caked soot and sweating a stream; and all the time singing loud and jolly enough to keep the cats scared out of the garbage.

"... la tumba de pobre Dolores," she sang,
"Rodeada de cruces y flores."

Poor Dolores' tomb, surrounded by crucifixes and flowers.

Haddad and I climbed up the dirt road between the almond trees. He trudged along despondently with the aid of a gnarled stick, the handle fashioned like a cow's head, down to the horns and ears. Along the ditches black fertile dirt was piled up and baked hard in the blaze. It was still early; sheep jingled through the orchards, clustered and blatting, with red smears of some chemical on their backs. Wc saw three black goats tied to a tree, three females, with banging black sags of udders between their ankles. Haddad had to rest half a dozen times on the way. He was not old, only about forty-five I judged, but he had had a hard life. That is, he never told the whole story, but was full of laborious hints about Yugoslavia in 1937 and running guns to Mikhailovitch and diverting P-51's to Chu Li in the China hills. His neck was covered with scars and several of his fingers had been broken and badly set. His main complaint stemmed from a kick in the kidneys dealt him in Munich by a blond lieutenant with an eagle on his cap, some twenty years before. It gave him trouble. Of course, a lot of this might have been fiction. All I know for certain is what Jack Pangs told me one day, that Haddad had had some success in Europe before the war writing Bolshevik plays, and some smaller success since in the United States. Haddad always talked about himself, but only obliquely, and he never explained anything. Not that anybody was very curious. Carol Bond, who gave everybody a nickname, used to call him the Dull Mystery Man, or Riddle-dee-Bore.

We arrived at Strangewolf's place. You had to climb an interminable flight of broken steps to reach it. The house was just a lot of flat boxes laid together without a pattern. Even the roofs were flat, like New Mexico ruins. There were hardly any windows and the front door was carefully hidden. There wasn't a sound, no farm noises, no birds or cattle, only the sheep bells a distance down the slope. Haddad didn't knock; he walked around the walls past blank shutters to a shed in the rear, where an old man was bending over an electric motor. In the same shed was the green Alvis, so I went directly to that. Haddad said: "El señor," to the old man. The old man said: "El señor no está."

"You know very well he's here, you silly beggar," Haddad said. "Call him out." So the old man wandered into the house by a back door and eventually came out again with a little old woman with a loaf of bread in her hand. "You like speak Mister Jock?" she asked. Haddad said yes. The old man and old woman stood close together and stared at us. They were both wrinkled and warped like the milenario olive trees along the road. After a time the woman said: "You get sick, señor, from the sun." Haddad immediately began to exhibit the first signs of heat prostration. "Pass to shade," the woman said. "Mister Jock come soon." She led him under an arbor where there was a wicker chair and a stone pot of water and a picture of Franco nailed to a post. Then she went in the house. The old man squatted down on his rope sandals and supervised Haddad, and I went back to the Alvis. It had a hundred thousand miles on it if it had an inch, but it seemed in perfect shape.

After another half hour the woman came out again with a bottle of red wine. "Take yourself wine," she said. "Look there—" and she indicated a narrow trail running on up to the top of the hill. "Mister Jock come soon," she said again. She poured cool wine in a couple of glasses and we drank it. The bent old man offered a brown-paper black-tobacco Ideal cigarette and I smoked it down to the last half inch, and that on a broiling hot day.

The woman went back in the house, leaving us the wine, and the old man squatted down and supervised us. Two carts went by at a dazed creaking walk on the road far below the house. We must have waited another half hour before Strangewolf came down the trail from the hill. He was tall and very thin, about fifty or fifty-five, and he had white hair and black eyebrows, which I like very much. He wore a blue work shirt turned dark under the arms with sweat, and a yellow handkerchief was tucked in his collar. "Ullo, Konrad," he said.

"Psst, you forget, I have another name now," Haddad said.

"Rot. Can't remember it," Strangewolf said. "Viper or Adder or What-is-it. Attention, boy: this is Konrad Prysbyshysky and he is an ex-Gauleiter. Thought you were coming up Thursday. Want to go hunt mushrooms?"

"No. Listen to me, Sir Jocelyn, I have come to talk of my problem with you; and I have brought Mr. Cord along so that you will not talk nonsense to me."

"All talk's nonsense," Strangewolf said. "What can't be conveyed by means of pantomime should be limited to one-syllable code words. Come off it, Konrad; you've been delivering your soul aloud for the last two months and still we haven't seen the end of it. What's the result? Where's your reserve? Who's this Cord? What's his name?"

"Cord," I said. "Hope I'm not butting in or anything. I just thought I'd walk up and take a look at your car."

"Help yourself," he said. "Keys are in it. Take a spin if you like. Konrad likes to jabber on."

I wandered around the Alvis for a few minutes, and sat in it, but the seat was pushed back too far even for my legs. Strangewolf must have liked to drive lying down on the back of his neck. A lot of English sports cars are built this way. On the dashboard were hundreds of buttons and gauges, including compasses and barometers and even an altimeter, in case you wanted to change your carburetors when you get up in the mountains, I guess. I wondered what would happen if I took him up on it and gave myself a ride. I had the idea the motor was in as good shape as the rest of the car, and I would have given an arm to go out on the highway with it. But that would give him the right to ask to borrow my car, and I don't like anybody driving the Jaguar but me.

They kept on talking and after awhile I went over to listen. Haddad was saying, "As I have told you, I do not read your work. Once I read a poem, but I did not like it, and all I need to know of *Sursum Corda* was in Claws Eggman's review. It is apart from your work that I consider you the supremely intelligent man. Because you need ask no questions. I must always ask them. But you have money, you have a pleasant if futile work to do, and a house in which to live; you have a life which would seem to satisfy you. Only extreme intelligence can finally arrive at this position. It is a recognized fact. It is probably for this that the young people come so far to wait upon your words. I am aware that you have only contempt for those who seek advice of you. I number myself amongst them, but I tell you it cost me much nervous tissue."

"Rot," Strangewolf said. "The kids don't bother me. All they want me to do is take their stories away overnight and tell them the following morning they've pushed the frontiers of literature a hundred years ahead. Nothing simpler. Sometimes I talk to them. I expect I'm old hat already in most quarters. What do you want me to do, read your latest play?"

"No. I thought you might know perhaps what life remains to an old man who has put everything important behind him."

About here I got up and walked around the house, looking it over. I gave a Chesterfield to the old man and he smoked it down to the end; I dropped a pebble down the well and spoke to some goats that were rooting in the garbage pile. Then I went back and sat in the Alvis again. I was figuring that anybody who kept his car in such good shape was probably a fiend for the sport, and if there is one thing I miss in Europe it is a chance to sit down and gab with the boys that hang around Harry's garage and talk racing and camshafts and stocks, et cetera. Hobbies are never much fun unless you know people who have the same hobby.

They went on talking for a long time. It seems Strangewolf had never read any of Haddad's plays. "I have written twelve," Haddad said. "Most of them were produced in Berlin and Paris. I have also written a book; perhaps you have heard of it: *I Chose Re-Defection.* It is in its fourth printing. Recently one of my early works was produced in New York. I have earned money, but it is not enough. I have a reputation and I am still writing plays, but it is not enough."

"Need money?" Strangewolf said suspiciously.

"Listen," Haddad said. "The plays, the books also, were weapons in the war. The war is over. Here in Spain I have seen many of my old comrades; they are dead men hiding in smelly rooms. In New York and Kansas and San Francisco are dead soldiers waiting on tables in impossible restaurants, or writing noncommittal articles for American magazines. There are old comrades of mine in prisons still, but most have finished even that; they have paid and are free again, to live in emptiness. The battle is over. There are old comrades who have sold out to one side or another, some are figurehead heroes in totalitarian states, some are repentant informers in the camps of the enemy. The old army has been routed; there are no slogans, no banners—there is no life."

"There's always life," Strangewolf said, swatting at a bee. I sat down by Haddad; the bent old man came around the corner and offered me another cigarette.

Haddad said: "To speak now of the bread of the workingman, of equality, of man's fate, to murmur against the guillotine, or against the inherited wealth of inbred feeble men, or to protest the weight of such money upon the necks of the poor, or on the other hand to bemoan the betrayal of humanity's greatest effort, the assassination of noble men . . ."

"Crocodile—" Strangewolf said.

". . . is to be ejected from nation after nation. It is to be persecuted, imprisoned, in certain states tortured, but in certain other states, worst of all, ignored or patronized. It is to hear the words History, Inevitable, Modern, used to demonstrate that man's invaluable spirit must be forever flattened, hypnotized, unlearned, and oppressed . . . Mr. Cord, would you not blow that smoke at me? It will give me a catarrh."

"Sorry," I said.

"—tears," Strangewolf said. "These bleeding bees seem to be making a concerted attack on me."

"But to keep silent," Haddad said, "is to live the life I seek now to avoid, that of the dead soldier. I have nothing to do. To write plays is interesting, but I cannot write about silly girls and ludicrous noblemen with monocles. When I write it is like *Sursum Corda!* Sombre, complicated riddles which seem important because they are incomprehensible, because there is nothing in them! I have no solutions to build into them. I have no theme. I sit on my terrace and think of men who are dead. Where am I at present?"

"Couple of American girls came here last year, haw haw haw," Strangewolf said. "Wanted me to have slow sexual intercourse with one while the other read aloud a certain lyrical passage from *Sursum Corda.* Then turn about. Do I breathe an odor of potential collaboration? You give me equal trouble. Is my success contagious? What am I to advise? I give advice only when it is not asked for. Besides, no one takes me seriously until I talk nonsense. Take time. Stay here. For heaven's sake, old boy, you've only been away from America three months. Everyone's confused in America. I'll take you out in my boat one day. We'll fish. The first year here is one of exasperation. Resign yourself. Write something to pass the time. We are only waiting to be superseded. Cease to live now; wait here for the end. Look outward to the world; it does not affect us now. Watch it from here to the end. You want to know what life is left for an ex-Gauleiter with no battle to fight? Vegetate, I say. And keep a eye on your line, in case you get a nibble."

"But I must correct one misapprehension," Haddad said, not much concerned. "I do not presume to speculate on how you spent the years of the war. However I wish you would not lump all the vanquished together and count me as one."

"Rot. Sticks out all over you," Strangewolf said. "Like these fat, unrepentant burghers who come down here to brown their fat necks in the autumn. Still read themselves to sleep with *Mein Kampf*, by the light of lamps with genuine Jew-skin shades."

"Oh well," Haddad said.

"Matter of fact, I wrote propaganda for the War Office those years. Gave me time to myself."

"I was in Washington, District of Columbia," Haddad said. "We arranged for Lend-Lease P 51's to miss Chiang's airfields altogether and fly directly to Chou En Lai's groups in the hills."

"Doesn't matter. If you think you are going to make a mark writing incendiary plays in this day and age, think again. Has to be something mystical. Mark my words. All the systems have been tried. They are finally waking up to what Shaw told them in 1921. Political man is a fart in a windstorm. Words to that effect. He doesn't know what's going on. And more, he doesn't care. If he did care he wouldn't have the capacity to do anything. Can't improve man's lot until you improve man. That will lead to a score of conclusions. Pick one and write a play about it."

"There is another misapprehension," Haddad said, "that I intend to write anything beyond what I must write to support myself until my death in the near future. As for framing answers to an infinity of pointless questions, the answers to which would benefit no one, to that I prefer the extreme of expatriate vegetation and desultory fishing."

"Not a bad lot," Strangewolf said. "Just what I was telling you."

"I shall respect your opinion," Haddad said with some irritation, "if you tell me that collective man, like the individual man which you seem to wish to represent, has no further interest in improving his condition."

"Old boy, if you yourself have the slightest interest in laying a finger on what is already a perfect social order, concerned only with the extension of money, you are indeed the Shavian superman. One might as well expect the great apes to become dissatisfied with their own climbing and turn to the manufacture of extensible ladders. Question of capacity, that's all. There hasn't been a social or biological advance in so long a time that we may as well begin to count on being supplanted. Good thing, I say. Every advantage our early human geniuses asked for has come to exist, in one place or another, at one time or another, without making our general lot one whit better. Rousseau wanted rationality; got it. Newton wanted scientific method; got it. Mill and Jefferson and others wanted universal literacy, an educated public. Such a public appears, everyone reads my novelettes and rape-and-comics newspapers. Who can read Mill? The English wanted a Bill of Rights. Well, they got it. Have no more rights than serfs. The Americans wanted rule by the people. Bedlamites couldn't have more difficulty discerning political arse from social elbow. You gentlemen wanted Communism. What have you done with it? Scared each other into funk. I once put the entire force of a fine-tuned human brain to work learning music. Never wrote a note. Do? There's nothing to do. Things are perfect, that which is to us perfectable. If a man with a round head, six fingers, and no appendix isn't born into the position of benevolent despot within the next few hundred years, make way for the rats, I say: next most intelligent unspecialized mammals on earth."

They stopped talking for about three minutes, and Strangewolf gave a big contagious yawn. Finally Haddad said: "If you have finished, then you are the complete pessimist, for there is a redeeming phrase which you have not used. It is: Cosmic Consciousness."

"Pretty idea," Strangewolf said. "Dim prospect. We are born of dullards and engender dullards. Even the super-dullard would hardly serve. I suspect there were desperate attempts at a super-dinosaur at the last moment. But the form was finished. I consider man to have raised a spectacular staircase to the scaffold of his own extinction. Surely no Spirit of Nature could ask for more than that her creation elevate her from the days of Grunt to the balanced technological civilization which existed at the beginning of the recent world holocaust—in which, to say the least, everyone was killed. You bear in mind, of course, that what we decide about the matter has absolutely no importance."

"That it is the aimless conversation of two old men killed in the early stages of the long war that burned up God's first attempt at men," Haddad said, nodding.

"Precisely," Strangewolf said.

Two

So WE didn't gab about cars that day. Haddad got morose and Strangewolf had talked himself out; he wouldn't say more, and went off up the mountain with Ernesto, the gnarled old man, to hunt for mushrooms. Later on, however, he and I got to be friends. I was right, he was a classics fan in a mild way, and had owned a lot of old Bentley and Frazer-Nash cars, the kind you have to be practically Sandow to drive. Among other cars he had once owned an SS Jaguar, and he was interested in seeing how the modern cars differed. Once he went out in my car and I followed along in the Alvis, which was reasonably easy to drive, although noisy with age and obedient only when you clenched it with both fists. We even diced a little on the winding road that goes down toward Barcelona—after we changed back to our own cars—but that was asking too much. He claimed afterward he could have caught up with me if he had had better fuel. There might be something in that; the government here sells all the gasoline, its a federal monopoly, and if you don't like what they sell, you can tank up on turpentine for all they care. And where there's no business competition there is usually no quality control. I never have any trouble beyond a little high-gear ping, but he claimed the Alvis was a very delicate and high-spirited machine and needed a pure, light, volatile gas. I left him a good distance behind me, especially on the corners. I was waiting to see him flip. In fact, I slowed down after awhile so as not to push him into killing himself. He has a nice sense of competition. At least, I never had to explain to him about going fast. Some people don't understand speed: they think a hundred miles per hour is just twice as fast as fifty and there's no sense putting yourself in such danger unless you are in a critical hurry. But a hundred miles per hour is a lot more than just twice fifty. There's a point about eighty-five where such calculations fall apart; you have to begin to figure differently. At a hundred or above, you are in a world where simple m.p.h. doesn't enter in. A hundred miles per hour is a state of mind.

For the rest, we lived pretty quietly. Es Cruylles was strung along the beach for no more than a quarter of a mile altogether, with a bulge in the center where the bars and docks and local houses were, and then a few tourist villas out at either end. Mari and I lived in the Villa Alegre, one of the last houses up at the northern end of town. We had a garage, where I did my tinkering, a bathroom, a terrace with the railing dynamited off, and a sort of grove of pine trees. The house was right at the edge of the sea.

I did a lot of swimming and Mari cooked the meals and we went down to the Bar Royal when we didn't have anything else to do. All this time we were getting used to each other and learning to speak a common language (not exactly Spanish at first, but near enough to it that I could use it as a base). Manuel came up to visit us sometimes. His mother never. She remained angry with me for a long time. You might expect her to be mad at Mari instead for running away with a foreigner, but it seems women aren't held as much responsible for their moral acts as might be. They are always pathetic victims, it seems. At any rate, Carmencita was not sore or shocked by Mari running away to the Costa Brava with me, she was mad at me for hiring her servant away; probably figured that foreigners come and go, and sooner or later she would have Mari back on her hands again, maybe pregnant. So for a couple of months we didn't go to see Carmencita when we went down to Barcelona to visit the kid (Mari's kid: boarded out with an old woman in the Barrio Chino, for the thumping sum of eighty cents a day, which I paid) but after a time she got over it, and we are friends again now.

When I got back from Paris I crossed Spain near the top and went along to Barcelona. I didn't have anywhere else to go. I thought I'd drop back and see the dog and then go up past Le Boulou again and make the right turn toward Nice, Cannes, and

Italy. Instead, I took a room in Carmencita's flat. It was Ramón's room, actually; he moved in with Manuel and left his room to me. A persistent odor of hair oil and underwear permeated the room; the cabinets were full of his sleazy pink shirts and verdigrised tie clasps, and the walls were covered with hefty Spanish calendar girls. Most mornings I woke up feeling suffocated, as there weren't any windows, and once or twice the feeling was so overpowering that I jumped out of bed and bolted for the front room in my drawers to gulp some fresh air. Those were the hot months.

One morning I went charging down the dark corridor between my room and the sala and sprawled headlong over Mari, who was scrubbing the floor. She got up at eight, three hours before anybody else, to start work. "Perdone Usted," she said, as though it was her fault. She irritated me, being so spiritless.

I was three weeks in the house all told. The first few days Ramón took me around with him and showed me his side of the city, but that got depressing, and besides he never offered to pay for a round of drinks in any of the joints we visited, so it got expensive, too. I was paying handsomely for my room and the nature-cure meals, and on top of that Carmencita was fond of taking me around to see the better class cabarets and nightclubs; and being no niggard of life's blessings, often brought a few friends along to share in her good fortune at having a rico Americano to pay the bills. The only one who didn't consider me a windfall was Manuel, and even he liked very much to go for fast rides in the Jaguar without worrying about how much gas was being burned. But at least he bought a drink or two. Once he even took me to his club, the Club Jazz. It was a neat cozy basement where well dressed young people sat around listening to American music. Manuel introduced me around, I don't know as what, and a couple of the young men practised their English on me, then everybody sat down to play a game. The leader started a question around in a whisper, asked it of the girl on his right; she answered and asked a different question of the boy on her right; and so on around the table. When it got back to the leader he compared his original question with the ultimate answer, and the result was apparently hilarious. I spent a dull evening.

But the following day Manuel took me for a ride on his B.S.A. motorcycle, and when we ended up in the country out by Sabadell, he offered to teach me to drive it. We came home exhausted by the nervous strain, but I had a fine time. In some ways a motorcycle offers an even more definite sensation than a car. You go roaring along very percariously at best, and the hazards are things you wouldn't give a second's thought to with four wheels under you: bits of paper, horse manure, gravel patches, and dogs. On a motorcycle any of them can kill you. It's all according to how you drive, of course. Scooters and motorcycles of all shapes and sizes are standard means of transportation around here, and it is nothing to see portly businessmen buzzing along with sample cases strapped on the luggage carrier; or neat clerks off to the movie with their wives perched cross-legged and nonchalant on the posterior seat; or for that matter crow-black priests scooting past on streamlined Lambrettas with their vestments streaming out behind. Manuel and I belong to another club, however; we wear out tires and frighten pedestrians and generally speaking travel at speeds that make hazards out of things the average motocyclista is going slow enough to steer soberly around. Manuel taught me to drive this way and he is covered with scars.

Within a week I could manage the B.S.A. pretty well, so one Sunday he helped me rent a Montesa and we took a trip down the coast to Sitges. The Montesa (it was a Brio Ochenta) will do about sixty on a good stretch. For a 125 c.c. it is a very well balanced and high-revving machine. On the way back I had gained enough confidence to let it out a little. Probably I should have started out learning on a Vespa or a 98 c.c. Derbi, but I came to no harm. As a matter of fact, all the time I was learning motorcycles I did no worse than jam into low gear sometimes when I wanted high (for some reason this blows out the headlamp) but now that I consider myself an experienced driver, having ridden a number of bikes at high speed, I am always falling off.

Well, motorcycling made the first two weeks pass like two weeks, which was all I asked for at the time, and after that Mari occupied me. The magic happened when I finally saw her standing upright, with the scrub rags off her head and her face washed. She came along on a paseo one afternoon with Manuel, his mother, and me. We were going up to Montserrat and we took her along for female companionship for Carmencita. In Manuel's saddlebags we had sausage and a slab of pork and some spareribs, bread, cheese, wine, and chocolate, the idea being to stop in the woods somewhere and have a picnic.

We left about noon. Manuel carried his mother and Mari climbed up behind me on the back of a rented MV Augusta. We sputtered out of the city via the Diagonál, which goes past Franco's palace. I wobbled along, more concerned with balance than anything else; I wasn't used to having a weight behind me, especially a girl gripping the back of my jacket and leaning every whichway in the corners. Since steering a motorcycle is mostly a matter of shifting weight, I fully expected we would run smack into a taxi or something, but we didn't. I underestimated her. She learned how to ride paquete in ten minutes, and by the time we reached Cuatro Caminos she was cramped up against my back, pushing us along, to see if we could get ahead of Manuel, who had a much more powerful machine. "Okay," I said, and waited for a downhill grade.

The MV, pronounced Emmy-Oovay, has a fourth gear especially for going downhill. We caught Manuel with his pants down and left him a quarter of a mile behind. Of course, a motorcyclist with his mother on the back is riding at a disadvantage. We stopped and waited for them in a little town of about fifteen houses and ten bars. It was a bright hot day; Mari and I sat down at a wooden table in the sun and ordered manzanilla. "Qué bueno," she said. "They are far behind." We waited about ten minutes. Manuel pulled up and his mother got off and said: "Capitán, you will die with your shoes on." I said Ha ha ha; I was making an impression, I thought.

(Incidentally, I am going to start recording conversations in Spanish as though I took a legitimate part in them, speaking a reasonable if simplified Spanish. There's no point going through the whole business of reproducing my pidgin as I learned. Or showing how I mostly didn't know what was being said to me until it was repeated six times and finally changed around to suit my vocabulary. It didn't actually take long. I have a certain facility for languages, or so my high-school teachers said, and besides, there is nothing like having only Spanish friends to talk to if you want to learn Spanish. In the three weeks I was in Barcelona I was able to talk a little and understand about thirty per cent of what was said. By special arrangement I was allowed to leave my pocket dictionary in the bathroom of Carmencita's place, where I spent a ritual half hour with it every morning. In addition, the Spaniards are very tolerant of learners, much more so than their

French neighbors, for example. Spaniards will always listen to you, deduce and calculate and watch your gestures, and finally they will rephrase whatever it is they think you are trying to say, and then all you have to do is agree. I think if I could find no other national virtue than this amiable patience the Spanish have, I'd still consider them the finest people on the continent.)

This town, the name of which I forget, had three bars, called the Bar of the Porrón, the Bar of the Two Porróns, and the Bar of the Three Porróns. We were in the Bar of the Three. A Porrón is a glass beaker with one open spout and one cone-shaped spout with a tiny hole in it, for drinking wine. Where we were there were three huge porróns on a table next to the road, each holding about five liters; and there was a sign saying that if you could hold one of them up in the air long enough to drink out of it, the wine was free. The house couldn't lose much on that bet. Manuel tried and couldn't even get it up. I tried and managed to squeeze about an ounce between my teeth, while the rest ran down my shirt. At that, a couple people applauded, and Mari got all excited. The thing is, when you suddenly notice you are making an impression on somebody, you automatically appraise the situation, to see if there is anything in it for you. This was when I noticed she had combed her hair up in a long roll, had put some lipstick on, and was dressed in a light blue dress and a tan suede jacket with a belt. She wore a yellow scarf and leather slippers. Her ears were pierced, and since with pierced ears you have to wear earrings all the time, she had a pair of gypsy silver circles about the size of a fifty-cent piece. In the grand tradition of the Groomed Appearance, she had modified the hairdo so that a few curls lay out in front of her ears. She had enormous black eyes. At the risk of sounding trivial, I have to report that the dress was not very well made and fitted too snugly across the indented front bones of her hips. She saw me looking, but instead of replying with a glance either offended, sultry, or coy, she patted herself on the abdomen and said: "Barrigóna." Fatbelly. There was a mild protuberance, but it was very symmetrical and soft. I was conscious of it when we got back on the motorcycle, her arms around my stomach and her chin on my shoulder.

She and I found the picnic spot. We saw a woods that looked cool and fragrant and we stopped, pulled the Emmy-Oovay off the road and went to look for a stream and a grassy clearing in which to build a fire. Again we were about ten minutes ahead of Manuel and his mother. After the intimacy of the motorcycle we were very much conscious of each other, and of being alone in the woods. It was worse because we couldn't make casual conversation to break the silence. I have to flatter myself a little to explain what was going on. I had recognized her for an acceptable sex object at the same moment she recognized me for one. Maybe I was only a large rich American, but I made an effect just the same. It was not absolutely pure sex tension in that clearing in the middle of the woods, because there were as many economic considerations on her part as there were psychological on mine. Or maybe I am making too much of what was actually only sudden blood in the head—the abrupt, gorged, throaty feeling that in some instances literally has an effect on your diaphragm and makes you snort air through your nose. I guess Bierce was right: we haven't descended so far from the apes as to preclude all hope of return. When Manuel and his mother came along and saw Emmy-Oovay parked at the side of the road, they came into the woods hunting for us and we were still standing in the clearing looking at each other. Manuel said Hoo hoo and his mother looked very dubious.

The rest of that day passed rapidly. We built a fire and cooked the bits of pig á la brasa, over coals, and sat around drinking wine. After everybody had had a brief siesta, we decided not to go on to Montserrat, even though we could see it straddling the road no more than two miles away. We turned around and went back toward the city.

All the way home I was thinking I would go back to my original plan: that is, stop somewhere and rent a room or a house and settle down for a time. I wasn't thinking specifically of Mari then, but I had it in mind for a girl to live with me, to do the cooking and entertaining and in general save me from being by myself. Probably in the back of my mind there was some such idea as: And she will fall in love with you because at heart you are not such a worthless fellow. But I wasn't sure I wanted that either—you have to pay for what you get, and when somebody falls in love with you, you pay by loving in return, or by suffering love, which is a sorry and unnatural state of affairs for everybody concerned. The alternative is to skip town. It's easy to imagine an arrangement whereby he lives with she and they have a fine time without complications.

However, it doesn't work. That's Free Love, and, as I have been at some pains to point out, it doesn't exist.

But I made my mind up in the next day or two, and evolved a plan. I woke myself up at seven in the morning, which is a trick anyone can do by concentrating on his wrist watch yoga-fashion just before going to sleep. I listened through the door for the noises that meant Mari was starting to work. The first morning she was up and around I got timid and couldn't nerve myself and it got too late: Ramón got up and went to the bathroom, then Carmencito came out to the kitchen and began making breakfast.

The next morning at about seven-thirty I heard Mari whish-whishing down the hall with a broom. I went out and put my hand on her back and said: "Come here." She came into my room and I shut the door and started to undress her. She was trembling and so was I. There wasn't any point explaining what I had in mind, as I would just have got tangled up in subjunctives. She was a mother and a widow and could be expected neither to scream nor have spasms. She was obedient. There are some who say woman's nature won't let her oppose a man who has his mind made up. It's only the triflers and the half-hearted who run into serious opposition.

Mari came into my room early in the morning whenever I told her to, which was once or twice more that week, but finally my dog caught on and started barking at the door, so we gave it up, and shortly after that moved on to the Costa Brava.

I am not apologizing for what went on, as that indicates I admit the right of people not directly concerned to make moral judgments. I consider the only people who have a word to say about any of this are Manuel, who once thought of seducing Mari on his own, and his mother, who employed her. These two are entitled to an opinion of us, so long as they don't bother me with it. Carmencita, as I said, was angry for a long time, but Manuel only thought it was funny. For myself, I recognize it was a cynical and grubby beginning, since all I wanted was a combination hired girl and mistress, and all I was willing to pay for it was money; and all Mari wanted was a chance to get out of the position she was in: scrubbing floors, pots, pans, and toilets for thirty-five cents a day. But neither of us lost by it, and who's to say that what begins bad won't turn out better, since everything always ends up different from what you expect anyway?

We got along well from the beginning, and we still get along well, although she's not nearly so spiritless now, and maybe that's a turn for the worse. We have arguments, and I suspect she takes me for granted, although she still has dreams that I am marching away in a sailor suit, or running down the beach with an American blonde (she hates all American blondes, makes spitting noises at them; once in Es Cruylles even threw a rock at Pete Merriam, and then ducked behind a house). She has turned out to be a personality in her own right, which I never bargained for. In fact, she is a tough little egg in some ways. The only time I let her go down to Barcelona alone to visit her kid, she came back with a big split welt across her face. It seems there was a riot on the Paralelo (two or three times each summer the factory workers run amok at the sight of German, French, and Italian middle-class tourists barging around in fancy clothes, with big cameras, in their own cars, when the Spanish middle classes, not to mention the lower classes, can't even manage to feed themselves, much less go touring). The mounted police were putting down this riot, and Mari saw an old woman carrying a kid get caught in the mêlée and fall down, so she walked up to the nearest mounted Guardia and cursed him. "Señor," she said among other things, "the goat-smelling and self-abusing rider is more beast than his horse." This got her a whack across the cheeks with a riding crop, which more or less proved her point, but she should have kept her mouth shut.

Mari is not what you would call a political thinker, but she has some pregnant observations to make about Franco and his government. Her father was on the other side, and maybe that accounts for it. At the time of the war she was very young, but she remembers some of the things that happened. One night some Falangists came to the door of her family's house and demanded to be let in, though they wouldn't say what they wanted. The two uncles and the old man wouldn't open the door, and said through the upstairs window that if the Falangists wanted to come in they could break the door down, if they were indeed hung with those appurtenances with which all true men are hung. Then the three, and one of Mari's elder brothers, stood just inside the doorway waiting, armed with sickles and axes. But the Falangists went away. All they were interested in was a little extra curricular looting. She says everybody whose name was on the black list was looted at one time or another. Toward the end of the war the army came through and dragged out everybody known to be in sympathy with the Republican cause, took them down to a bluff over the river, and shot them, shoving the bodies into the water. Eighty men from her village, a little place on the Miño River in Galicia, were killed this way.

On the other hand, she hasn't anything good to say about the Reds either. She says they committed just as many atrocities as the Revolutionists (Franco and his people were the Revolutionists, according to many Spaniards) and in a less straightforward way. She says if the Red side had won, there would have been a second war to get the Communists out. And she lumps in the young warriors of the International Brigade with the Reds. All this is ancient history to the rest of the world (except to certain of the Brigadiers, who are still being lumped in in some quarters) but to listen to her—and she is not the only one—it all happened yesterday, and isn't over yet by a long shot. "Do you think that the aims of the war were achieved?" she demands. She points out that after so much shooting, people are no better off than they were formerly, and I can't convince her that this is about par for the course. Being American, I spend a lot of time answering the question: What does the average American worker earn each month? Mari asks me about once a month. Translated into pesetas, the minimum daily wage for unskilled American cesspool diggers comes out to enough to support a Spanish family of fifteen in stupefying luxury for a week. There's no use explaining the international exchange to her either, or the fact that the average American laborer has to put his wife to work in order to pay the installments. Money is money as far as she is concerned, and she doesn't see why Spain has to be the only civilized country in the world where you can work ten hours a day and break your back at it and still not earn enough to blow yourself to a new suit once a year.

These things came later; in the beginning she didn't waste time on sedition, only concentrated on dogging around behind me, trying to anticipate what I was going to want next. You might call it the honeymoon. But it was a little more complicated than that. She was resigned to being a slavey in Carmencita's house, and probably came to my room out of habit of obedience, or maybe some loneliness, too (at least a little amor could hardly worsen her position, and she was a widow), but after I took her out of that and up to Es Cruylles she went to work making the best of it, which in this case meant studying to be her man's woman.

The Catalâns are fond of remarking that of all the animals, woman is the one which most closely resembles a human being. There seems to be the idea that the perfect woman is one which the true man automatically treats like a dog. There's no denying that it's psychologically very satisfying to a man to treat his woman like a dog. The Spanish women know this, so they are sometimes inclined to appear doglike. It doesn't happen in the upper city, but down in the harbor barrios when a woman sets out to get herself a husband she doesn't try to seem provocative, sultry, companionable, or interesting; she makes herself out to be a cipher, a house-cleaning, dish-washing, cow-brained bed warmer. But it's just as big a lie here as elsewhere. If any man tells you European women are more than superficially servile, nine times out of ten it only means he never got far under the skin of his woman. In the important things they govern just the same. No woman is herself in courting days. What you see is what they think you want to see. The only difference between American and European women that I can see is that the latter know there's a line they can't cross without getting whacked. American women can't imagine that they could ever marry somebody who might knock them down. In most cases they're correct. But European women seldom cross that line whether they think you are the woman-whacking kind or not. And they continue to take care of you long after they have you pegged for a rattlehead, because women are equipped to take care of men, and what's the equipment for if not to be used?

Well, one morning at the end of my third week in Barcelona, I took Mari out in the car, we drove up to the park, and I set to work trying to explain my idea. She understood what I wanted, but I didn't have the vocabulary to make her see that it ought to be a cooperative adventure. Here I was double crossing myself again. For myself, all I wanted was to put forward a business proposition, without committing myself, but I kept trying to make her say something compromising. It irritated me that she treated me like a business proposition too. She said: "You will have to pay board for the child."

"Of course," I said. "That is not the question. I mean, do you wish to go? Do you think that you will like the country? Do you think you will like to live with me?"

"Whatever pleases you." she said.

"Bat shit," I said. "You do not have to go if you don't want to. I do not want a sad woman in the house. I ask you if you think it will please *you*. I will rent a small house in the country. If you like the idea, I will take you with me."

"I cannot tell the señora," she said. "You will have to tell her."

So I dropped it. It gave me the same unsatisfying feeling I had had with Carmen the dancing girl. Something missing. We drove back to the house and went up the elevator standing shoulder to shoulder but not looking at each other and not speaking.

Carmencita wasn't home, she had gone out to shop. Nobody was there but Ramón and he thought the whole thing was a bad idea and tried to talk Mari out of it. She only shrugged. He sucked his teeth loudly and left before Carmencita came back.

We went to pack up. Or I packed; she had nothing to pack except the housecoat and the blue dress and the imitation suede jacket. Then we sat in the sala waiting. Mari got so nervous that I sent her down to the car. Finally when Carmencita came I met her at the door and helped carry her packages to the kitchen.

"If you have a moment to talk," I said, and then I explained my idea. I don't know what I said; it sounded clear enough to me, but when I finished she said: "You will return for dinner?" So I went through it all again while she unpacked her groceries, and then she said: "We will wait until ten, then we will eat. José María is coming tonight; we plan to play cards." So I let it go. Ramón would have to tell her. Afterward I learned from Manuel that she had a fit about it; she wanted to call the police or the American consul or somebody. Well, I tried to tell her.

We drove out of the city as far as Malgrat, and turned toward the coast. Mari wasn't used to my driving and she sat slouched down holding tightly to the sides of her bucket. At least it kept her from worrying about what she was getting into.

We arrived in Tossa de Mar about two that day. It's the first big town on the coast and has Roman ruins, a lighthouse, and winding streets. Cactus grow on the sidewalk some places, and the windows of the houses are full of flowers, something you don't often see. I liked the town and we might have stayed there, except there was nothing for rent. During the tourist season these places bulge at the seams; from May to October you can't rent a bath house. If you do happen to stumble onto something just as one tenant is leaving, the owner always wants two or three hundred dollars a month. For those prices I can live at Miami Beach.

We hung around Tossa for two or three days talking to rental agents, bartenders, and customers in the barber shops. But there was nothing available. We slept in a fancy hotel and had to eat in the fisherman's fonda to make up for it. Mari hid in the hotel room and wouldn't even come swimming with me. She said she was ashamed to go out in public because everybody seeing her with a foreigner would think she was a Whatever woman. A Whatever woman comes out different in translation, but it means one who is not exactly a prostitute, but who changes around. I pointed out various mixed couples: Spanish-French, German-English, American-African; but it made no impression. I showed her women in slacks and halters, with make-up all over them, who looked a lot more Whatever than she did; and I pointed out low-looking French types pinching thighs in the cafés, and fat old Germans accompanied by giggling teenagers, to prove that nobody would even notice her in such a crowd of miscellaneous broads. But I underestimated her; she said: "Even if they are all bad women, that does not excuse me." Then during the argument it came out that it was not only being mistaken for a loose woman that bothered her—it was also that she was born lower class and didn't know how to comport herself. This fell apart quickly, too, so she finally admitted that she was only ashamed because the foreign women were all so beautiful, and she was not. I decided that she needed a little self-confidence. We spent a whole morning buying her new clothes.

She liked that; she hadn't had any new clothes in years. It did her a lot of good. The clothes lasted her while we were in Tossa. The urge to walk around in a manner that best showed off her new dress overbore the urge to creep along with her head sunk on her shoulders and her hands clasped bashfully on her stomach, like an old woman. She even wanted to wear a hat, once she entered into the spirit of the thing, but we compromised on white kid gloves that reached almost to her elbows and made her arms sweat. Between the gloves and the swishy skirt and the tottering heels, she felt like a princess. It was her idea to go out after supper and sit in the sidewalk cafés. She sat in a basket chair with her legs crossed and a glass of sherry balanced on three fingers and had a hell of a good time. She looked good.

"This is a pleasant town," she said. "Son a beetch."

"Simply, you find yourself more pleasant."

"I am an International Woman," she said. "Got tam."

"Where did you learn those words?"

"From you. They come with everything you say. They are American, verdad? You must learn to swear in Spanish."

The next morning we moved on, and stopped in Palamós for lunch.

Afterward we sat for an hour in a café watching the bikinis—or I was; she was looking at the Jaguar.

She said: "A very beautiful car. There are few of these in Spain." I agreed. "They cost much money," she mused. "Everyone looks at our car."

When we got in to drive on she patted a fender smugly. She wanted me to turn the driving mirror around so she could see the people looking after the car. "I need it to drive with," I said.

"I will advise you when someone comes from behind," she said. "Duhty basteh. No, duhty basteh is he who goes in front and will not make room for us to pass."

In the next few days she developed a sort of chuckle. Pleasant to hear, but she came out with it at odd moments, like a person remembering old jokes. She would explain that it was a man (woman) in Tamariu (S'Agaró) doing something strange. "You remember that idiot with the red trousers and the green cane in the café de la Luna, glug glug glug?" she would say covering her mouth with her hand. At first she was simply laughing at all the unorthodox goings-on in the world that she had never suspected: the weird people, the bunting-covered cafés, the cars and drunks and summer costumes. It was a partly exultant, part possessive noise. High private entertainment.

Soon she was laughing just at foreigners, which, like monkeys, seemed to her to be almost human—especially Americans and English. Every time we saw some joker prancing around behind an easel, or swimming in one of those indecent leather bathing suits, or sporting a full beard and rope sandals, she asked if it was one of my countrymen. And usually it was, at that. Being the foreigner in plainest view I might have come in for my share of giggles,except that by virtue of eating and sleeping and traveling with her I had taken my place as an extension of her personality. By this I mean that Mari, like most uneducated women, considered herself and her immediate circle to be at the exact center of the universe. Such people are only bewildered and entertained by strangers; they can't even be critical. A very happy state of mind, to my way of thinking. We were rolling along in our little private two-ten horsepower world, and always just a mile or two ahead of us something outlandishly amusing was being prepared. It saved her from being bored to death, I suppose. And since I also got a kick out of watching how people behave when they are far from home, we shared most of the jokes. Although I never saw what was so hilarious about American shoes. But it put us on a good footing to sit together in the cafés, nudging each other and snickering at the clowns we saw go by in smeared smocks, bikinis, espadrilles, and beards.

One night at supper I asked if she was enjoying the trip and she said: "Por Dios! I hope we travel together for a long time before you go."

That same night in bed she made advances for the first time. All they amounted to were little tickles but that was something. I don't mean she was cold before that—on the contrary, she was very responsive; but always a little shy.

It was raining outside, but there were people in the patio under the columns, shouting and singing. Some English were singing *Old Tom Is Cast.* When Mari thought she had me in a weak moment she said: "Perhaps we will go to La Coruña some time. The country is more beautiful than here. And there are straight roads with good paving. La Coruña has many tourists. I would like to see my own earth some day."

"I'll think about it," I said.

Despite her new confidence, she didn't get around to asking me where we were going for another week. I didn't know myself. We just toured up and down the Costa Brava looking for a house to live in. We talked to foreigners and natives, bartenders and fishermen, but couldn't find a thing. We were offered two or three pig stys for a hundred a month, and all the rental agents had at least one baronial mansion in the center of town with six bathrooms and three gardens, but there seemed to be nothing of the right size and price that was furnished. The best the whole coast had to offer was the Villa Alegre in Es Cruylles, and they wanted a thousand five hundred pesetas a month for it. Thirty-eight dollars, which was cheap enough, but the house was huge, and the terrace had been half demolished during a wild party thrown by the Follansbees, a New York advertising couple. Besides, I thought the town looked dull. I didn't know then about Strangewolf and the literary types. We moved on that day, went clear up to Port Bou on the French border, turned around and came all the way back to Blanes, dispirited.

In the end we went back to Es Cruylles, only half hoping, and the owner said the house was still empty. I said I would take it. We hit him at a good time; he had turned down several prospective tenants to give himself time to have the terrace rebuilt, and the day we came back he had been talking to the contractors, and their estimate had made him gloomy. He was sitting in the Bar Royal with a bunch of foreigners who looked at us with hostility and told each other in undertones that we looked unreliable. That was at about ten-thirty at night. The owner, Pablo Noque, said we could move right in if we wanted. He went up to his house and got the keys. The house was a mess, he said, because the Follansbees had left in a hurry to go get a divorce, leaving dirt and food and children's toys all over, not to mention unpaid bills they'd left at Dolores Viñals' colmado amounting to over a thousand pesetas.

He said we could take the house as it was or leave it; he didn't care one way or another; the following season he would rent it for five times the amount we were paying. We took the keys and drove up to the house. At some point between the time we left the Bar Royal and the time we reached the house, the electricity went off. It often goes off in these little towns, but we didn't know that then. There was a moon up above the clouds, but when it went under, the whole world was black as a basement.

One thing about the Villa Alegre, it had a good sized garage. A lot of garages hereabouts will barely accommodate a Biscuiter. The only trouble was, I couldn't get the door open right away. The key was a yard long and didn't seem to work at all, until I finally tried giving it two turns instead of one. Mari was sitting in the car all this time, shivering. The villa was huge and dark and formidable and the wind whined through the pines. When at last I got the double doors shoved back against the wall, and drove in, the headlights frightened dozens of lizards out of a stack of old cement bags. Then we walked up the path with our feet crunching in the gravel and stopped at the gate.

"I do not want to go in," Mari said.

But I was tired of sleeping in expensive hotels and had already decided we were going to spend the night in the Villa Alegre. I unlatched the front gate and felt my way to the front door, with Mari clutching my shirt. We couldn't stand outside all night. While I was wrestling with the lock somebody went past crunching on the gravel and said: "Buenas noches." We couldn't see a soul. Mari made a shivering noise.

When the door opened, gusts of damp air met us. I lit a match and went into the vestibule. On a table just inside the door there was a stack of *John Bull* magazines, and I ripped the cover off one to make a torch. With its light I saw a fireplace in one wall, in time to throw the torch in before it burned me. I threw the rest of the magazine in and by its light discovered a couple of candles on a sideboard. When these were lit I saw a light dangling six feet in the air in a corner of the room. "Everything is solved," I said. But the light switch didn't work, even though I gave it two turns on the off chance it worked like the garage lock.

So we lighted the rest of the candles. Luckily, everybody keeps a few candles or a gasoline lantern around for these occasions when the system goes on the fritz. We were in a white room containing hundreds of chairs—rockers, straight-backed wooden chairs, and canvas deck chairs—all ripped apart. Beyond that were only a single table, a chest of drawers full of china and silverware, and a lot of plaster masks on the walls, with Ave María Purissima written on their bases. We didn't look in to the kitchen or go onto the terrace that night, just went to find a bedroom and the bathroom. The latter was bigger than the former and had a sink and a toilet crammed in one corner.

I shaved with cold water while Mari made up the bed with what she could find. There were some short blankets but no sheets; the pillows were all flat and hard and caseless. The mattress was full of almond leaves or something else dry and crackling. We lay down on it in our underwear and yawned and said good night and rolled over and couldn't sleep, either of us. A car went past, loud on the gravel, and the people in it were singing. It sounded like they were singing *My Grandfather's Clock* in Spanish. About ten minutes later a light jerked up the walls and I leaped out of bed thinking the house was on fire. Some people were coming along the road carrying flaming torches in the moonlight, and somebody was playing a guitar. They were equipped with bottles and wine skins and everybody was singing.

"—una simple cancioncilla de la calle—"

They went on up the road and a little above us I heard them saying Good night, Good night, and then all but one of them came back down the road. I wondered whom they had left up there, because there were no houses beyond us. They saw our open shutters and the car in the garage and a voice said: "Bigod, there's bodies in Sybil's house." They were talking about dynamite as their voices trailed away. I could hear music drifting from the bars down where the gasoline lanterns were burning. Then a fishing boat came all the way down the coast from Cerebére with its one-stroke engine thumping heavy as lead in a well. I sat in the window till I got chilly and then went back to bed and finally got to sleep about four.

Around seven the flies woke me up; a million of them booming around the room and lighting all over me, on my lips and eyes and in my nose. We soon discoverd that you have to sleep with all the shutters closed so that no ray of light enters in the morning, as flies apparently can't fly in the dark. If you do this, however, you sleep till noon. I covered my head with the scratchy blanket for awhile and tried to go back to sleep, but it was no good. I couldn't breathe. It was a boiling hot day already at that hour. So I got up and explored the house. Mari slept like a baby. I closed the shutters and the flies came out in the hall with me; then they went into the comedor and finally out the back door, which had been open all night.

I looked in the kitchen and it positively fumed with moldy food, stale water, garbage and dirty rags. Next to the kitchen was a small bedroom, for the maid I suppose. The other rooms, three other bedrooms and the bathroom, were laid in a line down a dim corridor. The main room, the dining-living room, where the fireplace was, had two large windows that looked out on the Mediterranean, where the sun was blazing up.

I walked out on what was left of the terrace and from the edge there was a drop of maybe twenty feet to the sea. The house was on a little cape; I could see the town a quarter of a mile to the south, brown houses and dirt streets, beached rowboats, a yacht or two, and smoke rising from the chimneys. Enormous clouds with turned-brown edges surged over the mountains behind the town. A few small boats were out on the glassy water with solitary men in them dangling fishlines in their inverted reflections.

I went down into the garden; we had a grape arbor among the pine trees, and the grapes were just starting to turn red. On a stone bench under the arbor somebody had assembled a collection of sea gifts: a dried starfish, a boiled sea urchin, the skull of a big fish, and hundreds of little white shells. Underneath the arbor and all around the gardens were stone boxes full of fatheaded claveles, pink and white. At the end of the garden there was a flight of stone steps down to the water and a short cement dock. I took off my sneakers and overalls and dove into the water and swam out far enough to look back at the house, the cliffs to the north, the town to the south, and the mountains. It was working out all right, after all; I could stop for awhile.

Mari woke up about eleven. I led her around and she was charmed. "Such luxury," she said but wouldn't go near the edge of the terrace because it looked crumbly and there weren't any railings. We wandered around the garden and tried the grapes, smelled the flowers, and then she jumped and said: "I must give you breakfast!" Before she did that she had to clean the kitchen. But that was an all-day job, so we went down to the village to have breakfast in the Bodega. Bodega means warehouse or wine bins, but this was just a bar, where the señora would also make sandwiches or even a full-course meal if you wanted.

I shot down the hill and did a four-wheel slide onto the main street, fish-tailed in front of the Bar Royal and screeched up to the wall in front of the Bodega with the brake flat on the floor, but made no impression on anybody except one old lady carrying a dead octopus. It was mail hour and everybody was up the hill in El Gaucho. We drank coffee with milk and ate a pastry, then I dropped Mari at the house and went over to San Feliu to cash travelers' checks. I had to pay Pablo Noque for three months right off the bat. By the time I returned, hunted him up, paid him and got a receipt, it was three o'clock. Mari had cleaned the whole house throwing practically everything that wasn't ours off the terrace into the sea. She was shining with sweat and accomplishment; she led me around in my turn and showed me how she had scratched the old grease off the stove, swept the garage, scrubbed the tile floors in bedroom, bathroom and comedor, and washed all the dishes and glasses and silver. "I am a good woman for a house," she said. She was full of contempt for women who didn't know how to keep their houses clean and tidy. "If a tortilla falls to the floor, you can pick it up and eat it without fear," she said. I pointed out a cobweb on the ceiling over the waterbox and she was covered with shame. "Never mind, negligente, I will hire a servant," I said. She stamped her foot and said she would not have another woman in the house.

"Look, you have not eaten," she said. "You will think I am worthless, but I am not." There was an aluminum pot on the charcoal burner, full of stew. She apologized for that too, because it was only potatoes, but while I was gone she was afraid to go down to the village alone, and besides, I hadn't left her any money. There was nothing salvageable in the house except the potatoes, one onion, and some olive oil. So after we ate we went down to do some shopping. That was at four-thirty or thereabouts. We loaded the car with staples and some meat for that night, and a bottle of wine, and two loaves of long bread. I wanted to stay around and have a drink in the Royal, where some foreigners were sitting, but she said: "Now we will go to our house." She seemed so pleased with the whole thing that we went straight home and did a third tour of the house, looking in all the closets and trying the light switches. Then we built up the fire and cooked dinner. We ate at seven: a green salad with tomato and olives, a plate of macaronis with garlic, oil and pimientos, fried pig's ribs with baker-warm bread and white wine, and finally pomegranates and coffee. I showed her how puffed up I was and how I had to loosen my belt, and she was pleased.

When it got dark we tried all the lights again and they all worked except one in the spare bedroom. We switched bulbs around a little, put a bright one in the bedroom and another in the kitchen, and then we went out on the terrace, staying close to the wall by the house. I lay on the tiles to look at the sky and she sat cross-legged by my shoulder, talking about her childhood.

She'd been in France once in a school run by nuns, and once they made her kneel for hours on a hard floor with sand under her knees. Most of what she said I didn't understand, and I wasn't really listening anyway, but toward the end she said: "Why should I stay in Carmencita's house? I would not have waited much longer in any case. I am not a bad woman, but I must pay for the child, and I did not want to work for so many years as a servant without anything of my own. I am young. Ramón said once that he would give me a job as a dancing girl in the Club Cairo. Carmencita said it was against God. However, God does not give me any money. He gave me the child and let my husband go away with my sister and die, and permitted his parents to put me out of my house. So, if He forbids me to earn my living by dancing, and I must die and the child too, this is a form of conscription I do not care for."

"Conscription?" I said.

"Do you think it is right for God to burden people to death, so that they will die and go to heaven to join His armies and sing His praises? If He kills me with sorrows I will not praise him, I will go up to Him and say: A ham for You, assassin and brute! However, I do not believe in God any more."

She didn't believe in Him, but she was always talking about what He ought to do if He was really up there, as though He was the president of a big collection agency; and if she thought about Him at all, He was only a swindle the door knockers were working. I think she hoped there was a God, but she couldn't see any sign of Him in the world, and she had violent ideas about His earthly representatives. She was particularly bitter about a friend of hers who had always been legal and devout but who had gotten a dirty deal anyway. I pointed straight up and said: "His stars are His burning candles. He sits up there by candlelight stacking the cards against us." I was speaking English. I pulled her over on my chest and she was quiet, but she was still thinking. "A woman who lives with one man who is not her husband is not so bad as one who lives with many men," she said.

"Clearly," I said.

"If we have children, I would be happy if you would put your name on the baptismal certificate. There is no one who would be interested except my brother in Burgos, but I would feel better if the children had your name."

I explained immediately that she was not to have any children if she could possibly help it. She said she did not want any, that one was enough, but that sometimes things happened. "They will not trouble you," she said.

"Just the same, let us not have any mistakes," I said.

It killed the conversation for a few minutes. Finally I asked if she were sorry she had come with me. That was cheating. Show me the man who hires a woman to eat and live and sleep with him, on a purely business basis, and I will show you a cheater. Sooner or later he begins to ask questions like this one, and won't stop digging until he gets the answer he is looking for. Everybody wants love. I was sorry the moment I opened my mouth. "Never mind," I said. "What's the difference?"

She got up and said she would make me some chocolate, and went indoors. I stayed awhile looking up at the stars, wondering if the Southern Cross was somewhere in one of the clusters I saw. Then I remembered I was on about the same latitude as Hoboken. When the cocoa was ready I went indoors. Mari was sharper than I had ever given her credit for being. While I was drinking she leaned on the back of my chair and said: "You must not ask me these questions in the moonlight, or the starlight. In return I will not ask you never to leave me while we are in bed, or dancing to sentimental music. We should talk of these things while we are eating bananas, or walking from the town with our arms full of packages. If I have anything of this kind to ask you, I will ask you while I am cleaning fish, and my hair is uncombed. If you wish to know what I think of you, you must ask me while you are shaving, or when you have a running cold in the head."

But a little later she said: "No, I am not sorry we are here, Señor Capitán. Look, what a splendid house. With the lights burning and the windows open we have no bugs. But you must run the pump. There is no water."

This pump deserves special mention. It was a little electric motor in the pantry over a resounding well. The house also had a rainwater arrangement, but it never rained enough, so we had to buy water from a man who owned a stream and a tank truck. Whenever the truck came we lost another piece off the garage wall, because the truck had no brakes at all and the best the driver could do was coast gently to the nearest obstruction. Once the water was in the well or cistern under the house, we had to turn on the motor to suction it up to a second tank in the rafters, from which it dripped slowly down through the faucets whether they were turned on or not. Whenever I forgot and let the upper tank run dry, air collected in the pipes between there and the bathroom and no water would run through until I climbed up among the spiders and lizards and poured water down the outlet tubes to prime them. When it did happen to rain, the little water we gathered in the roof gutters dripped into the well with verberating *ponging* noises that kept us awake all night.

That evening she fried me two eggs and we danced a little in the comedor to music coming faintly from the Bar Royal; and about eleven we went to bed. All the time we were in Port Crullers we went to bed at eleven or earlier, unless there was a party or something. Bed is the place we were always most simpáticos. Like an old married couple. Even when we were not rioting on the almond leaves we liked it in bed. During the day I worked on the car or read magazines or went off somewhere, while she cooked and cleaned or read Collección Bisonte westerns, by such authors as Drigulch Miquéz Masota and Tex Guittieréz, so we didn't see that much of each other; but in bed at night we jabbered on about one thing or another until one of us finally fell asleep, and it was very pleasant and warm and companionable, noncompetitive. Later, when we got to know other people in the town, foreigners, we put in some late nights, but usually we lazed around all day and went to bed with the birds and slept late.

We only went to Barcelona once the first month; that was during the first few days, when we needed sheets and pillow cases, an electric ring and a few other odds and ends for the house. We also had to pick up the dog, which Manuel was keeping for us. I left Mari at the house of the Yaya to visit her kid while I drove around doing errands. I went to the apartment to get the dog and stayed awhile gabbing with Manuel. He said he would motor up to visit us some time. I tried Carmencita to see how we stood, but at that point it didn't look as though we would ever be friends again. So I shook hands all around and bolted. I picked up Mari and we left, making only one more stop at a sporting-goods store where I bought a pair of fish fins, a mask with breathing tube, and a gum-band-operated harpoon. Then we drove home. The dog peed in the back seat.

"What are these things for?" Mari asked. I explained that they were for swimming underwater and catching fish. "Qué barbaridad," she said. It was too late to give the equipment a try by the time we got back to Es Cruylles, but I put on the fins and the mask to show her how funny it was, the feet flopping clammily and my breath roaring in and out the plastic tube. We ate supper and spent the rest of the evening training the dog to stop biting us when we weren't looking. It was about three months old by this time, and had tremendous feet. Nobody had ever named it so we tried to think of something suitable. Mari plumped for Rovár, the name of a dog in a novel she had read. I wouldn't have it because it was too ordinary. I liked Piar, meaning to cry or whine, which is what it was always doing, but she said it was ridiculous for a dog to have a verb for a name. So it didn't get a name that night. Later on I named it a Spanish adjective, Siguiente, which means Following, for the habit it had picked up of walking right between the heels of our shoes and gnawing us when we weren't aware it was anywhere near.

The next morning about nine I went down before breakfast to try the skin-diving apparatus. The dog came along, yapping and unearthing living things from the heaps of bleached almond leaves along the sand. Mari looked down from the garden and threw a couple of rocks. I put on the fish feet and the mask and sat on the edge of the dock contemplating the water. Never having been under water with my eyes open except in Y.M.C.A. swimming pools, and never having breathed through anything except my own nose and an anesthetic cone once or twice, I felt a little smothered. I stayed close to the dock, slid over and put my face under, and immediately got giddy. I held onto the concrete for dear life. The water below me was so clear and undistorted all the way to the bottom that it didn't seem to have enough body to support me. I felt as though I were going to fall. Four thin tiger-striped fish went by between my feet. I let go and worked the flippers and coasted away from the dock, breathing noisily in and out through the tube. It was easy enough, and seemed like flying slowly over the Amazon jungle. On my left hand was a topless mountain range, actually the cliffs rising to our terrace; and on my right was deep water, not thickening or anything, just turning a purplish color, with shafts of sunlight leaning down. I carried the dart cocked but didn't come close to a fish all day. I learned to work the fish feet and to breathe comfortably, without the strangled feeling, and I stayed down all morning, without breakfast, until I was chilled even in the warm water and had a runny nose.

It's hard to describe. The underwater world has all the ordinary colors of the spectrum and then some, but they are in unfamiliar combinations. The rocks look just enough like ordinary rocks to be eery; the vegetation is almost like earthly vegetation, but not quite. Some things that look alive are just weeds, and some things that look like stones leap away when your shadow touches them. I didn't actually swim much, only floated along face down over the bosques and designs and grottos, peering into the caves in the walls, down the deeps where the bottom slid away, under the stones where spiny fish hid and under the shelves where moray eels and octopi may have been hiding. (I didn't see any, but once I thought I saw a groping tentacle, and backed-water away from it in a panic.)

When I held my breath I could hear what was either trickling pebbles or millions of invisible shrimp in the tall weeds. I saw a rusty anchor that I couldn't budge, and found a wine bottle so encrusted with animalia that it might have been a drowned Greek amphora. Once I drifted around in a half circle and behind me there was a fish so huge that even if I could have shot it, it would have dragged me out to sea. Or maybe it was the distortion of the air in the mask that made it seem so huge. Another time I ran into a cloud of sardines scooting along just two inches below the surface of the water—I could almost have caught some of them in my mouth—but they flashed away so fast when I approached that the surface of the water boiled and turned silver. Then I went into a little cove where the waves didn't reach, and the water was shallow, and I drifted with the back of my head and my shoulders out of water, with my hips and legs and fish feet dangling in the grass, looking bloated and white. Just by my nose there was a transparent soft bag the size of a baseball. I knew it was a jellyfish and could sting me, but it didn't move, so I stayed and watched it. It had a round mouth on the bottom and short watery feelers. It looked almost too delicate to exist. On the way back to the dock I crept along the edge of the cliff where the waves were breaking and I scraped my knee and banged the palm of my hand keeping off the rocks.

"You must go down and look," I told Mari. "I cannot tell you about it. What things there are in the world! Fantástico!"

We ate and I sat in the sun for an hour and then went back down and spent the rest of the afternoon under water, so that by evening

I had a red-raw back from the sun, and aching arches and a headache. I still hadn't shot the dart gun. In fact, I never did catch a fish all that autumn.

Late that afternoon I was swimming down by the lighthouse and met another fisherman. I didn't know exactly where I was because I hadn't put my head up for the past half hour, but I gathered I had reached the lighthouse by the enormous range of subterranean boulders slanting mistily down to nothing. He was sitting on a rock, about halfway down to the bottom, legs crossed and one elbow resting on his knee, for all the world like a cane-pole fisherman sitting on the breakwater, except there was a tank strapped to his back and a line of bubbles ascending to the surface. He was looking into a deep hole. I floated above him. He didn't see me; I would have missed him except for the bubbles, as it was getting dark down below and he was dark skinned himself. I waited for about ten minutes, but he didn't move, so I swam to where the rocks rose to the surface and crawled out on land to warm myself. Some other people were sitting around in bathing suits. They all looked like tourists except one fat man and three fat women and a bunch of swarthy little kids. It turned out these were gypsies and everyone was snooting them, in hopes they would go away.

When the fisherman came up he had a big brown fish on his prong. He laid it kicking on a rock and the other bathers admired it while he climbed out and unhitched the diving tank. He was a big café-au-lait Negro with a white smile. I saw him glance at me and take in my gumband harpoon and plastic breathing tube and look away. He had a two-hour oxygen tank and his gun worked on compressed air. We never did get along well after that. His name was Charles Kolp and when he passed by me he asked if I'd had any luck. I was walking back toward the house and he was going to town, so we walked a distance together and he suggested that the next time I went out I try the far side of the mole, where there was a big mero that already had three rusty harpoon heads in him. "Nobody can beach the old bastard," Kolp said. "A fabulous fish." I stopped off at my gate and he said: "You must be the new folks that moved in last night. We saw your car. That's some car. Used to own a Packard myself. I like a big car. Join us for a drink this evening when you come down.There's a party at the Bodega after chow."

Mari didn't want to go, but I dragged her. We walked down to save a pint of gas. The bars were all jammed; it was a Saturday night. We only knew a couple of people by sight, and the rest were mostly weekenders on their way to or from someplace else. Kolp and some others had put a few tables together on the dirt street in front of the Bodega, which is up the street a little way from the Royal, and a big Texas oilman was mixing martinis with Cinzano vermouth and Larios gin. "Bring me lemons!" he said. "Olivos! Oniontos!" At eight o'clock he was already very much blurred.

"Come and sit down," Carol Bond said to us.

"Come and sit down!" the oilman said. He poured us two of his martinis, and I don't blame him; there wasn't enough vermouth even to give the brown color Cinzano has. ("He's drunk two pitchers by himself since three this afternoon," Carol Bond said.) It turned out we were crashing some kind of general party; I didn't quite get what the occasion was. The oilman had just come from Liberia or some place, where he had lost his job and raffled off his car, a Lincoln. He was able to sell eight numbers at a dollar each but the police said he had to pick out a number and give the car, or else go to jail for fraud.

Next to him was Pablo Noque, the owner of our house. He was the unofficial liaison between the natives and the tourists. He was also a painter; a visiting artist had once talked him into making a few water colors of his fishing adventures off the coast of Cuba, France, and Spain. His pictures were a big success with the tourists and souvenir buyers. He painted at night in what must be called a primitive style, and sold canvases to tourists who passed through. He claimed he had had exhibitions in Paris and London and New York, and it may have been the truth.

Fuhta Brag, the Finn, came and sat down by me and said: "Oh-I-am-too-early." I said not at all, things were just beginning, except for the oilman, who was half finished. "I-must-not-stay long," he said. "It-is-bad-for-the-discipline. If-I-am-to-work-at-all-I must-have-discipline. Today-I-went-swimming."

"So-did-I," I said.

"Ah-but-you-are-not-artist. I-see-in-your-face."

Then the music came. Frans and Hans, the two Dutchmen, arrived on motor-scooters, and Frans carried Jaimito, the chief musician, while Hans carried Santiago, who played one of the guitars. They indicated that the rest of the orchestra was somewhere behind them on the road down from the icehouse, where the instruments were stored. This meant Féliz and Pepe, carrying between them the jazban (a big drum) and three more guitars. They showed up a little later with old González, the town problem. Then came Francisco Viñals, who owned all the colmados, and he announced that by special dispensation some of the local maidens were coming to the party to dance. It seemed there were never enough women at the foreigners' parties to do much dancing, because most local mothers wouldn't allow their daughters to have anything to do with us. But Francisco said that he had arranged for three fat black-dressed aunts to come along as chaperones for the girls, who were a batch of cousins all of whom worked for Francisco in one or another of the town's colmados: Mari-Rosa, Maruja, Mariángel, Maribél, Mariána, two Marías del Carmen, a María del Pilar, one María de los Dolores, and an Asunción that somehow slipped in.

Lola Curtis (I am filling the names in; at the time I didn't know who a lot of these people were) pulled up on her bicycle, doing a neat skid. Her hair was bound up in a rag and she wore rope sandals. Gregory Kline and Pete Merriam drove up in Carol Bond's battered Volkswagen, and Tom Fast and Jack Pangs came down from María Molina's pension already drunk. Marcel Climant came, escorting Ingrid the gloomy Swede and Mrs. Johnson, whose husband had left her in Spain without enough money to get home on. A little later, in walked Kabut, the Ethiopian, pretending he was part of their group, but they wouldn't notice him. "Goom emening, emerywom," he said.

"Let us go home," Mari said. Jaimito and the others began to twang their guitars and laus.

It was dark then except for some last lights on the sea; the rocks and cliffs beyond our house had turned a pleasing mauve, and the beacon was blinking. More people kept arriving and there was noise from another party down the street in the Bar Royal, where things were more expensive (the oilman would have had to pay eighty cents instead of sixty for his bottle of gin, for example). I was having a good time and didn't want to go home. The band played and several couples tried to dance, sweating and kicking up dust. Old Mrs. Brewster went past and people called to her; she was leaning on a gnarled stick, and behind her came the three tubercular Malagueños, each with a dirk in his belt. I was listening to Pablo Noque tell Kline about his paintings: "This year I have sold sixty-two paintings. Every summer I charge more. Soon you will not be able to buy a Pablo Noque. I was a fisherman for thirty-five years and did not know that I had genius. It is because I paint as I see. I have the memory of the stone that has witnessed Creation. Ask the old ones of the village. They will tell you that the picture I have made of the dock ninety years ago is exact to the last detail."

On the other side of the table across from us Hans and Frans were explaining their movie scenario to Cobra Haddad, who had heard it before, I judged. "What is most difficult," Hans said, "is to wean the public away from this constant cretinous music. You must imagine the face of Bonaparte occupying the entire screen. He is grimacing bitterly, but there is no sound. He is screaming ear-splittingly, but no sound comes. There is only eery silence."

Sammy Carpenter showed up with three English girls from Palafrugell. "Hallo, everybody," he said. "I brought dancing girls."

"Wonderful," Carol Bond said. "We already have the foolish virgins and the three nanny goats gruff."

Mari and I danced a little, but it was too hot. Some more bottles appeared on the tables and two local boys tried to slip a white pill in the glass of a tall buck-toothed girl in a leather skirt. The boys were gigling and haw-hawing and daring each other but the girl did not notice them. "I-must-go," Fuhta Brag said, seeking me out. "I-must-work-tomorrow. I-thank-you-very-much-for-the-party."

"Not-at-all," I said. "Come-again-when-you-can-stay-longer."

We sat down again in different chairs, near Haddad and Ed Doyle and his wife. Lola Curtis said: "Listen to this, Snake."

"Don't call me Snake," Haddad said.

" 'At the beginning of my Indian Service I was a strong manly chap,' " Lola read. Ed Doyle had lost his glasses; Tom Fast had knocked them off the table and stepped on them. "Ga-lee," Doyle said. He had been reading the typescript of his memoirs aloud to Lola. "Here, you read out loud, Lolly," he said. Lola read: " 'At the beginning of my Indian Service I was a strong manly chap. A fellow said to me in a low bar in Lahore: Blimey, the Longarm Grenadiers are cowards, mate. I gave him such a punch in the face that his teeth broke and blood ran out his nose . . .' Heavens, Ed, that's a little strong, don't you think?"

A car went past slow in the dusty street and Fast and Jack Pangs stood up and waved their bottles and shouted in the glare of the headlights. Some locals came down the street in flapping skirts. Dogs and cats ran around under the tables. I was drinking more than I ought to and things began to get a little confused. I was introduced to the three Palafrugell girls and got a hard whack in the side from Mari for each one. "Let us go home, Merluza." This is a hake, a kind of cod. Mari had begun calling me fish names, maybe to imply that I am cold-blooded. I don't know.

Once I was walking around the table and old Mrs. Brewster caught me. "Are you enjoying the party?" she quavered.

"Oh indeed," I said.

"Parties out of doors are best," she said. "I like to look up at the stars. I can see God's majestic hand in every twinkle. His might and His love." As I moved on she croaked, "Look up! Look up!"

By this time Sammy Carpenter and Pete Merriam had gone off in the rowboat and everybody was talking about it, because Pallarés was expected to show up at any moment. "Sammy has become quite a Don Juan," Lola Curtis said. "He comes to the party escorting three girls, and goes off in a boat with another."

"He is not so very intelligent, after all," Haddad said. "It is a disappointment to me."

Kline said: "Sammy is just a dull young man. If you knew anything of the Midwestern towns in the United States you would know all about him. At the moment he is enjoying a Taste of Life."

"Good job that Pallarés fellow isn't here," Carol Bond said, "he'd give him a Taste of the Knout."

"Sammy now lives on the bright edge of danger," Haddad said. "Having lived there myself for many years in the shadow of possible sudden extinction, I know the sensation: it is an exaltation which admits neither scruple nor consideration nor prudence."

"Come off it, Snake," Carol said. "I thought you lived in the shadow of sudden possible liver trouble?"

"Or on the bright edge of dyspepsia," Kline said.

Meanwhile Kabut's huge black dog had appeared in the doorway of the Bodega and was standing perfectly still with the light behind it, watching everybody at once. Those nearest moved away. Some of the dogs under the tables started to whimper. The Ethiopian was nowhere visible. "Tell that awful nigger to come chain up this brute," Ingrid said. But the three old chaperones said that Kabut would not be seen again until the black dog had slunk off into the shadows and changed back.

"Look up! Look up!" old Mrs. Brewster chanted. She wound through the crowd tapping people on the shoulder and pointing up. Almost everybody looked, too. I got to laughing. Mari sat beside me with her lips pressed together, but I think she was having a reasonably good time. We danced some more and I made her drink some cognac. When she saw I wouldn't go home she concentrated on pouring my drinks on the ground before I could get to them. Good thing she did; the oilman was still mixing Killdog, pouring everything he could get hold of into his pitcher and mixing it with gin and insisting that everybody try a glass. Only the Dutchmen and he could stomach the mess. There were champagne and cognac bottles on the table, beer and aperitifs and falsified White Horse whiskies.

Once the power went off and the whole town was plunged in darkness, but the lights came on after a minute or two, just as the waiters had got the balky gasoline lanterns going well. Everybody danced at one time or another, including Pablo Noque, who didn't know how. They put him out in the dust with one of the Palafrugell girls and everybody laughed themselves silly. Jaimito and his men banged their instruments, and Hans and Frans did a routine they said they had learned from British sailors in Bangkok. The dance set everybody to trying the same thing: extending their arms and sliding their heads back and forth on their necks like marbles on a tray.

Some people from the party at the Bar Royal came along, Ace "Crash" Gibson among them. He came along on his motorcycle and I went over to look at it. Another of the arrivals was Luis Pallarés, but I didn't know him by sight then. The motorcycle was a big English works racing three-hundred-fifty cubic-centimeter supercharged water-cooled twin single two-stroke E.M.C., with throttle-controlled oiling, four-speed racing box, twin carburetors, swinging-arm rear suspension and telescopic forks. Nothing special.

Pallarés shook hands with the oilman. "May I present the Señora Bea Morgan," he said formally, and the oilman shook some woman's hand. "Get seats!" he ordered.

Marcel Climant was up on a table reciting Gide in French; then he hopped down and shook hands formally with Pallarés. "This other gentleman is unknown to me?" the latter said questioningly. The other gentleman was Gibson. He was about my age, dressed in blue corduroy pants tucked into short utility boots; he wore a surplus U.S. Army dress jacket dyed maroon, and around his neck was wound an endless yellow scarf. On his head he wore a flat black córdobese sombrero with a broad brim, bent up cowboy style; the cord under his chin was clasped in a small silver death's head. He also wore stitched blue suede gloves. "I'm Ace Gibson," he said. "Call me Crash."

"With pleasure," Cobra Haddad said. "Please take a drink, Crash."

"With pleasure," Gibson said. He lifted a half-full glass from Marcel Climant's hand and drained it. "Beard hairs in it," he said.

The band started again; Pablo Noque and Lola Curtis danced. Tom Fast had gone to sleep curled around a dog, and Jaume Pujol, the poorest man in town, sat by himself stuporously singing flamenco songs in gypsy. Pallarés looked all around, squinting in the bad light. "I do not see Mr. Carpenter," he said. "Is he here?"

Kabut had come padding out of the alley, in a red shirt. "He im gardem wim Mess Merriam," he said. There was a stricken silence near the Bodega door. Ed Doyle was about to correct Kabut and redirect Pallarés to the boat dock when Tom Fast woke up and started to scream: "Ah, ah! they're after me! It's the fits! It's Edgar Allan Poe's father, boys!" The dog that had been sleeping in the bend of his legs jumped up and ran through the crowd, startling the overdressed woman on Pallarés' arm. "Pardon me," Pallarés said. "May I present Miss Bea Morgan."

"Of course," Haddad said. "But I was under the impression you were en route to Vienna."

"I never saw you before in my life," the woman said.

"Are you not Mrs. Black from the T.W.A. Constellation out of New York?" Haddad asked.

By this time all three Palafrugell girls had come up to be introduced to Ace Gibson, and they gazed winsomely up at him from the level of his broad shoulders. Carol Bond went over to offer Pallarés a glass of champagne and she brought one for Gibson, too. "Thank you, ma'am," he said, flinging the cowboy hat back between his shoulder-blades. He looked at her hips and made a face at her graying hair and the wrinkles around her eyes. He looked down on the Palafrugell girls more favorably.

"Just passing through," he said. "A friend of mine talked me into coming down to Spain, but I lost her somewhere. She paid my passage. They're all looking for Crash, ha ha."

"And how did you stumble across our quaint little corner?" Carol asked. "Or were you brought?"

"What? Hello, ma'am, are you still here? Why no, I took a little drive this morning to shake the cobwebs out of ole Bessy Bee's pots, and it come dark before I knew it. I thought I'd look for a meal, so I stopped in a town up yonder, but it was pretty dead. I thought I heard a mouse creepy-creep behind one door, but I wasn't sure. Then I heard the mourning cry of the hooperhill from the castle keep. I took it for an evil omen and I come down here where there was lights. Where there's light there's life, I figure, and where there's life at night there's night life, and there's Crash."

"Crash," Carol mused. "Plate glass or stock market, do you suppose?"

Inez, one of the Palafrugell girls, subtly asked: "Are you traveling alone, Mr. Gibson?"

"Call me Crash," he said. "Yes, I come over in the spring to compete in the ole T.T. and I just thought I'd skip around a bit and see the place before my passport run out. No reason why not—got no ties, no strings on me. I wear boots and a T-shirt," he added obscurely.

"What's a T.T.T.?" asked Clara, the drunkest of the three.

"A motorcycle competition, sweetheart," Gibson said. "You know, one of them free-wheeling thingumabobs with a motor between her forks? They run cold, they run hot, they spin you dizzy, and you can't rely on them, but when they make their mind up, there's no stopping them. Ain't that just like a woman?"

Well, things went on, and the party got rougher. There was a lot of singing, and some dancing that was almost as loud. The jazban got kicked in and Madame de Mars came down the hill with a broom looking for her husband. I remember once Frans and Hans cornered old González and were explaining their film to him in Dutch, and later I saw them trying to induce Kabut to change into a black dog in the light of the gasoline lantern (it seems the power went off again at one point), and finally Sammy Carpenter came back and got in an argument with Ace Gibson, which I have mentioned before. He came up from the boat dock alone, tittering and nervous, so I judged he had had some success.

He mixed himself in with the crowd and tried to avoid Pallarés; he came just as Haddad and the Morgan woman began to shout at each other. "Me follow you?" she screeched. "I like that! I've been here six months. I'm following *you?* Who do you think you are—you sad old bald eagle—Robert Taylor?"

"I do not venture to imply a personal interest, Madame," Haddad said stiffly. "I am not interested in your libido, only in your employers."

"Oh go jump in the bay," she said.

That was when Sammy came along. Somebody handed him a glass of champagne; he shook hands with the members of the orchestra and said hello to Bea Morgan. "Hello," he said. "I believe we've met before. Aren't you Miss Kavanaugh from the B.O.A.C. flight to Paris?"

"Go ——— your ————— of a ——— with a ——— in it," she explained, and went to join a group that was singing. Lola Curtis, Ed Doyle, Gregory Kline, Charles Kolp, and Mrs. Johnson, and others were singing *I'll Go No More A-roving;* then, *There's A Shanty in the Town;* then, *The Curse o' Halle frae Me Sall Ye Beare, Mither*. Meanwhile, Mrs. Brewster was leading the musicians, singing *He's Just My Man Abraham, He Can't Give Milk But His Pelican,* while they played *Tú, Solo Tú.*

"I thank you for your courtesouly hospitalality and staggeroff," Jack Pangs said, and threw up on a brown cat.

Gibson was talking to the Palafrugell girls when Sammy wandered over to him. "Hello, girls, I'm back," he said. "I went rowing. I'll have blisters tomorrow," he added, frowning at his palms. The feeble ruse fooled no one. He was nervous but there was something of the turned worm about him.

"No, I don't race professional," Gibson was saying to the girls. "I don't do anything pro, because that can get to be work, and that gives me the urge to scat, sweetheart. I live strictly for kicks, and you get your kicks where you find them. That means you have to keep moving. In the States if they catch you sitting on your thumb they jug you for vagrancy. Always have a buck in your shoe. Get what I mean?"

"I peer through a positive *fog* of Americanisms," Inez said.

"Why, I raced stocks until they tried to get me to sign a contract, then I had to cut and run. They're looking for me yet. Leadfoot, I was called on the bricks. I used to fight preliminaries in Chicago, but I was afraid it would spoil my looks. I was a bush pilot in Canada for awhile—that's where I learned to talk you gals' lingo—but I broke up the ship. Now you know why they call me Crash. I ran a wheel in Reno once, and punched a few cows. Sometimes I hit up my relatives, sometimes I live off a woman. Money comes easy. It's room to breathe that comes hard. You got to stay loose."

I heard Clara ask him how it could hurt his looks to fight in preliminaries. "Aren't they American elections?" she asked.

"No, honey, preliminaries are fights. You know—where you punch the other fellow in the beezer before he punches you. That was a long time ago. When I was thirteen I—"

"What about punching those cows?" Clara said.

Sammy said: "That's where the good looks come in; he was afraid the cows might punch him back."

"—had to . . . run . . . away . . . What was that you said, son?" Gibson turned to Sammy, who was standing just behind him. Inez introduced them. They took an instinctive dislike to each other, as sometimes happens.

Then followed the colloquy previously reported: "Ace 'Crash' Gibson," Sammy murmured. "They're both nicknames. What do you want two nicknames for?"

"The same reason you got four eyes, Four-eyes," Gibson said. He went off to dance with Clara, who could barely walk, and Sammy sat down by Ed Doyle and his wife and Lola Curtis to sing *Lord Randal My Son.* After that whenever their paths crossed they bristled at each other.

About then the oilman came up to us with more glasses and said: "Whooooz this chaaaarming ladeeee?"

"That's my wife," I said. "Hands off." It wasn't any good though, once they started on us. Up to then we had managed to go more or less unnoticed. But Kline and Marcel Climant, Mrs. Johnson and some others came after the oilman, and Mrs. Johnson said: "Hello. You're the young man who has the lovely automobile. My husband had one of those. Quite terrifying. But it was taken away. What a lovely creature. Does she speak English?"

"No," I said.

"There she goes," Kline said. "Catch her, she's disappearing into your shirt again."

Mrs. Johnson spoke to Mari in Spanish: "You are enchanting. I see you two sitting alone by the wall quite content. You are aynamorados, no es verdad?"

"Eef I had theese automobile," said Climant, "I would go south to Jeebraltaire, voyage to Portugal and to the north by Biarritz, go to Sweden and Norway, down through Chermany, through Sweetzerland to Eetaly, to Chewgoslavia, Turkye, and return to Málaga or Cádiz in thee wintair, eef I had theese automobile, eef I had thee passport Américain."

I said I might, too, if I had the dollars Américain to finance all that trip. "Oh the rich Americans," said the oilman, who was one himself, except strapped. They started telling each other that I lived the life of a multimillionaire vagabond, dashing back and forth in a fast car and taking life as I found it. They said the present-day American was the true nomad in the best sense of the word. "For look you," one said, "the true nomad travels with his herds, his bassourab, his women, and his gold. So travels the American, taking photographs. No such silly hoboing as that of Mr. Fast in his cart. One must travel quickly! Live like a rajah! See nothing! Photograph all!"

"This young man," Kline said, "is the true International Soul. I will not admit the existence of the wife, in whom I do not believe. I prefer to see him wandering, fleetly, as a hugely magnified ant, without direction, without plan. To lack direction, and therefore goal, and therefore ambition, is to live a life uncrystallized. At each bend in the road he is on the point of becoming someone he has never been—depending upon what confronts him in the next town, the next vista, the next human situation. He is a body of malleable mental protoplasm, with the infinite potential of an unborn human brain."

Haddad and Carol Bond came over and the former said to Kline: "We saw you agitating your arms; you are declaiming." And the latter said: "Five to one he used the word crystallization. It's very much a la mode."

"We are envying our young friend," Kline said, "who has no master."

"Perhaps he lives for kicks, like our friend Mr. Crash," Haddad said.

"I know the type," Carol said. "He follows his wandering star to the brow of the next windy hill, whence he will see the distant beckoning horizon, towards which his itching foot will carry him wither it will over the open road, of which he will sing The Song."

"Very good, except for the itchy feet," Kline said. "Sounds rather public bath."

"Windy Brows, Beckoning Feet, Itching Hill; could equally be an address in Surrey," Haddad said.

"Look! he flies away!" Mrs. Johnson said, getting into the spirit of the thing as I got up and started to go, taking Mari with me, figuring enough was enough. We fought through the crowd. The party was getting sloppy around the edges. Some young men were squirting wine from their goat-skin bags on the three nanny goats gruff and Pete Merriam was having a loud argument with Luis Pallarés. The Dutch twins were trying to carry Kabut away with them, and a fuel-oil fire was burning in the middle of the street. Dogs barked, Jaume got up and sang some more, Jack Pangs urinated in the doorway.

We went up the hill into the quiet pine trees, scuffing at the gravel. "Ay, it is over," Mari said wearily.

We went home and straight to bed. Both of us were tired; my legs and feet ached from the swimming that day, my back was burned, and my stomach sloshed with mixed drinks. Also, I was in a bad humor about Kline and Carol Bond and Haddad making me out a pretty loathsome specimen, whether they knew what they were talking about or not. I couldn't get to sleep for a longer time than it should have taken. Anybody who is in a foreign country has recurrent bouts with the What-Am-I-Doing-Here? feeling. But what galled me was what Kline had said: that I wasn't anything; that I might turn into something depending on whom I met next, or what I did, but meanwhile I was just knocking around, a cipher in a big car. It was true; and I couldn't think what to do about it.

I could pack up and go home and let my father put me to work; or I could go back to the States *without* going home—get a job picking berries or something else with Experience Not Necessary. Or I could try to get a job in Europe and make it a modified knocking around loose. Or I could leap off the cliff to the moray eels and the octopi. But all in all I couldn't see any prospect more attractive than continuing to be a Nothing, until something happened. All very well to put me down as a no-good with no sense of responsibility, and an escapist to boot, but the only alternative was to go home and get a dead job and become a Charley Kenilworth. And I didn't have the incentive any more.

In my own defense I have to state that before the big blowup I had no objections whatever to what people who are stuck in it call the Normal Life. When Jennie and I moved into our own place, we both worked and talked about the house we would build someday (split-level, in a nice development, quarter-acre of ground, bushes along the sidewalk, modern kitchen and game room and nursery) when I got sufficient raise in salary or my old man came through; and I was all for it. Even down to the monthly installments on stuff we thought would make us happier to have. Every morning I got up at seven and carried the garbage out and ate an egg, then took the bus to the city and said good morning to the elevator man and went up to the ninth floor and batted the calculator around till noon. Then I went to lunch with George and Willis from the sales department and in the afternoon I batted the machine around some more, sometimes with the office manager urging me on. I drank coffee out of a paper cup at three-thirty and went home on the bus at five-ten; got there about five-thirty and turned the burner on under whatever Jennie had left ready to cook on the stove, and then sat down to read the paper until she got home from Sloo Brothers at six-thirty. We ate, and then watched TV or went over to Bruce and Amaris's house to play cards or watch TV or we went to the movies or we stayed home and made paper furniture for the model of the house we were going to buy some day. This was the life, at twenty-odd. What more can you ask?

But, now, I didn't have the incentive any more. The world can't expect me to work my eight hours a day and turn into a large TV-viewing callus for nothing, for the privilege of living alone and eating my guts out for the things I can't have. Only monkeys work for peanuts, as Charley Kenilworth used to say when he came back after drinking beer instead of eating lunch and surveyed the work piled on his desk. Not that it ever occurred to him to strike out for the South Seas. Because he had a good wife. He didn't want to do anything but work out the hours of his day so he could afford to go home and find food on the table and a paper to read and quiz shows to watch till time to go to bed. What made it worth it, or at least bearable, was a Good Woman. You can go on forever if you happen to have a Good Woman. If I wanted to take all the blame, I could say that I had all the best—the job, the TV, the woman, the incentive—and that I had spoiled it, but the point is that to go back to the States and try to pick up where I left off would either mean going back to live with my parents or going off alone to live a dead daily routine for the sake of coming home at night to an empty apartment full of dirty glasses and an unmade bed.

So I figured to hell with Kline and Carol Bond on the one side, and Charley Kenilworth and my father on the other. Any life is a good life, just so you realize you're alive.

To finish up: the party lasted through that night, trailing away to Pangs and Tom Fast and some others sleeping stuporously around the embers of a fire on the beach the next morning at seven. I heard about the end of it from Haddad, who stayed till four. Everybody got progressively drunker and those who didn't go to sleep got sick. About three-thirty Gibson was playfully pushing Pablo Noque into the sea and Sammy Carpenter said: "Cut it out." Gibson said: "Who's going to make me?" Sammy said: "You'll see who makes you." Gibson said: "Let's see you try." There was some confusion then, what with people throwing bottles and being sick and leaving the party. Somebody tried to push Sammy over the breakwater. He hunted up Gibson. "Did you try to push me inna water?"

"What water?"

"That water."

"Who?"

"You."

"Me?"

"Yes, you."

"What about me?"

"Did you try to push me in the water?"

"When?"

"Just now."

"Push you in the water?"

"Yes."

"Who?"

"You."

"Me?"

"Yes, you."

"What if I did?"

"Well keep your goddamn hands to yourself, urp."

"Who's going to make me?"

At the same time Mrs. Brewster was singing hymns and Jack Pangs was shouting: "Poke him one, Sammy!" Preparations were under way to move down to the beach for a sausage roast. The broken bass drum rolled into the sea and Jaume Pujol woke up and yelled: "I evacuate on all foreigners!" Sammy and Gibson arranged to meet the following day on the esplanade and slug it out, tooth and claw, no holds barred. Sammy stood on his toes and jutted his chin, trying to look like a more serious contender. And two of the Palafrugell girls were dragging the third away. "Wait a minute," Gibson said. "Hey, Clara, what about it? Do I get to drive you home?"

Clara was in the middle, being supported by the other two; her lipstick was all over her face. "Not on your tintype," she muttered. "I know you Americans and your big hairy things."

"Oh God, Clara, shh, for Heaven's sake," Inez said.

In the end these three went home walking, all the way to Palafrugell. Things were breaking up about this time, Haddad said. The drunks were reduced to a mumble and everybody else had gone home. The Marías and their chaperones were long gone; Benito Viñals, proprietor of the Bodega, had long since dragged his tables and chairs inside and locked up. Carol Bond and Ingrid drove off in the Volkswagen, Luis Pallarés and Pete Merriam took their argument uphill to María Molina's pension, where he beat her (Haddad said that María said). Jaimito and his boys folded the remains of their instruments and stole away, with several useless checks of the oilman's in their pockets. Pangs and Fast and the other members of the sleepless generation went down to the beach and built a fire. Kline and Haddad hung on for a little while longer talking about Dylan Thomas, and when they finally left there was nobody at the Bodega except Jaume, still singing bitterly in Gypsy, and old Mrs. Brewster, who had clung to a cup of cold coffee, was sipping it yet, and said she had to wait around for her Malagueños.

Three

There is no place so melancholy as a summer resort in winter. At the end of November we left Es Cruylles and came back to Barcelona. We hadn't intended to move; Pablo Noque said we could have the place at half price until spring again, when the tourists returned, and we had planned to stay on. But through the last month people kept leaving, until there was nobody left but Strangewolf, who kept to himself mostly, and Ed Doyle and his wife, and Lola Curtis. The days turned chilly, the nights cold—our house didn't have any arrangements for heating, only the little fireplace in the comedor—and the trees shed all their leaves without turning any color except brown. The stretch of beach below the town looked desolate and sad, and a wind blew in over the gray rocks from the sea, a corrosive gray wind that almost burned, a wind called the Canigó.

Es Cruylles had only two or three hundred inhabitants who would live there anyway, whether tourists came or not, and these, being Ampurdán to the core, were bitterly poor, gloomy, and somewhat querulous, and during the winter they shut themselves up in their houses and sat tight with the wind moaning around their calcareous walls. We had made few enough friends among the locals even during the balmy days.

There wasn't anything to keep us hanging around. Strangewolf and I sometimes sat gabbing about cars in the Bar Royal, but he only came down the hill once or twice a week and then didn't stay long; he had work to do. Ed Doyle and I had nothing in common, and Mrs. Curtis and I didn't get along: she was too snotty about people who weren't what she called Intensively Creative. "What do you live for, you people who have no purpose in life?" she asked once. It was drizzling gloomily, we were sitting around a fire Pepe had built inside the Royal, Lola and Mari and I. Mari said: "What more can one do except try to live as best as is possible? There are no rewards; the best is to never hurt another, to avoid distress and pain, to make improvements where one can, and to work as much as is necessary. Hah!"

"My child," Lola said pityingly, "without a plan of existence life is not worth living."

If you had asked me, I would have said Lola was the one whose life was definitely not worth living. What's the point in living alone in foreign countries, in drab little towns in winter, for the sake of writing dank stories for housewives to weep over? And selling all your rights and using so many pseudonyms you wouldn't recognize your own work if you saw it?

Mari went to buy some groceries, and went on up the hill. I mentioned to Lola that we were moving soon, and she said: "Do you mind if I speak to you quite frankly?"

"Go ahead," I said.

"You'll probably think I'm just a nosy old woman, but I've been watching you all this fall, and you seem to be quite an intelligent boy. I wonder if you realize that you aren't getting anywhere?"

"Where is there to get?" I said.

"Oh come on—you know that's old-fashioned. What do you intend to do with your life? You can't just waste it flitting hither and yon without ties or responsibilities, even though I daresay it seems very attractive at your age. I'll tell you one thing: I was contemptuous of security, too, when I was young, but it becomes increasingly important as the years go by. You'll find that a day comes when you haven't the energy you once had, and life on the loose seems one long frightening fight to feed yourself and not die of loneliness. All you want then is a chance to sit down somewhere and live a quiet steady life without surprises or adventures, without all the worries of being free. And mark my words, you'll never have a place to sit down and rest unless you establish one, and you have to start young."

"You may be right," I said. I didn't bother to take offense because it seemed to me she was talking about her own problem, not mine. The old maid's tragedy: she didn't have a rose-covered little bungalow with some wrinkling old clown around bringing home a pay check every two weeks, with a pension plan to take care of the final years. Everybody wants love.

"I'm speaking to you as an old aunt now," she said. "What are you going to do about this girl? Everyone knows you aren't married to her. I don't suppose that matters much nowadays, except that no matter how you slice it, you do owe something to any woman you sleep with. I daresay you expect to abandon her when you're tired of her, but even if you don't, what if something happens? What if she becomes pregnant? It happens every day, you know. Or if she gets sick. Such a poor little thing . . ."

Poor old Lola, she was saying. Somebody dumped her when she was young. I've never knowingly read any of her stories, since I don't often read Confessions, but I'd be willing to bet they're all approximately the same. Maybe by now she has made up a weepy story about Mari and me, with the names changed, and the scene a small Mid-west town.

Nevertheless it made me broody, and I sat around the fire the rest of the morning trying to figure something out. Something that sounded reasonable, practical—normal even. Something that didn't hold out such a despressing prospect as going home and getting a dull job and mouldering in it for the rest of my life. That may be normal, but it's not reasonable. You only get sixty or seventy years at best, and unless you believe in the hereafter and like harps, how can you bear the ridiculous business of forever working in order to eat in order to live in order to work in order to eat in order to live in order to work? If that's all there is, why not jump to the eels and the octopi?

But what Lola said about Mari was worth giving thought to. In the three months we'd been together we had made all the necessary little compromises and adjustments; we got along like an old married couple; she took my shortcomings into account as I took hers; we had a good sex life and laughed at the same jokes and had even picked up a few of each other's mannerisms. But it was true: she might get pregnant at any time, and as for getting sick, she already had a lump on the side of her neck that was touchy and swelling up; somebody had told her it was scrofula. She already had one kid, whose board I was paying. A kid of my own would be an even greater obligation, not to mention the legal troubles I might get into. And even if I wanted to marry her and take her to the States, she had never served her three months' government service, and her baptismal certificate had been destroyed during the war, so getting her a passport would be a year's work. Not that I wanted to marry anybody under any circumstances. Our arrangement was the kind that isn't supposed to last very long. When I asked her to come with me I didn't have anything long-term in mind; she knew that. While the arrangement lasted I was cutting deep into Uncle Fred's money, and I knew

I could stay a lot longer in Europe if I traveled alone. Then, too, I wasn't altogether over Jennie. There were moments, especially in fine weather, when I realized that, and the old urge to run came over me. I hadn't seen Italy, or much of France and Germany. I had an idea I would like the northern countries, too, Sweden and Denmark, where the people are a lot like Americans, or so I'd been told.

And another thing: I wasn't getting a chance to work out the car properly as long as I was stuck in one place. With everything well broken in and buzzing, the wheel had a live feel to it that gave me goose-pimples; I had an urge to open it up wide and see if it would really top a hundred and thirty miles per hour. But not on Spanish roads. For that I'd have to go north. And then there were the races. Europe is full of races, sports car and Grand Prix, and I was missing them all. I had been thinking for some time that I could go a long way on the money that was left, sleeping in the car and eating along the way, just me alone, between one motor race and another. Not that the sojourn in Port Crullers hadn't been fun, not that Mari hadn't been good to me, or for me, and not that I was tired of her. . . . It was just that I thought it was time I went on.

That morning I figured that no matter what happened in the future, the first thing I had to do was get out of the rut I was in. I figured that when we left Es Cruylles, with everything of mine already in the car, all I'd have to do would be drop her off with her few things at the house of the Yaya, where the kid was, and give her a couple of hundred dollars to fix up her neck and live easy until she found work. Then I thought I would go on up to Austria, which I hear is almost as cheap as Spain. Once there I'd reorient myself, take the back off the passenger seat, make up a bed, dispose my few properties around the floor and luggage compartment, and then light out to do some of the high-speed vagabonding Kline had accused me of. When I got tired of that I'd go home.

Once I made up my mind it wasn't but a few more days before we left. I was sitting in the Bar Royal about noon several days later and Strangewolf came in and said: "Lola tells me you're leaving. Pity. I've ordered a blower from England. Expected I'd have a chance to blow some dust on your Cougar or Hedgehog or wot-is-it."

"Jaguar," I said. "Have no fear. Whenever you think you're ready, just drop me a line and I'll come back and run you and all your superchargers into the ditch."

"When are you leaving?"

"As a matter of fact, this afternoon," I said. "Come to think of it, we don't own a thing we can't throw in the car in ten minutes."

It was storming again that morning—a good time for leaving. The waves were bashing around the moored boats and the wind blew straight in from the Gulf of Lyons. Strangewolf had brought along some chorizos, hard bloody pork sausages, and we charred them black in the fire, ate them with scratchy local bread (pan redondo), and drank wine from a goat skin belonging to Pepe.

Strangewolf said: "Attention: I have arrived at my analysis of your situation."

"Oh boy," I said.

"Your present situation, I mean. Analysis proper. Haven't the stomach for glooming over your psyche. Your predicament interests me. And your type is become rare. Walk away if you like, if you are he who can refrain from hearing himself discussed."

"Go ahead," I said. "I ought to be able to listen to anything by now."

"Yours is the problem of the insufficiently incorporated man. In these days, in which the personal crafts are no longer taught—except as a debased form of mechanics—one must either escape education altogether and become a self-taught artist—craftsman—or he must absorb education in its entirety and become a Corporation Man. Since you have no specific aptitudes, neither artistic nor bureaucratic, you should never have been allowed to escape total absorption of the three basic principles of Corporate Society, to wit: first, that the individual must integrate with the group, since all multiples of heads are better than one; second, that the inevitable law of life is meagerly recompensed labor for the proletariat; third, that the single justification for human life is the purchase of objects, and the single consolation for the human condition is constant entertainment."

"I couldn't memorize all that from a book," I said, "much less absorb it in conversation."

"These things are taught to Corporation Man by example," Strangewolf said. "They are fed to him with his mother's milk. They are never articulated because their falsity is apparent. You have observed already that eighty million heads are no better than one, and that idiot heads in whatever quantity can treasure an erroneous theorem for centuries without misgivings. Moreover, such a principle implies a headless society of democrats, as in the American plan, which is patently impossible; there is forever a board of directors, steeped in the ancient legal and moral immunity of the Zulu kings. As for the second principle, you have also observed that the natural law of unremitting toil for nothing applies to somewhat less than the total population. Such a natural law is automatically repealed, as would be the law of gravity were the élite allowed to fly on magic carpets. The final principle, that which aims at the evolution of the perfect Corporate Man, has already made tremendous inroads upon our individuality, through the inexorable progress of American technology. Nevertheless it is still possible to exist independent of the tradesman with his stanchless flow of gadgetry and the impresario with his eternal stupefying reiterations."

"What's the point?" I said. It seems famous men talk the same nonsense as Everyman in the subway, only using more difficult words.

"That you," he said, "insufficiently indoctrinated by the principles of Corporationism, which should be tattoed upon the soul of Corporate Man, have managed to detect these flaws, as you should never have been permitted to detect them. From chance remarks of yours during this autumn I have managed to piece together the following: that you have not inherited the money-extending aptitudes of your father and therefore cannot join the Board of Directors. Neither have you inherited the parasite configuration of your mother, therefore cannot with tranquillity and a whole heart spend money which you have not earned . . ."

"My mother's an artist," I said. "She sculpts."

"Beg pardon: she is a parasite. Women are particularly well fitted to this role, although it is by no means confined to them. To continue: that by means of desultory resistance through school, military service, and the university, you have developed outside the Sklavenmoral. This maroons you in the position of the autonomous personality devoid of inner resource. Upon perfection of the Corporation Society, through universal application of the three basic principles, you and your type of individual will be firmly dealt with: gassed, with sympathy; regretfully, gassed."

"Sure," I said. "Oh well. I guess you're right. Everybody's right. I have to run along now and start packing."

"Of course," he said. "No one listens unless I talk nonsense. I suppose I shan't see you again. Shake hands. I will miss you. You will never amount to much, but you never once asked me to read your manuscript."

Mari

One

As it turned out, it was just as well I didn't leave Mari and go north the end of that month. Up there they were having the severest winter in sixty years, I heard later. Already in late November people were dying of it. Between November and March all the rivers in northern Europe froze over solid; rain, ice, and snoring windy blizzards roved back and forth; the roads were ribbons of glare ice where they were ploughed at all. Trees were cracking and falling, and the temperature seldom rose above zero except in Switzerland, where they kept having heat waves, or so said the Spanish radio. In the Scandinavian countries, and even as far south as Münsterland in Germany, gray and famished wolves were prowling around country villages.

But it was not until January that the cold reached our part of Spain, by which time Mari and I were ensconced in another house, this time some twenty miles outside the city, in a little pueblo where the remnants of Yaya's family lived. We were fooled into renting the place by the sun streaming in the front windows in December, so we spent most of the time between January and March shivering over the wood range in the kitchen, drinking coffee, and smoking and trying to squeeze into the oven. Once there was ice on the top of the town fountain, and nobody talked about anything else for a week—there hadn't been any natural ice in those parts for ten years, so said the village baker. Sometimes I had to laugh, because Cataluña's severest winter in decades was actually only a little chillier than a fine day in early spring in Hartford. I often speculated what the Spanish would do if they were suddenly transported to some place really cold, say Utah or North Dakota in February. Turn rigid and particolored as so many barber poles and fall over dead, I suppose. The only thing that bothered me was that there was no place to go to escape the chill except to bed. It was a thin, niggling, nagging discomfort, as close and constant as skin. It was as chilly inside the stores, the bars, and the houses as outside, and considerably damper because of the stone walls and tile floors. Indoors and out, the people all wore several coats and wooly mufflers and flapdown caps. But it was only really cold at night, when the wind blew inland off the gulf; or, at least, that was when I most missed central heating; when I came home to relax and have a drink and eat supper and pass a quiet evening at home, and found it was almost as chilly in our kitchen as it was outside in the needly damp seawind.

Even bed wasn't warm, not at first. To take the freeze off the sheets so that we could climb in without perishing of shock, we would fill up all the old wine bottles in the house with boiling water and toss them in under the covers to radiate while we undressed. Sometimes we even turned back the blankets and pressed the sheets with the flat iron full of burning charcoals, then hopped in grinning and blue in the smell of scorch, the covers up to the nose, to press our feet against the hot bottles and begin the same old argument about who was going to leave his side of the bed to make love. Because obviously you can't make love on both sides of the bed at once, and whoever made the first move had to leave his nest of warm sheets only to return later to find it thoroughly chilled. Usually me. It was a source of acute domestic discord.

This was later. When we first came back to the city it was jacket or sweater weather, warm in the sun, and even in the early evening warm enough to sit outdoors at the cafés drinking grosella and Pepsi-Cola. The cold approached subtly and even after the first continuous week of shivers and rain we thought it was just a bad spell that would soon give way to Cataluña's ordinary winter of sun and brisk wind. The first cold weather in the pueblo was the second week of January, and we passed it mostly sitting in the Jaguar, with the heater—and the motor—running; but that cost too much, so we activated the wood range, which we hadn't been using because the charcoal pit was good enough to cook on. It kept getting colder, and it snowed half a dozen times, light wet snow, and when it wasn't snowing it rained.

I didn't move on immediately when we came down from Es Cruylles in November because Mari was having trouble with the side of her neck, and I didn't want to leave her in a bad spot with no job and the kid to support and medical bills to pay. That is what I said to myself, at any rate. The fact is, the lump was such a good, solid, noble, reasonable, even conventional motive for staying on a few days more that I couldn't push it aside to get at the real reason. I can't even guess whether or not I would have left her that same afternoon if it had not been for the carbuncle, boil, infection, or whatever it was. Anyway, that was the ostensible reason why we stayed in the Barrio Chino for the rest of that November, and why I rented the house in the country that I didn't expect ever to live in, and also the reason why the end-of-things feeling I had did not come to a head in a farewell or a death or any kind of ending but persisted without diminishing in intensity, making each day seem like the last, from that afternoon on through New Year's, when I finally did leave her.

Barrio Chino means Chinese quarter, though any Chinese in it would have felt just as lost and displaced there as in any other quarter of Barcelona. There aren't any Goths in the Gothic quarter, either, as far as I know. Our barrio happened to be where we felt most at ease, and where the Yaya pensión was, and where we knew the shops and bars and had a few friends; that was all. It was a bad-rumored district as ancient as the harbor itself, involved and seething and sunless, almost lightless, given over mostly to cheap movies, slum apartments, clothing stores, brothels, pawnshops, and shady venereal clinics. It was near enough to the docks that the small smelly bars were always full of Turks and Greeks and Frenchmen, Bolivianos and American merchant seamen, Peruvians, and Mexicans; but far enough from the nearest cuartel of the Policía Armada that these bars roared all night long with arguments and radios, agonized flamenco singing, gypsy songs, guitars, shrill jeering women, bottles and fist fights.

In the Hotel Paraíso we slept, or tried to, just above the Bodega Brasileño, on a reeking street compacted of similar joints full of drunks and seamen and prostitutes—slept, or tried to, through long relentless nights of close local noises: guffaws and groans and shrieks, iron cartwheels striking sparks from the cobbles, mysterious clanking noises, accordions, howling burros, rolling kegs, chains, klaxons, and castanets. The noise, movement, activity, could no more pause than the flow of a river can pause. Without rest the same streets in the morning were full of carts again, taxis and motorcycles, dogs, shawled and/or hooded women carrying grass and canvas market bags, beggar children, weaving loco prize fighters from Marseilles, lottery and/or blackmarket cigarette vendors, tight-button guardias armed with machineguns and bombs, garbage collectors blowing tin horns, enormous horses, fast cats, wisps of steam, fish trucks, flower carts, cripples, street sweepers, thieves, messengers, and lost infants, all suffocating and pushing in one long street scarcely twenty-five feet wide, everybody awake and alive and struggling, indignant and preposterous, as in one of those composite images of mankind at its most repetitious and superfluous.

Take for instance the hundreds, that seem like thousands, of cripples and infirms that stumble and limp and grope through the clog of the streets hawking their razor blades and cigarette papers and flints and lottery tickets and fountain pens. There are too many of them even to believe in, much less pity. Hundreds of tin throats and black bakelite hands and hook-shaped spines and blue dented temples and foreheads. Hundreds of men with huge prosthetic feet, lurching on home-made crutches; hundreds of blind or even eyeless men and women, victims either of the war or congenital gonnorrhea or the dust of the esparto grass fields; hundreds of hand-propelled velocipedes carrying legless cripples, swollen and skull-white; hundreds of arthritic widows with hands like dead spider crabs, selling old magazines in doorways; hundreds of spastics, idiots, rheumatics, paralytics, amputees, each with his vendor's license pinned to his coat, each with his cane or crutch or wheelchair or smoked glasses or peg-leg or steel-and-leather brace, and each with his folded strip of lottery tickets and his wooden box or tray of deteriorated commodities, which nobody buys.

Or take for instance a family of gypsies passing through the Calle Nueva, or what is now called the Calle de la Ciudad Condal: a diffuse, almost comet-shaped migration straggling along the sidewalk—a procession headed by the oaky, barrel-hard grandparents, surrounded by their legitimate sons and daughters, bizarre and barbarous in striped trousers and beaded rags and many-layered ankle-length skirts; followed by more sons, cousins, brothers, wary as wolves, with silver rings in their ears and bandanas on their heads—then girls, dirty and splendid bachelor gitanas, who dance and sometimes sing in the street, and demand céntimos. Then children and old people, strung along behind for many yards, almost lost to the group but always part of it, down to the last, the babies, mostly pantsless, at the very tail of the comet: brown and bright-eyed and melon-bellied, wanderers and thieves and fugitives before they have cut their second teeth.

Or again, for instance: once Mari and I and the kid, her kid, were going up the street early in the evening on our way to a movie when a gray little man, dried to an ash by his own inability to earn enough money to buy the food to give him enough strength to work, came pushing through the crowd trying to clear a way for a woman who followed him, bent over and paper-pale, her lips bleeding. The man kept crying: "Farmacia! Dónde hay una farmacia?" while the packed aching life in the street came to a halt and watched to see, and the woman, still running, began to scream; and she gave birth to a five month's miscarriage in the middle of the pavement.

After a time these come to be only a few sounds in a concert, a few colors in a kaleidoscope, single events in an endless, meaningless, panoramic, squalling, pointless moving picture that balks at nothing. Probably because it has not yet occurred to Nature, or whatever, that there is anything to balk at. No degree of comedy or horror murderous enough to draw the line at. People will stand for anything.

The Yaya lived in the Barrio Chino in the very middle of all this pointless preposterous fury, tragedy, farce, and misadventure which has no provable importance. Yaya is Catalán and means abuela, which in English means grandmother, but she was not the grandmother, she only boarded the kid. She and her two daughters, the one blonde and tubercular, the other brunette and almost blind, lived in a pensión on a side street, just off the Calle Nueva, not far from the Club Cairo. A pensión of this kind, in the Barrio Chino, is where some capitalist rents a whole floor of a down-and-out slum apartment and tacks up a sign that says Pensión So-and-so, then lets out the various rooms and halls and closets to people who can't afford to live anywhere else. Bachelors live four and five in a room, and even large families can't do much better; dogs and cats live in the patios and rats in the corridors, beggars and small businessmen set up shop in the downstairs doorways, the walls run slime, and the tenants throw garbage out the windows. Nobody bothers to sweep or paint or fumigate.

Yaya had one medium-size room with no heat at all, a single dim electric bulb in the ceiling, one small window, a ponderous armoire, and two narrow beds. The nearest running water was the common faucet down the hall in a reeking black toilet. Yaya did all her cooking on a brass petroleo stove and all her laundry in a zinc basin. Despite these conditions, the kid didn't seem to lack anything it could make use of at its age, with the possible exception of light and air. All three women doted on it. Yaya swept and mopped a neighborhood movie house every morning to earn her potatoes and oil, and while she was off working from eight to twelve every day including Sundays for a total wage of eighteen dollars a month, the two daughters tended the kid. When Yaya came home the blonde went off to the mine or whatever, that was ruining her chest, the brunette went off to the fluff mill that was putting out her eyes, and Yaya minded the kid. Considering life a rat race that has to be got through one way or another, it wouldn't be misleading to say that little Mercedes was what made it all worth while in that house. At two and a half she was already spoiled silly.

Both Mari and I arrived in Barcelona that afternoon in a mixed mood. The business of packing up our few things, closing the house, turning the keys over to Pablo Noque and driving away—away from what had been our home, no matter how you look at it, even though we left no marks of ourselves—had blended a certain amount of melancholy with the haste and irritation involved. The weather was damp and gloomy because of storms up the coast; my spark plugs were coughing; we didn't have any cigarettes; we were snarling at each other for nothing; and the dog kept making trouble in the back seat, where all our belongings were. It was about a yard long by this time, with huge feet, and it would keep fooling around.

When we came out of the city park and turned down the Paseo Colón that goes past the railway station, a traffic cop blew his whistle at me and I had to stop.

"Do not speak," I said to Mari as the cop approached. In situations like this I try to act as fuddled and aggrieved as possible, and of course I don't speak any Spanish at all. It seems I had gone past this cop's outstretched white arm. He was wet and ornery and made me roll the window all the way down so I'd get wet, too, not to mention the upholstery. As a matter of fact, I hadn't seen his arm in the first place, since he was at an intersection where there normally wasn't any cop, and besides, I had been keeping an eye on a trolley that was pinching me from the left. However, there is no point trying to explain circumstances to traffic cops anywhere in the world, so I only mumbled at him in English while he shouted excitably at me in Español Fácil, holding his white canvas sleeve under my nose and shaking it. "You see? You see? Lo comprende?" I just shook my head and smiled bashfully, as though he were presenting me with the keys to the city; and there wasn't really anything especially cogent he could think of to say, so finally he flung up his palms and said: "I have a thing for you!" He began rooting in his belt wallet, and for a moment I thought he was actually going to give me a ticket, which would have meant a trip to the Tenencia and a fine of maybe a dollar. But it turned out he was only looking for a special paper for foreigners. Obviously left over from the tourist season, and doubtless the only applicable thing he had with him at the moment. Apparently he felt it was just the thing to settle my malefactor's hash; having handed it over, he squared his shoulders and marched away, vindicated. It was a yellow card printed in French and Italian, German and English, and the latter read: "Esteemed Visitor! The City of Barcelona is Honored by your Visit. However due to Ignoring of our Parking Regulations you have Parked your Automobile in a No-parking Zone. The Municipal Council is not Fining you for First Offense, but Hopes you will take Opportunity to Acquaint yourself with our Parking Regulations. ¡¡Happy Voyage!!"

When we were moving again Mari said: "Why are you laughing, Flounder? You did wrong. Durty basteh poli."

Like most Spaniards she hates all kinds of police, but is abjectly afraid of them, with good reason, as they are very arbitrary and not above knocking your teeth out by way of demonstrating their authority. And they get away with it, too. Spanish subjects are subjects indeed, not citizens, and there's no such thing as habeas corpus or suit for false arrest or appeal against corporal punishment. The guardias in particular can never exceed their authority, as there's no limit to it when they are dealing with Spaniards. Both guardias and Policías Armadas are very proud and arbitrary and they will use the butts of their carbines to break the jaw of any subject who so much as gives them a dirty look. It is really not my business to comment on this, but I do bring it up in conversation sometimes with bright Catalâns who take advantage of my good nature to discuss our lynchings in the South.

Anyway, we cruised from there to the Columbus monument and turned up the Ramblas looking for a place to park. I was particularly anxious to find a good spot so as to reduce my chances of getting a ticket for running red lights. However, for a country that is supposed to have the fewest private automobiles per capita in civilized Europe, Spain has some pretty crowded streets. Whenever you do find an interval of curbing more than ten feet long, there is sure to be a motorcycle parked in the exact middle, effectively blocking your car out but not taking up all the space by a long shot. Besides, most of the downtown streets are so crowded that parking is prohibited anyway.

In the end I had to leave the car on a side street for the pedestrians to play with, as usual. And as long as I am criticizing Spain I might as well voice another long-standing complaint. I suppose it's too much to ask that the blind who go groping along the curbs refrain from rapping my body panels with their metal-tipped canes, but surely the sighted ought to be able to find some other place to toss their garbage and cigar butts except on parked cars. Then of course there are the kids who climb all over the hood in hobnail boots and play sliding board on my Italianate fenders; not to mention the irreconcilables with colds in the head who make it a matter of political principle to spit greenly on any vehicle which is in any way sleek or luxurious. Also, if your car is good and dusty after a long trip over Spanish highways, somebody is sure to write obscenities with his forefinger on the roof. In my case, whatever else they do, they never fail to shove the wing mirrors awry, and it is a drag to be always realigning them.

We parked, and sat still for a long moment. All of a sudden I was reluctant to leave the car. At that point I had made up my mind to leave her and move on toward the north, to Germany or Holland. In that long moment the old insanity of the previous spring stirred again within me like mud at the bottom of a pool; it seemed I had made a wearying journey and it was over, yet I hadn't arrived anywhere. I couldn't see any reason why I should get out of the car. There was no reason for me to halt in Barcelona. I wanted to let her out with her bundle of clothes while I roared away again on my search as though she had never existed.

I sat and stared through the windshield at the drizzling rain and the pale evening lights. She turned in her seat to look at me. She was dying to see her kid, and she looked at me wonderingly, puzzled that I made no move. Throughout that summer and fall our trips to the city had been spaced two weeks or a month apart, a month being the longest period of time she could exist without renewing her soul with a few minutes of sunny chatter with little Mercedes. We had not been in Barcelona all that month of November, and she could hardly contain herself. Nevertheless she waited, looking at me, and no doubt an inkling of what I was brooding about dawned on her. "You do not want to go see the nena?" she asked quietly. She was staring at me much too solemnly and I felt irritated.

"Where else is there to go?" I said.

"Wherever you want to go," she said, and put her hand on my knee, but took it away when I paid no attention to it. I went on glooming through the wet glass at the taxis and crowds until she said: "It depends on you. Where do you want to go?"

If I didn't want to go with her to see the child, she would go wherever I wanted, she meant. Wherever I went she would go, willingly. I felt tied, led, hampered, sucked into further complications. "Oh son of a bitch," I said and flung open the car door, feeling desperate and crazy. The moment came to an end, but I didn't forget the feeling; it stayed with me. The whole thing, morning to night and top to bottom, seemed useless and stupid and completely senseless.

The time was about five-thirty and all the inhabitants of the city seemed to be in the streets, in spite of the bad weather. Everybody was in a hurry. Taxis forged through the mist, nudging people out of the way with their fenders. Shop awnings ran water on us and the dog kept tangling its chain around people's legs. Mari led the way through the Calle Nueva and into the alley where the rain ran down the black walls to the cobblestones, turning the immemorial filth underfoot slippery as tide-washed rocks.

"Hola! Hola!" said everybody in the Yaya's place. As usual we surprised a riot in the dim smelly room. The blonde and the brunette had just come home from work and were full of the day's news; Josefa Nuñez, a bony woman from next door, was there, as well as two or three other neighbor women, and Luis, the sweetheart of the blind brunette (the two had been engaged since they were sixteen and seventeen, respectively, and were still saving money toward the trespaso on an apartment, so that they could get married). Also a collection of children, mostly nude, from nearby rooms, and a pair of off-duty waiters from the bar down below. Not to mention a live chicken, bought by the Yaya for the next day's paella. Everybody was surprised and pleased to see us, and Mari instantly grabbed her child up in the air; the two began to chortle. Yaya shook my hand and presented me to the people who did not know me, then brushed some stuff off a chair and made me sit down. She brought out a bottle of homemade mint liqueur and poured me a glass, while everybody talked at once and the petroleo burner puffed smoke and the dog crawled among people's legs and the single bulb swung slowly back and forth on its long cord from the ceiling.

"Ayay, mí madre!" the Yaya shouted in the uproar. "Callaos, I can't hear. Oye, Capitán, tell me what is happening. Are you here for a time?"

Yaya is just short of fifty and just short of five feet tall. She has a kind of soft hump on her back from working so many years with mops and brooms, and she darts around her tiny room like a monkey. She has a tough little seamed face turned slightly gray, with an irregular fringe of whiskers in the folds of her chin. Once she knows you she will give you the food off her plate, and if you are in trouble she will drop everything and work patiently for days to help you get straightened out. I never met anybody, in Spain or anywhere else, that I liked better.

"Well. Yaya, how does it go?" I asked, toasting her with the mint and evading her question. "How goes life, ha ha ha?" She and I get along very well, partly because she thinks that I am about the funnniest thing that ever lived; that is to say, a foreigner. She is both broad-minded and intelligent, but of course a little limited in her outlook. For instance, she takes it for granted that up until the time of the tower of Babel everybody spoke Spanish, and she thinks foreigners come from a narrow belt of land surrounding the Spanish peninsula and were put there to amuse Spaniards with their strange actions and barbarous clothes.

Mari was sitting on a low straight-backed chair fondling her kid, and as the confusion died down we told about the last few melancholy days in Es Cruylles with the Canigó howling through the cork trees. There was nothing else to tell except that we had left our house and were back in the city with no plans for the future. Mari said: "We lived very well, but the coast is sad when it rains and begins to turn cold."

"Surely," Yaya said. "What will you do now?"

She turned to me as she spoke and everybody else in the room looked at me as I opened my mouth to say something glib and suddenly found I had nothing to say at all. There was a long silence and it seemed to me all at once that they knew. Or maybe my guilty feelings convinced me that my traitorous intentions showed on my face. It was a perfectly ordinary question, and when I did not answer it I felt distrust bulge in the room. Particularly the old women; they certainly knew.

Besides Yaya, her two daughters and Mari, there were four other women in the room: Josefa, old Encarnación, and two other neighbors—furrowed bony women in plain black dresses that covered them up to the chin, and thick black stockings that covered their legs. All their faces were sallow and stern and only their eyes were active. Of the four, Encarnación alone was past fifty, but all of them seemed used and ancient, worn down by centuries of poverty and work and beatings and heavy husbands' unimaginative lust.

The four of them already knew about us, about Mari and me — Knew all they needed to know about the innocent poor girl snatched from their grubby streets by the dashing rogue foreigner who was leading her down the green road, robbing her of youth and honor. It occurred to me that I had been judged long before. These four had been looking, judging, ever since we walked into the room, relentless and wise, knowing from old experience what was to happen, what had always happened.

Mari said: "I suppose we will have to live somewhere. It is too much expense to sleep in a hotel and put the car in a garage each night." It had not yet occurred to her that the summer was over, the vacation finished. But it had occurred to the old women. There was another pause, and then Yaya said: "Capitán, you pay too much for villas. What you must do is find a small apartment or a single room with kitchen rights here in the city. Life is not too dear if one knows how to buy in the markets."

"Of course," I said, turning rather sullen under the weight of the hard Iberian eyes. "Frankly I have not yet thought about it, but that is what we will do. Or something similar, yes."

"Do you like to live in the city, or do you like to live in the country?" old Encarnación asked in a slow suspicious voice. Her full name was María del Pilar Encarnación Bogotá Mejias and she was married to a stolid jobless bum in the final stages of alcoholic dilapidation.

Another woman said: "Juanita, the sister of La Malagueña, has a room for renting. It has a mirror and an armario and an iron bed."

I had nothing to say and they stared at me with increasing antagonism. Mari also watched me, sitting with the child quiet on her lap. The hostility became so palpable that the two waiters lowered their chins and stared at their hands embarrassedly, and Luis sat silent and deaf in the shadow by the wall, leaving me alone with the women, the only male in the world. They would not involve themselves, they were neutral and unconcerned, because I was a stranger and a foreigner. But I don't believe the old women considered me even as a foreigner at that moment, only as the life-size brute embodied of the whole male principle, against which they were united in resentment and bitterness.

Finally Yaya said: "My brother Lorenzo lives in a small pueblo outside the city. He may know of a house that is cheap to rent, if you want to live in the country."

Yaya was born and raised in this pueblo where her family still lives, what is left of it. Lorenzo is the town baker and he also sells wines and charcoal. Yaya came down to Barcelona in the thirties with her husband, a beer official; he was killed in the civil war and she stayed on in the city with her two daughters rather than return to the pueblo, where they would surely have starved to death.

She said: "Tomorrow I will telephone, and if he knows of such a place, then you can go to see if it will serve."

I did not say anything because I was not interested in renting any more houses. Landlords ask three months rent in advance from foreigners and I did not intend to stay three more days, much less three more months. So I was silent and there was another uncomfortable pause until Encarnación suddenly said: "The house will serve, pues, any house will serve for fornication and afterward to abandon her."

I knew I should jump up and deny it, slap her, insult her, react in some way; but I did nothing. I just looked at her sullenly, waiting for her, for the other women, for all of them, to name me. I already knew the names they would call me. But it did not happen. Mari herself, who knew me well and saw that I had turned stubborn and angry and ashamed, put an end to it; she stood the child on the floor, came over to me and sat in my lap in plain sight of all of them. "We will do what seems best," she said. "It is not your affair."

That was the end of an embarrassing interlude. No more was said about our plans. The old women did not even glance at Mari, even though sitting on a man's lap in public was a very daring and meaningful gesture to make. They were not really thinking about Mari, neither pitying nor warning her; they simply sat in judgment—wise old tribal wives with all their fears confirmed, full of the bitter experience of the facts of love and bitterly aware that whatever happened, the woman would suffer for it, as she has always done.

It was almost seven and Yaya started to make supper. Old Encarnación heaved herself up and went off to her own cell—a great relief to me—and finally the conversation turned general again. Mari went back to playing with her kid and the dog resumed its furtive advances on Yaya's chicken, tied to the leg of the bed. We were invited to stay and eat, but I said no, we would go down to the fonda at the end of the alley when we got hungry. Poor Yaya, all she had for that evening was some boiled rabbit bones to make soup out of, and some noodles in tomato sauce. The only solid in the house was a piece or two of left-over mutton for little Mercedes.

People came and went in the pre-dinner hour. We talked about the snows falling on the Pyrenees, about the weather in Barcelona, about the student riots in the university, and about the bonuses the two daughters were hoping to worm out of their employers for Navidad. Luis told a repulsive joke about one Little Juanito who not only had relations with his sister but with his mother as well; Mercedes sang a gibberish song; and after a while Mari said: "I intended to ask you something, Yaya. Look at this that I have on my neck. What does it seem to you?"

She unwound the scarf she was wearing and everybody quieted down. Sickness of any kind is a serious matter on those streets. Yaya left the petroleo stove and aimed the light bulb at the side of

Mari's neck. We all had a good look. The lump was the size of a small egg and had turned red on top and looked chafed. Josefa tried to poke it with a long bony finger; it was very sore to the touch. The women discussed the lump in Catalán, with knowing medical airs, and Yaya said: "It is only a pimple, a grano."

"No. The wife of my eldest son had one of these," Josefa said. "It is an ulcer of blocked menstruation, muy serio."

"I can hardly turn my head to that side," Mari said. "For a long time it remained small, but now it has begun to grow."

Luis said it looked like a tumor. Margarita, the tubercular blonde, said it seemed more like flaming ganglions to her, and Mari explained that it had already been diagnosed by the women of Es Cruylles as scrofula and by a frivolous youth of our acquaintance as syphilis. There were further opinions as more neighbor women were called in for consultation, but no two agreed, so finally Yaya said she would leave the preparation of dinner to the daughters and take Mari down the street to a doctor she knew of. "Listen, nena," she said, "this can be a thing of much trouble. Already you have let it go too long. He is a very excellent doctor and I will accompany you so that he cannot throw you down on your backside."

Mari appealed to me and I said by all means. I gave her some money for the doctor. Up until then I hadn't thought much about the lump, because I ordinarily ignore what is wrong with me until it either goes away or kills me, and I sort of expect other people to do the same. But the swelling had been keeping her awake the past few nights and maybe it really was something serious. Or if it was not, if the doctor said it was only a side effect of a cold or something, then that would be one less obstacle in the path of my leaving. By all means go see what the doctor says, I said, so they left.

I decided to go up to Carmencita's place while they were gone. It wouldn't have done any good for me to go along with them, as the doctor would only have charged triple, seeing I was an Americano rico; besides I wouldn't have been able to understand what was going on in Catalán. So after Mari and the Yaya left I drove up to the new city to greet Manuel and see if I could trick him into taking care of the dog for a few days. If he had taken it he would have found himself stuck with it forever, but he would not even discuss the matter. "How have you been?" he said. "Hace mucho que te ví. We are all well here, with the exception of Ramón, who has a bad stomach."

"I am glad," I said. "I mean I am glad that you are all well except Ramón. But look, hombre, we must live in a single little hotel room for the present, and clearly it is impossible to keep such a large dog in a hotel room."

"A dog in the city is always a problem," he agreed blandly. "For this reason we have never owned one. Once we kept a cat, but it escaped. Well. Have you seen this new model of Ossa motorcycle?"

I saw it was no use, so I gave it up. We talked for awhile about one thing and another, till we discovered we weren't much in sympathy any more, not, at least, as we once were. It was just another reason for me to feel sick of myself, since I was sure I had alienated him in some way. We made arrangements to hit some of the winter hot spots as soon as things settled down, and then I said good night and drove back toward the Calle Estrecha.

My spark plugs were still coughing, my head ached, it was raining for real now, and everything seemed to have gone sour. I couldn't help thinking about old Encarnación's remark and it continued to gall me. It appears I don't mind too much being a bounder, but it definitely disturbs me when people accuse me of it out loud. Still, that was only part of it; the dog was only part of it; even Mari's grano wasn't as important as all that. It was just that everything seemed to have come to an end and yet was dragging on, like a bull that has already been stuck two or three times but refuses to lie down and die decently. All I wanted was just to drop everything and move on, but the moment had not yet come. The summer was over, the holiday turned sour, yet I couldn't seem to manage to thrash my way clear of complications. I couldn't think straight. A single idea kept occurring to me: of leaving Mari's little bundle of clothes and a respectable number of dollars in pesetas with one of the waiters in the bar below the pensión, with orders to make delivery to her a few hours hence. Meanwhile, I would simply drive away rapidly, not explaining or apologizing or anything. I wasn't in the mood for tears or rage or recriminations. The world's unwritten history is full of just such shifty tactics, but at least I had never made her any promises, not even of the tacit kind. As far as the dog was concerned, I could drop it off in Es Cruylles on the way to the frontier. Maybe Strangewolf would take it or Ed Doyle. If not I could just leave it in the town, and the natives would feed it as they fed old González, by turns, until it got old enough to look out for itself.

But even in the midst of making these furtive plans I was driving directly back toward the pensión, back toward my woman and my dog and the odd new life I had built for myself. Honor, conscience, the grano, lonesomeness, obligation—these were all good reasons for not leaving, but they weren't the half of it. If I had left that same night I could have forgotten all these things and Mari's face to boot in three hours of hard driving toward La Junquera. The reason I didn't leave was because way down inside I didn't want to. This goes to show what I mean about not understanding my own motives. My oddball friend in college, who had his whole philosophy of life worked out in algebra at one point, used to say that nobody ever did anything except what his psyche really wanted him to do, regardless of intellectual decisions. He used to say that both yes-decisions and no-decisions were only social gestures and had no survival value, since a man goes through life obeying only subvocal commands from the body and the id and the large intestine, all of which operate entirely independent of the apparatus of decision. To a certain extent I go along with this; at least, I am convinced that my subconscious is a lot smarter than my conscious. It has a better memory, it works a thousand times faster, it hardly ever makes a mistake when it has all the data, and on top of that it is, I claim, as moral, as considerate, as honest as any other modern subconscious. Just because you follow your impulses and reflexes doesn't mean you are an evil or degenerate person. It all depends on what kind of impulses and reflexes you have. And if, like me, you have a conscious mind that is always shirking, forgetting where it left its tools, checking in late and sneaking out early, making mistakes, and worrying at trivia and finally going off to pick violets, why not trust to the monster who broods in the bilge?

All I mean is, I didn't know what I was doing at that point; I just drifted down the line of least resistance. And when I reached the pensión, problems and complications climbed all over me again. Nothing you could put your finger on: a sense of things undone, a sense of threat. Mari looked at me as though she had never seen me before. Things came to a stop in the room as though everybody was surprised to see me there. The crowd had collected again, nude children and bony neighbor women. A mock wedding was taking place between little Mercedes and a gourd-headed little boy from down the hall, the former dressed in pieces of an old first-communion dress and the latter in a huge plug hat. Luis was the priest and muttered what fragments of Latin he remembered from mass. Mari held my hand and laughed up at me with something sorrowful in her eyes. I watched for awhile and said it was cute and then lay down on one of the beds. She hung my jacket up to drip and sat down beside me and I said: "Well, what did the doctor tell you?"

It seems all he had done was pinch the grano very hard between thumb and forefinger, so that she yelped. "He is a bruto," she said. His diagnosis was that she was frail, lacked strength, and had a weak chest. In short, general debility. She should eat more. Yaya could have told her the same thing; some of the neighbor women already had. Even doctors hereabouts seem to share with bootblacks and housewives and dukes and everybody else the conviction that layers of fat are much to be desired. A fat woman is not only considered beautiful, passionate, and healthy, but automatically rich and especially happy. So Mari should stuff herself and get fat. Nothing more specific could be got out of either her or the Yaya. It was the first of a series of bad experiences with cheapside Barcelona medicine. "You mean he did not tell you what it is?" I shouted. "He did not give it a *name*?"

"He is a dirty old man," Mari said, "but a very good doctor, and he charged only thirty pesetas. He made me remove all my clothes and I would have been frightened if Yaya had not been with me. Then he looked at all my body and down my throat and looked at my chest with the X-ray."

This made no sense, and after some more probing it came out that he had put her behind a screen, with the room-lights dimmed, and he had said hum hum hum to himself with a green light shining on his face. I don't know whether such a machine is always called rayos equis in Spain or whether this particular doctor called it that for his own reasons, but it seemed clear enough to me that he had looked at the lump and at her lungs through a fluoroscope, for God's sake. Even I know better than that. But this doctor was one of the best, Yaya said; he had cured the tubercular brunette of meningitis some years before, and for only three hundred pesetas. So Mari and Yaya and the rest of the women were all very happy to hear that Mari's trouble was only general debilidad, and the cure for that, and therefore the grano, was simply to eat like a hog.

It had been a long day. I didn't bother to try to explain to Mari that this doctor was either a fraud or a fool; it would have done no good. Try to tell any woman anywhere that her doctor has rocks in his head. Women think doctors are ordained by God, like priests, and have a direct pipeline to cosmic truths.

We said good night to everybody and promised to come around next morning to the movie where Yaya worked and have coffee there; and Yaya said again how pleased she was to have us back in the city. "I will telephone to my brother Lorenzo tomorrow," she said. "We will talk about a house."

"All right, all right," I said. "Tomorrow is soon enough." Just to add to the confusion, I might as well confess that it occurred to me that if Yaya did manage to find a good house, with a garage and some furniture I might even take it and stay on—maybe until spring, when the racing season opened up north and the weather turned warm. "Do what seems best, Yaya," I said; then we went out the door and down the gloomy stairs. But she wasn't finished yet. We didn't have time to pass out through the street door before she came clattering down after us. Apparently she had had an afterthought, one more thing she wanted me to mull over, and she wanted to tell it to me privately. Mari looked disconcerted and said she would wait in the bar next door. She said: "It seems that I am nothing of importance tonight. I am a birria."

Yaya touched my arm and murmured that she did not mean to presume. "About this of Doña Encarnación," she said.

"Nada," I said. "I don't want to hear about that."

"No. Not about that. Another thing."

It was raining hard. The rain blew in under the arch of the patio and she hunched her shoulders and gripped her elbows. Because she had always been a good friend of mine and had never before come at me with advice or criticism, I listened to her. And it wasn't advice or criticism this time, either, only a kind of philosophy that I did not catch the drift of till much later—how it was related to me, I mean. She said, rather startlingly, that love was like gamba shrimps a la plancha, in that the more you ate the more you wanted until you got sick and didn't want any more for awhile, if ever again. I can't say I had ever thought of it in this light. "Life is good enough without love," she said. "I mean to say that a man and woman can live together in armonía, simpatía, without love. Only songs are full of Corazón and Amor."

"Yaya, you are a cynic," I said.

"No. When I was a young girl things were different. We believed in the songs and waited to learn what love was like. Afterward we learned that love is for mothers and their children, and that the other thing is illusion. This has always been true. You will learn it, too, all you young ones who wait for love to come on the next autobus from the provinces, or to be waiting at the fiesta of San Juan. When you are no longer hurt because love is illusion, then you will see that a day passed without fear or hate is as good as loving, and a heavy supper and a warm bed are more to be valued than pretty kissing."

"Good, good," I said. "Yaya, everybody looks for love. What do they find?"

She was a little excited, shivering in the rain drift and remembering things she had not thought much of since the war. "Bah," she said, "bah, bah y bah! They find that a man must earn money so that his woman can put food on the table. I do not know how it is with your Americans, but here if a woman can find a man who works hard and does not always stumble home borracho, and a man can find a woman who can cook and who does not waste his money in tonterías or cheat him when he is gone from the house, then that is better than love. For love cannot last a year; it eats, it does not give nourishment. No one should live alone, but love is not at all of importance. Any partner is good enough, and luck is only the soup and good clothes and a fire and a little tranquillity in the night. A man and a woman who live together and do not hate are the loving ones, even if they never sing to one another in the light of the moon. They live together, and eat and sleep and work and fill up on the togetherness which is not Love, but Home, and when they are filled, they burst, and there is a child in the house. What else is one to do with all the years of life that no one requests to live?"

"Why do you tell me this, Yaya?" I said. "Vaya, a terrible way to live."

"To live is terrible enough," she said. "Es bastante terrible eso solo," she put her hand on my arm and pushed. "Anda, remember that I am not fooling you. Do not abandon what you have in order to run after fantasmas." She turned and scampered back up the oozing stairs to her cell, and as I say, I did not stop then to think about what she meant. Everything of importance waits on the stomach, I have learned; anyway I called Mari and we went down the alley to the fonda. I was hungry.

The Fonda del Mar was bright yellow, choked and steamy inside, out of the rain, and smelled of peppers. Fonda means restaurant or inn, but this was more a fonducho or figón, barely more respectable than a gypsy cave. The name is good though; when you say it fast it sounds like you are saying Bottom of the Sea, a play on words that is obviously intentional, because the proprietor is an expatriate Rumanian who has assumed the name Higado Caderas, Liver Hips. Nobody would adopt a name like that without having his tongue in his cheek. It is like the Catalán joke about the girl named Dolores Fuertes de la Barriga, Hard Pains in the Belly.

We sat in a corner watching the variously uniformed dancing bears drink beer and cavort with prostitutes of little success in life. I ate meat and omelettes and potatoes and round bread and drank red wine, while Mari drew lines on the tablecloth with her fork. "You should eat something," I said.

"I am not hungry."

"Your excellent medico of the instantaneous X-rays says that you must eat like a mule," I said.

She had ordered broth with the yolk of an egg in it and now she said the very sight of it gave her nausea. "Are you going to vomit?" I asked.

"I am not sick," she said. "Only my stomach."

She wouldn't look at me.

That night we slept in the Hotel Paradise, a grubby habitaciónes deep in the barrio. I've since thought that this might be where I picked up the crabs I mentioned earlier, but that's hardly credible since I didn't notice the first itch until spring. The only possibility is that I picked up some hibernating eggs. El Paraíso was not recommended to us by anybody; it had no ADAC plaques or American Tourist Rating on the door. In fact, unless you knew where it was you could hardly find it; it was only a door in the wall and did not even have an electric sign. You could rent a room there for half an hour as well as for all night, if that was what you wanted. For fifteen pesetas you could do your business and leave unhindered, and there were even a few girls hanging around the office in case you came unaccompanied. The water ran in the pipes all night and people fought and shouted in the corridors; there were painted nude women on the ceilings and grayish sheets on the beds. Looking back, it was such a favorable spot for it that I'm inclined to favor the hibernating egg theory. We only went there because we had to take the dog with us and El Paraíso is the kind of place that admits anything, just so you pay. There was a small sweet-faced youth named Celso on duty that night, and he did not even shrug when we said we wanted to keep a large German shepherd in the room with us.

We had to wait in the corridor while a room was emptied and a green old woman changed the sheets on the bed. We cowered in an alcove, feeling terrible, while dark muttering couples passed back and forth, staring at us, at our country clothes, our suitcase, and our dog. A man and a woman came up the stairs, arguing. The man said: "That's too much," and then the woman said he had also to pay for the room, and the man said he would not do it. "Ve te hacer puñetas," the woman said and went to go look for somebody less penurious. The man was left standing and he said: "What does one do?" A woman was just coming out with another man and Celso, the clerk, pointed his thumb at her and said: "Does this interest you?" The woman stood there while the client she was just finished with left, and the man who did not want to pay too much looked coldly at the woman and paid his price and the woman went with him, not having said a word. It was like a cattle market. I was thinking that the two worst evils in the world were there in the narrow hall outside Celso's office: the evil that lives because people do not care for each other, and the evil that lives because people will do anything for money.

We didn't even sleep well, what with the water gurgling in the bidets, the arguments in the corridors, and the creaking beds and the restlessness of the dog, obscurely stirred by the smells of the place. Every time Mari asked: Are you awake? it woke me, and I would thrash, keeping her awake. The pillow was hard and the mattress harder. Along about four in the morning we were both lying dispiritedly listening to a drunken woman singing in a room nearby, and suddenly Mari started to cry.

> ". . . Mujer que anda de noche," the woman sang,
> "no puede ser cosa buena . . ."

"What's the matter?" I said.

She did not want to tell at first; it was a thing of no importance. Everyone cries, she said, when he cannot sleep in the very early hours of the morning, which is when old people and sick people die. She had not supposed that I was awake to hear her. But in a little while "You are going to leave me," she said. "I do not know when, but it will be soon."

She meant it to sound resigned, but I knew she hoped for the passionate reassurance that even she realized I couldn't give her. I kept quiet; I thought it might make it easier for her not to be full of illusions when the day came. She had always known it would come. I was only sorry it had become important to her whether I stayed or went.

The woman sang:

> " . . . lo que has hecho tú conmigo,
> me las tienes que pagar . . ."

Two

So THAT WAS how it was, and that was where the matter rested. The uneasy moment of decision prolonged itself for almost two months, the mood of end and farewell floating between us like a foggy sea through days in which nothing much happened. We never discussed it again after that first time, never admitted openly that anything was changed, that anything was impending. We even went on automatically with what amounted to our domestic affairs; that is, we settled into the Paraíso and made arrangements with Celso to give us the same room every night. We couldn't rent it like an ordinary room because all the rooms in the place earned money at odd hours of the day, too; and we arranged with Carmencita to store for us the traps we weren't using. Manuel helped me find a garage that would guard my car for a reduced monthly rate, and we settled into an eating and coffee and bedtime routine in the Barrio Chino, all as though we planned to live there forever. We looked up friends and made dates, went to movies and an occasional play; we watched the frontón matches, bought ourselves some winter clothes, and called at the pensión regularly to get little Mercedes and take her out for paseo—to the Plaza Real to feed the pigeons, or on boat excursions to the breakwater in the harbor, or up to Tibidabo to ride the swings and things.

Mari was a little bit moody most of the time, but I think even that was largely due to the grano on the side of her neck. She did not like doctors or heavy foods or injections, and all the time the lump kept getting bigger and redder. Besides, she wasn't sleeping well. I was moody, too, but then I generally am, and on top of that the aimless life we were living wore me down. I kept thinking, just like any old married man, of all the advantages there are to being free of women. And then I'd think: one more day and I'll go. I slept and ate and dreamed my plans for further travel, unencumbered. Racing through the north of Europe, skidding in the snow and seeing new mountains, sleeping the nights in cozy German Gasthauses with the cold stars looking in the window, eating rare meat and drinking real coffee instead of the southern exprés—all the while booming along tight in the covered cockpit of the Jaguar, with everything necessary for my existence close at hand. At night the European roads leaping ahead of my lights, mile after mile, and the green glow of the dashboard and the wind in the wing windows and the rolls and coffee in strange places at dawn. It's the kind of traveling I like: a self-contained missile, self-directed and fast and free. It would have been good. Or perhaps I would have slid off the road the first day, smashed up the Jaguar and killed myself. Who can say? In any case I didn't leave; I kept waiting around with my stomach knotted up. Then Yaya caught up with us one morning in the Bar Infantíl and said her brother Lorenzo had at last found a house for rent.

It was the place I mentioned before, with the sun streaming in the windows and the farm next door, the black goats and lambs and Siamese cats, the lemon tree and the fig tree in the front yard. It appears that the family who owned the house, pueblo people and friends of Lorenzo, had given up farming some years before, rented their land to their next-door neighbors, and moved down to the village to operate half a dozen small businesses. It wasn't a villa or a bungalow or anything of the sort, just a big stone farmhouse built rather like the Escorial, with an unpretentious barn leaning against one side of it like a cowshed.

Old Manolo, the patriarch of the clan Falguera, said he had

never thought of trying to rent the place, since it was not a house anybody would live in if he didn't have to. What foreigners did was of course their own affair; we could live in it for five hundred pesetas a month if we wanted. Twelve dollars and eighty-some cents at the current rate of exchange. His sly look around him as he named the sum showed he felt no shame at taking advantage of us. He probably couldn't bring himself to believe that we would rent the house under any circumstances, so he figured he might as well shoot the moon. He and his relatives and friends, who had come to gape and marvel, politely withdrew to give Yaya and Mari and me an opportunity to talk it over. Yaya just scoffed and said that all Catalâns (though she was herself one) left both humanity and shame behind when they came to talk business. "A Catalán who has a thing to sell smiles at everyone but has no friends," she said. Mari only commented that the kitchen was adequate and looked sort of trustingly to me to make the proper decision. So I said I would rent the place.

Because there is one thing about living according to the dictates of your subconscious: that is, once the monster has prompted you to do something, it's no good asking questions. Just abide by the decision, then wait to see what happens. I said: "Well, this is as close as I will ever come to living in a castle in Spain. You must understand how strange and romantic is such a place to one who lives in America, where houses all come wrapped in cellophane."

"I think they must also have abandoned fortresses in America," Yaya said.

Mari said: "We cannot yet come here to live, however. Not until I am cured of the grano. Who will cook, and who will clean so many rooms?"

"We will come as soon as you are healthy," I said. "Nada; I have decided. I think I want to live here."

The sun, the cactus, the black goats, and cabbage fields and the mud-colored pigeon-smeared house with the ants on the balcony all added up to one thing in that moment: an illusion of peace and quiet. This is what I always think I want though I don't ordinarily know what to do with it when I have it.

But that is how I came to rent what everybody soon took to calling El Catafalco, after I was dissuaded from christening it Stonehenge. Yaya took care of all the final arrangements in my name, driving home the bargain with old Manolo, who glowered and shook his fists at the sky and finally appealed to all his relatives, living and dead, to assist him in calling down the wrath upon these Barcelonese who were diddling him out of his just returns. Lorenzo and Mari joined in on our side, and they all leaned forward from the ankles, arguing in shrill injured voices, hands busy as threshing flails. I had nothing to do, since the discussion was in Catalán, which to me is the original crackling of thorns under the pot, so I spent the time wandering around taking stock.

In addition to the lemon and fig trees, a concrete chicken-coop and a tin lightning rod came with the house, and also a grand inland view of the bare mountains and a seaward view of a blazing white haze pricked with ghostly fishing boats. A horse and cart hung with bells jangled down the track behind the house, where the almond trees grew in scraggly rows. The next-door people were out working the fields, bent over with their behinds in the air, inching slowly down long rows of winter colls. I had the same feeling for El Catafalco that I had had for our villa in Es Cruylles that first morning: here was a place where a man might pause and rest a while and meditate on whether life was worth it all.

"You must not take it seriously, our cockfighting," Yaya said as we drove back toward the city. "Everyone is happy with the agreement. It is the custom to shout and curse and pretend ruin. You see, from the start they were willing to accept less."

After so much name calling and despair, protestations of starvation, and thundering economic collapse, the terms agreed on by Yaya and Manolo Falguera were entirely verbal. After you have skinned, or been skinned by, a Spaniard in some ruthless deal, you can trust him implicitly to carry out his part of the contract, just as he trusts you to carry out yours. The only hard part is to remember all the ins and outs. Spanish acuerdos, even when you are only agreeing to meet somebody somewhere for coffee, are as complex and tentative as an international trade treaty, with endless clauses and provisos that take any number of far-fetched eventualities into account.

"We agreed that five hundred pesetas was too much," Yaya said. "So you will pay only three hundred for the present time, except that during the summer, the renting time, you must pay four hundred, if you wish to stay. In the meantime Manolo understands about the health of this child, and for so long as you remain in the city to be near the medicos you need pay only twenty-five pesetas each week, so that he will reserve the house for you. However, if he finds another tenant for immediate occupancy, then you must make a new offer. Of course, you may stay in the house on the week ends, but you must pay for water and electricity as you use it. This sum you will pay to Manolo. When you move permanently into the house you must rent for periods of three months, and pay in advance on the first day of each quarter. Then you must pay for the use of electricity directly to the company, and since all water comes from the well which Manolo has rented to the neighbors, you must pay them directly for the water that you use. Also, you must replace any article of furniture or utensil which you break or lose, and you must provide your own fuel for the stoves. Do not destroy much or have immoral parties, for then Manolo can evict you at the end of any month. Otherwise I suppose that you can stay forever, since who else but crazy extranjeros would live in such a tumba? Remember when you go to live there to bring light bulbs."

Mari and I sat in the front seat with the gear shift and hand brake between us. Yaya sat on the occasional seats in the rear, her feet on one, her fanny on the other, her head and shoulders crammed against the roof. She was pleased and elated at having had the chance to drive a sharp bargain and help us out at the same time. To make the most of her effort she kept calling our attention to the advantages to be found in living in such a fine house, which she had referred to as a tomb only a moment before.

"Solid as the church," she said. "You will not be troubled by thieves or high winds. Look how close you are to the sea and the beach. Or, in the summer when you are warm you can bathe in the pozo." (This was the big round irrigation reservoir in front of the house.) "And it is only a pleasant walk to the pueblo," she said, "where my brother Lorenzo will always receive you, and will see to it that you are given the best treatment by the local merchants. The market is in the central plaza, and it is open every morning. Wednesdays and Saturdays you can go to the cinema in the Café Miramar. I will come to visit you often because this is my pueblo and I know everyone."

Mari had not yet said anything. She doesn't talk much. "What do you think, baby?" Yaya said. "Look, he has given you a house."

"Perhaps we will live there," Mari said, staring through the windshield. "And perhaps it will be pleasant, as it was in the villa on the coast last summer." Then without warning she started to cry, silently and briefly. We were passing through Badalona on the outskirts of the city, and the locals were whistling and shaking limp hands of astonishment after the car, because of the long fenders and the noise of the exhaust. All three of us sat disconcerted by the tears; then Yaya flung her arm around Mari's neck and squeezed, Mari mopped her eyes with the heel of her hand, and it was over as quickly as it had begun. "Poor baby," Yaya said, understanding more than I did. "She has never had a home."

She never talked much. At least she always avoided explaining how she felt about things. I used to think she was fatalistic, or tried to be. She pretended indifference to what happened to her, often commenting that worse things had happened to her in the past. Her one boast that I can think of was that she always conformed to her life. This is an awkward way to put it, but that was the phrase she used, and she meant it to convey that life was bound to visit on her whatever calamity or felicity it had a mind to, no matter what she did, so her best defense was simply to accept and not complain. I don't know whether she deserves much credit for this or not, since that is what everybody does anyway in the long run, but she made a big point of it. Even in small matters she would come out with this phrase, as when she asked once for a new jacket and I said No, she stuck her lip out, shrugged, and said: "Yo me conformo."

By the same token she had never told me much about her past life, beyond a hint or two that it had all been one continuous catastrophe. Everybody thinks that about his life. But she seemed to feel it was not a very interesting story, just sort of monotonous, one loss or misfortune or vicissitude after another. Considering that most of the women an adventurous young man chances to meet have unvaryingly heart-wrenching tales of woe and injustice to tell, hers was a refreshing attitude.

I daresay I would never have learned much about the first twenty-odd years of her life had it not been for the long empty days we spent in Barcelona that month of November waiting for the grano to burst. We spent day after day just sitting around cafés in between visits to the doctor or the Yaya or Manuel, and we soon exhausted our conversation. For hours we would just sit quiet, commenting acidly on the faces and figures of the people who passed by. I happened to ask her one day how she had got the long scar on her right forearm.

"I fell off a trapeze," she said.

"Oh yes. Seguro. Claro. That is how I got all my scars also."

"It was not very high," she said.

"Are you speaking seriously?" I said. "What were you doing on a trapeze?"

"What does one do on a trapeze, Sardine? I was swinging."

You seldom learn anything important about anybody until they are ready to tell you. It appears she had once been a high-wire and trapeze artist with a shoestring traveling circus, or carnival, that played the Atlantic coast of Spain between the Portuguese frontier and Irún. "This is very interesting after so long a time," I remarked with great irony. "You should tell me these things, because it would never occur to me to ask. Must I ask if you have ever tamed lions or submerged in a bathysphere, or will you tell me of your own accord? Why have you never mentioned this before?"

"I never thought of it," she said. But a certain enthusiasm had come into her expression, and before long she was telling me all about those days with the carnival or circus or whatever. "I was a servant in the house of a rich doctor in Oviedo," she said. "I was fifteen. You must imagine: I had not yet become a woman, just a little child, but the son of the house would not let me alone. He followed me everywhere, and I said to him: 'Señorito, for the love of God, don't press me, leave me in peace; I am no good to you.' But he came after me each time I went into a closet. When his mother was present he was always very courteous and fino, since I was only a serving girl; but then he would lurk and wait for me when I came to make the beds; he would touch me in the front, here, to see if I was awakened, when I did not yet have breasts. Always coming up behind me when I did not suspect, and giving me great frights in the dark. He pinched and clutched like a very baboon, that little goat of a very fine family; and I could not slap him because he was the son of the master of the house. Naturally I locked my door at night, but then his father gave him a second key when he learned of his son's desires. A very gentle man, too, this important doctor; he gave his son a key to my room and said: 'Ha! ha! hijo mío, at least she can not become embarazada.' "

"Embarrassed seems a small word," I said.

"It is a way of saying pregnant. You see, it would have been a disgrace for a serving girl to be made pregnant by the son of an important house. But of course that could not happen to me, so the father thought that it would be excellent experience for his son. They are very fine, these rich ones."

"So he was the first," I said with a queer pang.

"Qué va, the first," she said. "When he entered my room I was washing myself, and I beat him over the head eleven times with the basin so that he fell down, and then I sat on his stomach and broke his front teeth with the heel of a shoe. Because, you see, I was harta, fed up to the top of the head. Afterward it was necessary for me to leave, or else they would put me in jail. I went down by the balcony, climbing by way of the shutters, and went to Santander to look for my aunt. I did not have any clothing, only the dress that I wore and a single pair of shoes, and I had no money at all."

Thinking back on the fifteen-year-old girl she had been, she grinned. "I remember I walked all the way to Santander carrying a piece of iron which I meant to use as a club against whoever approached me, excepting very old women: them I asked for bread. But it was a very bad time in Spain and no one had anything to give. Very often I walked for three days with nothing in my stomach. When possible I milked goats along the road, and once I ate several green figs and made myself sick. At Ribadesella, on the coast road, I met some gypsies, in the very early dawn. They gave me two small potatoes and half the leg of a rabbit and three matches, and then they stole my shoes. Therefore barefooted, I climbed down the rocks to the sea and built a small fire to cook the rabbit and the potatoes. This was the only full meal I ate between Oviedo and Santander.

"When I came to the city it was a ruin and there were very few houses standing, and the place where my aunt's house had been was a field. The people stood in the street with their children and sorry mules watching Don Bellorio and his dancing dogs in the field where my aunt's house had been. The dogs rose on their hind legs and shuffled in a circle, and when they fell forward Don Bellorio struck them with his cane. In the show was also a hand organ and a man who ate fire and puffed flame between his teeth. Don Bellorio had one ornate wagon but no horse to draw it, and there was a tight wire apparatus made of steel, but no one to walk on it; and his tent had long ago been taken away by the government, which had need of the tarpaulin material. After the spectacle the fire-eater carried his cap through the crowd, but everyone turned away from him ashamed, because they had nothing to donate. Poor people, they could not resist watching, there was so little amusement in their lives; and having watched, they felt an obligation to pay something, but none of them had anything at all to spare, and the fire-eater cursed them. But not very hard, for many of them were Vascos, who are dangerous people to maldecir.

"Everyone went away and when it became dark Don Bellorio built a fire and he and the fire-eater and the dogs sat down to cook. They had only a handful of rice and a few spoiled shrimp with which to make a small paella. It was very cold. When they seemed at ease and comfortable I crept to them and asked permission to warm myself by the fire. Of course, when they heard I had no home and could not find my aunt, who had earlier lived in a large house on that very same field, they were forced to offer me something to eat. 'Assuredly your aunt is dead,' the fire-eater said. 'Everyone is dead now.' I began to cry, and they gave me a pair of shoes and a red cap—both had belonged to a bailarina who had once danced with the dogs. She was the wife of Don Bellorio. 'Dolores has gone to Caracas,' he said. Many times in the months that followed I heard him murmur these same words, as though musing. I think he liked the sound of them, long after he had forgotten his Dolores and the reason why she left him. Caracas is in Venezuela in South America."

"Invariably," I said.

"After we had eaten the small paella I had an idea, and I said to them that I would walk on the tight wire and become a part of the spectacle, if they would allow me to live with them. They laughed at me, because they did not believe I could do any such thing, and in any case my feet, without shoes from Ribadesella to Santander, were swollen and bleeding. But I swore to them that I had learned wire walking in France during the war, and that my feet would heal in a day or two, now that they had so kindly given me shoes to wear; and I added that I would cook and launder for them, and help with the dogs and the costumes, and would even try to pull the wagon in place of a horse, if only they would keep me. Then the fire-eater said slyly: 'Wouldst comfort and warm our blankets in the night, renacuajo, and cushion us from the bare bone of earth with the flesh on thee?' He was mocking my small size and thinness and my earnestness; he was a common sort of man. I remember that I drew myself up before him and looked at him with contempt. Dios, still I remember with what pomposity and assurance! And I said: 'Señor! I will do what is asked of me, but I will not soil my honor. Besides, I have not yet begun to menstruate.' At that they laughed very hard, and Don Bellorio, who was a thoughtful, even a bitter man, though very kind, said: 'Madonna, a girl alone on this feudal earth has no honor subsequent to the first attempt upon it. Too soon thou wilt see that woman's honor only exists where there are husbands, fathers, and brothers to believe in it, nor does it survive beyond the charmed circle of their defense thereof. Sit thee down, and never again pose so before any man.' "

Up to this point we had been sitting quietly near the corner window in the Bar Alhambra on the Ramblas, and nobody had bothered us. A nice thing about Europe is that you can sit forever over one cup of coffee or one drink if you want, and the waiters never even scowl at you. This particular afternoon, however, the city was full of American sailors of the Mediterranean Fleet, and the tables were crowded with them and the usual percentage of them were half stoned and saying needlessly revolting things in loud voices, confident that nobody could understand them, or maybe not caring if anybody did. So we decided to leave, and got in the car to take a ride. I noted that somebody had written Yankee Go Home in the dust on the hood—probably one of the swab jockies.

We drove up through the park to the top of Montjuich, the mountain that overlooks the city, and parked on the ocean side to look out over the harbor. By this time Mari had clammed up again, as though she had only got to talking the first time by accident. "Oh it is nothing," she said. "Only stories. Long ago and boring." But I wanted to hear; rather, felt compelled to hear it all. I still felt the small queer pang of what must have been jealousy, and I was convinced I was going to hear a lot I wouldn't like.

"Finish telling about the circus," I said. "Was Don Bellorio your first lover?"

"Shut up, you Salmonete," she said. "Don Bellorio was an old man who had lost his wife, and the fire-eater was a thick-headed ugly fool. Besides, there was no spirit for that kind of thing amongst us. Seldom did we have enough to eat, and always it was cold, and we were weary. During the first winter I lived with them all the money that we earned was saved to buy a horse to pull the wagon. It was a bad time, and no one paid anything after the show. Don Bellorio sometimes had work in the office of the alcalde of Santander, copying out documents, for he had a very fine hand and there were no typewriters available to do the vast work of restoring the archives. The fire-eater, whose name was Agustín Zubiaurre de la Hojaldre, earned a little money treating the diseases of cattle, for he was a veterinary as well as a smith and a mechanic —a highly accomplished man for all that he had no culture and could not read or write his name, and who, according to this name, was born to a puff pastry rather than to a woman. It was Agustín who taught me to walk the tight rope and later to swing from the trapeze. I had told the truth, I had learned to walk in France when I was a child, but on a rope never higher than two palms from the floor. Even so I knew the way to walk on the balls of my feet and turn my toes, and I was not afraid. Agustín had walked high wire and had been a famous aerial artist known throughout all Spain and part of France before the war, but then he fell and broke both his legs, and when he was healed he found that he did not dare any more. He was seized by fear. But he knew how to teach me. When I fell he would say: 'Carallo! so thou wilt fall and dash thy brains and become a trembling husk like me, aha! If Jesus sees that thou art afraid He will throw thee down so hard thou wilt forever limp and shamble and whine in the image of His priests, carallo! Never let him see thee afraid!' "

Mari said: "These are the two lessons that I learnt from my starveling circus: one, that I must never posture or pretend before any man; two, that I must never allow God to know when I am afraid."

"They are very good rules," I said, "but backward. It is God Whom you must approach with naked soul, and men whom you must addle with deception and dissimulation. To appear before men naked and before God with hypocrisy, as in your system, leaves you open to assault on the one hand and eternal damnation on the other."

"No," she said. "I have thought more about this than you who have no code. God for me is not deity but only the doom, the nature, the force, that tears the weak ones to pieces. It is necessary to put up a brave appearance of scorn and imperviousness, so that devastation will not mistake one for a conductor through which to strike at earth, as lightning does."

"Ole," I said, impressed.

"As for the other, you know that to women is sometimes given a single compensation for their lives—although it is ordinarily brief and partial and painful—and that is the love of a man. In it are all good things, to greater or lesser degree: protection and merit, home, babies, physical pleasure, and respite from loneliness. Even if the man is a good one who goes away, or a bad one who will not, still love is better than nothing, and even pain is the pain of worthiness. So I believe that when I am sought I must respond not with pretense and pose, but with a naked body and a guileless spirit, as an earnest that I will not play false to my life, and also as a gift to the man if he will love me."

Jealousy is a very complicated as well as a very common feeling, a universal sort of gnaw. Unwarranted and unjustified as often as not. I was left entirely out of her philosophy of love. Any male will understand how I felt: mean and spiteful and contemptuous. To my resounding discredit I did not stop to think what she meant. "Slobber," I said. "Mawk. Schmaltz." All the things I didn't know how to say in Spanish. "I hope," I said bitterly, "that you have had great success in this offering of the naked body to these good men who have gone away. You will permit me to say, permit me to . . ." But what is there to say to a woman who has had other men ahead of you, especially when it is a woman you don't love, don't want to love, and from whom you don't expect or want love in return? It was none of my business in the first place. I mean, why should I feel cuckolded, of all things?

She was offended and then irritated. We sat in unbending silence. I ran my fingers around and around the rim of the steering wheel and muttered nastily in English, while she sat with her hands folded sulkily in her lap. It had grown dark. The Sixth Fleet battleships and destroyers on the sea outside the breakwater were no more than patterns of lights. After a while she said: "I only told you as a friend, when you asked me questions. You know that I have nothing to tell you when you do not ask."

"I do not want to know your secrets," I said bitterly.

"I have no secrets. It makes no difference to me whether you know or not. I did not ask to tell you anything. I will never tell you anything again! One cannot talk to you!"

"Hah," I said. "What happened to your guileless spirit?"

"I have many things to tell you," she shouted. "Many things that would not interest you, but also many things that would make you angry. And also many things that would give you pleasure to hear. But I will tell you nothing!"

"What are the things I would like to hear?" I asked, swallowing the bait.

"Nada! I will never tell you even one. I do not have to tell you anything. What have you told me, that I must explain myself to you? What rights have you over me? What right have you to ask if I submitted to the son of the doctor or if I was the lover of Don Bellorio? You ask if I have shown my body to men and you ask who was my first lover and you would like very much to know these things, but I will tell you nothing! Because long before, when we knew each other, you said that it did not matter to you who was the first so long as you were the last. You remember that, Macarrón?"

"Hah," I said for lack of something better. I never remembered saying any such thing.

She stuck to it; she refused to tell me anything more. In fact, wouldn't talk at all. So I bided my time, figuring she would get over it and talk some more when she was ready, the barriers being down now, so to speak. I believed her when she said she hadn't mentioned her past adventures before because she hadn't thought to. The present and its possibilities interested her far more than events long gone and half forgotten. Besides, she never had the easy access to her memories that some people do. But having once talked about herself she would talk some more. Even these laconic ones are hard to stop when they get going on their memories. One thing reminds them of another; they start talking about themselves and then they get interested in their subject, as is only natural. However, nothing more was to be got out of her at that particular moment, so we went on down the mountain and picked up the dog, which we had left with long-suffering Yaya, then went to eat.

It was about nine. I parked the car for the night and we went to the Casa Gallega, a tranquil undecorated bar in the calle San Pablo, run by a keg-of-beer who comes from the same province in

Galicia as Mari. They never knew each other there, but exiles are friends everywhere and love to get together and curse the place they are in. Though he didn't ordinarily serve food, Jorge would always get his wife to fix us something in the kitchen; then while we ate he usually sat with us and drank beer. His wife, Aparición, was Gallega too, and was pleased to feed us, since she could not only fix genuine Gallego platters for Mari, but genuine American dishes for me, too, because she had once been cook for an American family in Cuba. I used to wonder how those Americans ate, when she proudly served me boiled potatoes and soft-boiled eggs and fried fish all in the same bowl; but then I remembered that, to Spaniards, an American is anybody who lives somewhere between Tierra del Fuego and the arctic circle. The people I mean when I say Americans, people of the United States, are Estadounidenses. Those people she cooked for might have been Patagonians. Anyway, I never destroyed her conviction that fried artichokes and spaghetti were what my homesick stomach hungered for.

Jorge did all the talking while we ate, telling us about a sky-blue horse he had seen once in Estremadura, all the while sluicing down beer and whacking me between the shoulder blades when he made a particularly telling point. When he went out to the bar to wait on a customer, I made an effort to lighten the mood between Mari and me. I said: "Very good food. You should try to eat some."

"No," she said, flat as a flounder. I considered my peace offer made and rejected and so retired into my shell. I was not in a very friendly mood myself.

After our meal, while our dog ate its full out of the garbage pail, Jorge and I played dominoes in the bar and Mari went to the kitchen to chat with the wife—and probably filled her with tales of what a brute I was. Jorge made me drink a glass of a kind of Gallego aguardiente called orujo, which had a clean weightless bite and soon made my ears turn red and my upper lip sweat. "You like that!" he said. "After we have made the wine, of the first grapes, we crush the skins and seeds of the grape and make this orujo. In my country a man who takes a little of this after his breakfast will feel warm all day as he works in the field."

The domino game wore on till Jorge's score was ridiculously higher than mine and I had drunk about four copas of this stuff. Finally I went into the kitchen and got Mari and we left. I could tell she felt a little better for having unburdened herself into a sympathetic feminine ear, because when I bragged about the aguardiente I had been able to swallow, and recommended it to anybody who wanted to keep warm all day in the field, she offered to black one of my eyes, and she called me Merluzo.

One way or another, white fire or what have you, I had succeeded in pushing that afternoon's injured pride or jealousy back into the locker where I keep my conscience and other gear. On our way toward the Paraíso I sang and hummed, and then decided we ought to stop off for a nightcap somewhere. Mari didn't want to but I insisted. We went to a place called El Prócer, and I seemed to be the only male there, except the barman; the rest were women in dark dresses and gaudy make-up. "Have you got any of this stuff?" I said and breathed in the barman's face.

"What wants el Señor Gringo?" the barman asked. "A kiss? Or a copa of foul breath?"

Mari explained to me that the orujo was made by a secret process known only to Gallegos, and that Jorge got his personal supply from a friend in Villapedre. "Very well," I said. "But why does he call me gringo? He is no more Mexican than I am."

"Il est un poseur," Mari said. "Come, sit down. Drink dry anis, it is almost the same."

"Dry anis," I said. "In handy tablet form, I presume? Or instant?"

She would drink only coffee. We sat at a tiny table with a marble top and watched the multicolored play of light on a large jukebox, the only one I'd seen in Europe outside Germany. Except that the coin slot had been modified to accept rubias, which are peseta coins, it was just as it had come from the Wurlitzer factory, records and all. "I will play a fine old native American chant," I said.

"*You nothin' but a Hooouuuun' dog,*" the machine said.

"Perhaps I should explain," I said, "that this type of native ballad is called Oscilar y Ondular, although that may not be an adequate trans—"

"Drink and let us go; I do not like this place," Mari said. She drank her coffee in two swallows.

"Because you did not drink orujo you do not like this place," I said, although I knew perfectly well why she wanted to leave. The bar was one of those where the independents foregather to sit all night over coffee and be available. A whorehouse anteroom, so to speak. It is a practical arrangement, saving men shoe leather and the embarrassment of misdirected importunities on the public walks. The reason there were so many girls in El Prócer (the name means great man or hero) and other bars like it, was a recent police edict shutting down all the hitherto licensed houses, thus throwing thousands of indoor girls out on the streets to compete with nonaffiliateds. That night there must have been thirty or forty girls jammed up at the bar, packed around the walls, seated ten or twelve to each tiny table. So I pretended just then to notice them and leered appraisingly from one to another, simply to be irritating. The whores sat in listless graceful attitudes under my scrutiny. Mari propped her chin on interlaced fingers and stared at a point in space, as any honest woman ought to do in such a situation. I said: "Aha! Dirty women! Vice! Joy! Le clapoir! Fleshpots!" (Ollas de carne is what I said, pots of meat, which is meaningless in Spanish.)

"Will you leave now, Sardine?"

I said: "But you note how sullen, how bored are these pigeons. It is because they sit indoors all day and get no sun and fresh air. In my country it is different. There too it is the custom for las putas to appear enervated and bored, but it is only a convention. It is agreed upon that they be languid and cynical, but in reality they are healthy and happy girls who take long bird-watching walks and ride polo ponies for exercise of the lumbar vertebrae. In these days the women of my country all learn to behave by watching the sirens of the cinema, and it is increasingly difficult to tell one kind of whore from another."

"Borracho," Mari said and stared into her coffee cup and drummed her fingers on the table. I called her attention to a smiling veteran with three gold teeth and a fan-shaped henna hairdo, but she would not look. "Indeed," I said, "there is much woman. See what weight, what solidity, what body, like a fine Italian cheese. Or, by way of contrast, beside her is seated a fainting gazelle, a tiny bird-boned innocent witch, with eyes like chestnuts."

"We will settle these accounts in the bed."

"Meat. Steaming seductive meat. Lascivious, provocative, naïve, masochistic, gay, ethereal, sweet, mercenary meat. A meat for every taste. Pero vaya, there is none so beautiful as you, my little guileless grapeskin," I said with puling erotic airs.

Mari giggled. "You are drunk. I am going home."

"Sit down. Your home is where I am. I tell you, we will sit here all night watching the merchandising of the meat, unless you agree to my conditions."

She was looking at me again, and grinning. "That you be friendly," I said. "That we resume relations. You are angry with me, which is tiresome. In fact, I will not support it. You must return to normal, and be my fire and my food and my bed, or I will swell up your eye."

"Borracho. You are only friendly when you are drunk. I would have you drunk all the time. I agree to the conditions."

"Good. But I am not drunk. Wrong word. Illuminated. In English we say a 'glow,' an 'incandescencia.'"

"That is something else—that you are burning."

"As you will discover," I said.

The dog had gone to sleep, strangled in its chain, beneath the table. We woke it and paid and took leave of El Prócer just as the hennaed veteran said something raucous to the chestnut-eyed gazelle about the probable dimensions of my private parts. The painted panel swung shut on their brassy laughter. In the street a damp wind blew and the lights of the houses looked remote and late, like four o'clock in the morning. We ran, almost gamboled, holding hands, with the dog threshing at our heels; and tall twin guardias observed us inscrutably from the archway of Cuartel Numero Cinco. Deeper in the barrio, close to our hotel, more whores wandered in their masks of paint and kohl. A group of men, carters or sweepers or stevedores, wearing corduroy trousers and felt slippers, each with a black beret on his head, linked arms and straggled toward home, singing fragments of ribald songs. "Good night, good night," we said. They shouted: "Arrib' España! Viv' el Tio Paco!"

"Now they rush home to beat their wives and fall contentedly asleep," Mari said.

"A good wife will not mind."

"You will not mind if I beat you," she said, falling behind to kick me painfully in the calves of the legs and swat with her purse. "Because you looked so hard at the girls."

"That was part of the conditions," I said, "that I beat you because we are friends again."

"I will beat you for looking at the putas," she said and hit me in the solar plexus.

I held her arms. "You are my bawd, my trull," I said. "My artful hoyden and my slut and my houri, as well as my giglet and my strumpet."

She stamped on my toes, since I held her arms. "Name me in Spanish, Lujurioso." And then she said: "All the same, I think you will beat me tonight."

"It is a certainty. I have been contemplating it all day," I said. The dog, excited by our fooling around, had jerked loose and run away down the street, clamoring up at the windows and at the cats and drunks that crept in the shadows. "What a pity," I said. "We have lost our dog. Quick, down this street, before he sees us."

It was no use though; the dog knew as well as we did how to find the hotel. We had no more arrived at the door than he was biting the heels of our shoes. Loiterers of both sexes in the entrance to the Bar Brasileño threw little paper firecrackers at us and asked loudly what part the dog played in our amours. We did not take offense. Few people ever came to the Paraíso just to sleep; most did not stay long enough to take even a catnap; and the habitués of the Brasileño had a custom of commenting on the couples that came and went in the late evening, sometimes even placing small bets on how long it would take. As a matter of fact, Mari and I and the dog were well known to the regulars in the bar, probably objects of mild curiosity. And though they undoubtedly believed Mari to be one of the local working girls, at least they credited us with constancy and a kind of respectability, because every night we came home at approximately the same hour, usually sober, and always together, an odd little family.

However, entering the Paraíso was always a bit rough on Mari's remnants of rigid Catholic morality and on my Anglo-Saxon-Episcopal hypocrisy as well (it doesn't matter what you do in New England so long as nobody knows) and neither of us enjoyed running the gauntlet of sniggers in the street, or stepping aside on the stairs for descending whores and their crapulous clients, then climbing up into the stink that so excited our dog, into the lobby where little old ladies ghosted by, carrying sheets and towels while the house girls lounged around in the corridor with their hands on their hips and their feet hurting them. The saint-faced Celso, night clerk and bouncer, always greeted us faintly and affectionately, asking politely how we had spent our day, wanting to know if we and all our friends were well, and had we heard the latest about the olive-oil riots. Very friendly, but holding us up when all we wanted was to get inside our room and lock ourselves away.

This particular night, however, we both felt good and not embarrassed in the least. We greeted everybody we knew and felt young and genial in our own innocent world, like all young married couples who are just getting over the effects of an argument. People standing around grinned at us and patted the dog, which snarled. "How do you sweat?" I asked the whores. An ancient Egyptian salutation. The dog bayed ringingly at a bashful old man coming out of one of the rooms. Celso led us up the hall to our room. He had the only key; the doors only key-locked from the outside, though there was a bolt inside each one. We went in and turned on the lights and I gave the clerk his tip and he smiled fondly, ethereally, and shut the door on his way out. We were home.

El Paraíso makes no pretensions, does not even try to live up to its name. The room was about twelve feet square with one barred window and a tile floor. The bathroom had a shower and a bidet and laundry-frazzled towels. The bed had a wooden shelf on either side of it, and there was a dial for selecting the color of light to suit your mood. No other furniture, not even a stool. No closet, no rugs or shades or curtains or pictures. The bed constituted the only amenity there was, and the paradise, too, presumably.

Mari came up to me and kissed my neck and gouged in the token layer of flesh over my short ribs and put her leg between my knees. "Lecher. Shall I take a shower?" she asked.

I ought to explain that I had got Mari into the habit of taking a shower first not because I considered her dirty—she is actually a lot tidier and more hygienic than I am—but simply because I had recently discovered a pleasure very stimulating and at the same time profoundly interesting to the spirit—if that's not too obscure —in the kind of nakedness we brought to bed when we were both soaped and rinsed and still moist from the hot water, like a couple of steamed clams. It might be argued that this was just a mild form of erotic refinement, like black silk stockings or mirrors hung on the ceiling. But it was really nothing discreditable, I think—

only an elusive pleasure equivalent to, or at least akin to, the fine feeling you get sliding into fresh sheets on Monday night, that makes you squinch your cheeks and grin.

Not that the libidinous element didn't enter into it. Long ago we had discovered that both of us possessed big healthy appetites, easily and sometimes inconveniently aroused. As I have said elsewhere, we always went to bed early, even in the city; and on several occasions went to bed in the middle of the afternoon, once even at eleven-fifteen in the morning, which I consider somewhat depraved. In addition to simple enthusiasm, we also shared a mindless experimental tendency. Once in bed we were like a couple of happy monkeys, wallowing in the inexhaustible capacity for mutual stimulation which is one of the genuine joys of youth.

That night, however, we were otherwise stimulated. We were awake most of the night, almost until morning, talking, after an unpleasant interlude that I will tell about. For Mari, as I have said, it was the excitement and interest of talking about herself, which she didn't often have either opportunity or inclination to do. For me it was like meeting somebody new and fascinating for the first time—fascinating because her story, though perhaps ordinary enough in Spain, was bizarre and foreign to me. Not only that, but it seemed that after knowing her for so long a time I was only then getting a real idea of who she was and where she had come from. She was murmuring, off and on, all the time the red light shone, but I paid no attention until at the very worst moment—which you might call the Moment of Truth—she suddenly bit me very hard on the shoulder and shrieked muffledly: "I will kill you. I hate you!" I asked what that was all about, and she said: "What you want I will give you. There is no excuse to look at the girls of the barrio. I am the same as they are. Look at me. I cost you as much."

Later we turned the room lights on and were smoking cigarettes, and I said: "Well, if you are serious then I will tell you seriously. I was teasing. I have no interest in other women. I am monogamistic. One is enough. Yo me conformo. However, let us put one question, my little light: how is it that you are allowed to be jealous of me, when all afternoon you have not spoken to me because I was enough misguided to be jealous of your other men, hah?"

We smoked in silence for some moments. She said: "Why do you think I am jealous of you, Imbécile?"

"Um," I said.

We smoked and wiggled our toes at the bottom of the bed.

"It is different," she said. "If you go with other women, I can do nothing. If you cheat me, then I can only endure and say nothing. But if I cheat you, I will be beaten and thrown out in the street."

"Um," I said.

"You are not to say 'Um' like an ox. You are to swear that you will never cheat me."

"And if I swear it, will you believe me?"

"I believe nothing you say, Trout."

"Well then."

More thoughtful moments.

"Capitán," she said, abandoning pet names for the time being and resting her head on my chest, "do you want me to tell you everything?"

"Everything what?"

"I am thinking that you do not deserve to know, and that I do not have to tell you, but perhaps I will. I felt jealous of las putas and it is not a good way to feel. You wonder about men who have slept with me, and perhaps you feel the same. So I will tell you. It might be better that you know. I could explain in a few words, but I will not. I will not explain or apologize, I will only tell it in my own way, and you will think that it is important. You will have to wait. It is as well that you suffer a little, too."

"My pleasure," I said.

"Be quiet. There is no reason that you should not suffer as everyone suffers. You are entirely despicable and without morals or honesty, and have only a dirty charm. I do not see why you should always escape penalty. Yes, I think I will make you suffer a little."

"El placer es mío," I said. "You stopped as the fire-eater was teaching you to walk the tight rope."

"You see? You are only interested in the time when I was beginning to be grown, when I was still virgin, and you wonder who was my first lover and who came after him."

"Begin wherever you want," I said.

"I will begin with my ancestors and spend one week telling the history of my name, and then relate the lives of my brothers and sisters and the view of life of the village priest, and the medical history of my uncles' cows, and then I well tell all of my childhood before I turn again to the circus. Meanwhile you will wait and suffer to hear about my lovers. You were not the first; I did not try to make you believe that you were the first."

Her voice had risen and the dog, lying on the tiles under the window, rumbled irritably like an old man in a library.

"And I said that I did not care who—"

"So long as you were the last. Why should you be the last, Machute? By what right? Do you think I will never want another man? Or will you kill me when you are finished with me? Listen, I will tell you what you are so hungry to hear—when I'm ready. But in the meantime, remember that I am an old whore who sleeps with anyone."

"Forget it," I said. "I do not want to hear about it."

"Liar. There is no man who does not want to hear about his mistress's former loves. How do you know that I will not tell you in great detail all that men have done to me, all that I have done with men—perversions and vices that will make you sick with pain and jealousy and aversion and lust—until you sprawl over me again, pig! And grunt and struggle and root! But you cannot drive *out* all the men who have been *in*!"

"I said forget it!" Both of us were shouting. I didn't know where it came from, her anger swelling up out of nothing in half a minute, leaping up savagely out of apparent good humor, attacking me that way. "I told you to forget it!" I repeated, everything seeming foggy and distant as it always does when you really lose control.

"No. No. I won't forget it. Nor will you," she said. "Cabrón, do you believe that you can restore me with love-making that goes no deeper than the skin? Can you redeem me with coition that is no more than self-abuse? *Who has made me a whore?*"

"Shut up!"

"Go to the barrio prostitutes, they will squirm also, and whimper in your ear and complete themselves five times, and you will think you are a prodigy in bed, and beautiful and kind, because you give poor whores like me money, and they give you love!"

"Shut your mouth!" I shouted frantically.

"You are not a man, you are a *baby!*"

"SHUT UP!"

"Baby! COWARD! CHEAT!"

I smacked her then, and she screamed. The people next door pounded peevishly on the wall. Our dog sat up and howled. I hadn't hit a girl since I was about nine years old. Probably if I had been able to think fast enough in Spanish, if I had had the vocabulary to curse her, shout vile things back at her, I would never have touched her, and things would have turned out differently. I'm not sadistic or even hot-tempered. I don't like violent means to any end. Therefore it comes as a shock to me to realize that having hit her once I desired eagerly to hit her again and harder.

We were lying side by side on the bed and it's hard to slap vigorously from that angle. She rolled out of bed onto the tile floor, nude as an egg. I thought she was hunting for a shoe to hit me with, so I flung myself after her and grabbed her by the hair and struck her right across the mouth as hard as I could, off balance and a little blind with fog and dizziness. Her eyes went wide and out of focus. I cursed her in English. She fell down.

There came an immense moment of peace.

"That's good enough," she murmured finally. "You don't have to hit me any more."

I sat down on the edge of the bed. "Did I hurt your neck?"

Without getting up she fingered the patch of bandage over the grano, then gingerly felt of the cut on her lip. "You did not hurt me. Not much. Enough. But do not get false ideas—I am not a woman who likes to be beaten. You must only beat me when it is absolutely necessary."

"Throw a shoe at that dog," I said. "Lie down, you bastard."

Mari drew her legs under her shakily and got up and came to sit in my lap; she patted my cheek. Still a little frightened. "Ves tú?" she said. "I can make you believe in me when I want. Now there are two ways."

I said nothing; I remember I hung my head.

"Always I could quicken you and make you live in my body. Now I can anger you enough to strike me. Neither lasts long, but it is an improvement over nothing."

I just brooded. She tugged my hair. "Pobre niño. You do not know why you want to make love so much, nor why you hate me so much you want to break my head. Do you know?"

"I only want to know why you spoke that way."

She shrugged. "Perhaps I have a plan."

"If it is true that you feel disgust for me, then we should talk about it. That is very serious."

"*I* will not explain. Clearly it is serious. But you cannot have everything explained to you. Sometimes you must make the effort to understand by yourself, even if you do not think it is worth the effort. First you must wonder why. Then perhaps you will understand something."

I thought she was just being difficult; when I shook my head she sighed in despair. "Poor baby. It is no use. Well, I will tell you my life story. In a few minutes—if my lip does not swell up so that I cannot talk. First I will tell you two secrets. The first is that you make love to me with great frequency because I am very beautiful. I fill you with desire because I am a salacious grapeskin and I sit on your knees when we are naked. Moreover, I have the supple body and clever musculature of an athlete, which I am because I walked the high wire, and that is excellent training for the thighs."

"Good. What is the second secret?"

"The second secret everyone knows. It is that all emotions are the same, and can be interchanged one with another. That is, if you have an embarrassment or a grief it can easily be changed into anger. Just as anger modulates often into shame, or perhaps vindictiveness. If you have a fear, or a great sadness, or an ache of loneliness, you can make it turn into longing and passion. For passion has a cure."

Three

UNDER THE WINDOW the castanets made rapid cynical sounds.

There is another Spain that takes up space between the peaks of the Pyrenees and the African waters of the Gibraltar straits, a Spain that no foreigner ever gets, or wants, more than a peek into, a Spain that la prensa seldom mentions because nothing happens there. It almost seems that nothing of importance has happened there since the opening of the New World. Even the recent civil war exploded in this place like a bomb in the Sahara, immediate noise and smoke and damage but thereafter only a little local rubble and nothing changed. The farmers are still farming where they can find sufficient soil and water. The Murcians are still cutting esparto grass and the Asturians are still mining coal. Anywhere off of King Alfonso's highways, along which he used to roar in his Bugatti, transportation still moves on four feet or two. The French close their borders to Spanish trade, the U.S. sinks five hundred million dollars into the Franco economy, but in Almodóvar del Campo old Juan Fulano goes on feeding his pigs and bartering for vegetables with José de Tal, or getting into knife fights with him or going out with him in the sierra to hunt. Clowns from the Evanston, Ill., area, wearing sun glasses and traveling on foundation money, come and go, interviewing officials and taking notes for big books about The Surviving Axis Partner; meanwhile Albacete presses olives by hand and Porcuña herds goats on the hillsides and Esposende fishes for cangrejos from boats at least fifty years old.

The tourist can get a look into this feudal world if he wants, but the truth is that it is very sad and uninteresting. All that the word Spain conjures up, from bullfights to cantharides agreements, is concentrated in the dozen large cities. I will go further: the capital cities and the areas right around them *are* Spain, not only to foreigners but to a great extent to the Spanish themsleves. The spaces between the cities are nothing more than empty dry ghostlands, stony mountains and treeless plains, where a few ill-dressed and unintelligible shades plod through burning or freezing days of inland weather, sunk in apathy and the barbarous remnants of Iberian, Moorish, Roman, Celtic, or Arabic cultures.

I think I know as much about Spain, in these terms, as any foreigner with my temperament and my problems can learn in a relatively short time. But all I know is Spain, not the Iberian peninsula. By that I mean I know city Spaniards; I like them, and they like me. I have a feeling for their lives and problems. I've heard flamenco singing and cante jondo and I have visited gypsy caves. I've seen a few bullfights. I've argued politics with the gentry in their own cafés. I've lived like a Spaniard. Holy Week, Escorial, wine skins, Franco jokes; pastas, tapas and paellas; hidalgos and archdukes; motor scooters, beachwear, police brutality, business; whores, damas and dueñas—nothing much catches me unawares. I don't mean I am so perfectly acclimatized that anybody would mistake me for a Catalán, but only that if there's something I've never seen or heard about, I can accept it without thinking, like a tourist, that it's either picturesque or revolting. Nor have I seen only the presentable side of Spanish life—not after a couple of months in Barrio Chino. But all this is the city culture, the city-Spain. Which means everything you see or hear or read about that's Spanish. So what's left to fill up this connecting tissue of weather-brazened wilderness between Gerona and Cádiz, Cartagena and La Coruña? Practically nothing.

The best illustration of this point that I can think of is a story I heard. It was in the papers but I didn't read it myself, only heard talk about it, so I don't have all the details and don't even know if it's true, but it illustrates what I mean. It seems that somewhere in the lunar mountains of Castile, directly west of Cáceres and near the Portuguese frontier, in the area between the Río Tajo and the Madrid-Badajoz highway, they found a town. The country there is very wild and desolate, with only two other towns thereabouts besides Cáceres, and the maps show only a couple of roads and the highway; the rest is footpaths. This town was not exactly lost, only nobody had gone into it or out of it for the last hundred and thirty years, except a few priests. The people spoke a dialect no outsider could understand; they had only vaguely and incredulously heard of the war, movies, newspapers, the internal-combustion engine.

This self-sufficient little town raised vegetables and livestock, made clothes out of leather and shoes out of wood—the people never knew they needed anything that couldn't be grown, made, or hunted. The houses were of stone or mud and logs. Women working in their earth kitchens sang songs from the early Christian era. The men stomped around in their wooden shoes almost as speechless as their animals, big and black as Indians and juiceless as their precipitous pastures. They were all farmers and herders, except for two woodcutters and a smith. No tradesmen, no stores in the town, money almost unheard of. No cafés, no theatres, no banks. The only entertainment was a yearly religious festival—incoherent and stumbling and half in Latin, which nobody understood—a ritual or mystery practically pagan in its distortions. No books, no radios, no transportation except burros. Just a score of tumbling calcified houses, as unfurnished inside as they were out. By the time the town was rediscovered, if that is the word, there was a large proportion of idiots in the population on account of the inbreeding—something like a rousing forty-seven per cent, I believe. The other fifty-three villagers (roughly speaking there were a hundred inhabitants all told) would have to be classified as morons. The village itself—inhabited by these morons who probably would not believe there was enough water in the world to fill a sea—this village was named Barco de Guerra. Ship of War. Who can figure that?

Reaction to the discovery of this cloister was significant, too. The general public acted blasé, as though the find wasn't particularly newsworthy: probably hundreds of similar towns were isolated out there in the sierra, so what? And the government, far from setting its little head to the problem or reintegrating Warship with Spanish society, merely tackled the problem of how to go about taxing a people who had never heard of money.

I don't know exactly what I meant to prove by this story, now I have told it, except to show how little I know, how little anybody can know, about this enormous abandoned underworld, or overworld, that exists inside Spain's borders without being part of it. I was actually talking about Mari: she comes out of this feudal wilderness and has roots in it. But there is more to it than that. Let us reduce the thing to a proportion: Spain is to the rest of the world as Warship is to cosmopolitan Madrid, for example. And on another level, Warship is to Madrid as everything outside the cities is to everything in them. The whole rural world is just as lost and gone, removed from the stream of time, as that sad sunset pueblo of imbecile androids in the barren mountains.

Mari comes from the country and though quite developed by now, she is a child of that same prolific international race of submen and subwomen who grub in the ground all over the impoverished globe. Peasants, for want of a better word. They are the same everywhere and have more racial characteristics and rituals in common with each other than they have with the natives of the countries they happen to live in. No matter where they live, the main fact of their existence is that they bend over and dig in the ground. They are lower than the lower classes. They are slaves. They have faces like hairy walnuts, and piggish lackluster eyes. They don't know anything, nor do they know that there's anything they don't know. They have no escape, so they just bend over and dig in the ground. Because that's all they know how to do. And they beget series of doomed children on their cretinous wives because orgasm is the only unqualified pleasure in their lives.

If this sounds exaggerated, forget for a moment the Farmall-Cooperative-Combine-Subsidised agriculture which we and a few other hard-money countries rejoice in, and imagine how it is out in the vast spaces where there is scarcely any communication between towns, where there is no electricity, no gas, no motors, few steel tools, and almost no roads except animal tracks which are arroyos of dust and rocks in summer and knee-deep puddings in winter. Where half the time the farmer doesn't own the land he works on; where even if he does own it he probably lives in a medieval compound with two score other families and has to walk eight miles every morning to get to his holdings; or where if he does own a farmhouse on his own land it is no more than a stone tomb in which he lives on the second floor, his hogs and chickens and mules living in the apartment below, so they won't freeze in winter or be stolen in summer. Farming is tough when you hack most of your tools out of trees felled in the hills. Butchering is different, too, when you throw absolutely nothing away except the teeth and hooves, because even the entrails have to be worked into sausage with the blood and eyeballs, and even the bones have to be pulverized—by hand—to make fertilizer. Get up every morning at four in a stone room and spend all day digging out roots that are frozen into the ground, or ploughing with a wooden ploughshare through patches of sandstone and gravel, and then have the government people arrive to strip away thirty per cent of the crop in levy the same day it comes in, the same day the two remaining porkers vomit blue and die of erysipelas or something—and you, too, would end up some kind of mumbling imbecile if you lasted long enough.

Anyway, this pall of gloom and primeval rigor lies everywhere just beyond the feeble glow of white modern light shed by the cities; and it explains why Mari's story does not sound conspicuously Spanish in the telling: no guitars, no brave toreadors, no crenelated castles in it; no flamenco dancers, marquesas, or grandees; no serenatas on moony balconies with Castilian roses. She still knows next to nothing about frontón, about the Prado, the Inquisition, Blasco Ibáñez, Picasso, or El Greco. The only two characters in her mythology seem to be Quijote and Don Juan Tenorio, the Mocker of Sevilla. Sounds incredible, considering she was not only educated by the nuns, who subject their charges to an appalling scholastic discipline, but is intelligent and imaginative in her own right. The fact remains that she knows practically nothing except about her own life, which is perhaps enough.

That night (it began to rain about one, a few gusty drops, only enough to drive the celebrants in the street back into the Bar Brasileño, where they kept up the same noise but not so loud) we lay under the sheet and one blanket, and she did as she had threatened to do: told me the whole history of her family, or as much of it as she had heard. I remember nothing of it except that her mother's family was supposed to have come from Paraguay, or had gone back to it. She had no relatives in Spain from that side of the family. "My mother died when I was born," she said. "I did not know her. I have been shown pictures of her and she was extremely beautiful in the style of the time. You would not consider her beautiful because you do not like big women. She weighed seventy-two kilos. Notwithstanding, she died of tuberculosis. My uncles swore that she was very beautiful and either one of them would have married her if she had not accepted my father first. Once my Uncle Carlos tried to pretend that he had slept with my mother, but my father knocked him down. So did my Uncle Rafael. It was a silly lie."

This was in a place called Fuentevinho along the river Miño in Galicia. Hardly a town, more a hard dry outcropping of brown houses on either side of a rutted road. One of those agricultural compounds where farmers live together for protection and convenience and travel out at daybreak to their fields. In addition to the houses and the smithy there was a church, a one-room café, and a public fountain, built over the grape-vine-covered well which gave the town its name. The nearest city was Lugo, sixty kilometers away. No one ever came from Lugo to Fuentevinho, but everyone in Fuentevinho who possibly could went away to Lugo, preferably forever. Outside of going to mass and the plaza de la fuente to loiter around, nobody did much except dig in the ground and contemplate escape.

I've seen villages like this one, so low to the ground that they can't be seen from a mile away, hamlets beaten into the ground by a sun that seems to weigh tons. Bleached uncompromising houses that look as though they'd been chopped out of solid rock, and nobody moving, nobody at all, not even a mule during the day.

In the evening a few black-dressed women with shawls over them, drawing water from the pump; maybe a naked child or two in a doorway. Nothing else, not a bird or a snake, not even an insect in the copper grass, for all the noise you hear. People live here, live out their whole lives in such a place.

Mari's parents had half a house to themselves and their five children: Luis, Regina, Benito, Absolución, and Mari in that order, Mari being the last-born. The mother died when she was born, a mishap for which the father, true to form, always blamed the living child. Not that it mattered. Mari hardly knew her father either. What she remembers out of the early years is sitting in corn-colored dust as soft as velvet. A cow named Anónima, on whose back she used to ride, kicking her heels. Leisurely yellow scorpions on the window sills in summer, and gray mountain wolves in the village street in winter. Her happiest hours were spent at the farm her two uncles owned, where her grandparents lived. It was a house and a few acres approximately three kilometers from the village.

There was a memory of geese that pecked at her, something about carrying bread and garbanzos and bags of wine out to the field where her uncles worked. She used to have to help feed chickens and sheep; she got up very early in the morning to draw water and chop kindling. Nothing much happened to break the monotony. Her elders loomed and reared over her, stinking of boiled onions and livestock. She liked her grandfather best; he was seven feet tall and walked on a cane as high as her grandmother.

Her father gave her one ferocious beating with the hip strap and fork of a horse harness; she can't remember why, but still has little white scars on the backs of her legs to show for it. Her grandmother used to make her snacks of crushed tomatoes and olive oil on bread, while Uncle Rafael's specialty was wooden whistles. She says that she and Benito, the younger of her two brothers, were always fast friends, inseparable, and used to half kill each other with rocks and hoe handles or just plain biting and kicking. There is not much to remember because she was not very long in Fuentevinho before things began to change.

Affairs politic were coming to a boil, at least in the capitals. "In the village," she said, "it was not so much politics or revolution as bandit war. I do not think that there was anyone, excepting Don

Julio the curate, who knew which were the Republicans and which were the Nationalists, or if they were the same, or if the rebeldes were fascist or communist, or if Red meant Loyalist or Falangist, or which were bad and which were good. There were many names and epithets and terms in the war, not to mention abbreviations such as C.N.T. and F.I.A. and P.O.U.M. and others, and many long words such as anti-reactionary and counterrevolutionist. All that was known in Fuentevinho was that times were bad again. No one knew exactly why, or cared. But sometimes soldiers would come to the town to read proclamations in the plaza. They would ask for volunteers to fight with the rebel army. Those who answered the call were usually taken away to prison, for these soldiers were not rebels at all, they were the others. Bandits who may or may not have been Communists would come to the town to ask for contributions of food and clothing; then they would take what was to be found, whether it was contributed or not. My eldest brother Luis, who was then thirteen, was once taken away by a squadron of these bandits, who said they would train him to be a captain in the Army of the Republic. Luis escaped from them the same night and came home. Later he was taken away by foot soldiers and made a soldier in the government army—that is, the army of the Facist partido.

"One day the Guardia Civil came to collect all the firearms and swords in the village. Naturally the townsfolk had opinions about this banditry. Some said the government was bad. Same said that the bandits were bad, and wondered who they were. It is very unfortunate that because of these forays and collections and conscription raids the people of Fuentevinho began to develop politically. I mean, they began to wonder who were the Republicans, who were the Revolutionists, who were the Monarchists, and so forth. The men particularly began to take sides and have opinions, so that soon after, when men in helmets came and asked who was in favor of the king, a certain number declared themselves. These were then asked to point out their neighbors who were in favor of the republic. No one imagined that the king was unfriendly to the republic; therefore everyone was surprised when those who were denounced were taken away to prison. In reprisal, the guerrillas of the Confederación Nacional de Trabajadores came to the village the next week and led those villagers who were declared Monarchists down to the river. There they shot them. This was the first bloodshed in Fuentevinho, except for the apprentice boy of Máximo the smith, who had been kicked by a soldier's mule."

There was no more killing until the time Mari left for France, although a good deal happened later on and she was to hear all kinds of horror stories from the survivors when she returned. But she was just short of five years old when she left, so naturally she doesn't remember much. She has the impression that the male villagers at least were drifting toward the red side. Most of the villagers seemed to her to be more in sympathy with the Communists than the Facists, since these latter came along just as frequently, did just as much shooting and shouting, and moreover were in a position to keep upping the taxes.

Mari is quick to point out, however, that there weren't any real Communists in her area except for a few crackpots and a handful of Rusos who had come down from someplace north just to put one in Mussolini's eye and steal anything they could. Be that as it may, the alcalde and the priest, both dues-paying Fascists, were soon obliged to report to the Falange that Fuentevinho was a hotbed of communist agitators. Actually, these poor grubbers and hoers and herders were neither communist nor liberal nor republican; they didn't know what the terms meant. They were only mildly anti status quo. It was easier to blame their hard lives on the Facists and the Guardia Civil than on the rebel element seemingly made up of poor farmers like themselves, who were only fighting to preserve their lives. I also suspect that the menfolk at least were mightily intrigued by the fact that the Republicans spoke out in no uncertain terms against the Catholic Church. Which reminds me of a song Mari says was popular in those days. I quote it as a matter of record, because it is forbidden now and you can be jailed for even humming the tune. It goes:

Si supieran los curas y frailes
La paliza que van a llevar
Subirian al coro cantando:
Libertad! Libertad! Libertad!

It says: If only they knew, these priests and friars, the thump they are about to get, they would scamper up on their pulpits and sing Liberty! Liberty!

Poor farmers; there was some optimism at the time. But the

priests never did get their thumping, at least not hard enough to matter, and they are back now where they always were, and will probably outlast everybody.

Strangely enough, it was the C.N.T. who evacuated the children and French nuns who cared for them. I don't suppose there is any such thing as a communist nun, but after the Reds took Mari, along with hundreds of other refugee children, across the bridge to Hendaye, it was the French Catholic Church which provided food and shelter and clothing and schooling. Mari does not remember very much clearly about that time either, and I wish she could. She once met La Apasionaria—Dolores Ibarruri, I think her real name was—a very interesting figure, a slogan maker and symbol in herself: red as a boiled lobster but at the same time someone to stand alongside Florence Nightingale and Molly Pitcher and La Marseillaise as a heroic woman.

Later on a troupe of these refugee children, all girls, was taken out of the institution in Biarritz, where they were studying catechism and doing calisthenics, and put on a train to Paris. They had to sing and dance and speak little patriotic pieces in big nightclubs crowded with Frenchmen and Americans and Russians and Englishmen. It seems they were part of some big rally, possibly communistic. Some of the other performers were well known American movie stars. While in Paris Mari was picked up and kissed by a woman she claims was Marlene Dietrich. Not at a commie rally, I hasten to add. The troupe of little girls was also part of some kind of enlistment effort. Whether the International Brigades were forming up at that time or not I don't know. Mari did not understand what most of the uproar was about. As I say, I wish she could remember more.

What she does remember is things like M'sieur Bolte, who took all the girls down to the beach every morning at dawn and made them romp around in their bloomers doing barbarous calisthenics. It was this fellow who taught her and the rest to walk the rope stretched between two piles of sandbags, about a foot off the floor. Then she remembers the nuns caught her absently singing a child's parody of the *Ave Maria* and made her kneel for hours, her bare knees on sand and gravel, balancing books on the backs of her hands and praying for pardon from the Virgin. The rest was just study and institution food and being discriminated against by little Frenchies. But all in all it was a happy time, and she cried when they told her that she was going back to Spain.

That was in late 1938 or early 1939, when the Germans had either just invaded or were about to. The Spanish war was over below the border, and, while things were still bad enough that whole villages were starving to death, it was thought that the children would be safer in their own homes than they would be in France with the Boche galloping about.

So in groups of six, eight, or ten, boys and girls mixed up together, the refugees were sent home. The idea of the small groups, spaced a day or two apart, was to try to make it easier for the border guards and the customs people. However, all the children met up again in a squalling clot on the French end of the international bridge at Irún. The carabineros wouldn't let anybody in. None of the children had passports or documentation issued by the Nationalist Government. They had all been sent out of the country by the Reds and now the Reds had lost the war and were all dead, so the children were no concern of the present government. One must query Madrid, said the teniente-coronel. The French were only interested in getting rid of the children and closing their gates behind them. For a day or so it looked as if France were going to deport them and Spain were not going to let them in, so the only place they could live would be the middle of the bridge.

"All the far shore before us swarmed with people," Mari said. "Soldiers marched back and forth and fires were burning in the town. The muddy banks of the river Bidassoa were covered with people who wished to cross to France, in spite of the Germans, in order to escape hunger and the fear of the Falange. We saw a man try to make a dash across the bridge to safety. He was a Republican official proscribed by the police of Bilbao. The French douaniers pointed their pistols at him and made him return to the Spanish soldiers, who beat him down to the ground with their clubs and carried him away.

"All of us children were crying. No one waited for us on the far side. Our parents did not know that we were coming. They believed we were still in Biarritz. Many parents had forgotten their children and did not want them any more. And of course many of the parents were dead and their children were orphans without knowing it. We waited in the French town, living in barns and stations and sheds for three days, and then it was heard from

Madrid that we would be permitted to enter. We walked across the bridge and the common soldiers smiled at us and lowered their bayonets. Behind us the French soldiers cried: Adieu! Adieu! The carabineros opened a black and white gate and we entered into Spain.

"But we did not know what to do. Some of us lived as far away as Valladolid and Zaragoza. We had no money and could not find our way home. The older girls asked the soldiers: 'What shall we do?' The soldiers asked their officers and the officers asked the teniente-coronel. The teniente-coronel said: 'Come! Go home. Go back to France. What do I care?'

"We could not wait for the government to help us. There was no food in Irún. We went toward San Sebastián. Later Madrid sent telegrams to all families who had addresses, and some nurses to come to the frontier to help us, but no one was there. I think no one waited in Irún. One boy and two girls and myself, we walked to San Sebastián. The girls wore bloomers and blue academy jumpers and white cotton blouses, and the boy wore gray short pants and a gray tunic with a whistle. We sang our school songs as we walked."

From the international bridge to San Sebastián is twenty miles, more or less. They walked that far in two days on empty stomachs and did not complain, because the trip seemed worth while. But it was not worth while. San Sebastián was a ruin. There wasn't anything left of it, not even anything to steal. The four children could not even speak to the Guipúzcoanos who roamed the city streets hunting food. One of the girls—the youngest; she was five—got sick. The boy stayed with her, under a smashed bridge; he was eight. Whatever happened to them Mari does not know. She and the other girl, Amanda, decided to go to Santander down the coast, where Mari's aunt lived in a big house that might be expected to have survived.

The walk from San Sebastián to Santander is even longer than the walk Mari took some eight years later from Oviedo to Santander after busting her washbasin over the head of the doctor's boy. From Oviedo to Santander is about two hundred and fifteen kilometers. She had enough trouble hiking that distance on goat's milk and green figs when she was fifteen and tough. How she made the earlier journey of nearly two hundred and fifty kilometers on nothing but cheese when she was only seven, nobody knows, including Mari. Amanda lasted only thirty kilometers and then she gave up; she sat down on the edge of the road and refused to walk another step. Mari does not know what happened to her either.

Mari walked on. Not counting Bilboa, the only considerable towns on the road, which winds along the cliffs over the Atlantic, are Solares and Castro-Urdiales, both of which come toward the end of the trek. Most of the time she was in desolate underpopulated country where there weren't even any goats to milk. A man carried her in a cart for a distance on the third day and gave her a piece of his lunch: wet white Burgos cheese. She reached Deva: the first fifty miles accomplished. An old woman gave her a place to sleep and she slept fifteen hours, and then the old woman gave her another piece of cheese to carry along the road.

"In Bilbao," she said, "workmen were repairing a bridge and setting bronze tablets in the stone. They were cursing and sweating and talking about one Francisco Franco Bahamonde. I had never heard this name before. The men said: 'This bridge, little one, is not for the purpose of spanning the water, nor to knit the two halves of the city together. No, it is because Don Paco has pronounced the war finished, and his words are to be inscribed upon a bronze plaque set upon a stone, and the stone set in this bridge. Now we have this bridge only to hold this bronze plaque from falling into the river. La guerra ha terminado. Mierda!' "

When the workmen heard that she was going all the way to Santander and had come all the way from Irún afoot, they whistled and shook limp hands on limp wrists, which is Spanish for speechless astonishment or caramba. They wished her luck and contributed bits of their almuerzas to tie up in her handkerchif. Burgos cheese again. She left the city, somehow got on the wrong road and went twenty miles toward Vitoria before a man on a bony mule put her straight and carried her back to the city and pointed out the coast road. By this time she was getting sick, probably from all the cheese. Aside from the cheese there was nothing but water running down the roadside rocks on its way to the sea. "It is indelicate," she said, "but I will tell you. Never between Bilbao and Laredo could I empty my intestine. I tried and tried. I began to have a fever and that is why I cannot remember all the journey. I think that I was sick, because I dreamt even while I was walking. I thought that M'sieur Bolte made me run and jump when I was tired. Often it seemed that Sister Gloria offered me the café-au-lait and croissante of breakfast, and I wandered from the road to pursue her. At first I thought I was very fortunate because the weather was fine; I was not cold even in the night. But then the heat began to be terrible. I walked from shade to shade—I would hide in the shade of a tree and then dash to the next. The sun was like wool blankets burning and the shade was like ponds of cool water. But sometimes I walked where there were only thin low bushes with hard metallic leaves that threw no shadow. I thought I would stop and rest when I found a house.

"There was no reason to go home, because my mother was dead and my father did not want me, or he would not have sent me to France. Perhaps I would have stopped in Castro-Urdiales, but I was very young and could not think clearly. I believed that I could not be happy anywhere until I had kissed my brother Benito. He was thirteen years old and I had not kissed him or pulled his ears for three of his birthdays. So I went on toward Santander, for some reason thinking that I would find him in the house of my aunt. But I could not walk very far or very fast. I rested each hundredth pace. Sometimes I slept. Many times I slept through the whole day, waking only to walk a hundred paces and fall down to sleep again. I cried all the time. You see, I have forgotten the last part of the trip. My aunt said that I was brought into the city by woodcutters in their cart. The Sisters took me to sleep in the convent. Once I woke and found myself surrounded by their black habits, black mountains which moved. Since I could see neither their faces nor their hands, I did not know that they were persons. I believed that I was walking and I cried all the time."

She said: "I must have been a great molestia to the Sisters." According to my pocket dictionary, a molestia is a bother, annoyance, discomfort. "A child who always cries is a molestia," she said. "I cried for all time and for all the world. That is why I never cry any more. Except since I met you, Calamidad, for since then I have cried six times."

"I remember only two," I said. "What were the other occasions?"

"You lie," she said. "You cannot make me cry, Contagión. I have done all the crying that is in me."

She said that all the time she wasn't crying or throwing up the soup the nuns fed her, she slept. But at some point she must have mentioned her aunt's name or her address, because when she woke again her aunt was tending her and she was in the big private house. She lay on a pile of dry grass, her pillowed head on a bag of shoes, covered with a rough blanket. Soon she was able to swallow broth and keep it down. Actually there was very little else besides broth, made of water and dubious bones.

Besides her aunt, another fifteen or twenty people lived in the house, quartered there by the police, because many of the houses and buildings of the city were uninhabitable. The house itself, which had once been the next thing to a mansion, had been stripped; every last piece of the original furnishings had been sold or requisitioned or stolen, down to the wires of the electric circuits and the seats of the toilets. Each of the inhabitants owned one blanket; in the kitchen there was a single table and a few cooking utensils; in the vestibule hung a bamboo umbrella rack. The rest of the house was empty except for portable personal property. The aunt expected to have her own house back again when times got better; in the meantime she shared the echoing master bedroom with an ex-railroad conductor who had taken the place of her husband, the latter having died blind and noseless in an amateur attempt to blow up a Nationalist truck full of cotton pup tents. Mari remembers that policemen came around regularly to hound Tia Mercedes because of this husband. In the aftermath of war the victorious Falangists were rounding up all Republican sympathizers and shooting them. They kept trying to make the widow give them a list of the names and addresses of her dead husband's associates. Luckily, they didn't decide to shoot her, or Mari would have been left on her own again, since the ex-conductor was far gone in melancholy and vice and wanted no little girls running around his master bedroom.

"When I could walk again, he sent me out into the street to beg for potatoes and other things to eat. Usually I went to the beach and played in the sand all day and then returned to say that no one would give me anything. I could not beg; I was ashamed. He was always angry and sometimes he struck my aunt. It continued like this for several weeks. I would not beg, but often I tried to find something, or steal something, so that the bruto would not strike my aunt. There was very little to be found, but sometimes I was able to steal corn. Corn was eaten by people in those days, and cattle went without. Sometimes I would bring back little shellfish from the beach.

"In the meantime, my aunt had written many letters to my father, telling him of my presence in Santander. Some of these letters she sent by the stricken postal system, and others she entrusted to travelers, hoping that at least one of all the letters would reach its destination. None ever did, but after I had been in Santander almost half a year, a man who lived in the lower parlor said to my aunt that there was a boy in the street looking for his sister. The people downstairs would not admit him, because he came empty-handed and seemed to be a refugee. It was my beloved Benito. The telegram from Madrid, sent the day we crossed the bridge from France to Spain, had actually reached my home, and though no one knew where I was, Benito thought I might have made for Santander to find my aunt. I was so happy to see him that my nose began to bleed."

The ex-conductor rebelled, however; he would stand for no more hungry moppets cluttering up his master bedroom. Mari and Benito went down to the beach, intending to sleep on the sand, and there Benito told her all that had happened in the years past. "Our father is dead," he began. "We have a new mother. You will not like her. I hate her."

Shortly after Mari's departure from Fuentevinho, a body of soldiers had come and shot certain men and drafted certain others. Next, different soldiers came and drafted most of those who had not been shot, and shot most of those who had not been drafted. The village lay in sleepless confusion. All day and all night widows moaned in the street. Uneasily, Mari's father waited to see which way to jump. Finally a force of some fifty Fascist soldiers, convincingly uniformed, arrived in the town and were barracked in the stone church, so that the town was secure from further rebel raids. Things went well for a time, until one day, without warning, the Fascist commander, whose name was Santiago Plá, posted a black list of potential executees on the oak door of the church. Alertly discovering his own name high on the list, Mari's father, old Juan, expeditiously did an about-face, and sued for, courted, begged for, and won the hand in marriage of garrulous young América Torres, sole town whore, who also happened to be, and not by chance, the daughter of Señor Don Francisco Santos Torres Alvarez, alcalde of Fuentevinho and an important Fascist official. Old Juan considered his bets neatly hedged, coming and going:

a notorious lover of the Left, yet espoused to the Right. It was not the war that killed him.

After several years of prowling the local footpaths and sprawling in the potato fields with whoever had the price of a kerchief or a new pair of shoes, América Torres was as surprised as anybody when old Juan asked—indeed pleaded—to marry her. In little towns no man looks twice at a girl who has ever broken an engagement, much less at one who is allowed to go out of her father's house after nightfall. No girl has any secrets in a small town, either. América had never hoped to find a husband in Fuentevinho; she expected that when the time came for her to marry her father would send her off to Lugo to live with relatives and meet young men who had never heard of her. When old Juan proposed, she accepted partly because he owned land, his brothers owned land, the family owned half a house in the village and a whole farmhouse outside it, and partly because a home marriage would save her the trip to Lugo and spare her the necessity of disappointing a lot of steady customers. She was twenty-one; Juan was fifty-one. The wedding night proved the groom not only surpassingly smelly but well nigh impotent from lack of practice; proved the bride flabby and disinclined, contemptuous and witlessly jovial. A week after the ceremony she was walking the footpaths again.

Everybody knew about it, including Juan; he never said a word. Only once did he beat her, when he happened to overhear her rapping his children on the head and calling them illegitimate. One thing the old man would not stand for and that was to have anyone even mention the name of his first, his only true, wife: the Beautiful One. He caught up a stout cudgel of stovewood and laid América out on the kitchen floor and walloped her until she couldn't stand for a week.

Thereafter everything was calm for about a year. América fed the three children, Benito, Regina, and Absolución, and saw that they got to school when there was any. The war was far away. Old Juan worked all day and collapsed in bed after supper with Gallego soil thick under his fingernails. In the summer evenings the children went down to the river to wash themselves, while América prowled the potato fields.

Old Juan now being dead, nobody will ever know exactly what went on in his mind when he saw his wife going past with Santiago Plá, the Fascist captain who had published the blacklist. He just sat in the doorway of his half-a-house, whittling a new axe handle. Maybe he dimly remembered the legend of David and Bathsheba and thought he ought to assert himself in some way before Captain Plá had him liquidated. Maybe his Republican blood belatedly began to simmer at the sight of his wife carrying on with one of the despoilers. Or maybe he was just fed up, as every Spaniard gets once in awhile; or maybe the sly jeers of his fellows, almost all of whom had diddled his wife at one time or another, had finally worked under his skin.

At any rate, he followed the pair. They were accustomed to climb up into the squat tower of the village church rather than risk going out to the fields where the captain might be picked off by rebel guerrillas. Old Juan took his axe handle and followed along behind them. A sentinel made some move to stop him and got his scalp opened for his pains. Juan heard his wife laughing in the belfry. At that evening hour there was nobody about except a few soldiers, playing cards and joking. Juan was halfway up the rickety ladder when his eyes crossed, his hands opened, and he fell. His wife and the captain went on romping in the dust up above as the sun set over the cabbage fields.

Mari said: "I cried for my father even though I did not remember him, and even though I believed he had never loved me. Benito held me in his arms until the tide came up, and then we climbed to the top of the bluff and sat in the pine trees. Benito said that after my father's death the woman wanted to go away to Lugo, but old Torres, her father and the alcalde, would not permit it. He said (Regina, my sister, heard him): 'You are now the widow of Juan Quintero, and a respectable woman, a señora beyond all my expectations. Now you must respect his memory and guard his children. His property is now yours and we will sell it when the war is over. Soon after, the old parents will die and his brothers will die and you will own their land and the stone house also. You will be a wealthy widow, and then we will find you another husband.'"

So there were no more changes from then until the end of the war, except that after the death of old Juan, Luis, his eldest son, ceased to write letters; and when she was fifteen Regina vanished, taking nothing with her but an extra pair of shoes and a leather bag of wine. That left Benito and Absolución alone with the woman. Old Torres sold the half-a-house and Juan's land. América and the two children went to live in the stone house of Carlos and Rafael after Mari's grandmother died of old age. Grandfather lived downstairs in the hay with the two thin cows and the four thin pigs which the Guardia Civil had not troubled to kill. Carlos and Rafael, Mari's uncles, shared one room; América slept in another; and Benito and Absolución, twelve and eight years old the day General Franco ended the war, slept on grass mattresses in the kitchen.

Benito said: "When the telegram came the woman said that thou wert lost; nothing was to be done. But Grandfather and Uncle Rafael wanted thee to come home. Grandfather is too old to travel and Uncle Rafael could not leave the farm for fear that Uncle Carlos would lose everything to the Falange. I said to our stepmother that I would go look for thee, but she forbade it. She said: 'There are already too many mouths in the house, swallowing, swallowing.' That is why I come after so long a time. Uncle Rafael would not let me take the mule, because he was afraid I might lose it to the bandits. There was no money for railroad trains. The stepmother would not let me depart. Then one day Grandfather asked: 'Where is my baby María of the Angels? I do not see her in the house.' I told him thou wert lost but that I thought thee in Santander. He said: 'Why dost thou not go look for her?' I told him that the stepmother would not let me go. He went into the kitchen and struck her in the breast with his huge stick and said: 'Where is my youngest Angel, Ramera de los Embarcaderos? Whore of the Waterfronts, where is my baby?' He said that he would *kill* her if no effort was made to find thee immediately. She believed him. I believed him. The old man is terrible.

So Mari went home.

From Santander to Fuentevinho, on the river Miño to the south of Lugo, it is another five-or-six-hundred-kilometer journey. Mari and Benito covered the distance in only three weeks and four days, thanks to the ex-conductor, who finally came through with something good: he helped them sneak aboard a government train—the only kind running—that was bound for La Coruña. Nor did they travel hungry; Tia Mercedes provided them with a bag full of almonds, sausages, dry sardines, figs, and crusts of bread. Moreover, Benito had become an industrious and accomplished thief during his eastward journey, and he spent the afternoon before their departure stealing wine and flour cakes and eggs from Tia

Mercedes' neighbors. About midnight the ex-conductor took them to the railroad yard, was tipped the wink by a crony, and helped the two children climb up and hide themselves among the cargo. "Keep out of sight," he warned by way of Godspeed. "And don't come fornicating around here any more."

The freight on the trip was two dozen scorched and battered medium tanks. They had been the gift of Mussolini to his Spanish Fascist confrères, but now that the war was over they were being shipped to La Coruña, where an orange-bearded Argentinian military purchasing agent was waiting with a dark ship and bags full of pesos.

The train trip took a nonsensical twenty-one days, including stops to repair bridges and to lay track. And it would halt as night began to fall and not move again until dawn, for fear of the irreconcilables still roaming the hills. Benito and Mari slept most of the time, as dogs and cats will sleep when there is nothing else to do. Sometimes at night the boy would sneak off to scour the surrounding countryside for stray chickens or unguarded vegetable patches. Whenever he found something they built a fire and ate a hot meal. Not having any utensils at all, they cooked their eggs by building a fire on the metal deck of one of the tanks, letting it burn for awhile, then kicking it out of the way and breaking the eggs on the hot metal. Thirteen and seven years old: resourceful as a couple of smugglers.

After the brakeman had kicked them in the pants and given them a few deflated céntimos upon encountering them sound asleep on a flatcar at the end of the line, they walked the fifty-odd kilometers from the sea to Lugo, arriving in the capital late at night. A good time to arrive, as it turned out.

"We had no difficulty finding a boat," Mari said. "It was late and dark and very warm. No one was abroad, so we had only to walk along the bank of the river until we discovered a good boat, half out of the water, with wooden seats and four oars. Río Miño flows past the village. It was wonderful weather, warm even in the night, and there are few rapids between Lugo and Fuentevinho. The distance is no more than sixty kilometers, and we did not have to work—the current flows toward the sea at Caminha. In some places we had to hold our boat away from the rocks with the wooden oars, but that was all.

"After a few days the shapes of the mountains began to be

familiar. We saw men with burros on the paths along the shore. We hailed them and they shouted: 'Hola, hola!' My village has no dock, because no one goes to the river except to wash clothing and water cattle, but there is a point where the ground comes out and is covered with grass. We left our boat on the grass and spoke to the women washing, then we went through the village. The people looked out their windows and spoke to Benito. They did not know me. We walked to the farm of my uncles, and lingered on the way, singing and throwing stones at the goats. We ate the sausage that remained. It was early in the day; Uncle Carlos and Uncle Rafael and their two men were on the hill away from the house, cutting down an oak tree full of squirrels. My sister Absolución came to stare at me; she said she did not remember me. My stepmother was sleeping—she never rose before eleven. 'Grandfather has died,' Absolución said."

Benito had gone to look for Mari in the month of March. It took him forty days to reach Santander; he hadn't had a lucky break like a ride on the railroad. It had taken the two of them approximately three weeks to return. Grandpa had died sometime between March and early May.

"My mother was dead, my father was dead, Luis was gone, he never returned. Regina was gone. Absolución did not know me. I loved only Benito and my grandfather. Now my grandfather was dead too. I wished I had not come home. He always walked in the forest after he was too old to work; he carried a big cane and wore wooden shoes and sang the jotas of Aragón. When I was small he told me that he could speak to the birds, and I believed him, for when he whistled they seemed to answer. He said that when he was young he hunted wild wolves with only a club in the mountains of Navarra. My Uncle Carlos said that the evening of his death Grandfather went walking in the forest and night caught him unprepared; he returned home in darkness. He came back stumbling and pale, and they thought it was a stroke, but it was not. He told them that as he had walked on a dark path toward home, he had suddenly been dealt a terrible blow across the shoulders, and a deep voice had said in the Castilian language: 'Anda de día! que la noche es mía!': Walk by day, because the night is mine! But he saw no one. That same night he died. Yet he was not craven or sad. He was ninety-two years old and straight as a tree; and he died proud because he was an important man, to be struck down by the Spirits of the Forest rather than by his kidneys or his lungs, like an old bobo."

"How long did you stay with your stepmother?"
"Until I was eleven."
Four years.
"Well?"
"Nothing happened. Sometimes I went to school. I helped my uncles. Later old Torres found me a position as a servant."
Four years. She leaves it to my imagination.
A big stone house three kilometers from the village. Inhabited by two tall silent uncles who dug in the ground all day and shambled home in the dark to stick their jaws in bowls of bread soup and peppers and then flop into bed to snore and racket until four-thirty in the morning. Inhabited by the flabby village whore who was forced to cook and scrub floors and tend the three children of her dead husband's first wife; a garrulous whining young whore just biding her time until the two old uncles died. Inhabited by the three children slowly graduating from stock feeding and house sweeping to ploughing and at length the full twelve-hour day bent over double in the cabbage rows.
The deep little valley of the Miño River was a hundred and four degrees in the field in the summertime, with nothing within ten miles to throw a shade and nothing in sight higher than the squat church steeple in the pueblo, except the mountains like crusts on a burned pie. Everything the same dry color, like fried sand, except the skim-milk sky and an eye of sun burning like exploding magnesium. Heat cramps and whirling brains and running sores on hands and forehead and the back of the neck; mass on Sunday and pound shirts on the rocks in the river and mend harness and scrub and cook the rest of the time. The flat-bottomed little valley of the Río Miño was nine degrees above zero in the wintertime, inside the house as well as out. Freezing winds from the snow on the peaks of the mountains and the ice on the river, but the color of the fields just the same, the sky milk-white and the sun the same color but with no heat in it. Crack kindling and chop dirty ice off the stovewood, bend over and root in the dirt. Split black fingernails and burst fingertips and aching teeth. Agonized horses and sick pigs and dead chickens. Up every morning at five and drink a mess of red wine and honey

and all day claw frozen seed turnips out of the frozen ground. Mass on Sunday . . .

"Sometimes there was school," she said. She brags that when the priest gave classes she was always the brightest and best, because of having spent three years with the French nuns. She knew her catechism backwards and forwards and all the prayers, and was better at arithmetic than the priest, though her history and geography were spotty.

"The stepmother taught us to cook, Absolución and I; thereafter we stayed at home in the mornings and made hot food to carry to the uncles at noon, and the stepmother remained in bed until three."

Nobody sleeps that late in the day unless he has been up late all night. Whores as a species are notorious late risers, worse than actors. América turned up pregnant the year Mari was eleven, Absolución thirteen, Benito seventeen. She wouldn't say who the father was; probably didn't know; undoubtedly didn't dare accuse anyone in the village, or she would have got her teeth knocked out. Old Torres came to the house many times while Carlos, Rafael, and Benito were working in the fields. Mari heard them talking. 'When the child is born it will be heir to all the Quintero properties,' Torres said. 'After the old ones are dead, claro está. The other three are children of a communist father; they have no claim. Besides, if they are sent far enough away, perhaps they will never return. I will arrange everything.' "

Mari said: "Soon after the stepmother became embarazada, we were sent away. But he made a mistake. He arranged for Benito to be enrolled as cadre in a Falangist work camp near Zamora, on the lakes. For this reason I think that some day Benito will have the farm. Old Torres will not be able to cheat him, because Benito is a registered Fascist and wears a black shirt and has certain privileges. Absolución was sent to be housemaid for a family in Miranda de Ebro. I was very young and not useful, but old Torres found a place for me in a poor household in Pontevedra. I stayed there three years."

Until she was thirteen. Improving her usefulness in simple housework and child-minding. It was a pleasant enough time. In some parts of Spain it's common for even poor folk to have servants, though wages are not high—in fact, are usually room and board and nothing else—but the girls are treated like family, like adopted daughters at worst. Among the rich it's different. The people in Pontevedra, named José and Carlota Iglesia, were poor enough; they were up to their necks in hard times and triplets simultaneously. José was a dock worker and made good money for that day, but he had to work practically around the clock. Carlota was subject to mild heart attacks and generally felt faint. The triplets were a couple of months premature and consequently somewhat delicate. Mari learned all the oaths she knows from José. I'm not surprised.

José swore by the twenty-four testicles of the twelve Apostles; he evacuated constantly in or on the sea, the docks, the beard of the Pope, in the milk of the mother of the dock foreman, in the soup, on the ships, on the régime, in the skin-temperature soy-bean milk of Jesus, Maria, and José (the triplets). "You will teach the child intemperate habits of speech," Carlota would say mildly. "I void copiously on the speech habits of the child," José would reply. "Where do *you* void, niña?" And Mari would answer calmly: "I void copiously in your soup, Pig," stirring it meanwhile with a wooden spoon.

Again, in Pontevedra, she went to school—sometimes.

But things got worse instead of better. During World War II, unhappy Spain, exhausted by her own war, got no help from the outside. Reconstruction was slow; money would buy nothing. Few ships came into the harbor. José sat all day dangling his feet over the water, earning nothing. There wasn't even anything to smuggle. The triplets grew and ate more; they needed clothes, occasional medicines. Poor Mari, after three years she felt so much a part of the family, hardships and all, that it came as a shock when José said he could not feed her any more, that she had to go home.

They gave her enough money to ride the bus as far as Orense, then she followed the river to Fuentevinho. This time she couldn't go in a boat because it was upstream. Only some thirty-five kilometers, but it was winter and cold. She did not want to go home. She had never thought of the stone house as home. Nobody was there except América and the new baby and the two uncles who were slowly turning into ancient plough horses. Rafael never spoke to Carlos because there was nothing to say after so many years, and vice versa. Neither of them ever spoke to América because they had not yet recognized her right to live in their house. América never spoke to them because all she wanted was for them to go ahead and die and get it over with.

A cold house full of cold woodsmoke, ice in the stone sink. The upstairs was as dirty as the downstairs, where the single pig, the twelve sick chickens, and the surviving mule lived. In the evening the old men played wordless dominoes by the kitchen fire; América left the house, presumably to go to the village and her father's house; Mari sat alone in the straw in the cuadra underneath the kitchen, turning stubborn and fierce.

"I made the meals and carried food to my uncles where they worked, but I would not clean the house or wash any clothing but my own. I have never hated anyone so much. She slept until afternoon; then when I returned from the field I would find men in the house. Sometimes Máximo the smith, sometimes Pablo Guacho, the Orphan, who whispered obscenities to all women of the village, old or young. The stepmother and the men sat at the kitchen table drinking wine and cognac, singing songs and laughing. My uncles knew what took place in the house every afternoon, but nothing was to be done about it; old Torres was the chief of the Fascists in the village. The men looked at me and said to my stepmother: 'Send the child outside.' My stepmother said: 'Don't worry—soon she will be gone forever.' "

América probably knew that old Torres was hunting Mari a new job. But there were certain difficulties, because the poor people had no money to hire serving girls, and the rich could hire all the competent help they wanted for no more than meals and a place to sleep, so why bother with thirteen-year-old girls? Meanwhile Mari was determined never to leave the house again, not even for a minute if she could help it, hoping that her presence would deter the woman from bringing more disgrace to Juan Quintero's name. A couple of months passed. Finally things were brought to a head by the return from Lugo of young Guillermo Torres, old Torres' other pride and joy.

"I did not think he was so bad as the rest," Mari said. "True, he came to our house almost every day and did not work, and drank too much for his age; but he wore fine clothes and had the manners of the capital people. He had a thin blue mustache. During the war he was in government schools, which are like soldiers' training camps. Afterward he studied engineering, then he became the secretary of a provincial party official, but lost this place because of drunkenness. When he came to Fuentevinho he owned an automobile. You would not think it was a good automobile because it was old and made in Italy. But it was the only automobile in the village, as well as the only gasoline motor. He made a great impression with it and the old peasants saluted him and said señor and called him Usted, even though he was young and foolish. He was always very courteous, even with the old women at the fountain. He lived with his father, and it was well known that he had failed his life in the city. Every day he came to our house to drink wine and sing with his sister and her men. I thought that while he was present she would not dare do anything to bring more shame to our family.

"I sat in the straw one day and heard them laughing in the kitchen above me. I was waiting for my life to end; there seemed nothing else to do. A flea or a louse from the mule had flown into my ear and would not come out; I tried to tease it free with a wisp of straw. The laughter above stopped, and in a little while Guillermo Torres came into the cuadra. 'Hola, Prenda,' he said. 'They forced me out.' I could see that he was drunk. He sat by me in the straw. Then he put his hand between my legs. 'Open, spread,' he said. 'Muh ka'n dena!' My hand was near the harness belt hanging on the wall, a harness fixed with bells which my grandfather always put on the cart during Holy Week. I struck Guillermo about the head and shoulders, and 'Cling! Clong!' went the bells. 'Bing! Bang!' they rang, and Guillermo could not stop me because he was too drunk. I went to the fields and stayed the rest of the day with my uncles, until they came home at evening.

"The following day my stepmother rose unusually early and came into the kitchen where I was boiling potatoes for the midday meal of my uncles. She began to shout, and said that I had cut Guillermo's scalp in four places with the belt and, more, I had broken a front tooth. I was very sullen. I said: 'Good. The next time I will kill him outright.'

" 'Animal,' she screamed. 'It troubles thee too much to lie down on thy back for one moment?' You see, I had almost forgotten what Guillermo wanted of me. I did not know much and I was amazed that she did not understand. 'Por Dios,' I said, 'he tried to do things to me, do you know? I am only thirteen!'

" 'Hija de vergüenza!' she cried. 'Thou art pure, puta? Too pure for my brother? Vaya, why not tell me that thy puta madre waited even so long as thirteen years, bastard? Mother of improbables, wife to no one—show me the man of Fuentevinho who has not flung her across his furrow!'

"Like most prostitutes, my stepmother could not believe in the existence of virtuous women. I said that she must not speak of my mother in those or any terms. The knife with which I had pared the potatoes lay on the table. 'My mother was a respectable Señora,' I said, 'but you are not.' She cried: 'I vomit at the mention of the purity of thy filth of a mother! Five brats, five unlikes in ten years! Do I not know of my own experience that thy sheep-wiving father could not get five babies from five hundred women in five thousand years?' "

Mari sort of mumbled hurriedly over what happened next. It seems that she said: If my brother Benito were here, he would kill you. América said: Well, Benito is not here. Then Mari said: I am here. And with that she grabbed up the paring knife and took a long overhand swipe that very nearly sliced half her stepmother's stock in trade. While América looked down in crack-jawed astonishment at the copious and tomato-red blood running through the slash in her jacket, Mari just laid down the knife and went to spend the rest of the day with her uncles in the cabbage field. She told them what had come to pass, in full detail. Neither man said anything. Uncle Rafael jerked his chin toward the work still to be done, and Uncle Carlos gathered up the mule's reins. But that evening, before going into the house, Uncle Rafael stopped in the cuadra to select a stout pole from among several leaning in the corner. He sat down on a box and neatly cut off a four-foot length, then climbed the stairs.

América was raging to Carlos, exposing a bandaged breast. "I tell you," she said, "the animal nearly cut off my nipple." Uncle Rafael said nothing, he simply whacked her sidewise off her chair and laid it on just as old Juan had done some years before. He methodically pounded her blue and crippled, just as old Juan had done, and for the same offense. "Never again speak the name of the Beautiful One," was all he said when he was done.

Then, before América was on her feet again, Mari was out of the house and on her way to Oviedo, where old Torres had managed to find her a situation. "Be sure that you do not lose this place for want of energy or intelligence," he said as he ran her out of town. "Also, give thanks that you are not in jail for assassination."

The only kind word she got came, strangely enough, from Guillermo Torres, who came rattling up behind her in his old Aprilia as she was walking the road toward Chantada and the Lugo bus. "I mean to say that I regret the entire incident, chiquilla," he said. "I intended nothing bad."

"Una mierda!" Mari said.

"You are sleeping."

"No. I'm listening. Finish."

"I have already told you about the doctor's house in Oviedo. Now you are tired. You want to sleep."

"I said I'm listening. Go ahead and finish."

"You have been asleep. You were not listening."

"I heard everything."

"Yes, but that is enough for the present, and I will tell you the rest another time. About the circus and my lovers."

"Shut up. Finish now. It's early—only about three o'clock. Finish."

"You would not prefer to sleep?"

"No."

"You do not want to make cha-ka-cha?"

"No."

"Qué raro. You surprise me."

"Never mind. I want to know everything until I met you. This afternoon you said that the fire-eater taught you to walk the tight rope. Take it from there."

"Agustín Zubiaurre de la Hojaldre was his name. But first I must tell you more of my situation in Oviedo, where I was given only dregs of coffee for breakfast, with no milk, and one piece of bread. For dinner only one fried egg and wine with water and five fried potatoes. In the evening only white beans with onions. You will see that no one can eat only this much and live to scrub seven mosaic floors each day on all fours like a beast, and prepare meals and clean plates and serve at the table, then wash shutters and clean the gardens in the afternoon, as well as wash clothes for a family of five, then prepare dinner for El Señor Doctor and his family, all the while clutched in the buttocks on each dark stair by the lop-jawed son of the house. Clearly it is impossible. You must not be surprised that I seized my opportunity to escape and become an adventuress notorious throughout Las Rias Bajas and the Cantábrican coast. Also you know why I did not return to my home.

"It was the autumn," she said, "while we waited in Santander, and the wind came from the sea. We lived inside the wagon, and over the winter the bad weather dulled all the bright paint on one side and cracked the gilding; the wind roared and rocked us back and forth. The wheels of the wagon sank in mud, and then the mud froze and we could not move. Always it was cold and we could make no fire inside. We cooked on the ground and then carried the pot indoors to eat. We slept shoulder to shoulder on the floor, Agustín against one wall, Don Bellorio against the other, I in the middle, and the dogs in the spaces and crevices, all on a great sewn bag full of grass. The candles ran out in November, and then we had no lights in the evenings. At Christmas we went to the cathedral and Don Bellorio bought a tiny stable of carved cork, furnished with a Virgin and Child, a cow and a pig. For Reyes, the Feast of the Magi, which is when gifts are given, Agustín gave me a chain carved of links of wood to put around my neck, and Don Bellorio wrote a poem in his fine hand, that said:

Dos Tristes Viejos,
Com Memorias Malagueñas;
Morena Huérfano
Del Rio Miño;
Gracias á Dios,
Nos Vamos Compañeros.

Two sad old men with memories of Málaga; a black-haired orphan from the river Miño; thanks be to God, we journey in company. I was very sad, carai! I had nothing to give. But they said that children did not give gifts to their elders for Reyes.

"All winter we worked to find money to buy a horse to pull the wagon when spring came. Don Bellorio worked for the municipal government, copying documents; he wrote stories about history for the newspapers. Sometimes he went fishing. For a time he netted clams on the sandbanks thirty meters from the shore, standing in the winter ocean to his waist. He worked at many small jobs. Agustín painted signposts for the merchants, although he could not read what he copied, and he treated cattle and shod horses. He worked for the Fascists, repairing their trucks. I myself sometimes worked, after I had finished the work of keeping our camp. I washed clothes and scrubbed tiles and carried stones for workmen rebuilding the houses. Sometimes I begged in the street —what I would not do for the ex-conductor I did for Don Bellorio. When I earned or was given a potato or a fish or a piece of rabbit, I felt triumphant; I thought: 'This is two reales which we have saved! Soon we will buy a horse!'

"But when spring came we had only two hundred and thirty-five pesetas. Not very much. Agustín spent a little of this money to buy paints with which to repair the side of the wagon that faced the bad weather. Don Bellorio said: 'Look. In the country are people who will pay to see us. You know that the campesinos always have a gold coin hidden somewhere in their houses. But we cannot go to the country because we have no horse.' Agustín said: 'We will pull the wagon ourselves, coño! I will pull downhill, you will pull uphill. It is a thing accomplished.'

"But that was impossible. We thought and thought, but there was nothing to be done. Don Bellorio decided that we should stay in Santander and work through that summer and the coming winter; then perhaps after another year we would be able to buy a horse. No one wanted to wait so long, but there seemed to be no other remedy.

"Then one evening a boy—of my age or a little older—appeared at our fire while we cooked. 'Boas noites, senhores,' he said. 'With permission, I have watched you for several days, caballeros y senhorita, and I decide that you are to be trusted, that you are people of confidence. Therefore, know that I am Juan Bautista Maravillo Milagro Quijote de la Castillo y Salás, and I have come to join the circus.'

"Of course Don Bellorio roared with laughter, and Agustín sprang up to shake the young man by the hand and strike his back, and he said: 'Honored, honored, O Archduke of the Illustrious Name. Have the goodness to be seated at our fire and avail yourself of our poor food.'

" 'I will, with many thanks,' the young man said, and he sat cross-legged before the fire and warmed his hands, but he would not eat. 'With permission of the Senhorita, and of Ustedes, caballeros, I will smoke cigarettes. Listen, gentlemen; I have run away from home, intending to go to sea, but there are no ships. Therefore I have decided to join your circus. I hope that we will be mutually useful to one another. I have in mind a grand tour of the north, arriving at a grand culmination in Madrid!'

" 'Everything arrives at a culmination in Madrid,' Don Bellorio said. 'Meanwhile, O Fountain of Miraculous Baptismal Waters of the Castle of la Mancha, may one know what is your artistic specialty? I mean to say, in what light, other than that shed by your illustrious lineage, do you propose to shine?'

" 'Me, I am torero!' the boy said and smote his breast. It was some moments before Don Bellorio could speak again; he and Agustín clung to one another and laughed until they wept, and Agustín stretched out his hand to beat my shoulder and cry: 'Ay collóns! How good, how good!' The boy himself began to laugh and he made the sound of a burro: Aw! Aw! Awsqueek! Finally Don Bellorio wiped his eyes and rubbed the muscle of his jaws which were tired from laughing, and he said: 'With permission, thou of the Marvelous Incognito, I am afraid we have no use for toreros. If we had a bull we would eat it. If we did not eat it we would hitch it to the wagon. At present we have no horses on which to mount picadors, nor do we have banderillas nor monteras nor brass bands. Sit by the fire until thou art grilled, eat if thou art hungry, then go to sea, or return to the castle of thy fathers. We have nothing for thee, no work, no pay, nor opportunities for travel and adventure. As thou seest, nothing but two old gypsies and a foundling girl, a battered wagon and five hungry dogs. Look elsewhere.'

" 'O I am determined,' the boy said. 'Look, it is easy. While the campesinos watch the spectacle I will mix among them and pick their pockets; I am also an expert carterista. No one need know I am a member of the troupe. When I have enough money I will buy a yearling toro and train it to fight with me. That is a spectacle always exciting to the mountain people who cannot come to the plaza. They will not mind if the bull is not killed, for who but the very rich can afford a new bull in each corrida? Also, I can play guitar, steal setting hens, and speak Castellano.'

"But Agustín was tired of the joke. He said: 'Adiós, John Baptist. Already we have too many foundlings.' Don Bellorio said: 'You see, my son, there is nothing to do. We cannot find a horse for the wagon and we must remain in the city another year at least. We work and save money; there is neither spectacle nor show. This is no life for adventurers.'

"Upon hearing this the young man brooded for a moment with his chin resting on his knees, and then he said: 'And if I should happen to find a horse, then would you accept me as your associate? With permission—' he said, knowing already the answer to his question, '—I can get a horse; that is, I can get a burro. Will that be acceptable?'

"That is how we came to have Juan Bautista Maravillo Milagro Quijote with us on our tour of the Atlantic coast. At first we did not believe him, as is natural; he seemed foolish. To be rid of him Don Bellorio promised that of course the owner of a burro would indeed be a valued member of the company. Seeing that we mocked him, the boy was touched in his pride; he would explain no more. He wished us a very good night, restful, without dreams and free from preoccupations, and then he departed. We expected never to see him again. But in the early morning I dreamed of him, particularly of his burro laugh, and woke, and a real burro stood between the shafts of the wagon sunk in mud, and it said: 'Tee waw, waw!'

" 'He is named Llorón, the Weeper,' the boy said.

" 'Yaw. Yaw. Yaw-weee,' said the burro.

" 'And what is the real name with which thou were baptized?' I asked.

"Shamefacedly he said: 'Hyacinth. Of the family of Anacleto Azpiliaga.' "

"That same morning our caravan set out for Durango on the northern coast. Jacinto explained that he had run away from his home in Torrelavega, a few miles south of Santander, that very week, and that the burro was the same as his own, inasmuch as he had reared it from a colt. He said that he had left his cap to be recognized in the stall, so that his father would know who had stolen the burro and would not notify the Guardia Civil. 'I am sure he is glad to see me gone,' Jacinto said. 'Bear in mind that I have seven brothers and five sisters. Under these circumstances surely my father will not begrudge me one burro if it will speed me on my way?'

"Notwithstanding, Don Bellorio thought it advisable to journey on, away from the city. By traveling a day and a night without pause we reached Santoña on the coast, some forty-five kilometers distant from Torrelavega and the burro-bereft Anacleto Azpiliaga. I rode on the wagon and drove the burro, while the others walked, to make the load lighter, for Llorón was not very big, and though strong enough, he was grass-fed and so did not have the stamina for long labor without rest.

"Jacinto walked alongside me, singing and stroking an imaginary guitar. He was nineteen, he said, and very beautiful. 'In your travels, have you seen a chaval as beautiful as I, senhorita?', he asked. 'I can speak Castellano and play the guitar. I will be the music, if you will dance. I will play the barrel organ while Señor Bellorio el Maestro torments his dogs and Don Agustín the Sugar-cake breathes dragonfire; and you will dance. I am also a brave toreador. I have vanquished all the bulls, cows, horses, and infuriated goats on the filth of a farm of my father.'

"He was lithe and thin and he cultivated long sideburns down his jaws; his eyes were large and black and he walked lightly on his toes. At the very first he asked us not to call him Jacinto, although it is a very good name; he preferred to be called Juan Bautista, or Bautisto Salás. It made no difference: Agustín forever after called him El Incógnito, while Don Bellorio called him Holy Waters, or Sancho Panza, or El Milagro. Sometimes the men gave out to ignorant mountain people that the boy was a Marqués, or a Duque. I always called him Burro, because of his way of laughing, like the cry of Llorón.

"When we came to Laredo or Portugalete or one of the small towns along the coastal road, we would stop in the central plaza and send him crying among the houses the message that there had come to town the Combined Bellorio-Zubiaurre-Quintero World Carnival of Fiesta and Spectacle. '—with the Collaboration of Juan Bautista Maravillo Milagro Quijote de la Castillo y Salás!' we heard him cry like a roll of drums. He wore the red cape of the fire-eater and an old military cap, and carried the carved walking stick of Don Bellorio with which to rap on the walls. 'Venid Ustedes!' he cried in his fine Castilian, which few among the villagers understood. 'Fire and flame and performing animals, AND—ur—high-wire walking!' He ran through the crowd never ceasing to shout, especially at the girls, pushing and poking, trying to provoke laughter, curiosity or excitement, to make holiday. He pretended to light cigarettes from the fire-eater's breath; he mewed like a cat to disconcert the staggering dogs; he threw pebbles at me as I walked the wire. Whenever we earned a few coins, a loaf of bread, a handful of shrimp or a bag of potatoes, he took all the credit upon himself. 'Soon we will be the attraction of the eyes of the world!' he said. 'Drive on, Maestro! To Madriz, Parease, Londres! I sing and I play guitar, I dance and I torear! I speak Castilian and steal vegetables and I am expert pickpocket! Thou, Neska Policha,' he said to me (this in Vasco means pretty child), 'and when thou are grown, if ever, I will make heroic love to thee, under the wagon!'

"I said that more than one had already broken his head against this wall. Then he would pretend melancholy, to mock me. 'Ay, Salada, what can I do to please thee? I will give thee anything I have, saving my burro only.'

" 'Ask for his head on a platter, Salomé,' said Don Bellorio, who delighted to listen to Jacinto talk to me. Jacinto said: 'It was not Juan Bautista who cut off the head of Juan Bautista, but rather King Herodias, who cut off the head of Juan Bautista who baptized the Son of God.' Jacinto also spent the nights reading the collection of erudite books of Don Bellorio. This story of Salomé we had both read not in La Biblia but in the poetry of a maricón Inglés.

"I said: 'Do not worry, Burro, I would not have thee even at the price of thy head.' So that, unexpectedly as always, he was touched in his terrible pride, and would not speak to me for several days.

"I do not say that I never considered him for a lover—he was strong and young and kind, and he wore magnificent sideburns; but I was still unready, I was afraid. And above all, he was not serious. In every pueblo he ran shouting after the girls. Whenever we camped near a considerable population he was gone most of the night. Throughout the summer, as we traveled toward the northern frontier, he walked by the wheel of the wagon and boasted of his adventures. And never did he mention a girl by name or remember her face or what her character was. He was like you, he thought of the hide, the muscles, the legs, the capacities, as though his girls were burros which he put to his uses. As I have told you I was determined that when the time came I would give myself without reserve—but not without some hope of return. And though perhaps I could have forced him to believe in me, it would have been much work, and not altogether worth the effort, even though he was very handsome. So you are informed: neither was Juan Bautista my first lover, in spite of the fact that he was present, and declared himself waiting, when my time of womanhood came. It came that winter in the north. But it was not a very great occasion. I think I expected that a bottle of champagne be opened.

" 'Now you are happy, little orphan,' Don Bellorio said. We had all been much interested to see if it would ever happen. I was almost seventeen. However, there seemed to be no great changes in myself. I was ill for several days, and thereafter heavy and grumbling for a few days out of each month. We passed the winter in a town near Tolosa, a very small town where nothing at all happened except that we painted the wagon and bought a small straight-horned bull for the boy. Agustín hired himself out to work on neighboring farms. Don Belloria and I occupied ourselves with the costumes and equipment, while Juan Bautista worked for a smith. In the evenings we rested and played parcheesi, and Don Bellorio gave us lessons in cultural things from his old books. Very often the snow fell and covered up the mountains, the fields, and the village.

"Sometimes young Juan went out with the boys of the pueblo to hunt wolves. In the winter two of Don Bellorio's old dogs died of the cold or lack of proper nourishment, but we felt compensated for this loss by our acquisition of the bull. In its thick fur it looked brave and dangerous, and the boy taught it to charge the cape without harming itself or endangering the torero more than was necessary for realism. Feeling himself safe, Juan Bautista took many liberties with the horns, and by spring he could kneel before the bull, or turn his back to it, and evade its charges and guide its head, like a real matador. He felt great affection for the bull, which he named Shak-es-speary, after the author of one of Don Bellorio's books. Shak-es-speary is a famous English dramatist and is very well known in Spain.

"In March, although the roads were still deep with mud and the wind from the Gulf of Vizcaya was cold, we turned southward, passing this time along the inland roads away from the coast. We went to Vergara and Vitoria and Miranda de Ebro. In this last town I tried to find my sister Absolución. I found the household where she had worked, but the family told me that she had stayed only two months and then departed, saying that she wished to visit Jaca in Aragón, the pueblo of our grandfather. After Miranda de Ebro we went to Ona and Reinosa and Riaño and Pola de Lena and Belmonte and Becerrea and Mellid, all the distance down the coast toward Portugal. Juan Bautista fought the bull with flourishes and theatrics in whatever village would erect an arena of old fencing and broken crates and boxes. No one laughed at him except the few campesinos who had had at one time or another the good fortune to see a real corrida. Agustín breathed fire and offered to doctor any sick cows; Don Bellorio made his dogs dance and told fortunes and gave recitations and offered advice to those in dilemma; I swung from the trapeze and walked across the wire and then walked back. Sometimes I sang, if you will believe it. Young Juan was angry because they were songs I had learned from him, but Don Bellorio said that no one wanted to hear boys sing, it was better that a girl do it, even if she did not sing very well.

"For whatever cause, we had success and earned some money and always had food to eat. We were happy and laughed when everyone except the gypsies we met mistook us for gypsies. It is true that we were burned dark by the sun and the weather, and our clothes when we were not in costume were old and ragged. And our wagon was decorated as the wagons of the gypsies sometimes are. Juanito with his side whiskers and imaginary guitar looked like a prince of the gypsies, swaggering ahead of the burro and calling to the girls who worked in the fields. We had a very good time. When it came autumn again I suddenly realized I had been with the circus for two years, yet it seemed like one short week.

"Now I will tell you of how I came to leave the circus where I was happy. It came as a combination of two things. First, we arrived one day in Mellid, and I knew that I was only some thirty-five kilometers from my home, which I had not visited for more than three years. The second reason was that I had begun to have much trouble with Juan Bautista. It was not his fault, he did not even know it, but because of him I was struggling with my nature. All that summer as he walked by the wagon wheel he spoke jokingly about us and said that I was his little wife, and the two old men were grandfather and grandmother. He was not serious but he suggested that we marry and travel with the circus forever, and that our babies would be costumed in ridiculous disguises and advertised as mermaids, hermaphrodites, two-headed monsters, until they were sufficiently grown to fight bulls and walk the tight wire. He would say: 'Ay, niña, drop the reins and get down from the cart, old Llorón will follow the uncles and we will go into the woods and I will get on thee a twin joined at the navel by a golden bone, and our fortune is made! Viva!' And I joked with him and was not serious, and certainly he did not suffer with desire for me—in every village he rolled the farmer girls in the coverts of their father's fields.

"Only once was he serious, on an evening when we camped outside the village of Allaríz after the spectacle. Don Bellorio and Agustín had gone back to the village to play dominoes and drink aguardiente. I sat on the leaf of the wagon in the afterlight, as I often did when the camp was prepared for the night. The three dogs sat with me as it grew dark, and we played the barrel organ for company. Then I saw Juan Bautista coming through the grove in his red cloak. I suppose for once he had had no success with the village mozuelas, for he seemed dispirited. 'Niña, there is no end to life,' he said (he was then twenty-one and life appeared very long and futile). We talked for a time and he told me that he was very unhappy among Vascos, his own people, because they were rude and mountainous and played thunderous jokes and spoke a barbarous language, not fine and polite like Castilian. He said he knew of a Vasco who had eaten a motorcycle to win a bet. For sport Vascos lift stones of a hundred and twenty kilos on their knees and stomachs and chests. Juan Bautista said that his ideal was not great strength and loud noise, but fine manners and a dark blue suit.

"Seeing that he was in a solemn mood, I dared to tell him that which we had all ached to say, but had not dared because of his nettlesome pride. 'You call yourself Quijote de la Castillo,' I said, 'but Castillo is masculine gender and it sounds absurd to say La Castillo.'

" 'Bedbugs!' he said. 'Great scholar, knowest thou that the old poem of Don Bellorio of which thou art so proud that it hangs always on the wall, calls thee Morena Huérfano, which is equally absurd? Do I not tell thee that I speak excellent Casteliano?' At which he was happy, having scored on me, and he played the barrel organ and sang:

'Ay, Morena Salado de las Estrellos,
Todos los noches me muero de amores,'

changing all the genders. It is true that Don Bellorio made a mistake, but not a very great one, and I prized my poem for its thought, not for its literary merit.

"We joked, and sang a little, and it grew darker. Then he said solemnly: 'I looked at thee on the wire today. Do you know something? I think that thou wilt be beautiful. Not extremely beautiful perhaps, but of fine presence and great dark eyes. Thou art changing, niña, slowly as the tree changes. The blood runs in the womb now. Tell me, Morena, why came it so late?'

"I said that I had been often hungry when I was a child, and that I grew slowly. His seriousness disturbed me, but he was much like a brother, and without knowing why, I felt pity for him. He said: 'And the thing accomplished, still the waiting goes on. For whom dost thou wait, little wife? Am I not acceptable? You will see, it is a fine thing, and bursts the head, and liquefies the body, and the world explodes in gold. It is a thing we have only while we are young. Can I not teach thee? I will be gentle as a rabbit.'

" 'No. I will tell thee when I am ready.'

" 'Or art thou waiting for God, like a nun? Thou art ready now. Wait if thou wilt for the Blue Prince, but in the meantime I will have taught thee, and it is a fine thing to know.'

" 'Go away,' I said. Still I joked with him and he struck his chest and said: 'Bueno, I will not press thee. I am the hero and one day thou wilt come to me!' Then he talked about love, how it was accomplished, and what a great thing it was. I was young and curious, so I listened and did not go into the wagon. He said: 'I noticed today in your costume that thy breasts have grown round.' He talked of the mysteries of the flesh and the delights of the body, and he began to touch me. I allowed it because I thought no harm could come to me from only that. He lifted my breasts and touched my stomach and kissed me and put his tongue in my mouth.

"I had been near no young man since the doctor's son persecuted me some years before, and I found it was true, what Juan Bautista had said: my body turned to liquid and my head became thick and full and pleasant and I could not see and my eyes closed. I knew that close by my hand was the long chain used to tether the dogs all together—my angels always put something heavy close at hand—but I did not want to hurt him. He only kissed me deeper and stroked my legs. Then he stopped, and said: 'See? I will not force thee, because thou art asleep and have no warmth. But it will come, and we will practise, and in time we will explore all the world of pleasure and vice, when the old men are gone. Also, I will teach thee all the refinements I have learned from the village girls, who are virtuosi of excesses, caramba!' "

"You are tired," Mari said. "You are bored. The night is almost gone, and still I have not come to the aventuras picantes, the sins and amores. Wait a little longer, for I am coming to the time when I rubbed my belly against all the hard hairy bellies of Galicia and el Cantábrico.

"We came to Mellid. I was close to my home. I was afraid that I would succumb to my curiosity and my youth. So I said goodbye to the carnival. Juan Bautista begged me to forgive, to remain, but I could not. For two weeks I had not allowed him to come upon me alone. It was not his fault, but I could not tell him that even while my body cried out to him, my heart and mind despised him for his loudness, his foolishness, his shameless sexuality. Agustín wept; Don Bellorio reproached me. In the end they allowed me to go. But I would not let them travel with me to Fuentevinho. I left them in Mellid, and took Agustín's chain of wooden links and Don Bellorio's poem and a gold crucifix that Juan Bautista gave me, and I walked across the mountains to my pueblo, avoiding all traffic and all human beings. I carried cheese and sausages in a bag and wore a black dress and long stockings like a widow. I slept one night in the mountains and then came to the river. Again I thought my life was over.

"Now I will tell you very quickly what happened in my home. Regina had returned. She kept house for América and her child and my two uncles. The men of the village came in the afternoon as always, to drink wine and tell jokes at the kitchen table; and among them was Guillermo Torres, the son of América's father.

The baby, who was three years old, screamed all the time. My uncles seemed dry and ageless and spotted as toads in the field. No one was glad to see me. Guillermo Torres followed my sister Regina wherever she went. Once I saw her slap him. She seemed to hate him. Old Torres, the alcalde, came to the house every day; he called me a wanton slut, first for losing my place in Oviedo, then for roaming the world unchaperoned in company with gypsies and homeless boys.

"Máximo the smith one day tried to tear off my clothes. Guillermo Torres prevented him. I worked in the kitchen and in the fields, and one day Guillermo Torres kissed me gently on the cheek and asked me to forgive him for what he had tried to do to me in the cuadra some years before. I had forgiven him long ago, because I always forgive everyone, except that I can never forgive my stepmother. I heard from Uncle Carlos that Guillermo Torres wished to marry Regina. I believe it was at the instigation of his father, who had never ceased to intrigue for possession of my family's land. Land is very important in the country, more important than money, and people will steal or marry or kill to come into possession of a single field. Rafael and Carlos refused to convenience the family Torres by dying and going to join their brother, my father. Uncle Rafael was seventy-one, Uncle Carlos sixty-eight. They were juiceless and dry as the oak in the river field which, though dead, would not fall.

"Guillermo Torres followed me constantly. Whenever I turned he was there, and he always asked if I had forgiven him for his error, and many times he asked politely if he might kiss me. I did not think he was so bad as the rest. He said that he did not want to marry Regina, he wanted to marry me, but always I saw him talking to her and looking after her where she walked. And always she spurned him. When I asked her why she said she loathed Guillermo Torres and would not marry him for all the gold in America. Besides, she said that he was only interested in marrying the heiress to the Quintero properties. In bed at night I lay with my fevers and thick blood and curiosity and wondered if I dared marry Guillermo Torres. He argued with his father, they pointed and shook their fists at Regina. If my uncles died the property would go to América, or if not to her then to her child, a boy named Juan, so that everyone would believe he was the true son of my father. Or else it would go to Guillermo Torres if he succeeded in marrying either Regina or myself. In one way or another old Torres would have the farm and the stone house as soon as my uncles died. I did not care. When I thought of it I believed that soon Benito would return from the army or the Falange and reclaim what belonged to us.

"Meanwhile I lay in my bed and thought not of the property or América or old Torres, but of myself and the furry, feverish feeling of unrest that was entirely of the body, not of the intelligence. I was seventeen. After Regina hit Guillermo with a feed bucket he formally asked me to marry him. Old Torres had papers already prepared. Being alcalde of Fuentevinho, he was able to change the name from Regina to María de los Ángeles without difficulty. Don Julio the Fascist priest performed the ceremony.

"Guillermo took me to the empty house of my father in the village and locked the door and pushed me onto the bed of my mother; he caught hold of my feet and spread my legs and fell on me without removing his clothing or mine. I lay under his length and he hurt me. I knew that he hated me; he was bitter and shamed. Eight days I stayed in my mother's house and he would not let me go out into the street even to buy food to cook for him. He ran after Regina. Eight evenings he came back and fell over me and raged in my face with drunken breath and made me bleed. I would not cry. I tried to accept everything then, because it was my fault in great part. I tried to be open and honest as I had sworn to be, but he was not in the house ten minutes before he had torn off my clothes and completed himself and cried: 'I spit on the Divinity! I spit on everything!' and fallen into stupefied sleep with saliva running from the corners of his mouth.

"On the ninth evening I was alone. Too much afraid to go hunt for him, I slept alone, and waited all the following day, until Uncle Rafael came in the evening and said that the Guillermo Torres had run away with my sister Regina in his old Lancia automobile. No one came to the house after that. I would not go back to my house, because of América and her men, who would mock me unbearably. After a week Uncle Rafael came again. He said that the Guardia Civil of Lugo had brought word that the car carrying both Guillermo Torres and my sister Regina had gone off the road between Astorga and La Bañoza, on the highway to Madrid. The car had rolled down the mountainside and burned. Both were dead. I would not believe it. I thought that Guillermo Torres would come back and that slowly the rage and frustration would die away, and that he would believe in me after a time, and we would begin to love each other. We were man and wife, after all.

"But even this last was not true. Old Torres came to the house the following day. I would not let him enter, so he stood in the street under the window and shouted so that all the village could hear: 'The papers are not valid! The name María de los Ángeles is not admissible! The name Regina remains on the marriage papers! My son was married to Regina! Do not think that you were married to him! Whore!'

"I was sick. I had a fever. I remained in bed four days and dreamt of lobsters. I thought I was going insane. Don Bellorio tipped up the bed and Juan Bautista put his hand deep in my belly so that I screamed. I could not sleep again. Carlos came to see me and he said that I had best go away to some other pueblo where I was not known. He had no money to give me, but he said that he would sell what he could of Guillermo Torres' possessions and effects that were left in the house and give me the money secretly, so that old Torres would not know. It was Uncle Rafael who instructed Uncle Carlos, I am sure.

"A week later I left Fuentevinho in the night, riding behind Uncle Carlos on the mule. I do not expect to return ever again. I do not write letters, no one writes to me. So far as I know old Torres and América and her baby are still there waiting for my uncles to die. Then they will own the stone house and the four fields and the barn and the fruit trees. Unless Benito returns, or my oldest brother Luis, whom I do not remember, appears again. I do not care.

"I came to Lugo with four hundred pesetas—not very much, but more than an equal sum in those days. I used a part of this fund to buy a railway ticket to Madrid. I had no reason to go to Madrid, only wanting to be as far away as possible. On the train I vomited and dreamt that Juan Bautista was covered with snakes. In the compartment was a man who said he was a doctor and he would treat me; he felt my breasts and pinched my buttocks and said that he knew what I lacked. A woman also in the compartment said: 'Shame, shame, señor. The child is ill.' When the Guardias came through to inspect papers this woman said that I was her daughter, so I was not asked to show my permiso. I would not cry, but the woman was very kind and I told her what had happened to me. Then she would not talk to me. The old people are very severe. But at the station in Madrid, when I sat still and made no movement to disembark, she relented, and gave me the address of her husband's shop in the city. It was a photography salon and she said she would ask him to give me work tinting photographs, if I showed any aptitude.

"I will hurry now. I worked for the photographer, although I knew nothing about coloring portraits and have no artistic ability whatsoever. It happened that there sat next to me at the workbench an old man who had also taken the job on false pretences many years before. He colored my first photograph, a portrait of a child in communion dress, and allowed me to show it to the foreman as my own work. In a few days I learned to do well enough, with the old man helping me. I stayed for five months. I soon learned that I was pregnant. At that time I was too ashamed to kill myself, as I was still religious. At the end of five months I fell down in the street, and the police delivered me to the nuns in the charity hospital. My glands were swollen everywhere and something was wrong with my chest—not tuberculosis, from which my mother died, but only a congestion, a kind of pleurisy. I stayed four months in the hospital. The nuns would not permit me to leave because I was pregnant, and the Catholic Church always wishes to save the child. They were afraid that I would die before giving birth and the child would have to go to purgatory for lack of baptism. I was in labor nineteen hours when the time came, but the baby lived—you have seen it alive—and I loved her, even as I would have loved Guillermo Torres had there been opportunity.

"Then after another month I was allowed to leave the hospital. The nuns asked to have the child, wishing to raise it in their way; they believed it a bastard. I said: 'I will sign the certificate with the name of my husband, who cannot sign it because he is dead. I will take the child with me.'

" 'Very well', they said. 'If you wish to take it. But we do not know how you will support it. There will always be a home here for the child if you cannot support it.' They did not believe that I had ever had a husband. 'Before you leave', they said, 'a propósito de nada, there is a woman along the hall who wishes to speak to you; she is a patient. She heard you in labor and asked your name. She says that she is an old acquaintance'.

"I went down the hall, walking very slowly, and there I found Carlota Iglesia, wife of José the dock worker from Pontevedra. Qué alegría! My nose began to bleed from happiness, as it always does. I was so weak that I sat on the floor to laugh. Carlota had recently delivered herself of a second group of triplets. Two months premature.

" 'José will swear by the balls,' Carlota said mournfully. I laughed so hard that my nose bled still more, and the nuns had to put ether in my nostrils. Carlota said: 'Go to my home and care for José. He is mad with pride and anger and despair. We came to Madrid because there was no work in Pontevedra, and behold, there is even less in Madrid. While I am in the hospital please make him eat, and guard my other three children, Jesus, Maria, and José. Sometimes he beats them out of pure desperation and anxiety, though he does not mean any harm.'

" 'What will you name the new ones?' I asked.

" 'Fish, Meat, and Potatoes,' she said. 'Perhaps it will give them luck.'

"So I left my baby with the nuns, on the understanding that I could come for her on the day that I was established, and I went to the home of José Iglesia and helped him feed and clothe the first triplets. José did nothing but swear and sit in postures of misery or roam the streets looking for work. Finally he found a job in a factory where eyeglasses were made, while I stayed home with the three niños and scrubbed floors and washed clothing for all the women in that house, which was a six-story apartment and contained well over a thousand people, hard times having made for crowded conditions. In the house was neither heat nor electricity; I washed clothes in cold water by candlelight in the middle of the day. But you do not want to hear about that; you want to hear the aventuras picantes, the spicy stories. Well, there were none at that time. I was sick and weak and José was distracted, and there were no men in the building who had money to pay my exorbitant prices.

"When Carlota returned from the hospital with Fish, Meat, and Potatoes, I left, because she and the new three were no longer to be fed by the nuns and the government, and I did not want to be a burden to José, who was burning with pride at this further proof of his extraordinary virility, meanwhile writhing in agony as he thought of the additional expense. Also, I had my own child now. I took her from the nuns and used all but a little of the money which remained to buy a ticket to Barcelona. On the trip we were followed by an electrical storm and all the lights in the train went out. The thunder crashed overhead and great balls of fire danced in the trees along the way. This time I did not want to die. I prayed to God not to strike the train and kill my baby, not to kill me either, else what would happen to her, left all alone?

"I came to Barcelona and sat on the steps of the Estación de Francia all one day with the poor people and gypsies, trying to think what I would do. In the early evening a young man of short stature, with curly hair and bad teeth, came by and recognized me for what I was, by the country clothes and my long hair and the child in my jacket. He spoke to me in Catalán and I could not understand him. Then he spoke in Castilian, with the lisp of Andalucía. I told him innocently that I had only just then arrived, and that I came from Galicia. 'Muy bien,' he said. 'I will take you in my care, señorita. You are lost without me. First we will go to a hotel and I will try you. Then if you please me, I will hunt you customers, and you will have half the money.'

" 'No,' I said.

" 'Muy bien. In that case, I will take you to meet a friend of mine, who will give you employment as a dancing girl in the Night Club Cairo, where you will use your talents as you see fit, and pay me only a small commission, eh?'

" 'No,' I said.

" 'You are very proud,' he said then. 'Perhaps you are waiting here for your husband? Or perhaps the fellow who promised to marry you when you became pregnant? You are pure, of course. The baby is not yours, you are holding it for a friend, no es? Muy bien, I will tell you: we will go to the house of Señora Piedad, where you will have a room of your own, and she will pay me a fixed fee. De acuerdo?'

" 'No,' I said.

" 'Coño! I am only trying to help. I am a public servant. I am a pimp and macarrón. Were I a landlord I would offer you work on my farm. Were I a manufacturer, I would offer you work in my mill. Unhappily, being a pimp and macarrón, I can only offer you opportunity to spread your legs in my service. Perhaps you are seeking employment as a condesa? Be warned that if you do not find some job, the police will quickly give you employment as a prisoner.'

" 'Give me one duro to feed myself and the child and go away,' I said. This youth, as you have already guessed, was cousin Ramón. He was loitering near the station in hopes of making acquaintance with French or German tourists whom he could take to the street girls, or to the Club Cairo, or to the house of Señora Piedad. When I refused him he turned away, but he believed that in my hunger and distress and helplessness I would quickly surrender to him. He saw that I would not let him make a prostitute of me, but he thought that my position would not permit me to resist his personal advances. After a short while he came back and said: 'Mira, *Condesa.* I will get thee a place assisting a respectable señora in her housekeeping. Will that satisfy thee?'

" 'Yes.' I said. I did not believe that he could do any such thing.

" 'Claro, there is no extra room in the house and you will have to sleep with me,' he said.

" 'No,' I said.

" 'Me ca'n Deo, this insect is impossible!' he said and flung his arms in the air.

"I will be brief. After much push and pull of this sort, he swore to me that the woman with whom he took lodgings was a decent lady simply seeking a clean loyal girl to live in her house and help her, as a servant. I agreed to go with him to this house, provided that we walked, and entered no taxicabs. Then I said I would wait in the street until Señora Carmencita came down to interview me. I would not go into the house with him. As you know, it is a clean house in a respectable barrio, but still I did not trust him. But it was all right. The señora was kind and helpful; I knew from her manner that she was unaware of Ramón's activities in the Barrio Chino. She held my hand and said she would be pleased to employ me, if I liked her house. Ramón told her that I was his cousin several times removed, that he had been in correspondence with me and that I was a legitimate widow. Carmencita believed him, though later on I was forced to tell her the truth. Carmencita's son Manuel was also very kind and polite. He did not like me at first because I was very unsophisticated, and he is very cultured. But he was always courteous and chivalrous. To the point that while we were yet strangers, he rid me of the importunities of Ramón.

"Ramón said, that first day: 'See, Condesa? I have found you a place; I have saved your life. I suppose you will show your gratitude. Look, Manolo: this is my new girlfriend.'

"Manuel said: 'But not if she does not wish it. I do not see any evidence that she wishes it.' Manuel knew that Ramón is foolish sometimes, and that he is a pimp and means no good to a respectable girl, also that he is dirty and was once diseased by a Barrio Chino prostitute. While I was in the house of his mother Manuel would not let Cousin Ramón come near me or trouble me in any way. Ramón was not greatly determined. At first he whined and said that I was ungrateful. Afterwards we were friends. Manuel himself became like a brother to me. On days of fiesta he sometimes took me to the cinema. Last year he took me to the great industrial fair in the Avenida de la Reina María Cristina. That was just before a trout of an American arrived in Barcelona with a huge dog.

"I am finished. Now you know everything."

I stared at her in the dark. "You idiot. Why didn't you tell me all this in five words?"

"What is the difference? Why should you not suffer?"

"I didn't suffer. Imbecile, why did you try to make me believe that you were a loose woman?"

She said: "What do you care, Codfish? Now you know what I am."

"Batshit," I said. "Do you mean to lie there and tell me—tell me that you made love to neither the doctor's son nor Juan Bautista nor Don Bellorio nor Ramón nor Manuel nor anybody else—that you submitted to Guillermo Torres only when you believed yourself respectably married—as you were, I mean—at least by the priest, if not by their miserable papers—and the baby is legitimate and all—and you kept yourself—and I am supposed to *suffer*?"

"What are you laughing at, Bacalao? I told you that I am a woman who gives herself shamelessly. But I did not say stupidly. It is only accident that none of them convenienced me. The whorishness is there, the loose woman, as you say. The thought is the act. I would have given myself without hesitation to Juan Bautista."

"But you did not!"

"It comes to the same. If he had been serious. I gave myself to Guillermo Torres."

"You lie. He took you. You gave nothing. You had no pleasure."

"Burro!" she yelled, "one is the same as the other! For want of previous opportunity am I less the whore and kept woman today! Did I lust less after Juan Bautista simply because he did not come into me? Am I more virgin after Guillermo Torres simply because he did not give me pleasure?"

Her irritation had the effect of calming me down, though I remember I still sort of flopped my elbows and clenched my toes. I said: "You don't see—because you are not a man—where the difference lies. I will tell you. The two, both Guillermo and your Gypsy Prince, do not add to the sum of one husband or first lover."

"Oh shut up," she said. "I am tired of talking to you."

"You understand," I said, "that if you had been deflowered by Juan Bautista, after whom you lusted (but you were not) or if you had loved Don Guillermo, by whom you were deflowered (but you did not) that would have been a horse of a different color."

"Oh claro, I understand. You think that the man who will conquer me has not yet come along," she said.

"At least I see no evidence of him in your history," I said smugly.

"So now you are happy," she said. "Well, I am sick of you. Now let me go to sleep, curse you."

"Curse me," I said. "Now I am happy. I know the worst. Have you nothing more terrible than this to confess, mi vida?"

"I confess nothing. I have simply told you a story. All lies. Go to sleep."

"I only want to ask one more question."

She had turned on her side to put her back to me. "No more questiones," she said. "I have told you everything."

"This Gypsy Prince of the false names—I don't think that you were really in love with him. You were only seventeen."

"What do you know of love, Cabrón?" she said, and the contempt in her voice was real.

I lay awake for awhile with my hands behind my head, thinking long thoughts. Faint gray light began seeping into the room, and noise started up in the streets. Finally I half drifted off to sleep. But it seems she had an afterthought. I vaguely saw her up on her knees leaning over me with one fist cocked, and I heard her say: "You believed that I was a dirty woman, you pig!" Then she drove her fist into my solar plexus and I woke all the way and sat bolt upright in considerable pain. By the time I caught my breath she had lain down and turned her back to me again.

Then I Went On

One

There is not very much more to tell.

Christmas was that week and we all celebrated it together—Mari and I, Yaya, her two daughters, Luis the sweetheart, and little Mercedes—with a quiet party in Yaya's smoky cell. Everybody chipped in, including the little girl who had a sock full of céntimo pieces people had given her at one time or another, amounting to about seven pesetas in all. We drank sweet vermouth and ate mejillónes, which are big orange salt-water mussels, to perk our appetites; then we sat down to a dinner of chicken fried with tomatoes, potatoes, onions, garlic, olive oil and bug. Bug is a thin twisted variety of red hot pepper guaranteed to afflict any cold-country Nordic with brassy-belch heartburn and keep him awake all night. With dinner we drank Chablis from the corner delicatessen, and afterward coffee with anis. Luis and I smoked Old Poncho cigars. Conversation was mostly prices and politics. The occasion, as the English say, was rather dim.

Thereafter, only more waiting around, until the final deplorable events of the New Year, la Noche Vieja, and the morning after.

In all we spent some six or seven weeks in the Barrio Chino, mostly engaged with Mari's grano. From the evening we arrived in the city, when there was only one until the final day, when the first was healing, the second suppurating, and the third just rearing its ugly head, Mari's neck woke us in the morning and put us to bed at night.

The first one was the worst, because we let it go too long, and it was big and hard, frightening because we didn't know what it was; and it hurt. I was far from satisfied with Yaya's doctor's opinion; I thought there ought to be some way to clean it up from the inside with medicine, rather than wait for it to open. Besides, we weren't sure that it wasn't simply a form of mumps; that is, something simply swollen up. So the following day I myself took Mari to a doctor recommended to me by the American consulate (and if that organization doesn't get a kickback, they ought to arrange something, the prices their doctors charge). This doctor thumped her on the chest and peered in her ears and asked a lot of gloomy questions about our intimate relations: did either of us have venereal diseases and were we using home-made contraceptives? He poked in her armpits and groin to see if he could discover any other swollen lymph nodes; he looked down her throat and took her blood pressure and asked if she wet her bed and then finally he gave us a bottle of enormous mauve pills—one every two hours.

The grano stayed swollen. Mari was frightened. I couldn't blame her. Apart from the discomfort and mystery of the lump itself, the neighbor women insisted on telling her revolting stories about cancer and chancres and other maggoty indispositions that eat away the flesh.

A week later we went to a third doctor, after the mauve pills that were like golf balls had done no good, and the grano had only got bigger and harder. This doctor also said that she was débil and the cure was to eat more. But I had been feeding her steak and lobster for a week and all it did was give her indigestion.

The fourth doctor took an X-ray of her chest. It was a real X-ray this time, not a fluoroscope, but I was infuriated just the same. Granted tuberculosis can cause skin infections, but certainly not until the final stages, after much coughing and wasting away. Nobody was surprised when the picture showed a perfect set of lungs. It cost me five hundred pesetas to find out what we already knew: that she had a boil on her neck that was not caused by tuberculosis.

About a week before we went to the pueblo with Yaya to rent El Catafalco, I took Mari to the city hospital in the calle Casanovas. We had to wait a long time in a dull hall painted the gray-green color of poverty and illness; then when we finally got in, the doctor there gave Mari the worst time of her life, with a long needle. After some preliminary haffing and hawing and subtle smiles of omniscience, he sat her down in a chair and jabbed the point of a syringe deep into the lump. Poor kid, her feet rose right up off the floor and her eyes opened very wide—she was squeezing my hand with both of hers and my nails turned blue and the bones popped. He drew out about twenty cubic centimeters of terrible yellow-white stuff. She tightened up and her teeth began to chatter and her face paled and clammy sweat stood out on her forehead. He had to stop; he was afraid she'd have a nervous seizure. It wasn't the hurt so much as the sucking sensation of the extraction, she said afterward. But I think it just plain hurt. When he pulled the needle out she threw up a little and choked and turned away so I wouldn't see her ugly. Cleaning up his instruments, the doctor said: "That will give some relief. Of course, it is not finished. Within a day or two the sac will refill as the affected areas drain. When it is again hard and full, return to me and we will extract what has collected. Then we will see."

"Cuernos!" Mari shouted; that is to say: Horns! or, May all your wives and sweethearts cockold you without intermission.

We both figured it was no use subjecting her to this doctor's methods. Quite apart from the fact that he apparently didn't know any more about what he was dealing with than any of the others, he was only rushing a process of nature. The lump was obviously going to fill up and come to a head, open and discharge a certain quantity of pus, then close again, either leaving a scar or not. Nobody up to then had mentioned anything about organic causes, other symptoms, or possible complications, so we decided the best we could do was treat it like any other pimple or boil, only bigger. With twenty cubic centimeters taken out, the lump lay half flat and she could turn her head in any direction without discomfort; and that night she had her first good sleep in a couple of weeks.

We did go to one more doctor, when the swelling started again. I kept hoping somebody would prescribe sulfa drugs. They were available in Barcelona, and once when I had had a series of boils in my fifteenth year, sulfathiazole finally cleared them up. This last doctor we consulted was not exactly a doctor, he was a pharmacist. In Spain, I've learned, you have three roads open to you when something goes wrong with the animal. You can visit a doctor, who nods wisely and treats you like an oaf and prescribes placebos and recurrent consultations until your money belt has shrunk to a G-string; then he refers you to his cousin, a specialist. Or you can go to the practicante, usually a motherly woman who is also a cumadrona, or midwife, licensed to give shots and enemas and things like that; and she might be able to suggest something after a lifetime of dealing with minor ills, except that she is always furiously busy attending births. The last resort, and the best, is the nearest pharmacist, who is not legally authorized to prescribe or treat anything but cuts, but who knows from years of empirical evidence which powder or pill cures what complaint or eruption.

Our pharmacist was right down our own alley, not far from Yaya's. He had a humpback and a cheerful wrinkled head like a huge white raisin, and he was so deaf he had to read lips with one eye, the other being cataracted. He had no teeth and all the time he was not talking he coughed like a locomotive. In short, a walking negation of all medicine, scholastic and otherwise. Just the sort of old man you know instinctively you can trust. His shop was full of women who wanted medicine for backache. In the back room a kid was getting a penicillin shot and screaming his head off.

It turned out that while Señor Eusevio, the pharmacist, didn't know what caused the infection either, he had many times seen similar lumps. Nobody he knew of had ever died of one. Painful, but it went away, he said, leaving no aftereffects—something to do with diet. "Are you in a hurry?" he asked. "Good. It will take time. Dirty blood. The good fortune is to have blood, caugh raugh rah raagh!" He peered cheerfully at the hole left by the last doctor's needle and put a new bandage on and gave us a tube of belladonna to help matters along. "Have ánimo and courage and faith," he said. "Después de todo, life is a situation from which no one escapes alive."

We went back to Yaya's and stayed the afternoon, heating gauze pads smeared with belladonna over the petroleo stove and applying them to the lump. Nothing happened that day. But the following morning we came to the house with Yaya after she finished mopping up the movie theatre, and when we got upstairs Yaya gently lifted the bandage off and pus came pouring down into the neck of Mari's dress.

It was as exciting as if somebody had hit the lottery. Neighbors rushed in and the blonde and the brunette left off their sewing to watch while Mari sat patiently on a wooden chair and everybody took turns gently poking at the edges of the sore. Stuff flowed out for what seemed like hours. It soaked into all the gauze we had, and I went after some more, glad of the chance to breathe in the open. Pressing here, pressing there, wherever Mari could stand it, the Yaya extracted double what the doctor had been able to get with his needles and tubes. Finally no more would come and we sealed up the hole with unguent and gauze. "But it is not over," Yaya said. "More will come; it will fill up again. We must keep the wound open and keep the belladonna on it so that it will drain into the bandage and the gauze."

That was at about two in the afternoon. Mari and I walked over to the Ramblas to see an American cowboy movie I had not had the opportunity to see at the time of its first run back home on account of not having been born yet. Then we ate a late lunch and went back and Yaya took the gauze off and showed us how a little more pus had seeped out. "You see how it works?" She said. "Very effective."

"Estupendo," Mari said moodily. "I have always preferred running sores to festering ulcers."

The fact remains that all the time the sore was open and draining constantly she was at ease and could sleep nights. The sac hung unpleasantly and the opening looked nasty, but with a bandage over it and a high-necked dress on she could forget all about it and live a normal life. We spent many days at this process of salving and extracting, and several times she felt well enough to suggest that we go live in El Catafalco, but I thought we had better stay within reach of doctors in case something rare happened.

And every day the Yaya said to me: "Capitán, if the medicine is costing too much, I will pay and you can pay me back later." A dozen times I explained that my money was a fixed quantity and I could as easily lay out a few dollars for gauze and unguent today as tomorrow. Just the same, she refused to accept board for the kid. "You have other expenses at the moment; you will make it up later," she said. Yaya with her salary of eighteen dollars a month and her windowless rented room. Yaya is one of the world's best. Have I stressed that?

Most of the time we just sat around her house, since we only rented our room by the night and couldn't get in during the day. I read a few sports car magazines available on the newspaper kiosks of the Ramblas, and Mari lay on the bed indefatigably playing with her kid. The weather continued good up until the middle of December, when it turned gusty and raw and usually rained in the afternoons. Sometimes I went up to the new city to gab with Manuel, but it was too cold for motorcycling or anything like that, so finally I quit going anywhere and just sat brooding, watching the progress of the grano. It continued to suppurate, day and night, as though there were no end to it. At last Señor Eusevio took another look and said we ought to close it up, what little infected matter remained could be expected to pass off with normal body wastes. He gave us a box of sulfa powders, the first sulfa anybody had prescribed, and we substituted that for the drawing unguent. Every night we clogged the hole with sulfa and covered it over with gauze, and every morning the gauze was stuck fast and had to be lifted loose. By the time the suppuration was all over the hole was the size of a dime. Mari stood it all as best she could, playing the fatalist and stoic for all it was worth. Slowly the skin began wrinkling up, and slowly a scab began to form.

Mari sighed and said: "I am glad it is over. Qué horror."

To make a long story short and meanwhile muddle a metaphor, no sooner had grano number one begun to close its bloody eye than number two, which had been waiting in the wings, suddenly made its appearance. It was on the other side of the neck—no chance that the two were connected below the surface and would drain through the original wound. Mari told me about it one gray morning when there was no longer any doubt. She stared at me frantically and kept saying she was sorry, that it wasn't her fault, she couldn't help it. She knew what was on my mind.

"If you leave now, what will I do?" she murmured. "I cannot work with this thing on my neck."

It was the first time that either of us had said aloud what we were both thinking. It was also the first time she had ever said anything that might be interpreted as a plea.

"I'm not going any place," I said loudly, feeling nothing but decay and putrefaction. "Everybody gets sick. It is of no importance. For Christ's sake."

Under the window the bone scavengers and thrashmen blew

their tin horns, and Mari leaked three acid tears. "Ay, San Pedro," she murmured. "Always you make me cry, Catastrophe."

I would have left that same day, but then I decided a few more days wouldn't hurt anything, so I waited to see how the new lump would turn out. There was always the chance it would break up and be carried away in the blood, I thought. From then on we just sat around staring at each other, I at her to see what she was coming down with next, she at me trying to detect signs of instant departure. Grano number two now put us to bed at night and woke us up in the morning.

But as I say, the first was the worst; at least this second wasted no time in menaces, but forthrightly swelled up and burst, due perhaps to the concentrations of poison already in her system, or maybe due to the fact that I finally took matters into my own hands and prescribed massive daily jolts of penicillin. Moreover I dragged her down to the pharmacy every morning to make sure she got them. However it was, she didn't suffer half as much from number two. It stayed soft for several days, then suddenly puffed up and almost immediately opened, spilling volcanically, then quietly settling down to the slow routine of leaking a small daily quantity into the gauze. We were hopeful and started counting chickens, but it was too early.

This was the state of affairs that last day in Barcelona, some ten days after she told me her life story and a week after the Christmas dinner: number one grano had formed a scab and was healing over; number two had opened and though not yet starting to heal was draining nicely under the influence of belladonna; and number three grano was just then beginning to swell softly underneath her right ear.

We stared dementedly into each other's eyes.

I thought: All right. That does it. I've had it. Enough. I've done all I can. Nobody could expect more. It's over. I've been horsing around for two months not knowing my own mind, being taken advantage of, seesawing back and forth, getting mixed up, trapped, harassed, hampered, bullied and confused. Now it's settled so far as I am concerned. The vacation is over, the summer is gone. It's settled, and it's over. Open your mouth and tell her. Captain, you are in a dead-end alley if you stay another day. She is sick and might get sicker before she gets well. Maybe it's a blood infection or a tumor. What more can you do? She is already the mother of one brat and liable to get embarrassed with new brats any day. Your brats! What's the sense of that? She is below your station in life, and they say that kind gets worse and worse after marriage. She is uneducated and by God sometimes she even seems simple-minded. She needs all kinds of clothes from shoes to panties. It costs money to support any woman, even the cheap kind. She is passportless and untransportable; she could never learn English; and if you did manage to get her home to the United States she would be lost and miserable and worthless. Within two years you'd both be wishing you had never seen each other. Besides, your divorce isn't yet final, you can't get married, you haven't got a job, you probably couldn't get one, Uncle Fred can't provide any more, nor will Dear Old Dad. In fine, the season is over. Get the hell out while you can.

Of course, it wasn't that easy. Two or three times that morning I had my mouth open to tell her I was sorry, but it was time I went along. She seemed to know what was up; a couple of times she asked me what ailed me, and when I answered Nothing, she turned sullen. If that was a plea she had made the other night, it was all the pleas she would allow herself.

It would have been a good time to tell her when she asked me me what was the matter. But I couldn't. Apart from being an egotist and ninety-nine per cent selfish, I am also a coward (my mother says that to recognize your faults is to begin to correct them, but it doesn't work that way with me). I hate scenes. I will do almost anything to avoid unpleasantness. It makes my knees tremble. I could not spit it out, so I started making excuses. It seems I did not want to hurt her. Telling her I was leaving would hurt her, so I could not tell her. I did not want her hurt. More exactly, I did not want to see her being hurt. I preferred being halfway to La Junquera when she started being hurt. Having learned an unexpected amount about her in the last month or so, I liked her more, and allowed myself to believe that an unannounced departure would be easier on her. I knew it would be on me. Subconsciously I suppose I realized that she was getting an undeservedly dirty deal. She had always been good to me; she had an honesty and a virtue which are out of style in most places I've been. She cooked and cleaned the stove, she maintained my socks, which are constantly getting holes in them. She was bright, she obeyed, and she made love with her whole body and all her energy. She minded her own business and only took me seriously when I wanted to be taken seriously. And maybe on top of that she was truly in love with me, if such things be.

But whenever I even half thought of doing the honorable thing, as some smothered part of me kept urging me to do, I got an immediate horrifying picture of what it would be like: bean- and potato-stew and olive oil and foreign voices and woodsmoke and garlic and pus and rain and never a way out. Halfbreed kids and Barcelona in July and never a friendly word in English. Lost citizenship and outraged relatives, recurrent medical bills, homesickness, café exprés, police, and papers and desperate hovels and fetid beds and exile. I can't, I *can't!* I thought; and every once in a while there was this little interior voice that clicked its tongue and said: Such a fuss about a little whore.

It all boiled down to one incontrovertible argument: I had only a little over two thousand dollars left. A good two-thirds of that would have to go toward getting me and the car safely home. What was left would barely give me enough small change for a quick peek into the north countries and the international sports-car races before I climbed on the boat.

So my only real problem was working up good reasons for sneaking off without telling her. I could think of several just off the top of my head. In fact, after mulling it over a few minutes I had at least twenty good sound reasons for executing this convenient stratagem. But there was one needle-thin little objection that kept recurring no matter how much I concentrated: "You are just naturally rotten inside," said this still small voice with irresistible logic.

I made my plans. That same day I would casually suggest that we go up to El Catafalco to spend the rest of the winter. I would collect our things and dump them in the car. Then I would say to Mari: The car is full. You wait here while I take this load, and then I'll come back after you. And she would never see me again. I'd leave her stuff in our country house that we would never live in, and then with my belongings already in the car I would leave straightway for the border and never thereafter come within a hundred miles of Barcelona. There was no other way.

Just the same I felt that our impending goodbyes ought to be something more than just an indifferent peck on the cheek, as though I really were only going twenty miles up the road and coming right back. After so long a time together the end seemed to demand a more intimate and ceremonious farewell. So I thought I would give us a party that night, with New Year's Eve as an excuse. Everything had to be casual and ordinary or she might suspect. I would have to say my goodbyes in ways she would not recognize until afterward. Without words, in fiesta and celebration and the inevitable cha-ka-cha, I would say what I wanted to say to her, what I would have said aloud if things had been different: Well, my darling, it has been good, no matter how you look at it. Between the crazy times and the serious times the arguments and the adventures, we have lived a complete life and had what we wanted. Hungry youth turned loose in the horn of plenty, so to speak. I don't regret it. I will always remember these months with nostalgia and I will never forget you, doll.

Actually, I was expecting more than nostalgia; I was braced for remorse.

"You are thinking very hard," she said in a rather dead voice. We were having breakfast in a little bar in the calle Unión: café con leche with chulos. Normally we ate breakfast with the Yaya in the bar of the movie theatre where she worked, but that morning we didn't feel like socializing with anybody.

I roused, and shrugged my shoulders. "Oh it's nothing, nothing," I said. "Maybe a little bad humor. It is the disappointment of this morning. The new grano this morning was a shock."

"I saw. You were struck hard. A terrible blow."

"Don't be like that," I said.

"Do you think I am unconcerned, Mero? It is *my* neck. Would you like to have this neck? Then you would be struck even harder."

"What will be, will be," I said, patting her on the fanny. "It is necessary to conformarse, remember?"—giving her a quick lesson in resignation that might stand her in good stead during the next few days. I thought for a minute. "Look," I said. "It seems to me that we are both stale and disgusted. It is the infection, of course, but it is also boredom. I am sick of this city. We sit and do nothing. It is a useless life. Listen, let's give ourselves a change. Tonight let's go out?"

"Out of what?" she said. Sometimes I still use English locutions.

"Oh, out of what we are in," I said. "El rut. Los doldrums. You dig me, no? Out on the town, al pintar la cuidad roja. Tie a can on. Let your hair down and have a ball."

"Loco" she said; one of the milder names she calls me when I am not a calamity or some kind of fish.

"I am serious," I said. "I think we should have a good time. Tonight we will eat dinner in Los Caracoles and then go to a night-club."

"Do you wish to spend all your money at once because you have heard that the peseta is to be devaluated?"

"I am beyond money, mujercita," I said. "Tonight we will sing in the streets. Right now I am in disappointment, but I think that later in the day I will sing in the streets and kick the Guardias on the posterior and burn with passion."

"Will you put on an incandescencia?"

"I explained that to you before. An English glow is not the same as a Spanish glow; it is a euphoria. I mean a mild drunkenness of the happiest sort which is only achieved by precise mixtures and rigid control of quantity."

"I will go with you," she said.

"One forgets the troubles of the world and sings in the street and one feels good," I said. "Do you want to come with me?"

"I will go with you and get drunk, too."

"I've never seen you drunk," I said.

"I also put on an incandescencia when I am drunk. But it is not an English incandescencia, it is a Spanish incandescencia, and when I have put it on I am burning. You will have much trouble with me."

"I always have trouble with you."

"I mean in the bed, Trout," she said and faintly blushed.

"De acuerdo," I said. "A bargain."

Some of the bad mood was shaken off. We went from that bar to another and ate a second breakfast. That is, I did; Mari only had coffee. But the continental breakfast will not do for me. I need more weight inside so the morning breezes of December won't wither me away.

"How is the neck?" I asked.

"I am fed up to the nostrils. I am rabid like dogs with disgust. One is bad luck, two is too much, three is despair and helpless-ness. Perhaps I am to have a succession of these things from now until the end, like good Catholic pregnancies. But it does not hurt," she said.

"I was thinking about this, too," I said. "As long as they continue to open up and let the infection escape, they cannot poison you—I mean, they are only sores. Of course they are painful and ugly, but what I mean is, they won't kill you. Nor do they interfere with your life. We already know that doctors can do nothing that nature will not do by itself. It seems there is nothing to do but treat them as we have and wait."

"Qué mas da?" she shrugged. "Time will cure them or they will kill me."

"They won't kill you. Time will bring the last one. Meanwhile we can put the salve on the draining ones, put the penicillin powders on the healing ones, and the penicillin injections into where the world cannot see. I don't believe that the grano will interfere with your cooking or your reading of novels of Cow-boy del Far-Oeste, or with your incandescencia. We will take tubes of belladonna and boxes of the powders, and there will be a practicante in the pueblo to give the injections. You understand?"

She had been looking at me; now she looked elsewhere.

"We can go to the pueblo to live," I said.

She only nodded.

"You don't want to go," I said.

"I suggested we go there a month ago."

"Why don't you want to go now?"

"You know that I want us to live in our house."

"But—"

"Let us go then."

"You have an objection."

"I have no objection."

"Why don't you want to go?"

"I want to go."

"But what?"

"But what cuernos!" she flared. "I said let us go. We will live in the house. I don't like the Hotel Paraíso. I would rather we lived in our own house. I will go where you want to go. I said I would go. Why do you ask me questions?"

When she wants to she can be as uncooperative as a hangnail and give you no satisfaction at all. A couple of times she had specifically requested that we go live in El Catafalco, seeing we had it rented. And the week ends we were up there she was always reluctant to come back to the city. Now she apparently didn't want to go at all, or at least wouldn't give me the satisfaction of thinking that anything I suggested met with her approval.

"We'll take Mercedes to live with us," I said, thinking this might trap her into expressing some pleasure.

"When do you want to go?" was all she said.

Now that my fine plan was on its feet and walking, I wanted to get it over with as quickly as possible, with nothing going wrong. "Tomorrow," I said. "Why not?" She looked startled, but would not let herself comment that it seemed rather sudden. I said: "This morning I will gather our belongings and put them in the car, and then we will have our party tonight, and I will leave the car in the garage by the Comandancia Marina so we can get it and leave early in the morning."

"Only tell me what you want me to do," she said in a lampblack voice. I said that there was nothing for her to do; that I would get the car and go up to Carmencita's place for the stuff we had left there, then come back to Yaya's for the rest. I would garage the car in preparation for the morrow, then we would spend the rest of the day diverting ourselves. "You can go back to the house of the Yaya to wait," I said. "I will come in half an hour."

She nodded.

The next was the tricksy part—to see whether she would suspect. I said: "Probably our properties will fill up the car, because there is not very much room. And I have to take the dog, too. So tomorrow morning you can stay in bed for awhile, and I will make the first trip with our clothes and the dog and then return for you and the child about noon."

She looked elsewhere and blinked.

"What's the matter now?"

"Nothing."

"Why are you crying?"

"I am not crying. Curse you. I don't know."

Thinking back, I am persuaded that she saw as clearly as I that my early morning trip to the pueblo while she was still in bed was my perfect chance to defect. She must also have known that there wasn't a word in the world she could say if I was determined to go, which I was. On the other hand, there are few women who could keep quiet under such circumstances. It might be that she never suspected a thing. Or she might have suspected I was planning to desert but hadn't yet nerved myself to it. In fact, I don't know what she thought.

I took out my billfold, a present from her, and said: "You might as well go to the pharmacy for your injection while I go to Carmencita's house. Then we can forget about it for today. Also, I will give you some money for tomorrow morning. While I am carrying the first cargo to the pueblo, you go to the pharmacy and buy enough powder, unguent, and gauze to last one week. Ask the old man if penicillin is available in the country. If not, buy seven flasks. Next week we will visit the city and buy further supplies. Maybe you would like to buy some heavy clothes for yourself and Mercedes?"

"Dios!" she said. "What is all this?" I had given her seven thousand pesetas, or a hundred and eighty-some dollars, an improbable sum for anyone to own in the Barrio Chino, much less carry around with him or hand to women in bars. It was the money I meant to leave with her, to tide her over for awhile. I wished it were more, but I couldn't afford more, and to explain even this sum put a strain on her credulity. I said: "You will need it. I don't say you must spend it all. That's just what I happen to have in Spanish money at the moment. The rest is in travelers' checks. I want you to keep the pesetas for me because tonight we are going to celebrate, and no one goes to get drunk with so much money in his pocket. It might be lost or stolen or, more probably, spent."

Because we couldn't leave anything in our room at the Paraíso, we had our belongings stashed away in several different places. The trunk of the car was already full of stuff we weren't using: my underwater fins and goggles and dart, Mari's rubber boots and overalls, some papers and magazines and a couple of old blankets. Carmencita was storing our summer clothes for us, plus a bunch of souvenirs picked up on the Costa Brava. More junk was at El Catafalco, stuff we used when we went up there for week ends, like her old wrapper and some skirts and sweaters, my blue jeans and tools, and the guitar I had bought a while ago, always meaning to learn how to play. The rather inadequate trunk of the car was full before I left the garage; the summer clothes then filled up the back seat; and by the time I had put the stuff from Yaya's in the front seat, there was no question of Mari going with me on the next day's first trip. There was barely room for me and the dog. It's not that we had so much property, but that a Jaguar is not built for family traveling.

Mari carried down the last armload from the pensión and then just stood looking disconsolate, while the dog, sensing the excitement of moving day, cocked his leg and peed through my wire-wheels onto the right front brake drum. I drove down to the garage and locked up the car. When I asked the attendant if things would be safe overnight, he shrugged disparagingly at the mounds of junk in the cockpit and said, Claro, nobody would steal this.

I walked back up the block to the pensión. Mari was still standing on the curb looking dejected. "It's too early to begin getting drunk," I said. "How shall we pass the day?"

"However you wish," she said dispiritedly.

It was then about eleven-fifteen.

We walked over to the movie house where Yaya worked, and she came out to have coffee with us at the bar. "Why not take the baby for a paseo?" she said. "She has a new dress, she looks like a little angel, and it is a fine day. You can take her for a walk to the Plaza Real to feed the pigeons."

This met with nobody's enthusiasm. "What do you want to do?" I asked Mari.

"Whatever you want to do," she said, cooperative as ever.

Yaya said: "In the park of Montjuich there is a field where the boys fly gasoline aeroplanes on cords. You might go to watch."

"Or we could go bowling," I said.

"I am sick of movies," Mari said. "Please let us not go to the movies."

"Well, I don't want to sit in a bar all day," I said.

"Or else," Yaya said, "there is an exhibition of metal forgings in the museum in the Pasaje Virreina."

"Indeed," I said.

Finally it was decided that we would go to the zoo. Yaya said that the tubercular blonde could go with us to attend the child and that she herself would meet us there after she finished her work. In the meantime she would guard the dog, she said.

This zoo is in the pretty park just north of the railroad station. There is nothing I like better than taking three-year-old kids to zoos. "Maybe it's closed," I said.

"Oh no," Yaya said, "it is open all year around."

At least I didn't have to drive them up in the Jaguar; we went by taxi, and it was just as well, because little Mercedes promptly urped on the floor. Margarita, the blonde, said it was nothing, she threw up her breakfast nearly every morning. Luckily the driver didn't notice or I would have had to pay a staggering indemnity. We hurried away. Mari and Margarita were having a fine time pretending the kid had morning sickness. "Quien es el padre, nena?" they said.

We did a slow tour down the first row of cages, at the child's amble, smelling the bears and watching the monkeys at their nastinesses. We pitied a little elephant, mangy as an heirloom rug, that was trying to scratch its back against a brick wall, and we paused to watch the lions, who were being fed: mouthing and splitting big white bones in an oddly horrible way. By the time we reached Birds of the World (Chinese pheasants and blue peacocks and such exotic fowls as Rhode Island Red hens) little Mercedes had to be carried, and I had to carry her. We stopped at the kiosk at the far end and I bought her some almonds and a vermouth apiece for the rest of us, and we all sat at a little iron table to bask in the sun. The fine day, one of the last, had brought out flocks of pigeons and families with hordes of children. Mounted Guardias went by on coppery horses, dressed—the Guardias, that is—in plumed shakos and boots and silvery sabres. Now and then some caged animal moaned or sneezed or roared behind its bars.

We waited around, torporous, for Yaya to come so we could have another drink and go home. In coastal Cataluña in the middle of the day the December sun is warm as a New England spring, if you stay out of the breezy shade. Mercedes went to sleep on her mother's lap and got one side of her face sunburned, while the two girls talked about one thing and another and I read a sports-car magazine picked up on the Ramblas that morning. When Yaya came she disturbed us all by being full of pep. She had never been to the zoo she lived a mile away from for half of her life, and she wanted to see everything before she left.

At about three-thirty Mari and I wound up alone in a large indoor bar in the Plaza España, across from the airline terminal. Yaya and Magarita had gone back to the pensión, taking the child with them. "Don't look for us before morning," I said gloomily. "Tonight we make fiesta."

So now, the fine day dissolving into rain, we were trapped in the

Cosmos Bar, where we sat glumly over small glasses of jerezquina, sherry mixed with quinquina, whatever that is. Neither of us had anything to say. But at least it wasn't the usual December afternoon rain: it thundered and lightninged and hurled fusillades of hailstones like mothballs. Awnings flew and the taxis forged back and forth across the plaza, pushing mustaches of dirty water. We were at a table near the window, and we sat drinking and watching the rain and hail sheet past and bounce on the cobblestones. There was no question of going anywhere, at least till the hailstones stopped falling, so we sat not looking at each other and not talking. The bartender lighted the electric candelabras in the enormous ceiling, and then the storm put them out at the same instant it stopped the trolleys in the plaza. A group of old men playing remigio, the Spanish version of rummy, demanded a lantern; the rest of us sat in semidarkness. Every so often would come a tremendons flash and an immediate shattering thunderclap right over our heads. The storm was coming to a climax.

It was the storm that started things moving again. After about the fourth blast Mari suddenly got up and walked around the table and sat down next to me; she clutched the front of my coat with both hands and put her head under my chin. She believes that lightning will *not* strike her in about the same way she believes there is no God; I mean, the intellect is forced to that decision by what it sees in nature, but there are moments when the primal animal is not so sure. With me thunderstorms have a different effect; I am always stimulated and excited by them. I want to do something. When I was a kid I used to put my head out the window and get soaked and laugh like an idiot.

"Let's go outside and sit under the awning," I said. She just shuddered. I could not sit still, though, and after she had calmed down a little I went to telephone Manuel. "Let's see what he's doing," I said.

He wasn't home. His mother said he was supposed to be at his club, but she had tried to call him there and nobody answered. She said she would be glad if I could find him, because she was worried about him out in the storm, and besides she wanted him to come home because she was frightened, too. I called the Club Jazz anyway, and this time Manuel himself answered. We shouted at one another. He was exalted too.

"No one is here but myself and Paquita!" he yelled. "We have opened all the windows and the lightning bolts are hurtling in! She is screaming with fear!"

"Why didn't you answer the telephone when your mother called?"

"Ah—well," he said.

It seemed he was comforting Paquita while the thunder trampled around overhead.

"Come up to the Bar Cosmos in the Plaza España," I said. "We are having a party."

"Estás loco? Have you ever ridden a motorcycle in a hailstorm? It is death. I have a helmet, but Paquita would be beaten to death."

"The hail has stopped," I said. "Now it is only thunderbolts. Come get drunk with us."

"Why don't you come here?"

"I have no helmet," I said.

Mari asked: "Will he come?" Apparently he is occupied, I said, but he might come along later. "A girl is with him," I said.

"Most of his girls are bad girls, because he does not want to get married," she said.

About a quarter after four Manuel and his Bad Girl came in. The thunder and lightning had moved south toward Sitges, but it was still pelting warm rain in drops the size of grapes. The two had only Manuel's saddle poncho to cover them, nothing more, not even a hat, since Manuel had chivalrously declined to wear his helmet, seeing that she didn't have one. Their hair was plastered on their skulls, and their pants and skirt respectively clung to their legs. Manuel whirled the poncho around his hips like a toreador's cape and said: "Hai, Toro! Do you like our Spanish weather, Yanqui? In December we have summer storms, and next July we will have snow on the beach of Prat de Llobregat!"

"Astonishment has vanquished my hiccups," I said formally.

"Eet blease thee tour-eests," Manuel said. He studies English in the evenings, because according to him it is now the language of international commerce. Then he said: "With permission, I wish to present my friend, Señorita Paquita Trasera."

The Bad Girl left off picking the sopping skirt out of the copious folds of her gluteus maximus and without warning smacked Manuel full in the face with her fist. He shut his eyes and rattled his jowls as though unexpectedly beaned by a Texas leaguer. Trasera means rear or behind but I did not get the joke until later when he took me aside and explained the gleeful details of his conquest in the stormracked Jazz Club.

"Maybe she does not want it known," I suggested.

"Pero hombre! qué tensión!"

Paquita was about thirty, I guess. Unmarried but expensively dressed, with big black Moorish eyes and a pendulous lower lip. Manuel told us at the outset that we must not expect great things of her, as her head only served to keep her ears from snapping together. I daresay her mental candlepower was not much in excess of that of our dog's, but in spite of that, or maybe because of it, she made excellent company that afternoon. Even being insulted in public didn't diminish her good humor. Except when she was punching Manuel in the teeth she just sat there like a satisfied and somewhat cretinous cat, roaring with laughter at almost everything that was said.

Manuel said: "Señorita, these are my friends, Señor Don Nikolai A. Bulganin and his woman, both from America of the North.

"Hola," the Bad Girl said. "If you are Norteamericanos why are you in Spain?"

"Only I am an American," Mari said. "My husband is Spanish."

"Oh. You are tourists?"

"No, we travel on business," Mari said. "I am hangman; my husband is seamstress."

This passed without question, but later I heard Paquita ask of Manuel if I was really Spanish. "Then why does he have a French name?" she asked. Manuel said: "Because he is Vasco, and all Vascos have strange accents."

At any rate, I was glad to see Mari back in the conversation. She laughed and started to cheer up. Nobody can resist a dolt. We all took turns telling the Bad Girl fantastic lies. The waiter came and listened for awhile.

"Man, bring us sweet rum," Manuel said. "We have been drinking sweet rum all afternoon."

"Sí, señor."

I said: "I will drink carajillo; bring me coffee in a glass and two copas of cognac Carlos Primero to mix in it. You drink that, too," I said to Mari. "Coffee to keep you awake, cognac to arouse you."

"That's the same thing," the Bad Girl giggled.

"You make a mistake," Manuel told her reasonably. "The technique of this is to put the head of the red horse of passion in a black bag, meanwhile pricking it with the spurs." She giggled wildly at the mention of passion. He said to me: "I wish you success."

"We expect to be up all night," I said.

"Shut up, Tonguefish," Mari said.

The waiter returned carrying a tray with four coffees, four jiggers of cognac, and two glasses of ron dulce. Mari and I toasted each other and drank off one each of the cognacs. Then the four of us poured the remaining drinks into our respective coffees and sat in the grumble of thunder telling dirty jokes. Several times we had to grab the Bad Girl and hold her in her chair while she laughed. Some of the other customers started giving us irritated looks.

Actually it was in poor taste. The better Spanish bars are normally as discreet and decorous as a Boston dinner club, with even the rare drunks never raising their voices. If you do get over exuberant your fellow patrons are likely to mutter Nada de eso, let's have none of that. But we were beyond criticism that afternoon. We laughed at everything, and whenever the Bad Girl unbelted one of her mindless ululating carcajades it set the rest of us off and we roared till our jaws ached and we couldn't breathe.

Finally, although it was still raining heavily and the plaza had become a swirling lagoon, we decided to go elsewhere—our interior heat would keep us dry in any weather. "Today is the grand fiesta of the end of an impossible year," Manuel said. "We celebrate all night."

"Youth in flames," I said.

"Haw haw woo-haw-haw," the Bad Girl said.

"We will go to all the bars of low category in the Barrio Chino."

"I will go get a taxi," I said.

"Taxi? A ham for the taxis," Manuel said. "Do I not own the moto which wins all the races in England? Do you think it will not carry four? What idiocy! We will all go on my moto."

"It is a party," Paquita said. "I will ride on the handlebars."

"I would not consider going in a taxi," Mari said.

"Where are we going, though?" Paquita asked.

"All four together. Four comrades," Manuel said. "All night together, riding the red horse of passion. I will drive, Señor Malenkov will sit on the reservoir of gasoline, his woman will ride paquete behind me, and I have a short length of rope which we will attach to the ankle of Señorita Francisca. She will take it in good part. You are my guests. Where shall we go?"

"With permission, I will remain behind, if you are going to drag me behind the motorbike," said Paquita, who was capable of an instantaneous yaw from hooting hilarity to a kind of oatmeal solemnity.

"Well," I said. "We were only going to eat dinner and have a few drinks."

"That is no celebration, hombre," Manuel said, swirling his poncho around him. "We will visit all the bars, then we will go to Los Cuernos for appetizers, then we will dine in Casa Juan, and go afterward to the Nightclub Rio to dance and drink flaming rum. Are we all agreed?"

As we went out I said: "This is a very fine program you have laid out, my friend. How much money have you?"

"Fear not," he said simply. "I provide transport."

So I knew I was stuck with the bill, but I didn't worry about it then, since I could see that both he and Paquita were far ahead of us on sweet rum, and I couldn't believe that either of them would last beyond the first couple of bars.

First we went up to the Vista Mar on the top of Montjuich and had a symposium, looking out over the city and the storm. That ride is worth a mention. We actually did go all four on his motorcycle. The B.S.A. is a big enough machine, but bigness is relative when speaking of motorcycles; they're built to carry one person or, at most, two. It took some doing on Manuel's part to get us all up the hill alive, what with the unbalanced load, the traffic, and the slippery roads. Luckily, his bike had one continuous seat rather than two separate ones, so the girls managed to squeeze on behind Manuel, though Mari was sitting half on the rear fender. I being the most athletic of the passengers, had to straddle the gas tank, and such is the position of the instruments and the geometry of the front fork, that I had to sit backwards, staring into Manuel's foggy goggles, my feet out straight and nothing to grab hold of. It was a wild ride. I kept twisting my neck around, throwing us still further off balance; but it makes me exceedingly nervous not to see where I am going at thirty miles an hour with nothing behind me to break my fall except speeding asphalt. I say thirty miles an hour, but luckily we only achieved that on the level stretches. Most of the climb up to the park we were reduced to a second-gear crawl. The B.S.A. is a powerful machine, but close to six hundred pounds of people is too much to ask of the best of the one-lungers. It doesn't matter: a spill at even five miles an hour would have meant dozens of broken bones.

Getting started was the hardest. With everybody up Manuel could hardly keep the machine from falling over when he lifted one foot to kick in first gear. He kept us upright for the first twenty yards by skidding his shoe soles along the ground. At that we left a wild snaky track and almost ran into a monument. Steering a motorcycle is done largely by shifting weight, and our various weights were shifting in all directions.

We wobbled around the plaza and went under the Arch of Triumph and started up the hill by the Palacio Nacional. Before going fifty feet we were soaked to the skin. The girls squealed and leaned this way and that. Manuel, flying blind, started to sing exultantly, and then we all sang, the rain running in our mouths: "A lo loco, a lo loco . . . Loco es el sistema mejor!" Every time the back wheel slithered Mari said, Ui! Ui! Ui! but the Bad Girl did not even know we were in danger; she just flung her head back and sang up at the rain: "Loco loco loco, ay ay ay!"

It was blowing bitter cold on my back, which was serving as windshield for the rest of them. Rain hitting the exposed skin of my neck and ears felt like little pellets of sharp ice. As we groaned up the hill the exhaust pipes blew streamers of thick smoke. "Who says my moto will not transport the entire futbol team of Madrid?" Manuel shouted, peeking under my armpit to see where the next curve was.

When we wobbled to a stop in front of the Vista Mar, the café that overlooks the harbor and the city, we began to fall slowly over to the left, and all the legs on that side shot out to uphold us, like some weird kind of centipede. "Get off, get off!" Manuel yelled. He was doing most of the holding, supporting six hundred pounds on one leg. The rest of us scrambled down one by one until he could manage by himself. He and I hauled the machine up on its standard and felt the baffles. They were red hot. We shook hands formally and agreed that it was pure dumb luck the motor hadn't either caught fire or exploded.

"We want to dance on the terrace!" cried the girls, whose wet black hair, white faces, runny make-up, and soaked clothes gave them the look of splashy painted souvenir dolls. The terrace is the roof of the Vista Mar, where tourists come in summer to sit at iron tables under striped parasols. The tables were still up but there weren't any parasols, and Manuel and I decided to go downstairs into the bar, leaving the girls to dance on the terrace by themselves if they wanted to. I was already catching cold. "Ka-cheese!" I said, sneezing so hard that water flung off my head in a spray. I was only wearing slacks and the camel's-hair coat.

Nobody was in the bar except the owner and his old grandmother, playing dominoes by the window. Lights were out up there, too, but a small fire was burning on the hearth. "How may I serve you, señores?" the man said, pegging us right away for Flaming Youth. Manuel ordered a bottle of cognac and half a bottle of rum, a lemon, some sugar, and a bowl to mix it all in.

"We have come all the way from Paris, France, by motorcycle, and are dead of cold," Manuel said. The old man did not even dignify this lie with a smile. He went into the back room to get a bowl. To the grandmother sitting across the way Manuel said: "Allow me to present le Monsieur Victor Ugo and his concubine Mademoiselle Guillotine. Say something in French, Victor."

"Honi soit qui mal y pense," I said.

"I told you he was French," Paquita said confusedly. "Who has ever heard of a Vasco named Ugo?"

"Ay, what terrible weather," Grandmother said. I believe she was trying to be amiable. We talked about the weather.

"What crazy weather," Paquita said. "Será culpa de la Bomba H, no será?"

This is a remark that never fails to get my goat. If it is ever discovered that fission bombs have any effect on weather, it will be discovered by scientists, not by jokers who have picked up the easy habit of blaming everything on the United States.

We pulled a wooden table with a checkered cloth over to the fire and sat drying our shoes. The proprietor brought the fixings and Manuel said: "I do not know exactly how to make this, and I think we lack some ingredients, but I will make the punch myself, then if there is anything wrong with it, we will all blame me."

He poured the rum and cognac in and cut up the lemon in chunks, then added the sugar, all in a big shallow bowl painted with stagecoaches and red Indians. Then he mixed a little cognac and sugar in a spoon and set fire to it, and dripped the fire carefully into the bowl so that it precariously ignited the cognac and rum.

Thin blue flames leaped up and burned, detached in the air. We took turns stirring with a wooden spoon so it wouldn't go out. Meanwhile Grandmother had kindly given us a used tablecloth to wipe up with, as rain water was still running from our hair into our eyes and dripping off our noses. Everybody was sneezing, me Ka-cheese, Manuel Aw-phow, and the girls little Fichew noises like squirrels.

We weren't in the Vista Mar very long. Just long enough to dry off a little and drink the punch and recuperate from the ride on the B.S.A. before Manuel pooped the party. What with the fire roasting our skins and clothes, plus the interior heat working outward in red ears and flushed cheeks, we soon felt fine again. When the sugar burned off and the punch went out of its own accord, we leaned back grandly in our chairs with hot mugs in our hands and resumed the conversation. I could tell Manuel was feeling it; his eyes crossed several times and he kept lighting a cigarette that was already lighted until it was a charred mess. Then he started to monopolize the conversation. We were all talking, making jokes and carrying on somewhat, when he made everybody be quiet and listen while he told a rambling story about some incredible sexual adventure with an English girl on the island of Mallorca the summer before. It was a saga of consecutive thwarted attempts, the final one in the darkened patio of a strange house. The girl kept saying, "No, no. Bambinos." Wrestling away, with Manuel already in charge of her slip and girdle, the two had suddenly looked up to find the windows above them full of dark silent heads belonging to the girls of a house of joy, but that did not diminish the sudden horror of shame in which at least the English girl found herself. She fled, leaving half her underwear behind, presumably never to return to Mallorca again, possibly never to sleep tranquilly again. But Manuel stayed on to talk to the girls. He waved the slip and the girdle at them. They jeered at him for his failure to conquer the Inglésa. "Why don't you come up?" they said. "We won't fight you off." "Señoritas," he answered with profound hidalgo bows, "you ask why does the comely and virile young Spaniard risk rebuff and ignominy by pursuing the foreign lady? You ask why does a glossy and indefatigable galán like myself trot humbly after the Inglésa when your seductive selves are available for a modest fee? Well, may I be permitted to remind you, señoritas, that while failure brings shame upon all Spanish manhood, on the other hand, success—success does not cost me even a *single céntimo!*"

The punch was gone by this time. In all there were four mugs for each of us, but Manuel had dipped out a couple ahead of his turn, and I could tell by the meandering way he told his story and by the excessive solemnity with which he quoted himself that he did not have far to go before he got either sick or mean. Paquita made the unsurprising remark that men are all the same, and Mari said something bitter about what a man finished and forgot about in half an hour the woman had to live with for the rest of her life. Then in the discussion of sex that followed Manuel managed to surpass even his earlier dirty jokes, so that Grandmother left the room and even the Bad Girl looked disgusted. He summed up by confiding in a loud voice that he had only recently performed prodigies of endurance on the cooperative postern of a lady not far distant from us at that moment. The words were hardly out of his mouth when he received the best thump of the day, flat on his parted lips with a porcelain mug. A front tooth chipped and he spat blood.

The party fell apart.

Mari and I were alone.

"He has taken her to a house of rendez-vous," Mari said.

"No doubt. Among other things he will probably get revenge for his tooth."

"He has no right to strike her though," she murmured. "It was what he said. Besides, he did not seem angry."

"Only a little bloody," I said. "Maybe he is stimulated by pain. I have heard of such people. But what libidinous effect can it have to be hit in the face with a jarra?"

"I would be more than pleased," she said without much interest, "if at any time—"

"Please me some other way," I said, holding her hands on my knees.

It was seven o'clock, already dark because of the rain. We had come down the hill, by taxi, to a favorite little bar on the Diagonal, where it was usually quiet, the bartender knew us, and there was a miniature pooltable in case we felt athletic. Half the inconsiderable floor space was given over to resiny casks of wine; a tame pigeon sat on the cash register cooing while the customers quietly played parcheesi and one fellow stroked thoughtful chords on a guitar. The punch had sunk down in us and we had only just then gone back to cognac and coffee, a warming drink. Our mood had sunk, too, though not unpleasantly; we just leaned on our elbows and talked quietly, feeling smooth and mazy, forgetting that tonight was our last night together.

"We must drink very slowly and discreetly but without stopping," I said, "so that the blood will always carry a little fire, but not too much, to the brain, and the rest will be turned to sugar. That is the way we will put on both kinds of incandescencia but we will not become riotous or stupid, only warm and fuzzy."

"What is fozzy?"

"Cubierto de pelusa fina," I said, "like peaches. Like poodle dogs. But that is not what I mean."

"Hairy," she said.

"Not that either. Hairy is not it all. How can you be in a hairy state of mind?"

"Your legs are fozzy," she said. "Fozzy like poodle dogs."

"Never mind my legs," I said. "Have I ever told you that you are beautiful?"

"No."

"I have never told you? Often I think it. Your hair is like all the night, and your eyes are like grapes."

"Qué bueno! Thank you. What grapes, red or white, you Mackerel?"

"American grapes," I said. "Concord grapes, a purple-blue, with a faint frost on them."

"Well, your eyes are like bleeding prunes, hala! Now who has frost in his eyes, Flounder?"

"You are not helping me over the language wall," I said. "Without metaphors then: to me you are beautiful."

"Thank you," she said

We passed an hour or so like that, and then we decided to eat. Neither of us was hungry, but we thought perhaps if we followed Manuel's suggestion and went to Los Cuernos for tapas, it might wake our appetites. Los Cuernos refers to the bull horns which are the trademark of this establishment and hang on the wall over the bar. Tapas are the little dishes of Spanish hors d'oeuvres, which Los Cuernos specializes in. For instance, you can get practically every vegetable in the world pickled in brine or olive oil with garlic and hot peppers. You can get tiny octopi taken unborn from inside mama octopus and stuffed with anchovies; or snails cooked in their shells with wine or lemon sauce; or whole gamba shrimps in salt water; or oysters, dried, smoked, or fresh; or squids or sepias or mussels; or crayfish or goat's-milk cheese or fried larks or grasshoppers or I don't know what-all. We ate a little bit of everything in sight, washing it down with a sweet wine called Tears of Gold. Then, faint and reeking, and with stinging lips, we staggered over to the calle Escudillers to eat dinner.

"I can't swallow another thing," Mari said.

"You can drink champagne."

"Claro que sí."

"A bottle of Brute '67, buen hombre," I said to the waiter. He just looked at me inscrutably. "You know, the bubbly. Large economy size."

"Tell me what you want and I will explain," Mari said.

"What's the matter with my Spanish?" I wanted to know.

"It becomes a little equivocal," she said. "What do you want to eat?"

Los Caracoles is a very expensive and famous place, with chickens and pheasants roasting on a charcoal fire in the street outside. You have to walk through the medieval kitchen to reach the dining room, and the ceilings are hung with gourds and bulls' ears and strings of garlic. Any number of exotic and typical dishes are served, but the most I could eat was a bowl of bouillabaisse and some fried eggs. With the eggs came a chunk of pig fat, hard, white, and salty; I let Mari eat that. It was all she wanted. Tocino, she called it, which my pocket dictionary gives as bacon, but it was utterly unlike. We drank a quart of champagne between us, I think. We started to get somewhat riotous. Not really; just a little. Mari stood up halfway and proposed a toast to a side of swordfish roasting over the coals. "Noble death," she said.

"Let's go to bed now."

"Good."

"No. It's too early," I said.

"I want to go to bed now. I will drown you."

"It's too early. A heavy stomach interferes. First we'll go to a nightclub and dance. Are you drunk?"

"Yes. I am encendida."

The waiter brought us coffee and anis. "Drink some more," I said. "I have never seen you drunk."

"I have never been drunk. It makes me passionate."

"How do you know, if you've never been drunk?"

"I was drunk twice. Alone. With no man. You need not ask . . ." she belched: feep!

"Bon appétit," I said. "I believe everything you say."

"What did I say?" she asked wonderingly. We leaned our heads on our hands for a moment. "When I am drunk I also talk passionately," she said. "I forget to shut up. I talk too much. I was drunk on table wine one day in Es Cruylles."

"I think I remember the occasion."

"You lie, Perch, you were gone all night with Jaume Pujol and the Beard of an Englishman in a fishing boat, and maybe that blank blonde of an American also."

"I was not gone with the blank Blonde of an Anybody since I met you."

"Lie, you lie. I believe nothing you say. Go to bed?"

"Wait until we wake up," I said. "What's the use of going to bed if we're sleepy?"

"There speaks the reprobate," she mumbled.

"Well, do you want to go to bed to sleep?"

"I am awake," she said with pansy eyes. "Look how I stand straight. We will go dance. I am not drunk."

Nevertheless I noticed she weaved a little on the way out, like the B.S.A. with six hundred pounds up. Not drunk, but she tilted into a customer at the bar and joggled his glass. "Female reproductive organs," the man said in one word. "A life's savings spilt on the floor."

"Stand out of the way then," Mari said regally.

In the street between the overbearing walls and the lights, with the last raindrops falling in the puddles, we put our arms around each other and sang a song she had taught me a few days before. This song was prohibited for awhile; maybe it still is. It's a doleful dirge about King Alfonso XII, who came back from a hunting trip and found his bride dead in his absence. The history is that Alfonso married a dancing girl over the protests of his family and ministers, and she died; the folklore is that she died conveniently while he was away because the royal family poisoned her.

This is not in the song though, only how Alfonso comes back and hears the news. Then the ghost stops him on the stairs of the darkened palace. La primera hija que tengas, she says among other things, ponle lo mismo que a mi, para que cuando la nombres, tú te recuerdes de mí. Marry again, the ghost says, and treat the next one better. And the first daughter you have, name her after me so that whenever you call her, you will be reminded of me.

Maudlinly I thought that if I ever married anybody again and had a little daughter, I would name her Maria of the Angels, who was dead.

When I forgot the Spanish words I fit English in, with some difficulty: "Oh 'tis a far far fatter foul that I fry now than I have ever fried, ya ya yo."

People stared at us, not only because we walked with arms around each other, which is a rare thing, but also because we chanted this lugubrious song while laughing like idiots.

"Let's go in here," Mari said, listing toward a doorway in the calle Tapias. It looked like a delicatessen to me; the window was full of cans and dusty bottles, club-shaped cheeses and hams and sausages.

"What's this?"

"A nightclub. You will see." We went into the store where there was a display case and a wooden chopping block and a man in an apron; the shelves were full of bags of flour and canned vegetables and bottles of mineral water. The only evidence of nightclub was a streaked little cardboard sign over a door in the back; it said: Bohemia. I heard music and just inside the door I could see a waiter in a white coat. There were life-sized cardboard cutouts of Bohemians in beards and floppy hats standing in the passageway.

"Two?" the waiter asked, as waiters all over the world ask, no matter how well they can count.

Inside was a room with a ceiling no more than eight feet high, and at the far end was a platform with a piano and spotlights. In the center spotlight was a sexy stripling in a soigneé haircut and a suit of lights, the bullfighter's costume. He plunked a lacquered guitar and sang love songs to a storm of impatient and undeserved Oles. The rest of the by-no-means large room was a heaving mass of customers seated on each others' laps around tables the size of nail kegs.

"I thought you wanted to dance?" I said. "Even the waiters can't move around in here."

"Dance?" she said. "I only want to sit down."

"The lady is tiddly," I said to the waiter.

"M'sieur?"

"Tiddly," I said.

"News awrons oon taab toot sweet," he said.

"I'm with *you,* friend," I said.

Mari murmured: "He said he would find us a table." The waiter disappeared.

On stage, the bullfighter bowed deeply and went away. Then a barrel-chested old man in a cloth cap got up out of the audience and sang *Granada.* You'd think even the Spanish would get tired of this song sooner or later, but no, it's sung at least twice each night in every bar in town, and played on the radio even more frequently that the Ave Crem chicken-soup jingle; moreover, the natives seem to hum it under their breath all the time as though it was connected up with some involuntary reflex like the heart beat. Mari and I leaned against the wall in an amber fog, confused by the noise. She seemed about to pass out on her feet, so I tickled her thorax till she said: "Hoo ha ha, stop that."

"Why doesn't he look over there in the corner for a table?" I said. "Probably folks over there trying to fight a way out since last Guy Fawkes' Day."

"Speak Spanish," she said listlessly. The room went around and around quite leisurely. *Granada,* its lindas mujeres, was over, and the crowd yelled and everything seemed distant and weightless, like sounds and lights and distorted figures immersed in a globe of dark water. Mari leaned against my chest with her eyes closed and we swayed back and forth in woozy isolation. Up on the platform the old accompanist with a face like John Foster Dulles sat in the uproar waiting until he had to play again, a dead cigarette in his mouth, staring at his music rack as though it were a vista of twilit mountains.

Then a young man, another unpaid performer, got up from the audience, pushed up by his friends, and stood in the bleary spotlight. He wore cheap corduroy pants and a white shirt and had long sideburns. He looked like a gypsy. Layers of cigarette smoke drifted through the spotlight, and the crowd fell quiet, as though it recognized him. He wrung his hands and screwed up his face and began to sing the music called cante jondo. The old gypsy music. There are many ways to sing it, traditional and modern and mocking, but only one right way, and when it is sung right, as this boy sang it, and you are in the proper mood, it contains all that can ever be said or ever felt about pain.

This music is a mixture of Arabic and Moorish and Mediterranean-Hebrew and Andalucian and maybe even Egyptian, if what you hear is to be believed. But there is no sound like it in any other folklore. It is not even music in a way, just a cry, llanto, of unreasoning loss and distress. No need for Foster Dulles to play; the boy sang alone, his eyes closed, without accompaniment, almost without audience—there was no communication in the ordinary sense of the word. Whoever sings cante jondo the right way sings the same way a lunatic screams when he has a momentary insight into his own mind and knows the terrible thing that has happened to him. Not so much the words, which can be anything, but the Why? Why? of the human voice crying by itself, lost in a murderous world it didn't ask to be born into.

The songs are the consciousness of a race of originless, rootless, restless, dirty, thieving men and women and children who go from place to place in dusty caravans and have no destination they know, who eat when and where they can and lie down anywhere at night to sleep. When cante jondo is sung right, what are any of us but just that?

Walking, marching, running, and hiding, racing or escaping or vagabonding, what else is there to do except look everywhere for the Beautiful City of Earth that memory or instinct forever tells us does exist somewhere in our time, even if nobody ever finds it? And in the last analysis, what else is there to sing about, except that it was just over the next hill on the day we fell down at last and couldn't travel any further? Or that somewhere in the sierra we took a wrong turn and walked from there on into nothingness, with the City behind us all the time?

"I'm sorry I never called you beautiful before. I never will again. But every time I think about you I'll remember you as a little more beautiful than you ever were. Until I am an old mummy and you have turned into a sun. It seems I'm not leaving, but you are, and I can't do anything to keep you from going away."

"Habla español," she murmured, not much caring, turning her

face and listening to my voice rumble in my chest. "No sé que dices."

"I can't speak Spanish, you'll understand me," I said. "I have to say goodbye."

"Tra la la, I don't know what you say," she whispered. "I don't want to drink any more. Won't you kiss me?"

In the rear of the room, in the shadow, with everybody quiet except the singer, I bent down and kissed just the breath in her lips, barely touched; then kissed her eyes. "I am awake," she said. "Not drunk any more or I won't feel you. I don't want the night drunken and strange. Only like always."

Talking to herself, not me. I said in English: "Listen. The singing is how I'll mourn. Like that, without words. I'm sentimental. Anyway, I can't understand what he says. The voice says: Everything is gone that I had."

Neither of us was listening to the other; she couldn't understand what I said and I didn't listen to her, only knowing that her voice turned languorous and vague.

The boy with the sideburns stopped and the crowd screamed. He ran his hand through his long hair and shut his eyes and sang again. He sobbed and shrieked while Mari's hypnotized voice droned on: "We are different. I will not drink any more and it will be like always; he is not quick or brusque and I am not silly and frightened. Not whorish. Not drunk. It is not dirty. But lovers. I am his wife."

I could think of nothing to say. There was nothing to say.

"You won't take it wrong if I say Juan Bautista when I cannot hold back any more, indeed cannot contain any more, and the body turns to wine and I am blind, carai! If I cry and say Juan it is not a confusion—you know that every time there is the same blood and burst of rape, the first time in full womanhood, and always enormity and pleasure—it lasts too long, and the world is all vapor."

"What are you talking about?" I said finally.

"Codfish, you Pig, I wish—" she said mildly—"I wish you did not give me pleasure, then I could hate you—the whore and her hirer. What else are we? I talk too much. . . . Poor Pig, I knew that you wanted only a girlfriend for a time—that it was a caprice. I would not conform. I thought that if I did not bully, if I made love to you with my whole heart, you would see . . . Every man needs a woman, Capitán. One is as good as another. I am only poor whore, however. Loco, poor man, no woman can make him happy —he is too much craziness. But it is different, a woman asks not half so much. Only one man. I cook and clean, I look pretty, I laugh, I kiss, I breathe. . . . I thought you would stay. I am sorry, but of course I cost you much money, and pus comes out . . . ay, poor whore."

I said flatly in English: "I'm leaving tomorrow. I wish I could stay. I don't want to go. I don't want to lose you. But it's impossible. I'll never forget you. This is goodbye."

She was asleep on her feet. Her eyes kept closing, and she worked them open each time, looking up in perplexity and some grief. There were tears in them although she couldn't have understood me.

"Fish!" she said dizzily. "You could have changed everything. You never spoke. I didn't ask, I didn't force you. But it would have done no harm. It is not so much to say. I looked in your book of Spanish and English while you slept. There is a word you could have said. It is less than to love, it is to *like*. It is querer, gustar, to want, to desire, to *like*. Not amor, not amar, Pig. I do not ask you to say, 'Te amo.' But you could have said this *like* in Spanish. Only to care for and desire, te quiero, te quiero. Will you say, 'Te quiero'?"

"Te quiero," I said.

She closed her eyes. "See? What harm did it do to say that to me? I do too much. All. Finished. I feel sick."

"Come home," I said.

"Finished."

"Okay. Come to bed," I said.

"Now. I am burning. I will kill you."

By that time the cante jondo was over and a sad woman of the Piaf school straddled the stage and sang:

> "Adiós lucerito mío,
> Tierra y luz de mi sentido . . ."

Goodbye, my little light—earth and light of my sentiments. Just a coincidence.

We worked our way toward the exit. People were swaying and

singing like guests after the last waltz of the ball, when everybody holds hands.

"Que no tendrás en el mundo
Un cariño como el mió . . ."

"Are you awake now?" I asked.

"Oh, am I not!" she said, looking up at me with deep eyes like violets. "I am only waiting." We left the Bohemia without seeing the rest of the show, without drinking anything, without ever sitting down. We walked home fast and erratic in the cold, through crowds of drunks and clerks and wives, carts and smoke and streamers. At the stroke of twelve midnight. Old Year, New Year.

Two

AT TEN O'CLOCK on the first morning of the new year I was outside the city, rolling north. I traveled as fast as I could in the bad weather: rain, semidarkness, a film of ice at the extremity of the windshield wiper's arc. Heater going, the car full of junk, the dog whining and irritable in the back seat. My head a zeppelin-shape and mumbling with rumors of collapse; eyes like bleeding prunes; and a tongue like an old bandage.

Even so I felt better than I had expected to feel, after a night of no sleep at all. Most of what I felt, had begun to feel the moment I was in the cold street, was bubbling relief. Success, escape, the feeling of getting away unscathed. Everything going smoothly. There had been only one bad moment, when I was already dressed, coat over my arm and unlocking the door; when I turned to look at her one more time—and her eyes were open. Big purple eyes dizzy and tender with too recent, too much, too sustained love-making.

She didn't speak, didn't even seem awake; her body was sleeping and fluid under the sheet, and only the eyes were looking at me with an expression a man doesn't often see in his lifetime. I mumbled something about not being gone long and went out the door, knowing I would never see her again. And I went on seeing those eyes all the way down the stairs and out, eyes a man is lucky to see even once in his lifetime.

One wrench, one bereaved and agonized regret, and then the cold air and the bubble of relief had the same effect on my scruples that they momentarily had on my hangover. I ran down to the garage, with the dog clamoring at my heels and doing his early morning business virtually in flight, as if to demonstrate that while he didn't know what was going on, he'd cooperate to the extent of waiving his right to stop long enough to cock his leg.

There was no hitch at the garage either; the motor fired up right away and I did not wait for the automatic choke to cut off, but ripped out of the garage and roared around the Comandancia Marina and sped up the Paseo Colón through the early morning traffic, in and out the Parque de la Cuidadela where the zoo is, then north on the new boulevard they have just finished, and across the city line and over the primeval cobblestones of Badalona, and away.

The heater whirred with a fine domestic noise, the dog groaned and I sang:

"Give my regards to Yahweh;
Remember me to Elohim."

I can't say I actually felt good, but I had not yet begun to feel nervous, and the pain was all physical. Nobody feels good when his head feels oblate and smoking at both poles. But the car handled right and the road was open and I was away. I was poised on the threshold of new adventures.

The nervousness did not start until I had a little contretemps with the Hazards. The Hazards is in a little village called Monsolís, about ten miles north of Barcelona; it is where you ascend a long hill and at the top pass between canyon walls and can't see where you're going. At the crest there is a sharp downhill right turn, and then an even sharper left in the bottom of a deep dip, then a short-radius right, rising out of the dip to a left angle out over the cliff, and finally a dive downhill through a narrow street full of horses and children and large trucks. In the very worst part of the Hazards there is a bar called El Cementerio, where the locals come to sit in bad weather and watch the cars skid off into the sea. Even in good weather there is usually a cop or two on hand with a sharp pencil because of all the accidents that take place there.

Many times I had banged my right rear wheel against the curb coming through there, but nothing ever worse, as the Jaguar corners better than most cars. This time I came too fast, thinking about other things, went over the top of the first hill too fast, zipped through the first turn with my rear wheels slithering greasily across the cobbles, barely got around the second without turning over, and came to the sharp uphill left moving at about forty miles an hour, in third gear. My scalp began to sweat and itch. The wide cold sea was right in front of the car, just off the bumpers. In that moment I couldn't think of any good way to get around the corner at that speed no matter what I did. There was a Lambretta scooter coming around toward me in the middle of the road, afraid of skidding himself. I could see the driver muffled up in a leather coat and goggles and a furry hat, his hands in fur-lined gloves. It was the scooter that solved the problem. When I saw it I automatically stamped on the brakes. It was a reflex action. Otherwise I wouldn't have dared do any such thing.

My back axle floated airily across the corner and for a moment it looked as if I were going broadside into the sea sixty yards below. I trod the gas again as hard as I could, and by a miracle the back wheels took hold and the car bored up the hill in the proper direction, still too fast but at least on the road. I crossed the hump and got around the last corner and then the rear shifted over in the opposite direction, so I went obliquely down the hill saying, Whoa, whoa boy, to myself until the wheels caught again, just in time to fling me straight through the exit and down the narrow street.

Looking back, I can see that I might have spun like a top perhaps, but I didn't, and the fact that I didn't is due more to the factory engineers than to me. They had built a car that would forgive some very bad mistakes. So the spontaneous applause of the jokers in the Cemetery Bar, who had been absorbedly watching the entire maneuver, was undeserved tribute.

My scalp still itched and my heart beat loudly. "You can open your eyes," I said to the dog. "It's all over." But it took me a while to get my confidence back; every time I turned a corner I thought

I felt the beginnings of a skid. And that was where the nervousness started.

At first it was only that I imagined things wrong with the car—maybe the shift linkage—as though in reaction to the close call. Then as I got nearer the pueblo I began to be obsessed by the idea that our farmer neighbors would see me in the house and know somehow what I was up to. They would stop work to call me names and damn me for what I was doing. I even had the idea that in some way Mari had beaten me to the house, was there waiting for me, primed and desperate, to scream and cry and hit me and call me a cold-blooded fish.

It was just after eleven when I arrived. I drove furtively up the muddy track, grateful not to see anybody around, not even the Siamese cats. It was cold and misty. A fine sleet was falling. The cold wave had arrived. The lemon tree seemed to be dying, the lemons were shriveling up and turning gray. I unlocked, unbarred, unbolted, and unchained the several sections of the garage door, drove in and shut the door behind me, so that people passing by wouldn't know I was there.

The house was freezing cold; the dog scampered around on tip-toe looking for a warm spot to stand on. There wasn't any. Tile floors send shivering chills up through even leather or rubber soles; the best thing is crêpe soles or stilts if you have to live in a Spanish house in winter. Sleet was congealing on the windows as I moved hurriedly around the house throwing my things in the duffel. I knew one of my suits was at the cleaners in Barcelona but I figured the hell with it—maybe Mari could sell it for a couple of bucks. I also decided against taking the guitar, not so much to save space as because I was sure that the sound of even the few chords I could play would always remind me painfully of Spain.

When I had all my stuff sorted out and all of Mari's piled on the kitchen table, I sat down and scribbled something hasty to my mother, telling her not to write to me in Spain any more as I was on my way home. Then I realized that a telegram would reach her a lot sooner, so I tore that letter up and wrote another to Mari, to leave on the table where she would find it when she came to hunt for me. I wrote:

Querida: Thou hast been the love of my life. But it is impossible. Forgive me that I did not have the valor to tell thee. Thou wilt find a better man than I. Do not hate me. There is no other way. I will never forget thee.

I didn't sign it because of some vague idea that if I didn't sign anything I couldn't be sued. Then I went upstairs to our bedroom, where I had a cardboard carton full of old magazines and miscellaneous papers. When I hauled the box out from under the bed, a spider jumped off and scuttled away. I jumped a foot in the air. What the hell is the matter with you? I said.

I shuffled through the carnets and declarations and innoculation certificates and exchange coupons with hands that rattled like castanets. Get hold of yourself, Captain, I said sternly. And all the while I was waiting to hear a thunderous pounding on the door, half expecting to see the faces of Mari, Yaya, little Mercedes, Strangewolf, Lola Curtis, everybody I had ever known, suddenly lean down out of the ceiling and name me. Finally I couldn't stand it any more, and ran down the stairs and out to the garage. I piled my things into the car every whichway and unbolted the garage door and hurled myself into the car. I nearly backed into the fig tree getting turned around and aimed right.

Then, of course, the dog followed me. I couldn't have tied him up or shut him in the house or he would have gone mad. I had left food outside; Mari would be along before he got hungry. He came galloping and howling along behind the car as though prepared to follow me all the way to the frontier, but I knew he wouldn't get any further than the highway at best, because shortly he would have to stop and pee. I said goodbye to him under my breath.

So away I went and that was the end; except that I couldn't shake the nervousness.

After I left the pueblo behind, it was no longer a question of getting caught, kept from escaping, or even the fear of being seen. In fact I don't know what the trouble was. I kept on, thinking about all kinds of things, everything except the past. My plans were made: I was on my way to Paris, to arrange with the American Express to put the Jaguar on a boat the first of March or thereabouts. January and February in the Lowlands and Germany, and maybe Norway and Sweden. Then deliver the car a few days before sailing and look around Paris on foot. When I got home my folks would be glad to see me and I would look up old friends and play some golf when the weather got good, and make a sensation among the village maidens with the Jaguar all covered with stickers and escudos. Everybody would be impressed that I had finally learned something, even if it was only to talk Spanish with a Hartford accent. And so on and so on. Meanwhile steering the car with hands that would not stop shaking.

I stopped in a bar near Figueras, and while I was drinking coffee and eating a deplorable pastry, I suddenly thought: She is still in bed, and I could be back with her in an hour.

So then I knew what it was. I wanted to go back. A want so deep I hadn't recognized it. A want so strong it made my hands shake.

Without finishing either the coffee or the pastry I paid and left and jumped back in the car and spun the wheels in the gravel getting back on the highway.

It was almost two o'clock when I got to the frontier. Both the Spanish and the French customs offices let me through without bother, without searching, without undue haste either. Then I drove toward Perpignan. Spain is behind you, I said. You can't get back in. Time is up and by now she knows you aren't coming back. It's all over.

The job now is to think about nothing.

For another half hour or so it was easy, not to think about anything. Between French customs and the town of Le Boulou, good old Le Boulou, there is a fiendish stretch of road that lets you reluctantly down from the Pyrenees into that part of France which is called, I think, le Midi. This road viewed from the air would look like a fever chart, with convulsions thrown in. It was all I could do to stay out of the ditch and still make good time. Snow was all over the mountains and some of it had avalanched down into the elbow curves. I slipped and pitched along, muttering to myself and sometimes screwing up my face involuntarily whenever I thought, just as involuntarily: What is she doing at this minute? Oh blow the man down, I said; it's hi hi hee in the knockwurst industry; batshit. How will she take care of the kid? Oh yes those old-fashioned Back Bay oyster crackers, just lay your oysters right in here, gentlemen, while I activate the electronic mallet, I said. And the worst thought of all: She will need help—some other bastard . . . But that is all over now, the time has come to take a last farewell of this beautiful jungle paradise in the Islands of Langerhans, and as we sail reluctantly away into the sunset, let us listen one last listen to the horrid scream of the Buggabird as it is pinched to pieces pick by pick in the heart of the tropical rain forest, as we say farewell to the wood . . . Ay, me cago en la leche del mundo, is it too much to ask, to eat a few sardines and drink some wine, and lie down in the dark with my woman, that I found, that I had, that I left, that I lost?

Try *not* thinking about something that is on your mind once. In the end it was impossible not to think about her, so finally I let myself moan and maunder, not knowing where it would lead—to tears maybe. I thought about the good times on the coast and the week ends in El Catafalco and the long days in the city; about the early morning I stopped her in the hall with a broom in her hands and took her to my room for the first time; about Don Bellorio and the wagon and how she read all the old man's books; about the nuns and the International Bridge at Irún and beloved Benito and frying eggs on the steel deck of a medium tank; about Carlos and Rafael and América and the Beautiful One. I thought about Mari with the kid on her lap, about Mari on the back of a motorcycle, or cleaning out the stove in the Villa Alegre and singing the cats out of the garbage. But mostly I thought about the last night of the Old Year, breathing in each other's mouths all the night long in warmth and darkness, in a world, as she said, all hugeness and pleasure: a world of vapor.

Then thinking about that I thought how good she was—I mean virtuous, I mean chaste and honest and clean. I thought about how much she deserved somebody as good as she was. More, how much she needed somebody, because a woman alone in Spain has no recourse except to live miserably or become a prostitute, especially if she has one child by a dead husband and cannot prove she is a legal widow. So she would have to belong to somebody, whether he was good enough for her or not. And chances are he would be a dark-mustached side-whiskered garlic-reeking wine-drinking sweat-smelling Catalán, who would cheat on her, maybe hit her, or leave her alone too much and not understand her, nor make any effort to. Nor would he ever marry her, because of the kid, because of me; he would not marry her or cherish her but he would certainly sprawl over her and grunt and hurt her, then sit up and pick his teeth and spit and smoke Rumbos.

"I want to die," I said aloud in the roar of the car on the highway outside Perpignan, up in the hills over the Mediterranean inlets all gray and freezing. Then I thought about the Yaya, and the Yaya said: I want to tell you, Capitán, that a man and a woman can live together in sympathy and harmony, without love. Only songs are full of hearts and love. . . .

"You are a cynic, Yaya," I said.

. . . and a day passed without fear or hate is as good as loving—and a heavy supper and a warm bed are more to be valued than pretty kissing . . .

"That's a lie, Yaya," I said. "The comforts are the dividends you get on investments of capital, or something."

Then Lola Wingfelt Curtis popped up and said: Everyone knows you aren't married to her. I don't suppose that matters these days, except no matter how you slice it, you do owe something to any woman you sleep with. And old Jock Strangewolfe said: Upon final perfection of the corporation society, through universal application of the three basic principles, you and your type of individual will be firmly dealt with: gassed, with sympathy; regretfully, gassed.

"Gassed, deservedly; quite properly, gassed," I said mournfully. And Carol Bond said: He follows his wandering star over the brow of the next windy hill, whence he can see the distant beckoning horizon, towards which his itching foot will carry him, over the open road, of which he sings The Song . . .

And the Le Boulou man with the rotten teeth and cat smile said: You look for love? I find you it.

"Good," I said. "You have to believe in love at all costs."

The Yaya said: And they live together and eat and sleep and fill up on the togetherness which is not Love but Home, and when they are filled, they burst, and there is a child in the house—what else is there to do with all the years that no one asks to live?

"Love," I said.

—te quiero, Mari said. I do not ask you to say te amo. Only te quiero—

—I hit him over the head eleven times with the basin, Mari said, so that he fell down, then I sat on his stomach and knocked out his teeth with a shoe—

—when I cannot hold any more, indeed cannot contain any more, and the body turns to wine and I go blind, carai! If I cry in his mouth and say Juan, he will know that it is because each time there is the same blood, burst, of rape, first time in full womanhood—

—I laugh, I kiss, I breathe . . . I thought you would stay, she said.

—in it are all good things, she said: protection and merit, home, babies and physical pleasure and refuge from loneliness. So I believe that when I am sought I must respond not with pretense and pose, but with a naked body and a guileless spirit, as earnest that I will not play false to my life, and also as gift to him if he will love me . . .

By this time there were so many things in my mind that I decided to stop a minute along the road—actually afraid I would run square into something if I didn't. As it happened, this was on the lonely stretch of road between Perpignan and Narbonne where I had had my first look at the Mediterranean the year before. It had been high summer then, with the mistral rocking the Volkswagen; now it was winter, with the tramontane doing the same to the Jaguar. Flat desolate land and dead sea and hills like big gray boulders.

"I want to die," I said again, allowing the car to lose momentum. I shifted from fourth to third, then from third to second, all proper; then double-clutched into first gear, which isn't strictly necessary or even desirable when you are coming to a stop. Besides, it usually grinds teeth. But I was not coming to a stop.

By the time I was down in first I was making a U-turn.

From Barcelona to that forlorn spot on the coast of France is a little over three hundred kilometers, or say approximately two hundred miles. It had taken me five hours to get that far, traveling at what I considered a pretty good clip. An average speed of almost forty miles an hour, which may not sound like much, but counting in the constant hairpins, the bad weather, the stop in the pueblo to load the car, and then the stop at customs, it was very good speed. But it would have been better if I had not been unconsciously slowing down and slowing down from the frontier on through Perpignan, like a rubber band that is reaching its elastic limit.

It took me only from ten after three to quarter after seven to get back. I went back like that same rubber band when the tension is released. That four hours and ten minutes also includes a good half hour I was held up by the Spanish customs. They went over the car from stem to stern. When they stamp you out at two o'clock, and two hours later you are back again trying to get in, naturally they assume that you are returning with a trunk full of cocaine and Parisian condoms and Chanel No. 5. They even looked under the hood and in the tool kit, while I stood by raging. Finally they let me go. "You are in a great hurry," said one kindly carabinero who had wanted to let the air out of my tires to see if there was any marijuana in the inner tubes.

"I left something behind," I said.

"Mal asunto," he said. "Bad business. Americans are always in a hurry. Oiga, Senor, there is a policeman waiting here who wishes to go to Gerona. Will you carry him?"

"No," I said. "I intend to travel at one hundred sixty kilometers per hour and I do not want anyone in the car with me, let alone a policeman."

"Se va morir, chico," he said. But I had already made up my mind not to die: I knew what to do. At last I knew what to do. I said to the kindly carabinero that the thing I had left behind in Barcelona was a thing of the utmost importance. "El futuro," I said, starting the engine. "Porque la única cosa de valor que puede hacer, un hombre como yo, es ser padre."

I thought he looked doubtful. Maybe he thought I was studying to be a priest. There is no denying that on occasion my Spanish is a little ambiguous. I knew what I meant anyway.

"Buena suerte," the carabinero said. Good luck. I popped the clutch and spun the wheel again and made for home.

The journey back was without incident. By that I mean that everything happened inside my head. I thought any number of things I hadn't thought before. I should have known months ago. As I drove it got dark and turned colder, the rain becoming a thin damp snow that melted on the ground. The landscape skidded by so fast that I could hardly tell how far along I was, except by the passage of the larger towns. A cop stopped me in one place, flagged me down in a darkened village. I said: "This cat no speakee Spanish, officer." We saluted each other ironically and I went on.

I thought about love. I said: I am in love. But what does that mean? How do you prove it? How do you describe it? You say: I smell garlic. How do you prove it? Describe the smell? Prove you smell it. You say: My head hurts. Who knows what you mean?

Who sympathizes except yourself? All words are just assigned meanings. What is hurt? What is smell? What is love?

Love is where you must be with somebody, or you will die.

There were lights in the house.

It didn't occur to me that it would be Mari though. I don't know who I thought it was. Maybe old Manolo, the landlord, come up to fiddle with the water system; or maybe Yaya's brother Lorenzo; maybe even the Siamese cats for all I knew. I had figured that Mari would wait in the city another day or two, wondering where I was, probably calling the police to see if I had had an accident, or trying to get Manuel to drive up on the B.S.A. and look for me. I had already said to myself: Let's just duck in at El Catafalco and destroy that note and leave our stuff there, and then go to the city and find her, and when she says, Where the hell have you been? you say innocently: Who, me?

Of course it was Mari. She had found her things piled on the table, had found my things gone, had read the note. I was ready to be screamed at, reviled, punched in the old solar plexus at the very least. Despite this I felt half insane with joy, because I was seeing her twenty miles earlier than I would have if she had waited in the city.

I burst into the house and ran toward the kitchen where the light was, and stopped in the doorway. Mari wore her housecoat and a scarf on her head; she was slicing potatoes, apparently for frying. Little Mercedes was sitting on the kitchen table absorbed in the study of a smelly old sneaker. The dog lay near the stove.

I said: "What are you doing here?"

"Making supper," Mari said. "We came by train, to be here when you arrived. I did not expect you back so soon."

The dog was clawing me all over; it put its paws on my stomach, boisterous and forgiving, and peed on my shoe.

"Never mind that. Listen. Something has happened. I love you," I said. "Te amo."

"Ya yambo," our daughter said.

"Put the bag down," Mari said. "We will talk of this later when the child is sleeping. Now come and eat supper."

But her nose was beginning to bleed.

That was the first of January, the first day of the New Year.

Now it is March and spring has come staggering in after some struggle with the severe winter drifting down from the north.

Mari's nose still bleeds every once in awhile. "You must explain it to me," she says. "What connection exists between my felicity and my nose?"

We are still living in our ruin of a house, my Castle in Spain, which I have already described. We walk down to the town under arches of chestnut and pine trees to do our marketing and sit in the Miramar Café drinking vermouth and eating dried salt codfish and watching the misty sea. The town isn't a resort town, although it's on the beach; it is just one of the many small pueblos like knots on a string on Napoleon's Imperial Highway from Barcelona to France. Now that the cold wave has retreated back to Lapland and we no longer have to go to bed with bottles of hot water and bags of baked bricks, it is very pleasant and restful here. In the house we have a stuffed squirrel and several cross-eyed China lions and a lot of religious objects hanging on the walls. We have a fig tree and a lemon tree and in the middle distance there are other fruit trees, just now coming into flower. The old chicken yard has been converted into a species of garden where we sit in the evenings, drinking Tio Pepe sherry and listening to the herds of sheep and goats that go jangling through the pine groves behind the house. The black lamb and the white lamb from next door come to visit us every once in a while, and the Siamese cats are here all the time, so that even our dog is used to them.

Since January we have taken a couple of trips—the Andorra ordeal I mentioned and also an overnight trip to Valencia, where we slept in the big ritzy Hotel Inglés. And also a four-day trip to Madrid, with stops in Zaragoza both ways. But most of the time we work on our problems.

There are all kinds of problems in a mésalliance of this sort. Some are already solved, some are in the process of being solved, some only time can solve, and some are insoluble. A few minutes conversation with the Practical Animal on the night of my return made hash out of my fatuous original objections to the match.

When I said I was an American and couldn't stay in Spain forever, she said: "We will go to America when it is time." Sure, I said, but it wasn't that easy to get into America. "Yes it is, for the wife of an American," she said. "I am informed through a friend of a police captain who works in the American consulate." Sure, I said, but even so, America is a strange and perilous land and you would not be happy there. "I am happy when I am with you," she said. "Are you not happy when you are with me? I will go with you wherever you take me, and we will be happy together always." So I said that in the meantime I would need a lot of money, and the carnet on the car was almost run out, and to support a car and a woman both is a great burden. "Sell the car," she said simply. I said that our children would be halfbreeds and she said: "I would not care if they were blue." You will have to learn English, I said. "You will teach me." My parents are going to object. "A ham for your parents." We will live in poverty, I said, as of a certainty my father will cut me off without a tin farthing. "Have you ever considered going to work, Trout?"

So that is what I do most of the time, work on these problems. For the past few months I have been going down to Barcelona every Wednesday and Friday afternoon to give English lessons to six important gentlemen in the goatskin exporting business, and one pretty young girl whose ambition is to marry Captain Peter Townsend. I have written to all kinds of American companies that do business with Spain, and have written to both the Civil Service and the U.S.I.A. to see if they need any clerks or strong backs in their agencies hereabouts, or in one of the Sixth Fleet shore installations. Not only that, but I have approached some Spanish companies that do business with the United States and England. But Spanish salaries are nothing to shout about, I could do better pimping for tourists on the Ramblas in summer. And of course, I have written to my father to see if he has any good ideas. No answer yet, but when he gets over the shock of learning I am really willing to work, maybe he will come up with something. Chances are he has a controlling interest in the Falange too.

I also wrote my mother. Naturally she thinks the whole scheme reeks, but I am trying to placate her, as she is to be the dea ex machina of our International Problem. Sooner or later I am going to have to get Mari and little Mercedes into the United States and get them citizenship papers. As Mari made it her business to find out long ago, there is no problem about this where the bride is concerned, but the child is another thing again. While we wait, I am teaching Mari English and American History and the Constitution, and am trying to break the news gently about supermarkets, switchblade knives and TV; then when we have succeeded in worming a passport out of the entrails of the Franco Government, the rest is up to my mother to put a good word in the proper ear. Among her high-toned friends who send her deep-frozen steers and theatre tickets and come to her parties, there ought to be at least a couple of congressmen, if not a Supreme Court justice.

I wrote to Rudge. He said he would not only buy the Jaguar back, he would come and get it. It seems he has a vacation in August and plans to spend it on the island of Ibiza, off the coast of Valencia. So he will come down by air and drive my car back, then cable me the money; so I don't even have to go to Frankfurt.

Some other problems have solved themselves. The third grano was the last, for instance, and now Mari is healthy as a horse. My divorce was final in January, so we were married on San Blas' day, the third of January. By the time my copy of the divorce decree arrived we already had the necessary dispensation from Il Papa, so a Spanish Catholic girl could marry an American Protestant. The problem arising from the fact that I was divorced once was solved by simply mentioning it as little as possible and crossing a few palms with silver. I got a Christmas card from Jennie along about Lincoln's Birthday. Mari burned it.

And a lot of our intimate problems were solved the same night I got back. Just vows and affirmations and revelations that people who are in love murmur in bed at night. We said all the things we hadn't said to each other before and had a fine time, but rather abridged, as neither of us had had any sleep the night before, and it had been a big day. We decided that we were made for each other and never again would part; we agreed that our names were written in the stars in code, and that we would keep the romance of our marriage alive even unto arteriosclerosis and toothless doom. We lay in bed in each other's arms, two murmurous sponges of sentiment. I have something to say about that, too.

I can see how we got sentimental leaning against the wall in the Bohemia, in a champagne fog and listening to the gypsy boy with the sideburns singing cante jondo. Neither am I embarrassed by my sentimental feelings on the trip up and back from Perpignan. Sentiment has its place. But a couple days after I got back, while we were still talking things over, something occurred to me and I said: "What the devil did you mean, you wanted to be here when I got back?"

"I knew you would be hungry when you came," she said. "And the potatoes were not ready."

"Yes. Sure. Don't fool me, mujer. Why did you think I was coming back?"

"How far did you go?"

"Perpignan. A little distance beyond. Never mind that, answer the question. How did you know I was coming back?"

"Perpignan," she said. "That is not very far. Hardly enough to give the illusion of freedom. I allowed you until Paris, although I did not want to wait so long."

"Long? Do you realize I was going to America?"

"No, not America, Cod," she said. "Qué va, America! I gave you all of Spain and all of France until Paris, but not America. The net was flung wide, but it was sewn at both ends and closely woven."

So it seems it was not because she considered me cold-blooded that she had been calling me by fish names for the past six months. The note I had left her she used to wipe grease into a frying pan. So much for the guileless spirit.

One more comment. Several times in the past couple months she has made the illuminating remark that now we have things more or less settled between us, she intends to bend her efforts and devious energy to making an honest man out of me. I scoff, of course. She is kind enough to point out that until now in my life I have not measured up to a pinch of horse manure in the eyes of a good woman, but that with perseverance, maneuver, optimism, and a following wind she soon hopes to convert me into a person of stature: that is, a kindly, righteous, tough, humble, virtuous, and responsible citizen—her specifications. Well, a woman's reach should always exceed her grasp, I always say. Or, bukhra f'el mish-mish, in other words. Arabic for: Tomorrow it is possible there will be apricots.

Meanwhile, it is spring in Cataluña, and the earth is passing through its foggy gold stage on its way to burned grass. The people next door are out in the sprightly sea breeze, planting cabbages and shouting hoo-haw to their horses. In our garden, where we sit drinking Tio Pepe, we have calveles and geranios and dahlias, and along the fence there is a mixed bush of roses and grapes that Mari points to and says: "An inappropriate marriage, like ours." The cactus plants have put forth a bulgy kind of pear; sickly-looking bougainvillaea is climbing up the chicken-wire trellis by the garage. Sometimes we have thunderstorms and I go out in a big hat to collect the crop of edible snails that works up from underneath the ground.

But most of the time the sun shines and the blooming trees roar with honey bees. We have three cherry trees, two pear trees, an apple tree and a peach tree on the grounds, as well as the fig tree and the lemon tree. Everything is enriched and abundant, gorged with sap and bursting out in fruit and flower. Including Mari. Maybe it will turn out to have been a mistake, but we decided on it together. Well, decided is the wrong word—you can never really decide that sort of thing with much authority. It's in the cards or it isn't. We welcomed it. Willed it, at best. She wants to bear me a son—for her own reasons no doubt—and I am reconciled. More than that: I am enriched and abundant, too. What I said to the kindly carabinero at the frontier, or tried to: The only worth-while thing a man like me can do is become a father. There is always the chance that my child will turn out to be a better man than I. Quite possibly that is the road over the sierra to the Beautiful City of Earth.